D1110943

The Drowned Lands Stan Dragland

The Drowned Lands Stan Dragland

PEDLAR PRESS | TORONTO

ACKNOWLEDGEMENTS
The publisher wishes to thank the Canada Council for the Arts and the Ontario Arts Council for their generous support of our publishing program.

LIBRARY AND ARCHIVES CANADA
CATALOGUING IN PUBLICATION

Dragland, Stan, 1942–
    The drowned lands / Stan Dragland.

ISBN 978-1-897141-19-9

    I. Title.

PS8557.R275D76 2008   C813'.54   C2007-907114-7

COVER ART Michael Pittman, *'Liminality'*

DESIGN Zab Design & Typography, Toronto

TYPEFACE Galliard, Carter & Cone Typefoundry

Printed in Canada

For Rachel, Simon, Toby
and Beth

and in memory of Earl Meeks

Nothing I've ever read is like my life.
— STELLA BUSH

THE MAP

IT'S QUIET NOW, the Ontario country northwest of Kingston. Small-scale farming, acreages owned by commuters to the city, many lakes and a good deal of bush. But it was otherwise along the Napanee River in the sixty-odd years leading up to April 1913, what with lumber men, farmers and mill owners at each other's throats. It was lively. In the small hours of April 17th, it was explosive.

The Napanee River, or Depot Creek, as it is known in its northern reaches, flows south through all the Depot Lakes in turn, from Fifth Lake down to First, on into Bellrock, thence into the Long Swamp, long and wide, the heart of our story. Here it is joined by the other fork of the system, the creeks linking lakes of the lesser eastern tributary that reaches the swamp, the Drowned Lands, by way of Hardwood Creek out of Verona. Through the swamp, then, and out into the quieter southern course of the creek, now the Napanee River proper, which empties into Lake Ontario. Much of this marginal but once bustling territory, especially that north of the swamp, has gone back to bush. The remaining marks of lumbering are few: a rusted iron eye hammered into the river-edge rock to secure a boom of logs, a hole drilled in the granite for dynamite never punched down into it. Feldspar quarries and mica mines abandoned. The manufacturing boom long since bust, all those water-powered mills and factories gone. Except for remnants at

Petworth and Bellrock.

The roof of the Petworth Mill has rotted off, and part of the limestone wall has collapsed into the river, but the broken structure has majesty. The roof is gone, the floors are gone, the walls are as tall inside as out, and why doesn't someone buy it and engage a stone mason, and make something of it? The past is there in that building. There are stories in those old stone walls, and in the ruins of mills all along the Depot/Napanee. At Yarker, for instance, in Waterfall Tea Room on Bridge Street, you can order a piece of pie and a cup of tea, and sit at a table overlooking the river and watch it all rise up again, the log drives over the chase of that dam, the grumble of water-powered stones, the whine of wheels and saws and lathes. All that sad rusted metal out there was once machinery within a mill of which only the crumbling foundation remains.

Today's topographical map, veined with the orange of roads, is green for low-lying country, white for higher elevations. North of a line from Enterprise through Bellrock and Verona right across to Westport, the settlements are few, the country relatively empty. It was not occupied by settlers until the 1850s, land to the south being more open and happy, much of it offered to United Empire Loyalists. The Model T Ford showed up just before the Great War, but during the Depression it was still best to drive horse and wagon up the path north of Verona—just two ruts with grass growing between them. Except in the fertile river valley, hay and corn fields lay between outcrops of granite and thick stands of elm and maple and birch. Beautiful country, but hard. It was never all that good for farming, but farmers settled, expecting to stay, sending down roots into land that would not nurture them.

In spring, the whites and purples of lilac trees cluster around the foundations of houses long gone. The timbers of those houses are rotted, but the square nails haven't yet rusted away and may be scrounged, taken home, stored in a box. A box of stories that somebody ought to be preserving, stories of the time when all these little towns were bigger towns, when progress and prosperity were the watchwords. The 1878 *Illustrated Historical Atlas of Frontenac, Lennox and Addington Counties, Ontario* has maps of all those towns planned out with named streets you'd have a job to locate today. There are woodcuts of impressive stone houses built south of the swamp. Money was there to be made, for a time. Most of the fine houses are still standing. They are among the beauties of the area, constructed like the Petworth Mill of limestone quarried south of Verona, north of Camden East, cut and laid, laid and pointed, walls built and roofed, windows inserted, pine floors installed, staircases fashioned, furnishings installed, and almost all of this, structure and contents, manufactured right along the river, as were the wagons, the cutters, the sleighs, the wheels and runners and whatnot, everything needed to get you from one place to another, as was almost every implement required to work the land.

But wealth didn't flow north along the trail that became Highway 38. Near the Portland Township Dump just south of Verona, the pavement bucks and twists across the swamp. Deep down, long since sunk into mire—vestiges of the first corduroy road. The blacktop never lies perfectly flat just there, despite the tons of stone fill poured into the swamp below, so slowly do the Drowned Lands relinquish their sway. The Kingston and Pembroke Railway used to puff north across that fill. Locals called it the Kick and Push—'mostly push,' according to one old-timer.

The K & P whistle once cut the night with its moan, but the track has been torn up. These days, the trackless rail bed is plied by summer hikers, winter cross-country skiers, snowmobiles.

This quiet territory, 'Land O' Lakes' on the current tourist map, is gorgeous. It has the feeling of North, though it's just northerly, neither urban nor wild, a mixed rural country of small farms, acreages and cottages, where we entertain the illusion that we have time.

EARLY IN THE MORNING of Thursday, April 17, 1913, George Hudson drove his rig up to McCumber's Bridge. The bridge was covered with rushing water, but all Hudson asked of the woman standing at the side of the road was, Am I on the right road to Wagarville? Yes, she said, you are.

An article in the *Kingston British Whig* of Tuesday, April 27 eulogized George Hudson as a decent human being, respected and deceased. He lived with his mother in Centreville, the article said, and farmed in the area. It was a visit to his other farm fifteen miles north, above the dam at Fifth Depot Lake, that took him into Hinchinbrooke Township. He was 'a young man of the highest repute in the vicinity,' according to the *Whig*. 'Of retiring disposition, he still retained the regard of the entire community and bore the enviable reputation of a man who never spoke ill of anyone.' Death always elevates a person in the eyes of his acquaintances, but perhaps Mr. Hudson really was the paragon of humanity that his neighbours made him out to be.

For all that, George Hudson must have had a rash side. And why not? A reticent man might be impatient, even impulsive.

Have you heard of the Government Dam, Mrs. Sarah McCumber asked him, his horse grazing on the verge of the road with the high water rushing loudly over the bridge ahead. He had. Well, said Mrs. McCumber, somebody blew it up yesterday. You don't say, he said. I do, she said. My son Stewart was in the house at the time and that blast blew the front door open so it slammed against the wall. That's a caution, said Mr. Hudson. It is, said Mrs. McCumber, and I don't know that I would recommend crossing that bridge. There's debris caught there at the other end, rocks and rubbish. The water over there runs out of the chutes. It's always swifter that side. A word to the wise, young man.

Well.

Mr. Hudson sat with the reins in his hand, looking over the span. Pulled a gold watch from his waistcoat, flicked it open, flicked it shut. It's a long way to Wagarville if I don't cross here, isn't it? A long way round, said Mrs. McCumber, and we don't know what other roads are flooded. Though maybe some are not flooded now. Now that the river isn't spreading.

Well.

As long as there's hard bottom, said Hudson. The bridge looks strong enough.

Mrs. McCumber was wrong about one thing: Fifth Lake dam was never a government dam. At the inquest it came out that the dams on the chain of Deep Eau or Depot Lakes along the Napanee River system were built in the 1860s by Cook and Cochrane Lumber Company and later purchased by the Rathbun Timber Company for floating timber over the rapids, down the river to the St. Lawrence. Rathbun acquired huge parcels of land along the river, selling them at fifty cents or a dollar per acre, but always reserving the right to flood. This was according to B.S. O'Donohue, secretary of the Napanee River Improvement Company. Mr. O'Donohue willingly furnished the *Whig* with the Company's version of events. Why no watchman at McCumber's Bridge? Well, there was a watchman in place as recently as three weeks ago, Mr. O'Donohue stated, but his house was burned. It was razed to the ground. You can hardly lay that wanton destruction at the feet of the Company. He went on to insist that none of these farmers, none of them, mind, has any legal rights whatever along the river, because the Company has leased the water rights from Rathbun. There is a yearly rental.

They can't go to law, said Mr. O'Donohue, though they think they can—we are forever assailed by frivolous suits—and they also take the law into their own hands. The rule of law must prevail, he said, or what will keep us from falling back into the era of the cave man? Indeed I sometimes believe we have. Do you realize how many dams have been mischiefed, how many lost to dynamite or fire and machinery damaged? Our man on the river cannot be everywhere, and the Company has suffered this aggravation for well over a decade now.

Mr. O'Donohue went on to wring his hands over the release and loss of all that stored water. And Mr. R.W. Benjamin, of Yarker, interviewed while confined for some time in Kingston General Hospital, said the same. How, he asked, was his wheel manufacturing factory to operate this fall with water reduced to a trickle? The loss of cheap power, he said, would spell ruin for the village of Yarker.

Mrs. McCumber stepped back as George Hudson shook the reins and clucked at his horse. The horse showed reluctance. Hudson had to resort to his whip. Mrs. McCumber watched him go. In the near washout, the buggy wheels sank about a foot, but the horse pressed forward and gained the bridge easily enough. The water coursing over the span was also manageable, but the far washout was another matter entirely. The horse alone might well have made it through, but the buggy dropped into it and lodged, Hudson retaining his seat with difficulty.

For a few agonizing moments, the horse maintained a precarious grip, front hooves clawing for purchase on the bank, but the current was gradually lifting the buggy, inching it off the bridge. Mrs. McCumber's hand flew to her throat, her heart having leapt there. Then buggy, horse and Hudson were swept away, with Mrs. McCumber running along the bank and shouting, Jump, jump, catch some bit of brush. Jump, sir! Hudson did abandon his sinking rig then. He struck for shore, but the terrible current was too swift. He was down and up in it. Finally, down he went for good, and was lost from sight altogether.

A well-spoken, considerate, retiring young man, owner of two farms, quietly living with his mother in Centreville—a man with a promising future, if ever there was one. One rash act and he is no more. What he set out to accomplish with his life now falls to others. 'Spirits of steel,' saith the poet, 'in shells so fragile.' May spirit continuance in some wise balance such dire losses in the here and now.

Yes, the *Kingston British Whig* of April, 1913 has the story, including the farmer's side of it, a cautionary tale for the ages: lands flooded in the spring season of ploughing and seeding, valuable marsh hay drowned in the summer, fences lost, roads flooded, wells spoiled, all owing to the Company's 'indiscriminate' raising of water levels along the river; vain attempts to gain redress by law; promises of politicians forgotten after elections, though in 1907 two of them did—unsuccessfully—push for the removal of

Lott's Dam at Petworth. Frustration mounting and mounting over the course of decades during which prosperity in the region becomes ever more elusive. In the heartbreaking marginal Ontario country north of Kingston and Napanee, farmers were still discovering that from such rocky ground a living will always have to be scratched.

Crossroad grows into settlement, forest becomes farm. Growth, then decline. In hindsight, the all-too-familiar rhythm looks inevitable. But in 1913, the Company, in the person of B.S. O'Donohue, sees only that farmers, little more than savages, are spitefully interfering with hard-won commercial enterprises. The farmers are equally short-sighted. Stuffed-shirt, would-be big shots are all that stand between them and a prosperous future.

At the Hudson inquest, no farmer admitted to hearing any explosion. Sarah and Stewart McCumber excepted, every witness at the inquest held in Centreville testified that the force of twelve feet of pent water alone would have been sufficient to breach the dam. On this and every like occasion, the solidarity of the farmers was compact. No one was ever convicted of causing mischief to any dam along the Depot/Napanee.

It's a sad and fascinating event, the death of a man. On the day after George Hudson's drowning, the banks of the river were lined with over eighty observers watching efforts to retrieve the corpse. Frank Snyder and young Stewart McCumber had to be stopped from launching a rowboat unequal to the task, the current remaining fast and dangerous. They secured a better boat, and set out. The horse and buggy were soon located, but the search for Mr. Hudson's corpse went on all day Friday, and Saturday until just before noon. And then it was not the 'official' searchers who located it. The search party was at lunch on

Saturday when word came that Joe Compton was claiming to have located the sad spot. Mr. Compton was an Indian known to possess divinatory powers, and his reputation did not suffer on this occasion. The searchers, launching their boat again, found Mr. Compton in his bark, leaning on a pole to hold it steady in the current. The body is here, he said, and so it was, in eight feet of water.

Recovered, the corpse was conveyed to the vault in the Catholic Cemetery between Centreville and Camden East, where George Hudson was laid out. At a few minutes past 10:00 PM, led by the coroner and the constable, and with a *Whig* reporter in the party, the jury trudged two by two to the vault. The only source of illumination in the dark and chilly night was the constable's shaded lantern. The vault stood white in the side of the cemetery hill. The double plank and iron doors first resisted then yielded to the constable's pull. They swung open heavily, with a rasping squawk eerily appropriate to the grave moment.

Inside the damp, musty vault, the inquest party ringed the coffin. The coroner lifted the lid, revealing young Hudson lying among the folds of white satin. His smooth and youthful countenance was at odds with a body so cold and still. 'The faces of the jurors as they leaned over,' wrote the reporter, 'bore no sign of feeling, but they spoke softly in the presence of death.'

Soft indeed were the voices of these twelve impassive farmers, who returned their verdict as follows: 'That George Hudson came to death by drowning caused by the washout resulting from the breaking of Fifth Deep Eau Lake dam, and we are of the opinion that the owners of said dam should have had a watchman or someone there for the protection of the travelling public.' Nothing about the so-called 'gunpowder plot.' No mention, after deep deliberations lasting until the small hours of the morning, of any explosion. The blast might as well have been a dream of Mrs. McCumber and her son. A vivid dream, to be sure, so violently to fling open that front door. What emotions the jurors concealed behind their bland faces, what may have been stirring in the hearts of most of the fifty-odd members of the audience, one can but speculate.

Nothing whatever of tears welling in the eyes of Mitch Deeks, tender-hearted resident of Bellrock and custodian of all those dams for the Napanee River Improvement Company. He is the one B.S. O'Donohue has called "our man on the river." Nothing of hatchet-faced Dr. Walter Morse, of Verona, the farmer's friend. No one attends the proceedings more keenly than Dr. Morse. He has been appointed coroner, for one thing. For another, he knows the plot, while Mitch does not. The doctor's face reveals no more than the faces of those jurors, but his heart is harrowed. George Hudson, yes, an unfortunate sacrifice to the farmers' cause, but the smooth-faced young man, so beautiful in death, is not the only casualty. Hudson is not the only victim whose body Morse has examined this day, and what had the paper to say about that? A postscript to the Hudson story, a brief paragraph about a rumoured second death by drowning, appeared the following day. What happened to the *Whig* 'scribe' who followed Hudson so closely. Assigned to another story?

Hudson's death was reported in a month featuring also the recent Canadian visit of their Royal Highnesses, the Duke and Duchess of Connaught; the death in Rome of financier J. Pierpoint Morgan; the rejection of Home Rule for Ireland; the antics abroad of the pugilist Jack Johnson; the windbag foolishness of the Borden Tories in Ottawa and the dignity of Sir

Wilfrid Laurier in opposition; the opening of 'New Ontario' in the north; the expansion of the West, with seven million acres of CPR lands to be sold direct to settlers in Manitoba, Saskatchewan and Alberta; 'England's brazen women,' Mrs. Pankhurst's militant suffragettes; and item after item about widespread unrest in Europe.

In the same issue as 'Dynamiting of Dam leads to Tragedy' is another story, 'The Titanic Horror,' which recalls events of April 16th, 1912, one year earlier, when the unsinkable vessel struck a mountainous iceberg on her maiden voyage and sank, with 1,630 souls drowned. The loss of the Titanic was big news and stayed big news. Big news is history. Hudson is nobody. Buried in Centreville Cemetery, buried in the pages of the *Kingston British Whig* of April, 1913. What of all the feuding along the Napanee River that claimed his life? All but forgotten. Years after the troubles, in villages severely reduced in population, descendants of the combatants do remember a few bald facts. The doctor— Morse—who canvassed for funds to buy dynamite. The blast that blew Fifth Lake dam and Petworth Dam, the latter explosion heard and felt three miles north in Bellrock. Deep rifts in the Company, more and more manufacturers opting out because why pay annual dues for unpredictable returns of water flow? The complication of lumbermen, whose activities sometimes suit the Company, sometimes the farmers. Shards and shreds.

George Hudson may be nothing in the eye of history, but he did make the newspaper. What about the other drowning? The postscript was never followed up. Apparently that death means less than nothing. Where is the *justice*?

In opposite camps of the dispute that churned for decades until it blew up, Mitch Deeks and Walter Morse were united by grief on the night of the Hudson inquest, grief and remorse on the part of the doctor, because three young persons of Bellrock had also been mysteriously caught up in his flood. Who now remembers the story of Stella Bush, Mitch's young friend, and Michael Deeks, his nephew, and the third, the boy called Silas, deaf and dumb and seldom thought to count for anything, and yet, it turns out, the director of events, preceding the flood, that were tragically beyond his control?

Whole chapters of the story of 'progress' are so easily lost between the lines. Between is where it behooves us to look, when we can, because that is where we are right now, all of us. Between is where we always are, if we would only accept and embrace that truth. We are always, always, being swept along in a moment of becoming. Let us for once hold such a moment, brimming again with precious fragile life. Let us grasp and hold it. Dearly belovèd, let us open it wide and make sure that it lasts.

ONE

THE LOST VOICE

Silas

SUNDAY, APRIL 13. Silas rolls stiffly onto his back as the lights begin to show. The cat has been sleeping beside him. She screeches once and hauls herself out from under. Heart in his throat, beating out of his throat. The lights scroll by in mid-air—pulses of red, blue, indigo, green—in patterns he knows and does not. They come out of air and go back into air. He is seeing some code, a riddle. He is pinned to the bed of boughs in his hut, rigid. Because of what he is seeing, what it means that he can't understand, telling him. What? Lights, saying what? He is reading without comprehension the ranks of lights pulsing overhead as if sewn on leather, a belt, but they are not. Whose lights? Can't hear, can't ask. He swallows this as he swallows everything he can't understand. This is nothing. It scares him silly. Lights undulating in their patterns across the air, telling him so much. He can't understand.

How long, rolling up there until they fade? Until they lose colour and form and finally just pucker and churn with some great energy of something going. Or coming? Silas is not one for the clock. Time—he has no idea. They take an age to wisp away.

When the lights are good and gone and the air is healed of its thrashing he is soaked. His mouth is dry. There is a bad taste. He rolls from the bough bed and reaches his feet in one smooth motion. The cat stretches its body long. Sharpens its claws on the sapling floorboards. Silas steps to the edge of the hut and lowers himself into the creek. Relaxes his body and lets it rise. He dips his head and rinses his mouth. Lets go, drifts away, then strokes powerfully back, hauls himself up. How many days has he gladly sat out here by himself, watching the pool he loves and feeling the sounds of his own that throb or zag or flutter in his body.

Sitting out here. On his own. Clears away the thrum from town that clogs his senses and confuses him. Out here, even heart-sore, his own sounds are soothing. The air full of event speaks to his body. It's news, it's learning, it's better than Devil Rock. No lights there, not under the rock.

But there weren't always lights here.

Now he sits, dripping, refreshed, his body cool. He sits with his legs dangling in the water almost to the knee from his floating platform floor. Where he is usually content for hours. He is not content. The lights still pulse dully in his head. The fear is less acute now, but persists. He still feels, urgently, what he has been shown. He thinks and thinks. What is it?

He rises and enters the hut. Lies down on the bough bed. Then gets up and retrieves the sack. Sweeps the cat out of the patch of sunlight and spreads the contents on the floor.

Bellrock

March 29, 1912

D.B. Stegner Esq

Napanee River Improvement Company

Newburgh, Ontario

Dear Sir

I thought I would write you as spring is about at hand to find out what the prospect is for the seasons operations on the dams. You will remember I was laid up from a fall on Burnt Mill dam. Just after I maild you my last letter I saw Long passing my place I called him in and gave him your order which he said he would carry out.

I saw him again about a month ago he said he had the dam in good shape and the stop logs in and no fish hole in them. That fish hole spouted off an emence lot of water at the wrong time last season.

So Mr Stegner, plese advise.

Your Obdt. Servant

Mitch Deeks

SILAS SPREADS THE CONTENTS of the sack on the floor of the hut. He needs the comfort of his things, laying them out, looking at them.

First the driftwood stick, forked at one end and with two rounded stumps at the sides. A tiny armless man. A manikin.

The little pail with the smooth stones.

His arrowheads.

The snakeskin, tightly rolled and secured with a loop of rawhide.

The little machine. He turns the movable part round and round with his forefinger.

The bones of the kittens. Tiny skulls, tiny backbones. Most of the bones are detached now, from carrying them in the sack. It doesn't matter. He knows these bones. He knows how they were. How the kittens were. He knows where the fox crunched them. He knows which fox, he watches it. He has it traced to a burrow beneath a huge rock by the creek. The fox has young too. From the tree in the meadow he saw them come out. He saw them playing. The kittens fed them.

His papers: newsprint clippings and a note scrawled on a torn envelope. He unfolds them carefully, because the creases are becoming cuts. He spreads them out side by side in the arrangement he likes, same each time. Mostly black lines on yellowing paper, but in the middle of everything, a man. Picture of a man. You can't see the man's face, not clearly. He is reared back. In his one hand, behind his back, is a ball. The other hand, raised up high, has a big glove on it. One long leg raised in the air, bent at the knee, the knee right up under the chin.

Silas studies the picture. He used to study it without knowing. It made no sense at all, not for years. The old man showed it to him, the picture and the other pieces of paper. Now the old man sleeps all the time and Silas took the papers for his sack. Old man don't care. A long-legged man with one long leg in the air, flexed at the knee. Silas used to practice standing that way, holding a stone instead of a ball. If he tried that, maybe the meaning would come. Standing on one leg like the heron, the other leg up. He would stay that way for a long time, then the planted leg would start to tremble and he would switch to the other.

The meaning did come, but not any way he expected. He looks at the picture now, knowing what he knows about it, longing for the meaning of the lights. How can he understand the lights? Not that the picture worried him. He just puzzled at it. He liked to. He needs to know about the lights.

He was hurtling past the sports ground, one place he never stopped, not since he was small and Ronnie Pilk hauled his pants to his knees. Ronnie was bigger, but he would not have tried that except where others would egg him on. Some things you learn a hard way. Silas knows many such things. He knows never go near the sports ground, never closer than the road past, which is where he was, passing, when he happened to glance at the field. There was a man in the middle of it and he lifted his leg into the pose. Silas couldn't help stopping, though he knew he should not. He has learned to keep moving everywhere but at the hut and Devil Rock where he is safe. He stays away from the shanty now, as much as he can. The old man always sleeping there, and the stink.

But he had to stop that day, stop and gawk. He watched from the road as the man's leg swung down and around and out into a big step while the arm with the hand holding the ball came out from behind his back and flung it at another man. This one was holding a big stick behind his head. The ball sailed by him. Another man stopped it with a big glove. He threw it back to the first man, who stopped it with his glove. He picked the ball out of the glove. He took off the glove and tucked it under his arm. He rubbed the ball between his hands. He put the glove back on and stood holding the ball behind his back, bent forward, looking hard at the man with the stick.

Silas stands up. He raises both hands, just like the man on the field did, lifts his leg, takes a long step along the floor of the hut, and makes as if to throw a ball, or a stone.

Back then there was a crack, as the stick connected with the ball, but Silas never heard that, never saw the ball streak between two of the other men on the field. He didn't see all the men go into motion. He had his answer! He stood on the road, lost as he knew he should never lose himself. He assumed the leg-up pose, stepped out of it and followed through. He was in the picture. The picture was in motion. Raised his hands, lifted his leg, stepped and followed through.

By which time, hangers-on at the game had reached and surrounded him, pointing and grinning. He straightened up. He rushed at Ronnie, stiff arms outstretched, knocked him flat, and ran. Nobody followed. Nobody wastes time trying to catch Silas. Nobody can. Behind him, the bunch had shifted their attention. Ronnie hit his head on a rock and was crying and cursing. Hard to beat that kind of fun.

Silas has nothing to throw today. He can hit the tree across the pond three times in four when he remembers to bring a handful of stones from the road. Arms up, leg up, step, throw. Once more. What are those lights?

DOROTHEA HAS THE COPY BOOKS piled on one another, all of them open to the latest page. Out in the sun on this beautiful April morning, copy books on the small drop-leaf table that Tom pulled out of his loft. Too small for the lot of us, he said, but it'll do for you. It's walnut, heavy. A struggle to haul it outside by herself, but worth it. She has taken care to lay down a cloth. She would hate to leave a mark. If Mrs. Ritchie ever gets her dining room, she might need the table in there. Useful and beautiful. For now, it's the long pine harvest table in the kitchen, where she takes her meals with the Ritchies. Tom doesn't care much for the walnut table one way or another, but he should. It's from the Old Country.

In the Old Country, they make a different breed of woman than they do here. So it says in the *Whig* she has kept to look again at 'No Votes for Women.' Well, who expects a Tory government to pass a franchise bill? A good many women, apparently. 'The women who crowded the galleries of the house,' the paper says, 'those who constituted the deputations Sir James heard while they pleaded for their rights, looked down on him reproachfully.' Of course reproachfully. Dorothea flushes with resentment. We can raise their children and teach them, we can nurse their sick, but when it comes to the vote – 'And only that dignity,' she read on, 'which distinguishes them from the suffragettes in England saved him from their wrathful challenge.'

Old Country women. Mrs. Pankhurst, the 'Queen Mother of suffragettes,' is in jail now. And in response, her supporters blow up a train at Stockport. Where is Stockport? And they blow up Oxford Station in Surrey—that is south of London—with, the paper says, 'nitroglycerine or dynamite.' Blowing things up! Dynamite and destruction to convince men that women deserve the vote?

Who gave men the power? God-given power. Now *there* is a gift.

There was a man injured at Stockport. A train hand. A man with no power. It's the innocent who suffer when people take the law into their own hands. But oh, Mrs. Pankhurst. She would starve for the vote. They're force-feeding her. And why should we not have the vote, Walter Morse? Why should we not?

Walter Morse? Doctor Morse and dynamite and Emmeline Pankhurst. Strange bedfellows.

Bed! She shivers. Stay away, she counsels herself about the impending visit to Walter Morse.

But it's hard not to agree with the writer of Editorial Notes in the *Whig*, up to a point. 'The militant suffragettes are becoming more abusive, indecorous, and insulting,' he says. Undignified, they are, un-Canadian. But then he goes on, and this is too much. 'They are simply insane, and should be immured in the asylums.' Insane! Lock them in the madhouse for wanting the vote. She tosses the paper down. Those silently reproachful women in the visitor's gallery at Queen's Park—keeping their place, kept in their place, by virtue of their Canadian dignity.

The air is awash with scent. Wood smoke, greenery, something sweet. If this were June, it would be lilac. She takes Ronnie's book from the pile. Ronnie's book is on top, Stella's on the bottom. She has learned over the years how to treat herself—best for last. When she gets beyond Mister Spit-ball, things will go better.

But it's not easy to start with Ronnie today, not with the rich, sweet smell in the air, and the leaves newly opened in all their light greens. It's not a day for brooding on suffragettes either. Dorothea Asselstine, a suffragette? Well, what would be ruined if women could vote? They're still punishing us, men are.

35

They don't trust us. Not since Eve. You'd think the eviction from the Garden took place yesterday. But we have had no congress with the serpent. Not since then. No, the serpent has moved on. Moved in.

It was Cecil Spencer speaking with the forked tongue. Thank the Good Lord the others saw fit to vote him out. Even a single false and ignorant trustee makes her job far more challenging than it needs to be. Thank God the chairman is Tom Ritchie.

She leans back in her chair, raises her face to the sun, closes her eyes. The intricate melody of a rose-breasted grosbeak abruptly sends her elsewhere. To Ottawa and school. Ottawa and Emily.

Emily and Paris. Dorothea and Emily in Paris. That was the sweet dream, Emily's idea. Finish school and rendezvous in Paris and live together in that small hotel in the Rue de la Montagne, the same one Emily stayed in. And then: the Tuileries, the Louvre, the cafés, all of romantic Paris, the Paris of Emily's stories. Emily's Grand Tour, she called it, two weeks in Paris pretty much on her own, assigned to the care of the stiff uncle who lived down the *rue* but saw her just twice. The English uncle, who was something for Barclay's Bank. He had a large but well-trimmed beard and a monocle. Nobody could ever be more English, Emily said, with his tweeds and his 'I say' and his 'Jolly good.' He was certainly the opposite of anything French. And he wore a deerstalker.

A deerstalker?

It's a cap with a peak out the front, out over the eyes, and another peak out the back, over the neck.

Well. How would you know which way he's headed?

In my uncle's case, the nose would tell you.

Being always at the front?

36

Also large and red.

Emily and Dorothea. Paris. It was a beautiful dream and Dorothea let Emily dream it. Don't worry about money, Emily said. Lots of money in my family. We will come for you, well, I will, and I will spirit you away. In the night, if necessary.

Spirit me. I like that. But my school?

My dear, this is kidnapping. It's out of your hands. Emily flicking a strand of hair away from Dorothea's eyes. Dorothea shaking her head against the gesture.

What if I resist. What if I raise the alarm?

My love, are you saying you could resist me? Those eyes with their mischievous twinkle, the lips that drew Dorothea's eyes to them, always. Irresistible.

Teasing, Dorothea assumed, and she gave as good as she got. Teasing was all it could be. Eyes closed, savouring the April sun, she sighs. Two years of Normal School in return for five years teaching in Bellrock. A ward of the township after her parents died, and the township took care of her. She would never, she *will* never, break the bargain.

But five years has stretched into twelve, and a move to Sydenham High School, and where is Emily now? Her last letter was full of plans for the Florida wedding. Dorothea still has the fancy invitation. The honour of your presence at the wedding of Emily Elva Harris and George Anson Barrett II. There was the middle name Emily hated. She had caught a II. Lots of money, she said. Money draws money. Somebody's money paid for the honeymoon, anyway, a real Grand Tour. A few postcards, from Ghent, Paris, Florence, and Emily never heard from since.

Emily didn't pass. She missed Trig and Maths. Dorothea couldn't help her enough in those subjects. Helping Emily was

37

helping herself, though. She saw how you really had to know things to explain things, know them inside out to explain them to someone barely interested and with a mind that skipped. Loving Emily, Dorothea worked all the harder for her sake. And, it turned out, her own.

Emily was her first pupil. And Ronnie Pilk will be the beneficiary. Dorothea's mouth tightens. She doesn't love Ronnie, no, nor Brendan Reynolds. The Bible enjoins her to love thy neighbour as yourself. It is so very difficult to emulate the saviour. Thank the Lord she knows where true love lies, having experienced it once. It helps her. Oh, Emily.

Twelve years now. Emily married and gone. Perhaps she's a mother now. Perhaps she has her own children, as Dorothea never will. Only she knows that. Spinsterhood is just a few years away. She looks forward to it. A spinster might be left alone. A confirmed spinster would be free of fools like young Barton at the Picadilly School. The most pathetic of her suitors. She has difficulty giving Barton so much as the time of day. He scrapes along with a minimum of effort, and admits it, for goodness sake, even boasts of it. Better cadaverous Walter Morse than a smooth, superficial twit like Barton, the fatty, with his 'thikke knarre.' Break a door by running at it with his head, could Barton. She used to think that was funny, like so much of Chaucer's Prologue, until she met the man it fit and the brute wanted her. Walter Morse is not thick. He might even be interesting, he might be decent company if he weren't so tiresomely gone on her. No conversation with Walter Morse is ever just a conversation. Patrick Lewis? He's young. All the girls moon after him. He'll survive.

She sighs again and opens her eyes. They light on Tom's boar, rooting in the pen outside the barn. She chuckles. Porky Barton. For Walter Morse, she is sorry, and that is all. There is a conversation impending with him that she has been dreading, both because he is who he is and because of Mrs. Pankhurst. Why? Why the suffragettes? She will not be discussing women's suffrage with Walter Morse, the secret revolutionist. She doesn't quite know why the most intelligent man of her acquaintance bears the brunt of her growing outrage. He doesn't deserve to be a symbol. She can't help it. Leave me alone.

But Tom Ritchie will not, or cannot, carry his own message. Head trustee of Bellrock School conferring with the chief plotter? Too risky. He hated to ask her, she could see that, but she had opened herself up by asking a favour of her own. She could not say, I cannot abide the man. Not a good enough reason to refuse. And she *can* abide Morse. At a distance.

Ronnie, now. Ronnie has been promoted every school year for one reason, and one reason alone: Dorothea. Miss Asselstine, the crone, the battleaxe, the witch, keeps him after school and drills him. In gratitude, she knows, he calls her Miss Asshole. Ronnie and Bren need the extra help, and once in a while dreamy Michael Deeks. Left to himself, Ronnie would have fallen by the wayside long before this. But even Ronnie Pilk, sparrow number one hundred, yea, even he, the very least of these my brethren, he will lift up his eyes to Miss A from whence cometh his help. Or else.

She opens the book on Ronnie's wretched fist.

Bellrock

May 9, 1912

D.B. Stegner esq.

Napanee River Improvement Company

Newburgh, Ontario

Dear Sir

It being my birthday yesterday, I took the morning to visit my fathers old place on 13 Island Lake. Manys the year has past since I travelled so far up on the lake, though you know I have often these years been to the dam at the bottom. Well Sir, it being sutch a fine day yesterday, and seeing a deer swim from the point out to the near island, I borrowed Mr. Simon's bark, who lives at the old place and I paddled myself out to see could I get a closer glimpse of it. Mr. Stegner, there is no finer time of the year than Spring in this country on a fine day with the leaves all new and the sun shining on them. I got no sight of the deer, though I paddled as silent as my old father taught me how. I kneeled at the thwart as well, with the bark tilted, that no wave might lap on the bottom and betray me. Well, no deer as I said but soon I could hear the sound of an axe and it was louder the nearer I came to the dam. I thought very little of it. I thought the girls people might be splitting some firewood. But when I come round the top of the last island I could see the chopping was coming from the dam. I seen the girl sitting nearby while two men worked on the stop logs. Mr. Stegner it wasnt enough to lift them out. These characters were seeing to it that our fine squared cedar planks were cut in two. Approaching nearer I could see the girl was weeping and I checked my anger against her. What could a slip of a girl do I have asked before. Well Sir, those men took no notice of me until I was almost aground. One of them looking up, a hard customer I thought though I never laid eyes on him before he leant on his axe like it was a walking stick and watched me come. But the other man seeing him rest looked out at me and said a word and the two of them hightailed it. Who it was breaking up our dam I could not tell. I asked the girl, she didnt know. I told her to tell her parents not to leave her alone with the dam. She said she would but I lay you she doesnt. Shes a timid little stick. But if I find out anything further I will let you know.

Yr. Obdt. Servant,

Mitch Deeks

DOROTHEA PICKS UP the second last of her copy books. One more writer, this one a dreamer, before she treats herself to the words of her star pupil.

Dorothea has written to the University of Toronto on Stella's behalf. She wants shy, irascible Stella tested. Stella of the birthmark, the averted glance. Stella should be tested. She must have her chance at higher education. Dorothea wants for Stella the opportunity she had, that or the equivalent. She has been pestering Tom Ritchie about it. She wants Mr. Ritchie to help. His problem with Stella Bush is Stella's own problem. The birthmark. How, he wonders, is Stella ever going to muster the confidence to stand before a class? How is she ever going to convince a class to pay attention? She always hides her face in her hair, Stella does. She never meets your eye.

Privately, Dorothea asks herself the same questions, but that way lies defeat. She has lately been telling Mr. Ritchie about the other Stella.

In class, no, she never speaks. But get her alone and give her time. She needs time for the self-consciousness to fall away. Give her a subject she is passionate about. Then she'll look you in the eye. And then. Oh, Mr. Ritchie, you should hear her.

Stella?

Yes, Stella. The very woman, the same young woman we have been discussing.

Stella Bush.

Mr. Ritchie, I have never been more serious in my life.

Well, Dorothea, if you say it's so, it must be so. But what can be done? I'm sure I don't know. What about the mother?

That woman. She's smart enough herself, you know, though nobody thinks so.

Well.

I know. But oddness does not preclude intelligence. But she can't be reached. Any teacher who sends work home with her pupils, she says, is just admitting her incompetence.

That was in the paper. I bet she saw it there. She's not alone, you know.

Let's not argue about that, Mr. Ritchie. She'll end up in that factory, Stella will. You want her condemned to a life like that?

Tom shook his head. His sister has been making cheese boxes half her life, ever since she lost her husband to the mechanical rock picker. Nobody has the heart to use that rock picker any more. It just stands idle. But he knows what Dorothea means. Mary is not Stella. Cheese boxes are fine for Mary.

He took off his cap and scratched his ear. Dorothea hates having to load this on his back. He has trouble enough these days. He and almost everyone else along the river. But it looks as though he'll carry it. It looks as though he'll think about what to do for Stella. He does owe Dorothea something. She has more than repaid her debt to the school board. The community knows her value. She is loved. She knows it.

I dunno, Dorothea. I dunno. Let me sleep on it.

That's all I ask, Mr. Ritchie.

Oh, I know all about your asking. Thin edge of the wedge.

She pestered him about Silas. She pushed him and others hard for Silas. Nothing came of that, poor lad. No deaf school for Silas. No Jesus, either, to stick His fingers into Silas's ears and then spit and touch his tongue, and Lo! The world of sound opening up, pouring in. She will *not* give up on Stella. She could not picture Stella at high school in Sydenham without her, or she might not have requested the move. She might have been content to stay in Bellrock. For all intents and purposes, she is all the mother Stella has, though mother – what is Stella to her, exactly? Not a daughter. Mrs. Bush – why do they call her that? She never was married. She has never divulged the identity of Stella's father, though people never tire of guessing. Mrs. Bush's mind is up in the clouds or down in the dirt, always one or the other. A laughing stock she is, oblivious to the fact. Which Stella is not.

A cup of tea now. A good cup of tea.

This good, good man, Mr. Ritchie. She wanted to embrace him but knows better. He'd never come nigh her again. She let it go. Once in our lifetime together, she thinks, I will find a way to thank this good old courtly man, and I'll do it right. I'll do it so he knows he has been thanked and so he stays thanked.

She pumps the kettle full, pokes up the fire. Out the kitchen window she can see SS No. 11, her first school. She tries to imagine Stella in front of a class in there. Stands her up with the blackboard and the world map behind her, but Stella won't stay. She slides back to a desk in the last row under the windows. Hunching there with her hair over her face, hands over her hair. Stella is a knot of deep grief and fiery curiosity. There is steel in her backbone, coiled steel. Nobody touches her, nobody goes near. Nobody but Miss A.

Emily with all that money could spare tuition for Stella. Married to Whatsisname II. Lots of money and, it has to be said, little brain. Oh, but brain enough to get by, to have graduated, if she had only applied herself. Flibbertigibbet. She got her Latin. Dorothea could sometimes interest her in that. It was the stories. The stories and the sounds. Emily retained enough to pass; Dorothea held it all.

Emily and Dorothea. Dorothea and Stella. The kettle on the hob. Camomile tea with Stella. Just as soon as she deals with Michael Deeks's unpredictable effusions.

Dorothea and Emily on the green sward outside the college in broad-brimmed straw hats. Emily's hat with daisies in a chain all around the brim. Straw hats and long white dresses, two young ladies reclining under the college's huge old flowering crab on a spring day much like this. A round red cloth, with white embroidered curlicues, spread out on the grass, dainties arranged on it. All purchased in town by Emily, who insisted, who pooh-poohed Dorothea's objections. Such extravagance! The air alive with songs of cardinal and robin. A blue jay bold enough that afternoon to flash down and snap up a peanut astonished and delighted them. And the rose-breasted grosbeak, right over their heads! It was almost too much, that song. Dorothea so happy, it seemed that the bird had snagged her heart and poured it out in melody. Examinations still more than a month away, and study over for the day, and Emily in charge.

Close your eyes, she said, ostentatiously picking up a paper bag. Something precious in it, judging by her manner. Close your eyes and open your mouth. I have a surprise. When I say 'Now,' bite down, but not too hard. I don't want you losing a tooth.

Well, no! What are you feeding me?

Never you mind. But when your teeth meet something hard, don't try to bite through. Just hold it tight.

It? With my teeth?

With your teeth. Ready?

Dorothea closed her eyes, opened her mouth, braced herself. She wouldn't put it past Emily to pop something in too far. You could choke on a nut. Then: Emily's soft lips on hers. She opened her eyes, astonished, drew back. There was a brown and sticky-looking something protruding from Emily's mouth. She took it out from between her lips.

You're looking, she pouted, then brightened. But anyway, I can't say 'Now' with this in my mouth, can I? Let's try again. This time I'll touch your arm when I'm ready and you bite down. This surprise is getting less surprising by the second.

Eyes open, this time. Again the meeting of soft lips. Dorothea felt faint. She was melting. Then the sharp taste as two sets of teeth slid the dainty off its pit.

How do you like that? said Emily, chewing.

Um. What to answer? Dorothea chewed and swallowed. She was blushing, flustered. What was being asked?

The kettle whistles. Dorothea pours water in the pot, swirls it, swishes it out. Now the tea and more water. Pot and cup on the tray. For the pot, the cozy knitted for her by Mrs. Abruzzi in the green, white and red of the Italian flag. Dorothea carries the tray outside.

You mean – do I like – the taste?

Of course the taste. What else? Do you know what that is?

She didn't know. It was a date. Yes, she liked it. Then they ate too many. Too much Asia, Emily said. Next time, let's just have a couple.

Next time. Let's be a couple. There was no next time. Not for dates, not for anything like that. Irrepressible, irresponsible Emily. Who never knew what she stirred up in her friend.

Outside, Dorothea sets down the tray, drags the table across the grass, out of the shade back into the sun.

Yes, she has had love. Felt love. She sits down.

A whole group of suffragettes was chased by a crowd off the Brighton Pier. They took refuge in a house nearby, and pursuers broke every single window in that house with beach stones. Dorothea crouching in a corner of that besieged house. A day at Brighton Beach ending like this? She and Stella crouching in a corner, weeping and clutching each other. She and Emily, their Grand Tour poisoned. Where is Stella going to find love? Oh, Mr. Ritchie. Higher education, maybe; the vote, maybe. But what about love?

Michael Deeks, now. He shows flashes, Michael does, but he's lazy. No, not lazy. Well, what else to call it? He goes along, he gets along. He seldom puts himself into his work. He might be something if he did. What would light a fire under that boy? Not his father. Not for school. No getting through to the father.

At the interview, Mrs. Deeks was the one listening, listening closely. Emma, she said warmly, call me Emma. Beautiful Beleek to praise during the tea. My, but your cups are light. So lovely to look at, and so light to lift. Emma Deeks blushing as she smiled. Yes, they are nice, aren't they? They're just about all I have from my mother, the cups and the pot and the cream and sugar. Yes. Beautiful.

Right away she saw that Mr. Deeks was going to be difficult. There was no 'Call me Des.' She could see resistance on his face, though he was polite enough. These fathers, these farmers. Nothing but work on their minds. She respects it as much as she can. Work a-plenty to do, and help very scarce. A strong young boy is an asset.

Asset, a word out of bookkeeping. Credits and debits. She never cared for Bookkeeping. She can teach it, yes, but she never liked the procrustean model, everything cut and dried. No, give her the inspired games of mathematics, the dance of figures, that beauty. Or history or literature. Other kinds of dance, with fact and fiction. She likes introducing them one to the other. *War and Peace* meets the actual Battle of Borodino. But you don't want a boy to have to be an asset and not a person. You want him whole.

No Michael to be seen that evening. She had expected him to be present. Emma Deeks flustered slightly, explaining why not, while her husband stared at the floor. Chores. A perfectly good explanation, but apparently not the real one. One purpose of these visits is discovering just such tensions. Dorothea likes knowing what burdens or advantages her pupils bring to school. She can adjust her approach to each one. She summoned up all her charm to enter the subject of Michael's lacklustre performance by remarking on the guitar resting on the arm of the settee in the parlour. Deeks just glanced at it and grunted. The man has a creative side. Of course he does, though he is a very wooden performer. He seldom so much as smiles, playing for dances. Where is the joy a person ought to feel in the music? He and Jim Shibley—same programme of music every time. Reverend Smart never needs to worry about 'vulgar contortions' with these two in charge. No Turkey Trot, no Bunny Hug out here.

It's about learning, Mr. Deeks, she said, abandoning her strategy. It's about learning on his own. He has to practice, he has to do the exercises and answer the questions. Otherwise, it won't stay with him. He's a dreamy boy, she said. Emma lowered her eyes, but Dorothea could see the smile. No corresponding smile from The Father, as she was denominating him by now, in her mind, so she said, He's smart, sir. He has a good mind, if he'd only use it. But he doesn't pay very good attention.

Oh, I know all about that, was the sharp retort.

The three of them sat in awkward silence for a few moments, then Dorothea decided to cut her losses. Well, she said, if there's any way I can –

Thank you, he said gruffly, I do appreciate –

He looked up, saying that, looked her full in the eyes for the first time. Ah, she thought, he's not a bad man. He's troubled. And he doesn't have words.

Emma, standing up, was quick to echo, Yes, we appreciate everything you're doing, very much. And I know Michael does too.

The interview was over. Emma Deeks's eyes, as Dorothea took her leave, were filled with some sort of appeal. Woman to woman, what would she say? It's the women you have to talk to, and when might she catch this one alone for the necessary heart-to-heart?

She can see through the page that Michael's composition ends on the next page. Half a blank page under the first. Is it brevity, the soul of wit? She scans the two pages, and sighs. Mere brevity. B- or C+? 'This is well enough expressed,' she writes, 'but you need to review the use of the semi-colon. Several of yours (see my marks) should be commas. The semi-colon, remember, separates grammatically complete sentences that are, however, closely related in meaning. It may also separate items of a list, of course, but you have no lists in your composition. Your composition has, in fact, scarcely any content at all. It has clearly not caused you any strain whatever.' A trifle sharp, perhaps, but he has it coming. And she has talked herself down. A spade should be called what it is: C.

That is disappointing. The marks should have climbed at least to a high B by now. Well, one more essay left. She tosses Michael's copy book onto the finished pile and glances up at the sound of wheels.

There is Walter Morse. Come away from Buzztown on a Sunday afternoon. Again. He turns his head stiffly to look in her direction. Has the man no natural movements in his body? He is holding the reins stiffly out in front of him. Can he not rest his arms on his legs? Can he not relax? His touch to his hat in greeting is forced. She can see him flush all the way from where she sits. If she were to draw him, Mister Skin-and-Bones, she would require straight lines only. But of course she is the one making him self-conscious. He is blushing for her. She returns no smile, but raises an acknowledging hand. Doctor Morse, visiting Bellrock again. What would it take to call out to him? Oh, Doctor Morse, would you mind very much stepping over here for a moment? I have a message for you. She should. Save herself the trouble of going to him. She considers it for too long, and misses her chance. Just as well. Risk raising the fellow's hopes and spoil this beautiful day into the bargain. More than it is already spoiled, by the mere sight of the man. She must conquer her aversion, and soon.

His buggy stops at the hotel. She watches him climb down awkwardly and limp out of sight. He would not stop here on his own, she thinks. She has a good idea what he will say to Jim Shibley and not, not ever, to the likes of her. Not unless she beards him. He would have been one of those gallants standing casually back from the lifeboats of the Titanic, tamping their cigarettes on their silver cigarette cases. Women and children first. First to the life boats, ladies, last to the vote. If ever. Forcing her to horn in.

She picks up Stella's booklet. Please, God.

IN EARLY MARCH, just a year ago, Silas was passing behind the hotel, between the hotel and the creek. His usual route. A late snowstorm, followed by a melt, had left icicles hanging from all the eaves in the village. If he had his ears, Silas, he would have heard the icicles dropping all over town. There was a huge one right above the back door of the hotel where Jim Shibley is often seen peering out. Summer or winter, Jim likes to open that door, step out, look this way and that way, refresh his eyes with a view of the creek. Passing, Silas happened to glance at Jim's back door exactly when that huge icicle let go. It plummeted and shattered on the step. Jim was not killed by that icicle. He would have been killed had he stepped out just then. Silas knows this, Silas and no other. Not killed that March day. Spared to sit this April day in the lobby of his hostelry, Dr. Morse shortly to open the front door.

Silas is no calculator of odds. He has not totted up the frequency with which Jim looks, this way and that way, out his back door, nor the number of times an icicle with Jim's name on it will form and form and finally release and plummet from his roof. How many days of how many years, the years of Jim's occupancy of the hotel, minus the time before he got into the habit of looking out back? What is the likelihood of Jim Shibley dying by icicle, assuming that nobody notices the threat and calls his attention to it? He won't be hearing anything from Silas.

Silas is not familiar with the operations of numbers, but he does have the notion of luck. Icicle shattered into a million pieces. Big one. Jim not killed. Lucky. Silas smiled, nodded to himself, and continued walking.

And what are the odds of Silas passing by at that exact moment, passing by just then and glancing at Jim's door precisely when that icicle dropped? Big numbers, wouldn't you say? Huge numbers. Hundreds of millions of years ago a meteor smacked into the earth at what is now Holleford. Holleford is about seven miles south and east of Bellrock. The crater was thirty-four miles wide and three hundred and ninety-two miles deep. Ouch. What were the chances of *that* collision happening? Astronomical.

But what are the chances that today, next week, somebody of your acquaintance, remarking on some striking coincidence, will ask the rhetorical question: 'what are the chances of *that* happening?' You'll have to admit, if you've been paying attention, chances are pretty good.

THE LOBBY OF SHIBLEY'S HOTEL is a small, low-ceilinged room with a table for a desk. Jim sits beside the desk in his creaky rocker. Does he have any sense of his luck, any inkling that last spring he was spared from being impaled by a huge icicle? Any notion whatever? He does not. Behind his chair is a door to the living quarters. Three rooms for a family of five. No wonder Jim likes to sit in the lobby through the day. He seldom misses the spittoon on the floor beside him. He's got a crusty cloth slid under the chair for when he does, because Lila can't abide spit on the floor. Not much for a man to do but chaw and spit through the day, with the river drivers in camp up to Fourth Lake. Down here in a week or so, then she'll be busy. Not Lila, the hotel. For now, not much to do in the chair but rock and chaw and spit and dream. Get up and look out back. Pick up the fiddle once in a while.

A shadow falls over the glass of the front door. The bell over the door jingles. Jim sits up straight. A bony hand grips the jamb, and a fist, holding a cane, pushes the door wide open. Doctor Morse. He deposits his cane in the umbrella stand.

Morning, Doc.

Jim.

Have a seat, Doc. What brings you out here? Never get used to the sight of the man. Walking skeleton. On a quiet day like today, almost any diversion would be more than welcome, but Doctor Death? Jim is going to have to work at being cordial.

Thanks no, Jim. Sitting a lot today. Walking and sitting. Making some rounds.

Nice day for it. Now, you been in Toronto, Doc, haven't you?

That's right, Jim.

They get any satisfaction?

It was a farce, Jim. Doug Stegner is a good man, but I wouldn't trust that BS as far –

BS was there!

Far as I could throw him. Yes, he was there and did most of the talking. The Minister just listened. BS never gave an inch. He had a copy of the Company charter, from back to 1866. 'That water is ours,' he kept saying. 'The government said so, and here it is.' He waved that charter. 'We got it in writing.' I knew it was a mistake to take Des along, but Des was appointed. Don't get me wrong, now. Des is a brick, but he's not so cool-headed, not any more. 'So you can flood us,' he blurted, 'so your dams can just – ' BS cut him off. 'You ought to know, Mr. Deeks, the river has got to be regulated, you of all people. Now correct me,' he said, 'correct me if I'm wrong, but your brother, I'm right, am I not, your own brother is our man on the river.' Well, Des came back with 'Don't you drag Mitch into it, you four-eyed fuck,' pardon the language, and the meeting just fell apart. Shouts and recriminations. Worse than a game of hockey between us and Wolfe Island. It was depressing. I believe I will sit down.

He limps to a chair and lowers himself into it, his left leg straight out in front. How does a man get around, Jim wonders, on pins that skinny and a gimpy one to boot.

So, he says. Nothing.

Waste of time, a complete waste. Nothing could have been accomplished, it turns out. That charter is federal. Of course, nobody thought of that. All White could do—he's the Minister who had the pleasure of presiding, nice enough fellow, no help whatsoever—the most he could do was urge all parties to work it out between themselves, the Company and the farmers especially.

What about Ottawa?

What do you mean?

Shouldn't they be meeting with –

Jim, we're done with meetings. You think there's anything to choose between one politician and another?

You got a point.

The only interesting thing, the only thing we learned in Toronto, was from Scanlon. He was there representing Rathbun, and I don't know why.

Well, the logging.

That's what I would have thought. But Scanlon says there's a year or two of logging left. At best. 'She's just about played out, boys.' Those were his words.

Jim stops his rocking. No more logging, he says.

A year or two.

The doctor has stood up again. He's a restless stick. A stick man who walks with a stick. Never settles for long. Something eating him.

You know what it means, Jim, the logging all but done?

No more driver business in the spring, and during the winter cutting.

That's what it means to you, Jim, and I appreciate that, but it means something else too. You know the water is always lower now than it used to be, and the river silted?

That's right.

Well, those trees that went for lumber, they were holding the soil. They were keeping the skin of soil together all over that Shield country. When the trees go, the soil goes too. And the soil holds the water. Less soil, less water. Yes. That had me almost convinced, and one more futile meeting did the rest.

Convinced?

Yes. Walter limps to the outside door, looks out through the glass. Motions to Jim, close that door, the door to his quarters. Jim raises his eyebrows. What kind of a show is this? Walter nods. Jim rises and tiptoes to the door, eases it shut.

Yes, says Walter, low, Stegner and the others don't see it. BS doesn't see it. He doesn't have two good eyes in his head, never mind four. Well, you can't blame them. They don't want to see.

They're done, finished. It's just a matter of time. And there isn't much time for Des and the others. We have to do something, and soon. I'm asking you for a donation to the cause. Whatever you can afford.

The cause.

I think you know what I'm talking about. It's time for direct action. Two dollars. Fifty cents. Whatever you can spare.

Jim sits for a moment. You mind me asking you something, Doc?

Not at all.

Why you?

Why me collecting?

Walter takes a breath. He has prepared his answer to this question, and it still takes him by surprise.

BALLAD

(Malvolio)

WHY WALTER? The deepest reason is hidden from Walter himself.
Hauled too soon off the tit, as they say. Money always did the
work of love in the Morse family, propriety trumped affection.
Morse money put him through medical school at Queen's, and
that was where shame for his family's wealth and pretensions
took root and began to grow. He began living the austere life
he still cultivates. Why not become a monk, his mother spat in
their final argument. Why don't you go the whole hog and take
orders? That was bad enough, but the unforgivable followed. We
are idle shallow things, she mimicked, aren't we? We are not of
your element, are we? How—if she had even a trace of maternal
feeling—how could she ever have thrown that in his face, *that*,
of all things, the mistake of his life: letting himself be talked into
playing Malvolio in the school production of *Twelfth Night*. He
was a laughing stock both in and after the play. And there stood
his father before that ridiculously expensive Dutch painting of
cows, the gold chain dangling from the expensive watch in his
waistcoat pocket, hands clasped behind his back, rocking heel to
toe and smirking at his mother's withering wit.

It was Emma Goldman's inspiring lecture in Toronto that
furnished him with a philosophy. Capitalism is a scourge of
humanity, she said, all forms of government rest on violence.
Order is derived through submission and maintained by terror.

Amen, said Walter. Science was by then joined in his mind with an ideal of service. He repudiated his patrician parents, but not before they starved him of all social warmth. He knows that a good country doctor is no sophisticate. A country doctor should be a man of the people. That is Walter's aspiration. His hesitations gall him. Family is what he craves.

He craves to be gathered into the bosom of his adopted community, but the arms never open wide enough. Not even after he prevented the infant Bren Reynolds from strangling on the umbilical cord, in mysterious circumstances that, years after the event, trouble him still. If he hadn't somehow—he hates the illogic of this—if he hadn't *felt* that Mrs. Reynolds was in difficulties and made his way there uninvited – If not for that act, he'd be a complete misfit still. Dorothea is the key, his open sesame. If she would just give him the least bit of encouragement. If she would only give him some kind of an opening.

WHY ME? WELL, says Walter, I'm outside. Outside is the telltale word, scar over a deep wound. I'm not involved, he goes on, at least no one thinks I am. I won't be suspected. That's one thing. And I'm sick of it, Jim, that's the other thing. Sick and tired of seeing the people in this township, yes, and Hinchinbrooke as well, seeing them ignored and taken advantage of. Capital commands and labour jumps to it. When I first came here there was none of this animosity. Remember? Now it has the country poisoned. I happen to have the cure.

Cure is a bit much. He worked himself up to that. Otherwise, that's about right, he thinks. He got it right and kept mum about his revolutionist principles. Jim wouldn't understand any of that, common sense though it be. The masses seldom do. In San Diego, in the US of A, after one of Emma Goldman's speeches, vigilantes kidnapped her manager. They didn't get Emma that night, but they did catch Reitman. They tarred and sage-brushed him, and wrote IWW on his backside with lit cigars. Industrial Workers of the World won't fit across a man's buttocks, apparently. No, in rural Ontario, revolution must be covert.

Jim sits still. Yes, he knows what the money is for. Those dams. This will be bad for the Company. He shouldn't get involved, but what can a man do? Finally he clears his throat and says, Well, you're the doctor. He slides out the drawer in his desk, opens the cigar box, hands the doctor a dollar.

Thanks, Jim. I appreciate it.

Well, Doc. Good luck to you.

It's worth a dollar to see the back of him, Jim thinks. Doctor Death. What good ever comes of all this naysaying? He's wrong. How could you log a country out? Yes, millions of logs came down that river, so many over the years that they punched out the waterfall above Camden East. Back when the first settlers were moving in, back in the 1840s, they say it fell thirty feet. You could hear it miles away. There's a painting of the falls as it was in the lobby of the Colonial in Newburgh. Now it's just a long rapids. Spring after spring of the drive, those big logs wore it down, the rock elm especially, but the pine as well. They used to square off the logs where they were felled, out in the bush, so all the logs had corners. Little by little, they gouged out the limestone. Now they run easier down that stretch, and a good thing. And there's millions of trees up there yet. Got to be.

Year after year of those logs floated down to mills in Napanee and cut into timbers and sent overseas. For just the hull of one of those seventy-four-gun ships of the line? Ten thousand, six hundred tons of timber. Jim relishes the figures. That's seven hundred big trees right there. For the one ship. And those three-hundred-and-twenty-foot masts, with all the fittings? Some of them came right down the Napanee and out the St. Lawrence too. White pine. No better wood for those masts. That's our wood floating the British navy. It makes a man proud.

But Jim feels a chill, like somebody walked over his grave. He shivers. I've just given money to blow those dams, he thinks. What's going to happen to us?

The Doc don't know everything. A few things get by him. Maybe this is one of them. He probably thinks nobody knows he's sweet on the teacher and she's not sweet on him. Village this size, there's not many keeps a secret.

Lizzie Murphy couldn't. She tried to keep from telling who knocked her up, but they got it out of her. What in God's green acre she sees in Bob Henry, who could ever tell. Of all the possible men to pick for her ruination, she got the absolute worst.

She's a soft one, Lizzie, soft in the body, soft in the head. Murphys hardly ever let her out of their sight these past couple of years. Not hard to see why. Body of a woman already when she was thirteen, and that lazy flirty way with her. Flirt with anyone, she would. But you can't stop these things happening. Easier to dam the river. Damn sight easier.

No, you can't stop nature. She'll be burning at home, Lizzie, and then one day, or one night, out she goes—can't lock a girl up always—out she goes, and she runs into a snake, and he turns her head. Sixteen years old. No more school for her. Only good thing about it, Bob isn't going to make an honest woman of her.

Rocking, rocking and thinking, Jim's stomach is churning. What's he going to do if the Doc's right. Probably he's wrong, but what if he isn't? What would he and Lila and the young ones do? What good is a hotel with no customers?

After the other hotel burnt down, Lila wrote Stegner that Bob Henry had been spied passing Oak Flats that same evening. Of course, she wouldn't leave it at that. She had to drag in all the youth of Bellrock running wild, as though a big hat in Newburgh could do anything about that, or would. Young lads on the rampage in the back of the township, what's that to him? 'The morals of the youth is being destroyed every day,' she wrote, 'and will be as long as the older generation is permitted to go unpunished for crimes committed in their presence day after day. The writer has had occasion to travel through the locality several times and always could hear of some criminal offence that was committed or about to be. Chicken stealing, or turkeys and fowls of all kinds is not safe unless under lock and not even then.' On and on. She went after Mitch Deeks, too. That's just foolish. After all, who burnt up Mitch's house? And why? Well, why is not so hard to figure out, but none of the trouble along this river is Mitch's fault. Mitch is doing his job the best way he knows how. Everybody knows that. Everybody likes Mitch.

Well, there must be somebody that don't.

No finer man alive than Mitch Deeks. Good man in a bad job. Sad about him and Des. Brothers on opposite sides of the river, both senses of the word. Not speaking.

Jim is cautious by nature. He keeps his own views under his hat. He tried to keep Lila from sending that letter. What good ever comes of getting involved? That's what he said. She did send the thing, finally, but signed 'A Wellwisher.'

His own establishment filled up the night of the fire. No wonder the constable paid a visit. Who profits more from a fire at one hotel than the landlord of the other? Lila was his alibi, fine, but why mention snoring? Wash our dirty laundry in public, he said after the constable left. Why would you do that, woman? It's you calling it dirty, she retorted, and one word provoked another and he wouldn't have been welcome in her bed even if he hadn't decided to sit watch in his beloved chair. His chair, *her* bed.

He sat in his rocker all night for a couple of weeks after the fire, waking and sleeping, a couple pails of water handy. Nobody going to fling open *his* door and splash down a crescent of gasoline and light it up. Something terrible about that shape of a flame. It came out at the investigation. Nothing but a flaming horseshoe at first. Orville Stamp, his opposite number, woke to the smell and leapt up to find that horseshoe of flame snaked around on his lobby floor. I couldn't help staring, he said. I couldn't believe it. A great big horseshoe of fire. I was mesmerized, he said—big word for Orville—and it cost me time. I never got the water in there before it was too late, he said. She had took, he said. Nothing I could do, just raise the alarm and get out myself. I got my life, he said, and nobody else hurt, that's all I can say. But why? Somebody done this to me. Why?

Yes, why? Well, somebody, and maybe it was the same body, set the stop logs afire at Burnt Lake Dam same night. Bob Henry? Nobody proved it, but trust Bob Henry to be lurking wherever anything suspicious is going forward. Well, he buggered off after that business with Lizzie Murphy. Good riddance to bad rubbish.

Full many a jest is spoken
Full many a foul pest, choking,
　　To hide an aching heart;
　　Conceals a breaking fart,
And lips oft part in laughter
As cheeks do part hereafter,
　　Lest the hot tears should start
　　Phew! the foul fumes dart.
For oh! The springs of feelings
And through the cracks of ceilings
　　May oftimes deeper flow
　　Odours higher go
Than we, in our careless judging,
Than we, our noses grudging,
　　Can ever, ever know.
　　Can ever, ever know.

Judge not, judge not, my brother;
Grudge not, grudge not, my mother,
　　But know that every heart
　　But know, with all your heart,
Hath some close-fastened chamber
In some close-fastened chamber
　　Where sorrow sits apart;
　　That gas awaits a spark.
And from her crystal fountain,
And from that foul fountain
　　The tears unseen oft swell
　　My fears await a smell,
With grief, whose thrill of anguish,

The stench that makes me angry:
No words can ever tell.
The putrid in the dell.

— ANON
   Stella Bush

Dorothea slaps Stella's book down on the table and sits, glaring
at it, breathing hard, her cheeks flaming. The outrage! How
could she do this to me? Why? Dorothea is withdrawing all
support, abandoning the ungrateful wretch. Let her make her
own way. Try to be a woman in this world, Stella Bush, just you
try. See how hard it is to cope without your prop, your only, *only*,
support, you with your – she won't say birthmark. She won't say
curse. She has acted as though she is blind to that mark. She has
all but erased it from her thinking. It's not important, it's not real;
you look past it. Why does it come flaming out now? Her own
face aflame. Oh, Stella, she thinks, what are you doing?

   She picks up the book and looks over the pair of poems again.
She knows the source of the doggerel. Her eye brushed it in the
newspaper. She reads it through now, skipping Stella's interpola-
tions. 'Lest the hot tears should start.' That awkward line gives
her pause. If you're going to dum de dum along, then at least
be consistent with the rhythm. Otherwise, the thing flows well
enough. And yes, and yes, to the sentiments. Yes, the aching
heart, yes the hidden, the hiding. But the sentiments don't hold,
not in those words. They rise up and drift away. To the ceiling
and through the cracks.

She reads Stella's parody again. It's vulgar. Fart is not a word that has ever passed Dorothea's lips.

Passed. She feels a reprehensible smile forming on her lips. She feels laughter gathering somewhere in her mid-section. She gathers her pedagogical sternness to force it down. She marshals her disapproval. Something else that will not hold. The poem, the poet, had it coming. Waste your time stringing together banalities. She has to let the laughter come.

Nobody is listening to Dorothea on this beautiful morning. Everyone in the village is occupied with their own affairs, casual or serious. Too bad. That laugh is like water sparkling over stones. It is the sweetest sound to be heard on this morning or any other morning, in this or any other township. But there is nobody within earshot to feel the lift of that contagious laughter. Nobody to ask, smiling involuntarily, What's so funny?

What would Dorothea answer to such a question? Because this is not funny. This is serious.

Back to the original poem. That aching heart. No words for it. Why dismiss this honest, failed attempt to say something true?

Oh.

Stella is telling her something with *these* words. These are the words she wants Dorothea to take note of, not that she knows it. Of that, Dorothea is sure. Why this shocking outhouse humour, unlike anything Stella has ever shown her, unless the original words have struck home?

It's one thing to lend Stella books and discuss them with her. Words and ideas. It's not enough. A cry for help has to be answered. Throw out the lifeline. Someone is drifting away.

A terrible disappointment, yes, and a cry from the heart. What to do?

Dorothea feels tears welling in her eyes. Selfish tears, she thinks. I want my world to stay as it is, I do not want this complication. I am myself holding on, holding by the skin of my own teeth. The sun sinks out of her morning. To find herself thinking Not fair! A petulant child, that's what she is. The tears are falling freely now. Sorry for herself, when Stella needs her compassion. She dabs her eyes with a napkin. She sighs deeply and picks up the copy book.

First the doggerel. Resentfully, she feels it tugging at her. Oh God, she is saying yes to this—She will absolutely not sink to Stella's level. This—ordure.

Then Stella's answer. She puts the book face down and ponders. Opens it again and writes.

> I would say that the genre within which you are working, and I wonder if you know this, is the *palinode*, or poem of retraction. Of course, the palinode is normally written by a poet who has something to retract, or take back. You are not the composer of the original poem; the sentiments are not yours to retract, or subvert in that way. As for your *parody* (I don't need to tell you what parody means), it has a certain poetic virtue. I would call into question at least one word, though. Fumes can hardly be said to 'dart.' The word is chosen for the rhyme alone, and thus is not organic to your poem. Perhaps together we can choose a more appropriate word when we discuss this, at which time I would be interested to discover what happened to the original assignment.

Oh, Stella.

OFF THE CHAUMONT ROAD just north of Bellrock, over the fence where the posts are anchored in cribs of rock, Silas moves into the shadow of Devil Rock. Which doesn't mean brimstone and demon light, not to Silas. He hasn't heard the stories. He is drawn to what the others shun. He has never heard the rock named, never heard anyone speak of the Devil. He lowers himself down the sheared side of the crevice into the cold, dark chamber beneath.

They say the Devil punched out that big cube of rock, punched it up out of the granite of the Shield. They tease themselves with saying how the Devil got mad one day, tired of his damnation for eternity, a huge number, and pounded out that rock with one punch. The sides sheared off smooth as limestone quarried and dressed. That rock is the plug of Hell, they say. Nobody human could pull it out. Something escaped the night it happened, according to the story. Pete Swenson's house, just down the road from the rock, almost jumped its foundation. Pete ran outside, he said, and there was this terrible bright glow over at the rock. Hard on the eyes, he said, like somebody welding over there. Hell gas, they say, hell gas leaking out. Goes to show you: people will say anything.

What others shun is a refuge to Silas. It was his only refuge before he found the lost canoe and then the lost channel and built his hut in there, and it's the only place now where the lights don't come. The sun does not penetrate the deep darkness, nor does any other kind of light or lights. Maybe the darkness has nothing to do with it. Maybe it's the rock so close to Silas's eyes, as he lies slid into the body-sized slot down there.

Silas has no stories to turn over, none that he can speak to anyone else. His ears don't take words. No words, no sounds at all—not a cicada rasp or the trill of a veery—let alone stories. Never a whisper or a curse does he hear. Nothing wrong with his eyes. His eyes take in the world and they take lights, but that is different. Say the lights were a kind of talk, what would they be telling? Silas has no idea. He wants to be free of lights for a spell, today, long as he can tolerate the cold. Eventually the cold will work its way into his bones and he will have to slide over and stiffly climb back up.

Why is it that under Devil Rock and nowhere else he can always hear a sea? *His* sea, not the great ocean of which he has no conception. The sea in his ears. Under Devil Rock, there is always a wash, a pulsing, soothing, ahh-wash of a sea that never dried up. Everybody's ocean dries. Everybody's ears clear. Not his. Lying cold and stiff under Devil Rock, he listens to his sea, relaxed into rocking by the wash and wash of unseen waves.

Nothing forms out of the sea. Sea is a word he doesn't know. Nothing to see in the dark his eyes never adjust to. Lying so still, like a snake beneath a rock, he listens and listens. For what? For himself? There is something he so very badly needs to know.

Silas and the stone are one. He is not exactly thinking in his sea of sound that never dries, never clears. He is listening and listening. For a shriek and a sudden flip of sound into white silence? Brief shriek or sharp whistle, then a gentler shhh fading into silence cold and blank? An emptiness, a clearing in the dark, held open with enormous difficulty. Can he lift, by the power of his mind, a sash in the darkness under Devil Rock?

No lights. Mercifully, no lights. But for once Silas is not calm under Devil Rock. He is not relaxed. There is not and never could be any trace under Devil Rock of the light or heat of the sun—or any heat. So much for hell gas, so much for burning in hell. No, it's not the sun making Silas sweat for the first time under Devil Rock. He needs to know. He is listening, concentrating.

So. He slides out, clambers up. The sea-sound mutes in the afternoon light. It's more buzz than wash. Was Silas meant to be a troglodyte? He knows nothing of the limestone caverns near Centreville. Few do, yet. Eventually somebody will have the bright idea to call them Hell Holes and open them up to tourists. Picnic Area, Snack Bar, Mini Golf. Why is any fissure in the earth's crust consigned to the devil?

What is any of this to Silas? On the earth and beneath the sky, where other people roam, he has his troubles, he even has joys.

April is uncharacteristically humid and hot. The sweat won't be drying soon. Across the grass and over the patches of crocus he goes. Over the fence, on to the Chaumont Road and down the road to Bellrock. Entering the village, he moves along the creek, behind the houses. Through the village, across the road between Enterprise and Verona, down the Swamp Road to the bridge. Under the bridge, his canoe is tied up where he left it.

At the bow end of the canoe, just in front of the seat, which faces the stern, is a drinks cabinet and a platform designed to hold a gramophone. Silas would shake his head if he ever saw a gramophone there, because the canoe is narrow and inclined to tip. You do have to wonder what the designer was thinking. Imagine. You're out in the lake. A calm enough day on First Lake. There is a lady in the bow seat. There has to be a lady. No gramophone could possibly be meant for a solitary paddler. No, you want the lady in the bow, for romance, yes, but also to wind the gramophone and very delicately place the needle in the first groove of the wax disk. Also for balance. That canoe and that gramophone have to be level and they have to stay level. The lady has to be calm, well-balanced by nature, and even so she will have to be tactfully advised not to change position abruptly. Otherwise, there goes the needle, scritching across the record. If that needle slides right away over and off, it cuts an arc across the circles of those grooves and the scratch so made will hiccup into the speaker once in every revolution of that disk. Or the arc might be so deep as to shunt the needle right across the record every time. There goes your 'Whispering Hope,' your 'Home Sweet Home.'

Silas keeps a piece of driftwood on that platform, a figure a little like the homunculus he has in his sack. This one has its arms spread as though flying. The head is grotesque, with a long, twisted snout on it. He didn't like that snout, at first. He thought he might take a knife to it, whittle it off. But he got used to it. Now he likes to look at the figure while he paddles.

There is something comforting about it, like the things in his sack. It is most like a person, a bosomy woman, many-breasted, and at the same time a beast. Not quite a person. There are no legs and no hands at the ends of the arms. It's changing, that's what. It always seems to be passing between shapes as he looks at it, watches it. It might change before his eyes.

No, you wouldn't really want a gramophone on the shelf, not even if you were an expert canoeist. Which Silas now is. You'd be better off carrying a ukulele, supposing you could play one, for music on the river. To serenade the lady. But where does the ukulele come from? Hawaii, that's where. And where else does it show up? Oh, anywhere people have nothing better to do than tinkle out silly little tunes on gut strings. Wearing straw boaters, in rowboats on small, placid, artificial lakes in the centres of cities and towns. Just let any one of Scanlon's men catch you strumming a ukulele along the Napanee. Never hear the end of it. George Hudson? Ukulele-strumming Mama's boy. No river swallows a real man. Well, what about poor Frank Deeks, riding that log down the river? Oh, he was a man all right. Too bad he had to prove it.

There was no music machine aboard when Silas caught up to the canoe, submerged, half-concealed with branches, snagged on a deadhead.

Best day of his life.

He'd been standing in the fall of water over the lip of the dam at Bellrock when he glimpsed it first, almost sensed it. Something dark, oh! A huge fish? gliding over his head, blocking the sun. Late May and high water. A log? The front drive still at Second Depot. A log might have slipped out of the boom, though. If a log, he'd have been a goner. It would have crushed him. But there was no time to think log or fish or anything, just flinch away from the nightmare shadow apparently descending in broad daylight. He shrank back against the dam, well behind the fall.

Then the shadow was gone, like a fat cloud had cleared the sun. He stuck his head out of the water. He could see the thing, tilted and foundering, sliding around the bend of the creek. He hopped to the bank, caught up his shirt and jogged down the road. Missed it at the first bridge. He padded down the Long Swamp Road, then. Waited and waited at the second bridge. It never showed up.

Paddling back to the hut now, Silas is looking for his good feeling. His finding that canoe, the good of that. He can't get the comfort from his beast-woman stick. Something is gathering in him. He's familiar with that, at least. He will see something soon. It might tell him what to do. Make him feel better. Right now it's like being sick to his stomach, but the trouble is not in his gut. Or is it? Yes it is. There and also in his head, his light-afflicted mind, so just throwing up won't help. Back at the hut, whatever it is might show itself. He could decide, then. What to do. Even now, something is forming, just edges. Gold. Soft gold and purple.

He walked back toward Bellrock, to trace the canoe from where he'd seen it last. This was three summers back. A hot day and no one else at the dam. Good day for a good soak and then lie out and dry off. Then that canoe came down the river. From where? Silas doesn't think much about origins. He knew Mitch's bark, he knows it, but never a real cedar beauty. Such a beautiful vessel lost on its maiden voyage—that's right, first time—down the river below Burnt Mill dam. A bad decision that, trying her out in the river. Why not in the lake above the dam? Ask young James Wilson. Didn't want to be humiliated if he tipped and dunked.

Better to be embarrassed and not lose your canoe. That's what young Wilson told himself after the event. Saved himself, that's a mercy, but there went his father's brand new Peterborough Comfort Courting Canoe. Nothing came of the reward poster tacked up in stores and post offices in Bellrock and Verona and Petworth, nothing whatever. Brand new canoe. How off the face of the earth, how from the sweet-flowing waters of the mildly turning earth, meaning Depot Creek, does a brand new Peterborough just up and disappear in the year nineteen and ten? Owners of less fancy, more stable canoes, one hundred and twenty Peterborough models to choose from, seldom find themselves asking such questions.

73

James Wilson never set foot in a canoe again. He settled on the other side of the Portland Road and gave his name to a short stretch of country road in Bedford Township, beauteous in summer for the overarching nave of the trees that meet above it.

When Silas found the escaped canoe, it was submerged, snagged on a deadhead, half concealed with branches. Three springs ago. It changed everything.

Another change coming. Silas can feel it. Sometimes it seems that he thinks with his skin. Information comes in where his skin meets air. He has never been to school. The old man never knew what to do but give up on him. Give up and lie down on the daybed in the shack. Pull that ratty blanket up over his shoulders, turn his face to the wall. Silas to shift for himself.

Somebody has to think for Silas in the ordinary way, putting words to his thoughts. Of course Silas *can* think. Some things he knows and accepts. They never trouble him. The old man, his grandfather, the only kin he has ever known—wasn't he a young man once? Certainly he was young. We all were. Few of us were warriors, though. Few of us had the good fortune turned bad to be born and raised in the Mohawk Nation. Gabriel Monture used to run with Tom Longboat, for god sakes. Well behind Longboat, yes, but then Longboat was not the baseball player, was he? Longboat never had those years of semi-pro ball. He didn't have the arm. But Tom stayed sober. Oh, the bottle is a long and a deadly tale of decline. Just as well Silas has no way into it. He has the old man's papers. He took them, he doesn't know why, not to this day, but he took them the day he came home and found the old man lying on the daybed by the stove, but facing the door for once. His eyes were open but he closed them quick.

Don't want to see me.

Silas took the papers. No idea what they are, though now he knows windup, step, throw. He doesn't know the old man is the young man depicted in the photograph, the caption reading 'Chief Sets Down 18 Batters. One Out Shy of a Perfect Game.'

And then what to do with the canoe, turned up, drained and newly floated. Varnished so golden, inside and out, that it might have floated out of the sun. So light on the water Silas could send it off with a finger, stop it with a finger.

Hide it.

Silas was shoving the canoe into the bushes at the margin of the cut. He rammed it into the willows there, expecting it to catch, expecting to have to draw it back and shove again—just get it out of sight for the time being. He has little sense of ownership, of stealing. What if he did? Should he have pushed that canoe back to Bellrock? He couldn't paddle it then, even if he knew how. There was no paddle. Push it back to Bellrock and look for the owner? Young James Wilson to regain his new cedar strip courting canoe? Forget Wilson. He's much better off than George Hudson, who lost his horse and buggy and his life. Not to mention poor Frank Deeks. And Silas has, well he *had*, nothing.

The canoe just disappeared into those bushes. It slid easily through them and they closed behind it. Silas was left standing waist-deep in the water. That beautiful wishbone-shaped bow and narrow body penetrated the bushes much more easily than Silas, splashing after it. The branches caught at his arms and shoulders. He turned sideways and forced his way through, into an overgrown, sand-bottomed channel, and there was the canoe, nudging the bushes in quiet, shallow water like a horse that bucks off its rider and is satisfied with that. Now to snatch a few mouthfuls of grass.

Silas reached the canoe, placed his hand on it, pondered. It was safe, already hidden right there. But out beyond it now was this narrow channel. Where does that go? The draw was irresistible. He started walking in the shallows, pushing the canoe ahead.

Pretty soon it was no longer a channel. It was swamp. There was no bank as such, just patches of land where tall trees had somehow taken root. That was what kept him pushing on, struggling past fallen trees and around hummocks raised on the ragged edge—the feeling of shelter under that canopy, shelter and solitude. Sand underfoot, at first, and, high overhead, all that green. The bottom was not solid everywhere, though. One spot looked safe enough, but gave way so he dropped waist-deep into black muck, bubbles plopping out of it with a stench that made him want to retch. If he hadn't been shoving the canoe over that stretch, and held on when it gave way, he might have plunged right down. That stinky muck might have closed right over his head. He thrashed his way out of there.

Beyond, the small channel opened again. Now he could walk in the creek wherever it was shallow. There were places where the canoe passed over wave-rippled, sun-gold sand. Sun canoe, sunny creek bed. He could see his moccasins advancing like slow water creatures. He laid full out to let the water clean off the muck. There was grit inside his clothes still, and in his moccasins, but the water relieved him. Soothed the scratches on his face and arms. He took his time. He might have been many miles away from the dam at Bellrock where all this began.

He stood up and began wading again, shoving the canoe ahead, catching up with it, shoving it on. He pushed it on into a pool before he realized that the channel was opening out. There it went, floating away, and here he was, footing suddenly gone.

Does not having a word for panic preclude the experience of panic? What was it Silas felt back at the dam, when that shadow appeared overhead? An instant hollowing. He had been solid, flesh and bone right through, and then he was empty. He was there, then he was not, and then he was again. Like surviving a lightning strike. How is it you could have been hit, lifted bodily, flung onto your back, plucked right out of your shoes, which lie there precisely where you were standing at the stove when the lightning rushed down the stovepipe into the stove into you—shoes right there, side by side, laces still tied tight—how could that ever have happened unless you had dematerialized and then reassembled when the chain at your neck, the one with the locket on it, the locket with the tiny picture of your parents in it, when that locket chain deflected the charge from rising to your brain? The mark of that chain burnt into the flesh of your neck for weeks, the burn sensation with you for years. It's not panic when you are lost to yourself. And I say it was not panic when Silas was launched into deep water for the first time in his life, and the water closed over his head.

It was a surprise, the first in his life that he actually liked, and now he stayed within himself. He gave himself instinctively to the water. Not for nothing has he been a watcher. He had watched the others at the mill pond often enough to know what their arms and legs do in the water. The familiar motions came to him. Limbs churning, he surfaced, sputtering. He thrashed and splashed. Found he was not sinking, though his feet were not touching bottom. Then he made himself fall forward in the direction of the canoe, now drifting lazily in the middle of the pool. Paddling awkwardly, he made way through the water. When he reached the canoe, he grabbed the gunwale with one arm and rested.

Then he uttered a great Ahhh that could have been heard for a mile had any ears been cocked to it.

That's right. Nothing wrong with Silas's vocal cords. He just lacks instruction in using them. What is *that*, a listener would have asked herself—Katherine Bush, for example, weeding the patch of potatoes behind her house. What on earth is that, she might have exclaimed out loud, straightening up, automatically pressing her fist to the small of her back. That is no cow. That is no bossy bellow, and yet. What *is* that? But Katherine was in the house at that very moment, grumbling to herself. It would surprise no one to know what only Stella knows for certain: her mother is a private as well as a public grumbler. So Katherine Bush, the neighbour nearest to Silas where he was latched on by his elbow to James Wilson's father's lost canoe, did not hear that howl and ask herself what soul was just then sucked into the bowels of hell. Would the tot, her mother's little daughter, have risen up in her? Would she have crossed herself?

Ah, but the howl was for joy. It was a laugh. It was the lost voice in full cry. And then Silas gulped air, released his grip on the canoe and let himself sink. Down, down to the bottom, the rich, thick mucky bottom, into which, when he bent his knees and sprang, his feet unexpectedly sank, absorbing half the thrust, so he arrived at the surface with no breath to spare. But he was up in the sun once more, then down, then up. Splashing and thrashing with his arms and legs. Swimming. He struck off awkwardly across the pool, away from the canoe, and fetched up against a fallen tree. Arm hooked on a branch, he rested again. Across the pool he saw the beaver dam snaking through the woods. He saw the root structure of a great fallen tree, still clutching soil and stones in the widespread network of roots, a solid wall levered into the air. He saw something else. Home.

Silas is master of the swamp now. He has his hut with the raft floor, built against that vertical root structure. He has new channels, channels of his own. He will take the canoe as near Bellrock as the bridge over the swamp road, no farther. He has no thought of ownership, no concept of stealing, but he is no fool. He knows how long he would retain the use of that canoe if anyone ever found him with it. Now he glides up to the hut, steps onto the floor in one smooth motion, turns and looks back the way he came. He always does. The V of his wake is spreading in waves across the pool. He is completely alone. The sun is still hot, unusually so for this time of year. He lies down on his bed of boughs and closes his eyes.

Something coming. He needs to see it.

MONDAY, APRIL 14. 7:30 AM, Dorothea draws a deep breath and pushes open the door to Walter Morse's surgery.

Dr. Morse, she says, in a deliberately neutral voice. Even so, his eyes widen and he smiles broadly before regaining something of his professional manner. Not all of it. Of course not. Not given this sudden angelic vision of the woman he adored the moment he clapped eyes on her. And she has come to him!

Please, Miss Asselstine, he says from behind his desk, Walter.

He is dressed in his customary black. Behind and above his head, on his wooden cabinet, is a small plaster cast of The Thinker sporting a tiny red skullcap. The incongruous flash of red briefly catches Dorothea's attention. Then Walter lurches to his feet and gestures toward one of the two chairs. He has a reflector on his forehead. With his long face and prominent cheekbones, it lends him an Egyptian look, a look of something angular carved in low relief on a stone wall. A statue, smiling. Which she is not, not smiling, and not accepting his invitation to sit. He catches hold of the desk to steady himself. His smile fades.

Bum leg, he says.

Why does that enrage her? Why can she not restrain herself? I know about your leg, sir. Everyone – Enough. She is not here to fight. But it's already too late.

Ah! he retorts. Everyone in town? So much anatomical interest. It certainly does people credit. And your leg, your legs? I suppose the whole township –

That will be quite enough, sir! She colours and whirls to the door.

What are you, Doctor Morse, one might ask, a Pisces? Where is your consistency? In fact, he is a phlegmatic Virgo. His consistency is as would-be lover.

Now his tone is wheedling. Please, Miss Asselstine. I apologize. She turns, her hand still on the knob. That was uncalled for, he says. I am very sorry. He gestures once again at the chair. She looks at it. I'm afraid you provoke me, he continues.

I provoke *you*!

Well, you are provoking. Provocative.

Doctor Morse, I am not here to be provocative or anything else to you. They stand, facing each other, eyes locked. There is snap in hers. His expression passes rapidly through outrage, disappointment, resignation. He sits down, heavily. She removes her hand from the knob. He gathers himself, summoning his best hearty office demeanour.

Well, he says, well. Well, what can I do for you. Are you well? He raises his hands just off the desk, a tentative gesture that she sees is repudiating the banality. The pathetic, silly creature.

I am perfectly well, thank you.

Then –

Doctor Morse –

There is no chance of Walter?

And you have the face to call me provocative!

I'm sorry, Ma'am. I'm sorry. Will you please sit. Please sit down and tell me what brings you here on a Monday so early. She hesitates for a moment, looking hard at him. Is he going to continue so? Then she relents and seats herself.

You won't come collecting to me, Doctor Morse, she says, so I have come to you. I don't have money. If I had any extra money I know what I'd do with it. But I know what you're collecting for.

Now he looks hard at her.

You do.

Let's not pretend, Doctor Morse. I teach their children. I hear the talk. I know what is afoot, and I cannot stand by –

Miss Asselstine, this is no business for a lady. He makes to rise again, but she lifts a hand to stop him. Exactly what she expected. Bitterness floods her voice.

Not for ladies. I can teach them – I teach history, you know. I know something about history. I know about war, for example.

War!

Don't trifle with me, Doctor Morse. War along the Napanee. Let's call it what it is. 'War on all oppressors and all despoilers.' I can't stand aloof while this goes on. Stand by helplessly and watch? No. I'm offering you Bellrock School.

The school.

Yes, the school. For your meeting.

He looks at her, calculating. If he involves her – But she is involving herself. But if he accepts this gesture, does he put her in jeopardy with the trustees? He would not put her in jeopardy for the world. She sees his hesitation.

Where else would you gather?

His eyebrows raise. The point has hit home.

I'm a serious woman, she continues. I am very serious about this. I will not attend, but the school is yours.

Tom Ritchie?

Mr. Ritchie will be there.

Ah. So the trustees are with her. At least the chairman.

The school, then.

Tomorrow. Thank you. He hesitates. She stands up. I thank you very much, he says.

You're welcome, I'm sure. She reaches a gloved hand towards him. He takes it.

A truce? He holds on to the hand. He has not touched her hand since the day they were introduced, but he has never forgotten the feel of it. Slender fingers, soft palm. A soft, dry, small hand.

Truce. She smiles now, for the first time since entering his office, if rather grimly, and it undoes him. Dorothea, he says, and her face instantly hardens.

Let us understand each other, Doctor Morse, she says, allies need not be intimates. May I have my – He releases her hand.

I would like to understand you, Miss Asselstine. Very much.

I thank you for your interest, sir. If I could reciprocate –

I see.

She turns to the door. Good luck, she says over her shoulder. Then she is out and the door clicks shut behind her.

Sir, he repeats dully.

Still standing, he stares at the closed door. It closes him in. What she has just said is unsatisfactory. It diverges so radically from his own desires that he will not, cannot, credit it. Not at this moment.

She rules her classroom. He knows that. No one with any brain to speak of ever fails a grade. Not unless they refuse to work, and she drives even the dull ones. She has intelligence, authority. It was there on the day they met, all of it, all there in her bearing, her deliberate, graceful movements. She is more, much more, than the sum of her parts, much more than her physical attractiveness. The attractiveness is more than physical. That was a terrible slip about her legs. He should never, never, never have let that slip out. But why was she angry before the interview began? She has closed more than one door on him. He is devastated.

In the shade on the walk outside, Dorothea pauses and rests her back briefly on the wall beside the door, hands clasped behind her. Her eyes close. They are misted when they open. Then she squares her shoulders. Her heels clip the boards smartly as she walks to the station. She can hear the locomotive releasing steam. She is expected. Train to Harrowsmith, trap to Sydenham. Time to gain control of herself, change the conspirator back into a teacher.

Bellrock

May 25, 1912

D.B. Stegner Esq.

Napanee River Improvement Company

Newburgh, Ontario

Dear Mr. Stegner,

    I never in my life saw sutch a fearful drought at this time of the
season. All the little creeks running into the lakes have been dryed
up nearly three weeks. I have fixed the dam at Third Lake without
causing the Company much expense. The river being low beyond the
dam I got most of the materials out of the river. The drive is moving
rather slow. Mr. Scanlon had a spat last spring with Rooke the man
who owns the old saw mill above Bellrock and Rooke tore down the
old mill and dam last fall and would not let Scanlon build an other
dam as it is a bad place to run. With out a dam they are having a
pritty hard time of it. Rooke is determined they shall pay him before
they build a dam and Scanlon is just as determined to put the drive
through without a dam. The tail is in the creek above Burnt Mill. The
back drive is small, only one small gang of men on back drive, but 100
men at the front. Scanlon was at Davey's hole Tuesday the thirteenth

and give his men who are camped there orders to open the dams and keep them open.

Please tell Mr. O'Donohue not to do any more sharking on my account. I know it was him said it was me keeping the dams open. The reason Scanlon is in sutch a flurry about Burnt Mills dam is that he has done a lot of damage along the river by drowning it and he wishes to blame someone else. And who does the blame fall on but the Company.

Well Mr. Stegner I have tryed not to bother you with my aches and pains but I guess I will have to do so yet. I have always felt for years happy when I could be in a camp but my canvas camps and the cold weather in April has pritty near fixed me this time. I have had siatic rheumatism in my left hip and leg since the last of April. Dr. Morse in Verona can do very little for it. I am going back to camp as soon as it stops raining and will try and tough it out till river driving is over. Then it's hospital in Kingston for me. Wish me luck.

Mr. Stegner, it was Bob Henry one of those individuals breaking up the dam at 13 Island Lake. Mr. Stegner, nobody in these parts knows any good of this character. I don't think the dams can be left. I will engage a replacement Mr. Thomas Long from here while I am away.

Yours respectfully,

Mitch Deeks

HERE IS BUSY WALTER, out on his rounds again, driving north from Verona, turning west onto the Snider Road. Without tonight's errand, what would he be doing? He'd be up in his rooms above the surgery. Well, that is where he will be later on tonight. He will have to pierce that emptiness and rustle himself up a bit of a meal. Then? The usual. Sit at the chair drawn up to the window and look down on the street, where he might be lucky enough to see a person or two pass. Most evenings a few people make their way to and from Walker & Genge. Sophie Whan passes every night. Set your clock by the Widow Whan. Sometimes she comes back along carrying nothing but whatever fellowship she managed to find at the counter. She can seek it out, she has that advantage. The Doctor can no sooner set up to loiter at the store than Sid Smart could. Of course Sid is married and has a child. What would a flat-headed parson want with loitering? He can stay at home, contentedly ignoring Walter, who is not of his congregation, not of any congregation. To Walter, who cannot risk saying so aloud, religion is what Emma Goldman calls it: 'one of the pernicious influences which have so far prevented the harmonious blending of individual and social instincts, the individual and society.' Religion aside, though, Walter is The Doctor. The Doctor does not gallivant among the people, not even a doctor with proletarian sympathies.

Walter sits at his window of an evening, peering out, despising himself. When it gets too dark to see, he rises, brews himself a cup of tea, dips into his pamphlets. If he would only review the one entitled 'Stateless Socialism: Anarchism,' he might realize that Dorothea has that very morning quoted Bakunin to him. Walter hasn't gone to drink yet, not beyond the drop medicinal. He hasn't yet found how a few drinks can lift a solitary and a few more smash him down. He doesn't like living inside himself, but at least his mind is still sharp in the mornings. So far. He needs it to be so.

In the slant evening light, he drives up the Snider Road, turns off onto First Lake Road, continues along the twisting and undulating road to the hill above the lake and down it to where the lake opens out. It's normally a pleasure to greet that water vista through the trees, not tonight. Then up the hill on the other side. Just at the top, he spies Gladys, Lachlan's famous cow, Gladys and her boon companion grazing on the verge. Can't keep her home, Lachlan says. She likes to get out. Likes to wander. Bit of the wild goose in her, you know, and she always takes Beulah with. Never seen one cow and another cow get so friendly. Lachlan is proud of that cow. Smartest cow he ever saw, he says, can't hold her, can't keep her in.

Doña Quixote, Walter thinks, pulling back on the reins. Gladys is tall and gaunt, with a look of slightly mad intent about her. She swings her big head around to inspect him: just where do you think *you're* going, Mister? The short, squat companion grazes on. Sancho Panza. Sancha? Walter's Spanish is shaky. One tall bovine, he thinks ruefully, one gangly cow in search of better wheat than is made into bread, and a foolish tagalong with a mind as deep, and no deeper, than the cow mind of the ages. 'Lambent dullness played about her face,' he thinks. The line is about people, not cows, and he has had ample opportunity to think it about people. Why is it that those who govern are so often not only dull, but narrow-minded and self-interested? If you could get these minor officials to do anything, ever, ordinary people might rest in their own lives. They would not have to step out. They would not have to take corrective action. He would not be visiting Lachlan on this beautiful April evening.

Heartbroken.

He would be at home, he reminds himself flatly. 'Home, sweet Home.'

Whoa. Walter climbs down from the buggy, picks up a length of dry sumac from the roadside. He smacks Gladys on the rear with the stick, throws up his hands and whoops to shoo the partners away from their grazing. Gladys starts and gallops off up Lachlan's lane. Beulah looks up suddenly and tears off after her. Walter can't help but smile. A perfect image of foolishness, the pair of them. He drives up the lane behind them, past the dilapidated outrider sheds, through the gate and into the yard. He stops to shut the gate. Easy to see how she gets out, he thinks, seeing the chain hanging loose from the post. He nudges the gate closed, snugs the chain around the gate and the post and onto the hook. If Lachlan were just to pull the chain tight, at least. She'd have her work cut out for her then.

But that's Lachlan's business. Walter's business is with the worker of dynamite, who steps out onto his stoop in combinations, trapdoor flapping.

Walter nods at Lachlan's rear end. Am I interrupting?

Interrupting? Lachlan snorts. He doesn't follow. No, no. Come and set. Get you a drink?

Little too early for me, Lachlan.

Noo, Doc, no. Never too early. Too early for a drink? He cocks his head to one side, reproachfully, places his hands on his hips. C'mon, Doc. Good for what ails ya.

You prescribing, Lachlan. You after my job? That's a good one, Walter thinks. *Nota bene*, he thinks: the lighter note is the more winning.

Lachlan's chuckle reinforces the insight. He has heard Walter's capitulation. He pours two cups of clear liquor from a jug of shine on the porch.

There ya go, Doc. Here's mud in yer eye. He raises the cup in salute and downs his own drink. Walter takes an appraising look at the cup. Washed last month, maybe. Maybe never. Hard to say how long it takes a vessel to get that filthy. Well, for the sake of negotiation. He knows better than to sip. He closes his eyes and throws the liquor back. It burns all the way down, then hits him back of the head with the force of a fence post. Whoo, he whistles through his grimace. Lachlan grins, picks up the bottle, raises his eyebrows. Another? Walter's voice is gone. He can only shake his head. Lachlan shrugs and refills his own cup.

Nice evening, he says pleasantly.

Walter is waving his hands in front of his face. He holds up an index finger. Hang on, Lachlan, hang on. I need my voice back.

Lachlan grins and lowers himself to the stoop. Stands up quickly, sets down the cup and fastens his trap door. Sits again, picks up the cup. Gladys clops past them down the lane. Beulah? Ah, there she comes.

MORNING

THE SHED DOOR squeaks and then whooshes open on its sliders. Tom Ritchie's boar rises heavily to his feet and trots heavily out into the pen. He pushes his snout under the bottom rail. Nothing, nothing. He trots to the trough. Nothing, nothing, nothing.

That pig knows a lot, Tom says, and he says the same of the house cat. Maybe he's right about them both. But all of that pig's knowledge this morning is appetite. Tom will hurry breakfast from the other side of the pen. Get between Norman and his slops, he don't go around you.

SILENCE IN THE DEEKS KITCHEN. Emma Deeks at the stove, scraping the griddle. Des and Michael at the table. They've had their eggs, they're at the pancakes. Maple syrup from the sugar bush. The cows are on their way in. Right now they'll be about at the arch where last month Des and Michael were busy at the sugaring. Michael and his mother spelling each other at the fire all night when the sap was flowing most freely. All that work: it's a wonder Michael still likes syrup, but he does, and so does his father. In fact, though Des would never, ever, say so, he loves the taste all the more for loving the idea of syrup. For nothing but his own labour and the labour of his wife and son — cutting the firewood in winter for the fire under the vat, keeping the fire fed, gathering and pouring in pail after pail of clear sap, boiling and boiling it down—for muscle and time: such bounty. From the land. The young lad don't understand how to value the good Lord's gifts, he thinks. He is always picking at this bone with Michael these days, this bone or that, worried he isn't growing up right, remembering Frank, his flashy irresponsible brother. Waste of a wastrel when he drowned. But he might have made something of himself eventually. The good Lord has been a teeny bit niggardly these last few years, but not with the syrup. With the rain, yes. And the marsh hay washed right out. Not blaming the Lord for that, but the Company. The Company better pay. And the young lad better listen. He'd damn well better listen.

Look at the closed faces. Not that of Emma at the stove with her back to the others, scraping at the griddle to clear it for batter. The batter for scones, for lunch. Her face is merely sad and grim. She harbours unreasonable hopes for those scones. She wants them to melt in the mouths of her men. She wants those scones to soften them to each other. But right now, some flint, something mean, infects the air of this beautiful April morning.

Lately it was Michael trying to sleep in, imagining he could sleep late on a Saturday. What kind of a dairy farmer gets a morning off, ever? Michael is no kid now. He's old enough to be a man around the place. Be grateful, his father thinks, be grateful to them who – what is that? He's heard that before. From his own father? Never mind. Be grateful. Period. The air of the kitchen is charged with unexpressed anger.

Des's chair scrapes back, he rises. Michael waits a couple of beats, this morning's brief, sullen protest. Then he pushes back his own chair. Father and son, one after the other, pass into the summer kitchen, lift their jackets off the hooks by the door and step out into cool morning air. Mist rising off the duck pond. Cows bunched at the barn door.

THROUGH THE WALL, Stella hears her mother still wheezing and whistling in sleep. She swings her legs out of bed, slides into her clothes, tiptoes down the stairs, grabs an apple and a bun and heads out the door to the creek. Along the path by the creek to her favourite rock, the one shaped like a throne. Well, anyway, a seat. Meditation Rock. Her straw-coloured hair, the purple birthmark livid on her left cheek, her lithe slender body in the faded hand-me-down blouse and skirt. Down the creek, perchance to dream a little before school. Before facing the music.

MITCH DEEKS IS OUT the door, favouring his hip. He limps down Perry Street to the creek and his bark. He has orders from Mr. Stegner, remove two stop logs at Burnt Mill dam. He posts his response at the post office, through the slot in the door. May it not be lost this time. A change of government might do some good, he thinks. Dead wood in the government, rot in the township. Let them keep their family squabbles to themselves, away from the mail.

At the dam by the mill, Mitch unties his bark, steps in. With a relaxed, economical motion, he strokes away towards Second. Going to be another beautiful day, beautiful. No relief for the hip, though, neither walking nor sitting. He is getting too old for this.

IN THE ROOM ABOVE his surgery, Walter Morse is frying bacon and toasting bread. 6:15. He has an hour and a quarter before surgery. Bacon and bread. He should have double. He should have fried potatoes and eggs and molasses, put some meat on those bones. But he tried that. Nothing sticks to him, howsoever he packs it in. Bony he was bred, skinny he remains, skin and bones his fate. Why waste time and provisions trying to fatten up? Steak or pork or chicken, he has little interest in preparing these things, these comestibles. Fish. What about fish? How to cook a fish? He had fish last week, at The Tallen House. That was good. Maybe he should eat out all the time.

At the edge of his thought, and he holds it out there this morning, will not regard it squarely, cannot bear to, is the vision of a bright kitchen with a small table set for two, a checkered tablecloth, immaculate. A steaming cup of coffee at his place, on his side of the table, where he seats himself, and Dorothea's slim hand, protected by a quilted lavender potholder, setting down a heated plate in front of him. Eggs, sunny-side up, two thick slices of bright red tomato, two fat slices of buttered toast.

He throws another strip of bacon in the pan. He's giving himself a bit of an appetite, at least.

And then her plate, as she sits down opposite, still wearing her apron. No. She removes the apron, folds it carefully, places it on the sideboard. Now she sits, smiling at him like the sun.

Her shining eyes.

Not for him. Not ever. Never.

DOROTHEA'S EYES ARE CLOSED, but she is awake, sun on her eyelids, warm under the covers, beneath her quilt. She loves that quilt. It marks her 10th anniversary at Bellrock School. Many careful hands in many a bee made that quilt. With these remnants, these scraps of home-sewn clothing worn past use and wasted not, something of each of their lives is carried into the squares of fabric log, browns and tans for the day on two sides, blues for the night on the other two, with a bright red patch at the centre of each one. Red for the hearth. Thirty square log houses, each with a warm hearth, a heart. The houses of her community, her love for it returned.

In ten minutes, when she rises, she will make the bed carefully, lovingly, tucking in the nurse's corners of the sheets, remembering her mother in those corners, folding back the quilt at the head of the bed and plumping up the pillows. She will carefully place the throw cushion Emily embroidered with the Old English D, place it right side up, having first held the satin cool against her cheek.

SILAS WAKES ON THE NEW BOUGHS he laid down in the hut last night. His eyes open and he looks up at his roof. No light leaks through that anywhere. No light, and no rain, when there is rain.

The spiders began to crawl out of the boughs as soon as he laid them down. He knew they would. He sat with his arms around his knees to watch them crawl out and away. Interrupted lives. How long do you live before something goes wrong that can't be fixed? Spider families. Well, no little ones until the summer. In these branches. That he cut from that tree, that living tree. The blood of a tree is sap. He has sap on his hands. The tree will heal itself. What about the lives of the spiders? They have to start over.

He nudged the spruce bed with a foot. Make sure all have left. Squash nobody. It was not such a tender watch, not like the first time he laid boughs down on that floor, nor most times since. Something coming. He can't fix it.

The cat lying on his chest stretches, begins to knead. Wait. Unhook there. Ow. That's better. He strokes the cat. It's the only one left of the kittens Jeb McMullin put in a bag to drown. Tossed the bag into the creek. Using the creek that way! Silas hauled the bag out and untied the string. Let the kittens go because he couldn't keep them. They were small. The fox got two. He found the bones, bits of fur. Gathered the bones for the sack. Swamp sack. Bones and bits of other things. Silas's sack. Did the other kitten, this one, did it watch, behind a tree? Couldn't the fox smell it? Silas almost stepped on it, crossing Miller's hayfield. He picked it up and carried it back to McMullins', opened the drive shed door, dropped it gently in.

Next day he was passing the field again. A mother skunk was crossing. She was rushing through the open with about a dozen baby skunks scurrying with her, spread out around her, but close, like they were attached, their little legs going like mad. It looked like one black and white creature with a wide, rippling fringe.

Silas stopped to watch. He was startled by something brushing the back of his leg. It was the kitten, winding now around his ankles.

You got out? Here you are.

So he took it into the swamp. He had to feed it, at first, bring it along. Not now. It learned to hunt. Kitten takes some care, not a cat.

He lies with his eyes open, stroking the cat, first light rising over the creek. Shifts to his side, the cat slides off. There is the beaver pool. A first heron humping by. The bullfrogs that grumbled and snapped in relays up and down the creek last night are quiet now, but Silas never heard them.

He is delaying. It will come. Lying on his side on the new cut spruce boughs, he can't delay it for long. Once, he could lose himself in that sharp bough smell, breathe deep and inhale that sharp green scent down and down into grateful lungs. But not now.

Bellrock, May 15, 1912

D.B. Stegner, Esq

Napanee River Improvement Company

Newburgh, Ontario

Dear Sir

This is good weather for black flyes. I have not seen them so thick in ten years.

Scanlon's men did not close the Fifth Lake dam as they said they did. They abandoned the dam last Wednesday and my friend McCumber under stood how matters stood and closed the dam for me. Someone opened Fourth Lake dam and I no sooner got that shut than Fifth Lake was opened again. I shut that when Fourth Lake dam was opened again. I did not lose mutch water however but I had to play sharp as I did not want any of the water from the back lakes to get into Seckond Lake as Scanlons men have opened Seckond dam three times since I wrote you last. They kept it open about three days each time.

But I must say the river drivers have acted mainly with me. They have not tutched any of the dams since back drive. It is not the river drivers who bothers Fourth and Fifth Lake dams but those savages who live near there on account of Marsh hay and fishing.

You say Mr. O'Donohue thinks it was not Scanlons men who let off the water. I think Mr. O'Donohue talks very provoking and unreasonable sometimes. He blamed me the day I was in Newburgh for not reporting sooner when the water was let off and then when I do hurry down from the lakes to report he does not credit what I say. If Scanlon's men had not let off the water I would not say so.

Now Mr. Stegner I do really hope the company will do something and do it as soon as conveniant to recompense Granny Rundle for drowning her spring. Of course it is Scanlon's falt that it is so but it is flooded and will be so for some time unless I have good luck with Burnt Mill dam. Someone cut the brackets off the dam Sunday. They were not off more than three hours. I think it was Bob Henry but don't know for shure. The old woman has no other way of making a living ondly with her cows and as her spring is full of lake water it is bad for her butter business. Cant you get Mr. O' Donohue to run up and arrange the matter. The old woman is hopping mad and wants the water let off at Burnt Mill.

Yours respectfully,

Mitch Deeks

THE MEN ARRIVING at the school in knots of two or three are all preoccupied. They pay Silas no mind where he sits in deep shadow created by the sharp angle of evening sun.

But who ever pays Silas any attention? Stella Bush. Michael Deeks at times. Miss Asselstine tried to get him assessed at the Deaf School in Belleville. Other than that, he might as well *be* a shadow. At this exact moment, only Dorothea has any inkling what has been lost, to Silas and to the society that shouldered him out to the edge, and Dorothea doesn't know everything about him, not by a long chalk.

She can see him, though. She will not show herself tonight, but a sharp eye might detect her curtains twitching, as she watches from her kitchen window the men arriving at the school. Silas, sitting tense on that stump, with his back arched and his chin in one hand. He reminds her of Dr. Morse's Thinker. That was a strange sight. A splash of bright red anywhere on that man's person would be most incongruous, so what might it mean on his statuette? Anyone else, she might have asked.

Silas was probably twelve, eleven or twelve, the time she managed to insert him into the sixty-yard dash for twelve-and-unders at the Verona Empire Day Picnic. 'One King, one Flag, one Fleet, one Empire.' There was Silas, leaning against a tree by the lake. Only a restless eye could have picked him out over there, a restless eye and an unsatisfied heart. Oh, the trouble in the world, Dorothea thinks. Her own loneliness peaks at times like this, viewing with compassion a fellow solitaire and empathizing with these farmers, now themselves pushed to the edge, like poor Miss Pankhurst and her suffragettes. Miss Pankhurst now being force-fed in Holloway Jail. Dorothea couldn't get anyone to care about Silas, not enough. He will be outside all his life. As will she. And what of those others of her sex, unadmitted to the circle? Pursued, incarcerated, force-fed. There is no level where people of all sorts may meet as equals, in mutual respect. And nitroglycerine is a blunt instrument for levelling.

Wait, Dorothea said to the Reeve, hold the race for a few minutes, would you please? He inclined his head respectfully, patronizingly—humour the lady—and she headed off through the throng of Empire Day celebrants, off to the margin of the lake.

Silas instinctively backed away as she approached, not so much from her as from the eyes of the crowd now following her. She knew that. She might have been approaching a fawn. One move too abrupt, off it bounds. But she had engaged in silent communication with Silas. She had often seen his head appear in the rear window at the school. He would never show himself to the others. He would watch and she would allow it, her heart pouring out to him. On the days when Silas was there—she had a line for him in her day book, to mark him present—she was at her most ardent. The others would benefit then and never know why.

Come here, she beckoned. Come with me. Pointing back to the crowd. Making motions with her arms. Head down, serious expression on her face, one quick high step, arms pumping. Nodding at the crowd. Over there, You. He was enthralled by her performance and almost relaxed. She took his hand, then, and he let her. She pulled, he resisted. She held tight, smiled her most persuasive smile.

Walter Morse, now approaching the school, limping up with Lachlan, who is carrying something in a box covered with a bit of canvas—the doctor would have sold his soul for one of those smiles. Sweet Dorothea, make me immortal with a kiss.

At the starting line there were objections. I'm not running with no eejit! spat Ronnie Pilk, perilously close to describing himself.

Scared he'll beat you? Patrick Lewis taunted from among the spectators. Ronnie blushed and scowled, but shut up.

But is he eligible? asked the Reeve. How old is he? Another of your projects for the lad, Ma'am?

That's a politician for you. Never take a risk.

There was acid on Walter Morse's tongue when he spoke up. Eligible for the sixty-yard dash at the Empire Day Picnic? Look at the boy. He is of a size with the others.

To place a stumbling block in the path of Miss Asselstine! A self-important, bureaucratic blowhard! Bulging out of his suit!

These men will be at each others' throats in a minute, Dorothea thought. She backed Silas into the line. Now, gentlemen, no harm will be done if Silas runs with the other boys. Make room there. A wide space opened in the middle of the line. Shoving and elbowing commenced. Turn the other way now, she said to Silas, rotating him by the shoulders until he was facing the finish line. Ready, she said.

The Reeve's expression was severe. I capitulate to honour a lady, it said, but I condone this unorthodoxy under protest. He turned, cupped his hands around his mouth and shouted down the field. Ready there? A wave from the finish line. Ready here? The boys toed the line.

All right, then. One for the money, two for the show, three to get ready and four to—GO!

The boys took off. All but Silas. Dorothea put a hand on his back and shoved.

She smiles to herself now. Silas the swift. Watching the watcher from her kitchen window, she is remembering that race and smiling. Smiling, yes, and then her heart is smitten. Oh my God, she thinks, the least of these thy brethren. Why?

The gap in the line that had opened for Silas was closed. He had lost a good ten yards. The trailers were scuffling along, dust rising from their feet in the dry grass. Gaining rapidly, Silas changed course, apparently to outflank them. Oh my! He *was* a deer. His legs were pumping but his feet seemed scarcely to lift off the ground. It was gliding more than it was running and the speed of it was astonishing.

But he held to his own course, at perhaps a forty-five degree angle to that of the others. Heading for the rhubarb, said one bemused observer. Nobody in that race could run like Silas. That was quite clear. Other things were not. Phil Leonard, charged with picking the third place winner, was standing open-mouthed with his back to the finish line as the other boys crossed, watching Silas gain the trees. Some of the claims for third place were patently baseless. It took almost fifteen minutes to reach a decision which did not satisfy everyone.

Back at the starting line, one hand against her cheek, Dorothea breathed, Did you see that? Did you see that? They had. They had all seen what she saw, but the spectacle had not impressed everyone. Yes, said the Reeve, I saw it. That runner is disqualified.

O, I know, said Dorothea, but –

Walter Morse interrupted. I must agree, he said pompously. If this were the sort of race in which the winner is first to the rim of a circle, why yes, that youth would be –

Dorothea turned on her heel and left. Enough roostering

for one day. Walter Morse dropped his sarcasm and stomped off in the opposite direction. Let somebody else marshal the egg-and-spoon race.

Silas is on his feet. No one has entered the school for some time. He is padding toward the rear window. From there, she knows, he will be able to see the backs of the farmers, all of them squeezed, two by two, into desks meant for more compact bodies. Big Lachlan had better not sit or he will be trapped. At the front, she imagines: Walter Morse. Behind Morse, the blackboard and, on the windowless wall, the Map of Canada and the Map of the World, with all those pink possessions of the mighty British Empire. The maps she herself acquired for the school. What brings Silas to that meeting? What ever brings Silas to the school, for that matter? Does he want to be near the others unobserved?

Well, if Walter Morse spots him, as Dorothea always does, he will not be alarmed. Silas will carry off no news of conspiracy. What *will* he carry off?

Dorothea could not resist incorporating that race into her Mathematics class. She felt just a little bit reprehensibly triumphant, doing so. There are few subtle ways of rubbing the community nose in community folly. Her demeanour for the entire day was severe. She wanted it perfectly clear that she was not joking.

If Runner A heads straight down a race course, and Runner B, for reasons of his own, adopts a course at an angle of forty-five degrees from that of Runner A, how much faster than Runner A must Runner B run to cross the finish line a winner? One question of ten, the only one with a topical application. Let them see it for themselves, and let them take the problem home. Michael Deeks twigged. She caught his broad, delighted smile. Who among the alerted parents would then ponder, remember the race, and call to mind her campaign for Deaf School? Few. For most: completely different matter. Chalk and cheese.

Like beans it is.

BUMP ON A LOG, Silas. Nobody sees him watching them come. He knows them all, only not by name. He knows who doesn't come. Nobody from the mill or the store. Nobody from the cheese factory. Not Jim Shibley. Not Mitch Deeks. Only farmers. All men. Then the doctor, him and Lachlan. Thin as a rake, the doctor, and limping. His cane has no hook on it but a knob carved in the shape of a head. Silas knows the doctor with his axe face and those eyes that bulge slightly and look deep into you. He knows that energy. Lachlan carrying something.

The doctor's cane was sticking out of the umbrella stand at the hotel. Silas could see it through the window in the door. He risked stepping up on the porch for a closer look. There were horns, curled back. There were eyes drawn back around the curve of the knob. Eyes in the wind. A terrible blast of wind. But wind would never close those eyes. A wind so strong it stretched the whole face back, tugging the eyes into slits. Wooden eyes. Ears too, pointed ears wrapped around each side of the head, under those horns. Hair waved neat but still wild. A man? With horns? Silas stepped back and returned to his prowling. He drew no parallel between the horned man and his driftwood lady beast.

Last to arrive is Tom Ritchie. He looks furtively around,

opens the door of the school, enters.

Nothing came clear about the lights back at the hut. Is the answer in the village? Silas has been prowling, looking in windows and doors. Is it here?

He was startled by a huge display of flesh at Stella's. It was her mother's bum. She was bent over, looking at something on a table, wearing a blouse, but nothing beneath. He backed away quickly, tripped over a low bush, fell, scrambled to his feet and slid away.

He stopped on the street outside Mitch Deeks's house. Something wrong. The house looked the same as always, but there was an aura to it, a glow. But nothing was happening. Something wrong at the river, at the dam. There was a man on it with a gun. He looked hard at Silas and waved the gun threateningly. There were angry men in front of the store. Red faces, angry gestures.

Something. Is it the water? What about the water? His canoe came down the creek. The water was spilling over the dam. The horned head on the doctor's cane. Tears at the corner of those eyes. The wind. Water swelling deep behind the dam.

Peering in the window, Silas watches the doctor, seated at the desk, talking. On the desk is whatever Lachlan carried in, still covered. Now Des Deeks is standing and talking, raising an arm and chopping the air with it. The doctor answers. Des sits. He is twisting his cap in both hands. Tom Ritchie stands. He talks for some time. The doctor doesn't answer. Instead, he rises unsteadily and sweeps the cloth away. Stands looking at the crowd, one hand on his hip with the other still holding the cloth aloft. He drops it, picks a stick of dynamite out of the box and brandishes it with a challenge on his hatchet face. He looks at Lachlan, who is leaning against the wall at the side of the room. All eyes follow. Lachlan salutes, touching a forefinger to his temple.

That is it. No more to see. Silas turns from the window and leaves. Once he saw the doctor halt in the street, unscrew that knob of a head and draw out from the cane a long glass tube. He uncorked that tube and lifted it to his lips. Bottoms up. Poison. No one else could drink out of the tube that came out of that cane.

Stella

STELLA'S THRONE IS A TOOTH of limestone upthrust, with a few layers cracked off and weathered smooth. The whole thing is tilted slightly upstream. Stella sits down, placing her breakfast on another rock. Queen Stella.

Bella Stella, Mrs. Abruzzi said to her once, years and years ago. It made serious Stella smile, which made Mrs. Abruzzi's face light up. She took Stella's small hand in hers and squeezed it. Stella had no idea what 'bella' meant then. She was smiling at the rhyme. Understanding came later, and then she began to wonder. Mrs. Abruzzi's round face had shone. She meant it. But in nobody's eyes is Stella bella. Stella is no belle. What was Mrs. Abruzzi looking at? Bella Stella. Ridiculous.

Queen Stella is ridiculous too, but in certain frivolous moods, here on her throne, she will play with the notion. Today, on the edge of the creek, under the tall trees, where princes are frog and fish and muskrat, Queen Stella is ironic. Water creatures for courtiers. Nary a naiad.

In *King Lear* there are too many queens, and one king too few. One king in exile. 'Blow winds,' he says, keening fiercely into the fierce wind on the heath.

What is a heath?

She hooks one leg over the high edge of her seat to keep herself from sliding sideways. She runs a thumb over the trilobite exposed by the split in the stone. The heath must be some kind of a plain.

'Blow, winds, and –' And what? *What?* She has the play all but memorized, and where is the rest of Lear's rant this morning? Where? And why? Why is she on the verge of panicking, not to remember this? She doesn't need it now. She does. She needs all her information always. Wrapped around her. Or else. Or else what?

She should not, she should *never* have passed in that composition. 'Composition.' Parody. What is Miss A going to think? Miss A will not be impressed. To say the least. There is only one wind here along the creek. Not winds. Wind. If winds, plural, were to blow on the unsheltered heath, what would that mean? So much wind, it seems to be coming from everywhere? Wuthering wind. Heath and Heathcliff? Heath and cliff. Now *that's* interesting. A man might be more than a man, mightn't he? He might be a force of nature. She'll ask Miss A.

No she won't. Miss A will hate her now. How could she have handed in that excrescence?

The wind is gentle along the creek today. You want to lift your face to such a wind and close your eyes. And the sun almost warm again. Already.

The wind could pick up. It could grow and grow into a storm wind. Banshee wind. It won't, but it could. And even so, all of that new green would stay put. All of those lovely new leaves. Their delicacy fills her with awe. All the evergreens have light green new growth, little bursts of new needle that will darken in a month. It's as though you can actually see the trees growing.

Most of that new green will stay put, even in a howling wind that nobody commanded to blow, most but not all. Because look, there is an oak leaf, not even full-grown, already lost to the water. It's trapped by the rock she sits on, where it juts out into the creek. So weak a stem so early in the year. Now it rests on the water, rocking gently in the water where it kisses the rock. Sometimes that water looks still. On a quiet day. But it never is. By definition, she thinks, ironically aware of the language of the classroom invading her thoughts once more.

She won't go to school today. No. She'll stay here. She'll stay home. Miss A will be apoplectic.

What if she frees that leaf, pushes it out in the current? Where would it go? Not far. No, a small leaf like that one is at the mercy of the waters. It will go where the water takes it, the water and the wind. A big wind could tumble it, pick it up and skitter it, even against the current. King Lear shrunken, dried up, desiccated, tumbled across the heath by the wind. Ridiculous.

But a leaf or a Lear would come to rest. Everything but water comes to rest. Is that true? Everything but water comes to rest. It sounds well. It must be true. So, little leaf, I see your place, your resting place, with patches of light pouring down through the cedars. There is no tree more beautiful than the cedar, no tree more aromatic, and cedars guard your place. On the golden sand, beneath you there, you throw your own tiny shadow that rocks as you rock. Is this movement rest? Yes it is. Nothing could be more peaceful than this gentle rocking, nothing in the world. Lost from the tree, your brother and sister leaves, your parent tree, alone in the deepest solitude, but rocked. There is a white birch angled over your place, white with those flecks of black up the bark, and a lover of cedar might well be a lover of birch. The cedar grows those lacy needles so like leaves, but the birch has bark that peels off like paper. You have your beautiful birch, and I have it too.

The rock beneath her is warm. In the unseasonal warmth, the rock is holding heat. She draws her legs up, wrapping arms around knees, head resting on her arms. Birthmark side down, automatically.

A birch-and-cedar fastness, little leaf. The final resting place, as they say, of an unregarded leaf, lost from an otherwise strong oak rooted on the bank of Depot Creek, in the Township of Portland, part of Lot 18, Concession 10, this day of Tuesday April 15, 1913.

This is silly. But it's too late to stop. Little leaf. You have no – voice.

Oh.

That is more than silly.

Bless you, little leaf. Bless you.

Everything loose is going somewhere. Who knows where? What eye follows to its haven? What eye—*is* there an eye— watches Stella?

All that green, that beautiful green. The colour will change. It will darken. Then in the fall comes that explosion of rich colours, gold to yellow to rust and red. Then all of it falls, and the snow comes, and the trunks and branches are stark and dark against the white. Damascene: would the beautiful word be true to that bleak beauty? She wants a dictionary.

A movement downstream catches her eye and she lifts her head. Mitch Deeks is nosing his bark around the bend. On his way to Second. No one else she might see this morning could be so welcome a sight. He smiles at her as he passes, driving that canoe surely against the current, and she smiles shyly back. She watches his progress. Mitch belongs on the creek. He might be a part of that canoe, the paddle an extension of his arms.

What eye follows Mitch? Well I, said the spy, with my little eye, I see the lake spreading and spreading behind the dam. Behind all the dams, stepped up to Fifth. Where once that water would have been free. To seek its own level, Miss A. *I* know. And I see the lake drowning Crowley's well just like it drowned Granny Rundle's spring.

'And crack your cheeks!' 'Blow, winds, and crack your cheeks!' That is it, Miss A. But there's no school today, no school for Stella. For Stella there may never be school again. Stella in disgrace.

'Crack your cheeks.' That is a picture, something to see. Stella can see what King Lear is seeing. In one of the books Miss A lent her there was a picture of Boreas, just a big round face, round like the moon, and frowning with the effort of blowing a gust from the O of his chubby lips. Big rosy cheeks rounded full of wind. '*Crack* your cheeks,' though. What is that? Crack. Would that be lightning?

Stella hopes there will be no swell of water rushing down towards Mitch. She can see Joe Crowley prying up the stop logs again, or else that horrible Bob Henry. How her mother finds these things out is beyond her, but she does. And without ever setting foot in Hinchinbrooke Township, where Joe Crowley lives. Ear to the ground, she says, fly on the wall. A word to the wise, Mitchell. Joe Crowley is a bad one, but that Henry fellow, he's your nemesis. She mutters to herself in rhythmic phrases, many of them hanging in the air with quotation marks clearly around them. It's as though she's – not exactly a witch—never stirred a potion of her own—but it's as though one of the old ones has her ear. If it weren't for talking to the crone, or *for* her, what would she say at all, any more?

It could be bad if Bob Henry is at the dam again. Stella crosses her fingers to keep Mitch from catching him at it. It's not Mitch's fault that Crowley and the others are mad. They might hurt him.

The leaves become so beautiful in October. So beautiful and so fragile. They just crackle into colour, so it seems, then fly. A big storm, wind and heavy rain might take the most of them in one day. Crack your cheeks.

October has a sad soul. The soul of October is the Vs of Canada geese, honking their lonesome ragged honks overhead, heading south. Stella has been right here, sitting on her rock, when a gaggle—gaggle can't be right for wild geese, no, a flock—when a flock of wild geese has glided right in to land. Stella sitting still in thought, composed enough not to start as the geese, wings raised, braking, carve the water, and settle. Raising her head slowly, slowly, to watch them where they paddle in the shallows, feeding, with tails pointing straight up and heads below. They must be exactly balanced to be able to do that. One or two will occasionally step onto that little flat rock out there, and stand on it. Why? Their stick legs look funny out of water, though not so funny as the heron's. Then, at some sort of signal, up they all rise and off they go. Some don't get past the point where the lake opens out. The men waiting there in boats behind the blinds.

October in April. Stella carries her autumn within. There is no frost on the ground this fine spring morning, but autumnal frost there is. Having betrayed herself, she can't go to school. 'Bad side of human nature,' she says to herself. In *Great Expectations*, which she is reading, Pip, the prig, has just insulted Biddy with that remark, thinking her jealous of his unearned rise in fortune. Biddy, of all people. Biddy and Joe are the salt of the earth. Pip is a fool to say such a thing to either one of them, but to Stella it sticks. She has betrayed her self, exposed her bad side. She'll go get *Great Expectations* and come back here and read all day. She will crawl deep inside the book and not come out.

She rises, sees the forgotten apple and bun. So much for breakfast. Well, she can eat them on the path.

A pair of cows are grazing on the road where the path almost brushes it, a very tall skinny one and a squat round one. Gladys and Beulah, having walked down First Lake Road and right through the village. A pair of restless cows. Does she have to consider cows? Cows don't come to rest? Not these ones. Gladys has the wrong name. They should have called her Trouble.

Stella pauses at the bottom of the stairs, one hand on the bannister, cocks an ear. No sound above, no creak of floorboard or bedspring. She climbs the stairs. The door to her mother's room is closed. She tiptoes on by, checks herself, returns to the door. Puts her hand on the knob. Thinks better of it, knocks lightly. Listens. Nothing. She opens the door.

The bed is made. Where has she got to so early?

It has been a very long time since Stella sat down on the seat in front of the vanity and surveyed its contents. The brush and mirror and comb, all matching, the lamp made of a lady, a porcelain dancer with delicate lines, posed with one silver toe emerging from under her long dress and pointing, her hands joined in a graceful oval above her head. The lamp part comes out the top of the oval and the shade has a lacy fringe. A round black lacquer case of powder with a powder puff inside. The jewellery box with her grandmother's ruby ring in it, and a necklace her mother said was diamond. Also a sheaf of papers tied up with a red ribbon.

Stella picks up the brush, and seats herself, back to the mirror. She draws the brush through her thick, sandy hair, drawing it back above her ears. She will not risk the mirror, not today, not now that Miss A is lost to her, her mentor lost forever.

She arranges herself, knees together, legs shifted to one side, one ankle crossed over the other. Fingers linked, hands resting in her lap. Her face will be mostly in profile. Looking into the round eye of the lens. Behind that is the bellows, the big box.

Someone is there. Someone is peering through the lens, hunched under that black cloak. Patrick.

The cold eye dilates, and yes. It's as though you could say his eyes are smiling. Patrick's Irish eyes? That's a silly song. Even sung by Caruso. Why Caruso would lower himself to 'When Irish Eyes Are Smiling,' who could ever tell? Leave it to an Irish tenor. Leave the Irish tenor in Ireland.

What is she on about? Has she mistaken Enrico Caruso for John McCormack? John McCormack *is* an Irish tenor. It isn't like Stella to get such things wrong. Of course she's right about the song.

She is gazing at Patrick, looking him right in the eye. And what is it that she detects, as his expression alters slightly? What is he detecting in her that calls out that, yes, that flicker of admiration? Well, hauteur.

Of course. The word lifts her chin slightly. Her eyes flash, she knows it. 'Her dark, flashing eyes.' How dare you! she snaps. How *dare* you inspect me. Am I livestock, to be inspected so? Stop it, do you hear! Stop it this instant!

Crimson pours into his cheeks. His eyes blink rapidly. His fingers absently comb through his hair. His gaze wavers and falls.

That is more like it.

Again. What is it he sees? What can it be that those blue, blue eyes are seeking, as they search her face so ardently? It must be the yearning, the speechless smouldering in her eyes. 'We must not' is on the tip of her tongue. Inner fires, banked for him.

The bedroom window is open. A soft breeze flutters the sheers. Oh, if she could paint. The light pouring in, and the delicately shifting shadows. How would you capture that? You'd have to find a way to render the peace. The rest, the peace. A block of light across the bedspread, the ridges of chenille broadened by shadow. Lines of piping, lines of shadow. Peaceful. And so full, the scene, so plumped with beauty that you feel, looking at it—gazing is a better word—you feel full yourself. It's not movement you feel then, no. But what is it?

Fires within. Oh, turn the damper down. Nothing must feed those fires or we are lost lost lost. And he knows, oh, he knows. A questioning enters his eyes. His lips part slightly. He is breathing shallowly, quickly. Now he is going to ask, and what will the answer be?

The answer? Well, what could the answer ever be but yes, oh yes, yes.

But wait! Should that passion—she can feel her face flush at the word she has permitted herself—passion!—should that passion burst forth, should all that pent-up ardour burst its banks –

How can a fire be a flood? She should go back to the fire. Or the fire should have been flood in the first place.

A sound below. She freezes, listens hard. Is that the door? She waits a long moment before relaxing.

The fire is doused. She is back to looking at the sun on the spread. Resigned to her failure. There will be no drowning in a storm of passion today. No pale, lifeless body, face down on the strand, with the waves gently, heartbreakingly, lapping beneath his chest, his waist, his knees, the slaked tide receding. It's gone. He's gone. Resigned, she picks up the brush and sweeps her hair forward, restoring the helmet.

She swings around. Catches a glimpse of herself before she can avert her eyes. What could be harder than not looking into a mirror when the mirror is right before you? Even when the last thing in the world you want to see is yourself. But she knows how to see past herself. She knows the mirror will be a window if she uses her other eyes. She is by herself. She is not going to school. Why not?

The mirror doesn't have to disappear. Here it is still, with the sticker in the upper left-hand corner depicting roses and bearing the words, 'Let all see Christ in me today.' That's where her mother has gone, no doubt—out and about to shine forth the Jesus. A stranger Jesus few will ever behold. The mirror, the sticker, the girl in the mirror, the flowered wallpaper behind her—she still sees it all, but her eyes glaze and she enters the other real.

She is marked in purple by the beast. Marked to be his beldam. But the beast is every bit as gentle as he is repulsive. If only he weren't so exceedingly repulsive. Well, that is what he wishes too. With all his tender heart he wishes for a smooth, human face, a visage clear. Poor ugly dear.

Come, Beauty, he says. He extends his large paw, she grips his pad. His claws meet around her hand, which has never until now seemed small. Come, he says, in the rough tone which sounds so terribly like tearing canvas, come see the chambers I have prepared for you. He hands her—pawses her? Oh, Stella!—he hands her through the arched door. And Ah! The sight takes her breath away. The little kitchen decorated softly with bright tones borrowed from the sun, the welcoming sun pouring in through the ivy-framed window in a shaft that strikes the steel-grey cookstove and actually bounces—phht—right off it. And then, in the adjoining room, the cool blue sleeping chamber. White and delicate blue with sheers and flounces everywhere.

Not everywhere. Tastefully here and there. The bright vanity mirror gives back her perfect complexion. It need hardly be glanced into.

Beast, Beast, what have you sacrificed to gain all this for me?

The four-poster with its canopy, the canopy a mimic heaven, so to lie afloat on the eider quilt, looking up, is to survey the whole night sky. Lying there, lost in the milky way, she is drifting when her hornèd paramour steps discreetly outside. Her eyes close. The latch clicks and the key turns in the lock –

The front door! She rises quickly, hooking the stool on her calves, catches it before it topples, slides it in quietly, steals to the door, wrenches it open to avert the squeak, slips out, wrenches it all but shut. Turns the knob, pulls the door softly to. She hears the latch snick home.

She turns to the stairs.

Mother?

Bellrock, June 1, 1912

D.B. Stegner Esq

Napanee River Improvement Company

Newburgh, Ontario

Dear Sir

Any man who will say Third Lake dam holds less water than
Fourth Lake is a liar or a fool or never saw either but Bob Henry saw
both so he is a liar. Mr. Stegner, why does the Company send Bob
Henry to spie on the dams. I write you every month myself is that
not enough. If not please tell me and I will do my best to write more
often, though my hands are full here. I know you cant afford two
managers but I have told you before this there is too mutch territory
for one man. In times gone by there wasn't so mutch meddling with
the dams. It seems every year there is more and more lawless behaviour along the river and I can't keep up. But Bob Henry sharking out
here makes it worse.

The water is good in the drownded lands but when it starts to
fall it will go fast unless the Supply is kept right from the lakes. I will
do my best. Crowley can go to thunder. The water don't hurt him at
all. I don't say there isn't drownded hay and fences washed out and
some of the roads under water. My own friends are not so friendly in

Bellrock and I fear you will be hearing from them. I inclose a paper
I found tacked to a tree.

Notice i hereby Forbid Any person

or Persons

Building a Dam

on this Bywash

Henry More

Now Mr. Stegner I am going to ask you as a great favour to me
to come up and see for yourself just how things are. I know you don't
feel like standing one of those old time hard trips. You need not do so.
Start from your place at half past six A M come to my place. I will meet
you there drive to First Lake then you can step right out of your rig
into the boat. Not the Bark boat. Then ride to Burnt Mill. I will row
and carry over. I would have to do that if I was a lone. Then to camp
at head of Seckond Lake and have dinner. Then ondly a short carry and
clear water to Fourth Lake dam. Then you can take in the whole
situation without going further. Then return and be back to Bellrock
by five P M. Then if you are tired stay all night at my place. If you
wish to return home you can do so convinantly. I could meet you
here next Tuesday A M at 10 o'clock or earlyer if you come. Now come
if posable.

Respectfully,

Mitch Deeks

ONE FOOT ON THE FIRST STEP, one foot on the floor, she halts. Not her mother.

Silas.

Impossible.

But there he is, one hand on the frame of the kitchen door, peering into the parlour. What is he doing here, glancing nervously around? What's he looking for? Then he sees her. He beckons.

What?

Asking her to come with him. Silas in her house! She can't get over it. She folds her arms. Go with Silas? Where? Now he is nodding his head vigorously. Yes, yes, yes. She smiles at the spectacle of this nodding fool standing where he never stood before, where nobody else but she and her mother and Mitch Deeks have stood for years now.

Company! Sit down, Silas. We'll have tea. Tea and crumpets, whatever they are. Tea and crumpets for Stella and Silas, with the little finger crooked off the teacup just so. Wouldn't Grandmother English be proud. The height of civilization, a proper cup of tea. She breaks into a laugh.

Silas has been growing impatient. She can see it in his body, which has begun to rock side to side. What is it? Her laughter dies as the rocking halts and he comes straight for her. The smile is still on her lips when he stoops, clasps her behind the knees and pushes his shoulder into her waist. He is picking her up! She shrieks and stiffens, feels him stagger backward. She is overbalancing, they're both going to fall! She stops flailing for the moment and allows herself to bend at the waist over his shoulder. He regains his footing and lurches for the back door. He is through it, leaving it ajar, before she has thought to claw at the jamb.

Out the door, down to the river and along the river path. He is moving easily with his burden. Whoever would have thought him so strong? Well, strong, yes, but manners? No. Manners! Hoisting her up and over his shoulders like a sack of potatoes. This is ridiculous, riding over his shoulder, limp, bent at the waist, while he trudges along, swerving with the path, ducking under low branches, turning the two of them sideways to step over a fallen tree.

The shock of it! Her mind is tumbling. It isn't functioning properly. Abducted, abducted—she sticks on the word. She can't think. And then she can, and the tumbling spirals in on one word. She shouts it: *No!*

She is drumming her fists on the small of his back, his buttocks. That has got to hurt. It does. He stops, staggers, backs up against a tree. She barks the knuckles on both hands before her hands are pinned. He leans there a moment, as she writhes and wriggles in protest, then sets her down. She straightens and goes for him, her whole body clenched in one savage thought: *tear you*. It's not fists now, it's fingernails.

Tear Silas? Well, who laid hands on her?

If Stella had wings, she would soar up and dive at him. She is harpie now.

Threaten a child and you uncage the beast in the mother, nobody raises an eyebrow. Regrettable, but natural, such descent into savagery, perfectly natural. But a ferocious girl? Well, what if the girl has to mother herself?

BALLAD

(Wild Music)

SHE WAS FOUR when Silas appeared. He was suddenly there beside a tree at the back of the yard near the river. A boy of about her own age, looking at her. He stood with one hand on the tree. He might have stepped out of it. She thought he did.

It satisfied Stella to think that about him, Stella now frozen for the nonce in her mask of ferocity. Even then she was more at home in stories of her own making than out in the world. The world, intricate, marvellous, infinite, has offered her so few signs of welcome. If not for Miss A – but oh, that is gone now too.

The elm that Silas came out of is lost now, fallen into the river when the bank collapsed with the high water. Scanlon's men had to go at it with their big two-man saws. She cried to see it fallen and to watch its limbs lopped off. That was just three years past. Silas was the tree boy for ages. He might have been her invention.

Want to play, she asked, the first time. He said nothing, just gazed at her. It's rude to stare, she said, but he stared on, so she stuck out her tongue and turned back to her doll.

But she knew he was there. She looked over her shoulder now and then to see if he still was, and he was, still watching. And when she looked and he was gone, she felt a twinge of disappointment.

It was always the same. He never wanted to play. He just stood there, watching, beside that same companion tree. He might squat and dig in the soil before him with a stick. Sometimes she went over after he left to see if he'd been drawing, but whatever marks he made were always scratched out. Maybe all he did was scratch.

She got used to him. He was company. He stayed company, even after she went to school and he did not. Her play changed over the years, and he came less often. By then she knew her mother's version of Silas: a savage, just a savage, deaf and dumb into the bargain, left down the Swamp Road by the gypsies.

Gypsies!

Stella couldn't see it, not even at the age of six when her mother said that, not then and not since. She could not have said why, though she came to have some experience of gypsies, the people who come through—*came* through—every spring about the same time, sharpening knives and selling notions. Putting on their queer puppet shows in the front of one of those wagons fixed up for a puppet theatre. Never much story to those shows, mostly the puppets getting mad, hollering, and whacking each other with sticks almost as big as themselves.

Lucky for Silas that Stella hasn't got a stick right now, suspended as they both are, quite a tableau for a Grecian urn: harpie launched in attack, hero recoiling, poised to parry.

The puppets always brought down the house. Not that there was a house. The audience was seated on the ground in the open air of the sports ground. Then, later, that wild music from the wagons camped along the Sand Road. Wild, yearning music from violins played by the campfire. You never hear that kind of music from Jim Shibley. Jim is a fiddler, not a violin player. His music is infectious, but not haunting. Those people, her mother said, they're just like water. They never stay in one place. Here today, gone tomorrow. Turn your back, they'll steal you blind.

Like water. Once in a while her mother has something interesting to say, interesting to Stella. Something Stella can use. Some people *are* like water, she came to think, and not only those who shift from place to place. Miss A, for example. You never know what she's thinking, you can't predict what she's going to say. Like water, she is. Does that mean she never comes to rest? If so, so much for Stella's theory. And some people are like stones. They just lie there, heavy. Hardly worth trying to lift them, not worth the effort. Ronnie Pilk, Bren Reynolds. Or pebbles: most of the girls. Chatter, chatter, whirr. A handful of pebbles tossed into the river.

Some people are like trees. Stella will come to see Silas rooted, now that he has strength enough to lift a young woman bodily and spirit her away. She will see his strong trunk lifting into the air, his branches reaching every direction, stretching myriad twig-fingers everywhere. That may be just a fancy, but it began in Stella long ago. Silas is a tree. He is not and never was a gypsy.

A gypsy woman spoke to Stella once. Stella liked to lurk in the shadows just beyond the light of the fire, watching and listening, where she thought she couldn't be seen. Once or twice she caught sight of Michael Deeks out there. She pretended not to see him, and he did likewise. Why didn't the woman talk to him?

You ask your mother she wash my clothes, she said imperiously, I pay her well. Stella did not reply, just ducked away from the firelight and left. Of course she said nothing to her mother. Why provoke a tirade? Then she couldn't go back to that campfire

127

for fear the woman would fix her with those dark eyes. Well? she would say, hands on her hips. And what would Stella answer?

She saw the woman the following year, wearing what might have been the same long black dress with a shawl of some enchanting material over her hair and shoulders. It shimmered in the firelight. Stella could see that even where she stood, well back from the circle of light.

SILAS SEIZES BOTH her wrists and clamps them tight. She is spitting, words she hardly knew she had. You fucker, Silas, you prick! Goddamn it, let me go! I'll scratch your goddamn eyes out. But he has her firmly. Hurting her wrists with his grip. Goddamn you, goddamn! Her legs are free. She kicks his ankle, his face knots up in pain. She pulls her leg back to go at him again, but he throws his weight forward, they topple backwards onto the grass. There they lie, Silas on top, arms lifted over their heads, because he still has her wrists, and now her legs are pinned with his. She wriggles violently, but his dead weight is too much. You arsehole, she cries, you potlicker, you freak of nature! Let me up! Oh, the foolishness. Cursing at a deaf man. Calling him a potlicker. That's disgusting. Bastard! More like it, just as foolish.

She can feel his breath on her cheek. Bite your ear, you bastard, bite it off! She twists her neck to get at him, but he anticipates and arches his back so he's looking her full in the face. Now he is shaking his head. No more nodding. He can't hear, no, but no more can he speak. Nodding and shaking, what kind of pathetic language is that? And he's heavy, the shit, the bastard! He's got her pinned. She can hardly breathe. You Picadilly prick! You dog!

The stab of her own laughter takes her by surprise. She throws her head back and crows. You knave, Silas, you eater of broken meats, ha!, you base, proud, shallow, beggarly, three-suited, ha! three-suited! she can't keep it up. Her body is convulsing in laughter. Silas purses his lips, watching her doubtfully until she subsides, lies limp beneath him. He looks closely at her, raises his eyebrows. Is that it?

She considers. What is the alternative? There is none.

She nods. He keeps on looking, assessing. Then he rises on his knees, with his ankles still pinning hers and his hands still gripping her wrists. She nods at each one in turn. He releases them, quickly gains his feet. She lies there, chafing her wrists. He bends, lifts his pant leg. That's a nasty gash. That's going to bruise. Well, that's what you get, you abductor, you son and heir of a mongrel bitch. She is impressed with herself. That's the way it should always be: total, instant recall. None of this slack forgetting. Crack your cheeks indeed. Crack your cheeks for you, you – too late for that. That would have worked too, but not now. She is done with this round of cracking. She is still smiling, invigorated.

Silas is repeating the beckoning motions. Come along. Come with me. What is making him so vociferous? Is that the right word for a person who can't speak? So – urgent.

Well. Her school days are over. She memorizes the cursing in *King Lear*, she hands in filthy writing. She is not fit. She never was, now they know. She gets up, brushes herself off.

He steps closer, takes her hand. All right, Silas. Show me. Whatever it is.

She doesn't resist now as he pulls her along up the path, limping slightly. It already seems like ages ago she was sitting at the edge of this river, not happy but peaceful. She feels almost empty now, so much ugliness has spewed out of her. That language! Not the Shakespeare, the other. She *is* a filthy beast.

Holding hands with Silas! Lying in the grass with Silas! Nothing intimate about any of it, nothing nasty, not the fate worse than death. No, she knows Silas too well. She can trust him, pulling her along in such a rush. Stella purged, convalescent. Stella gone.

Bellrock, July 4, 1912

D.B. Stegner Esq

Napanee River Improvement Company

Newburgh, Ontario

Dear Sir

I received a letter from Mr. O'Donohue which I consider the meanest and most unreasonable thing I ever read by post. The fact of the business is that Mr. O'Donohue is dissatisfied with me. He wants a man in my place that will slash off water every time he winks at him. He don't care a snap for anyones interest on the Napanee River excepting his own. Mr. Stegner I tryed not to say a word to one member of the company over another but I will not put up with Mr. O'Donohue's mean talk when I am not to blame in the least.

Respectfully,

Mitch Deeks

THERE YOU ARE, says Stella to the calico cat who greeted her and Silas, when they arrived, like the proprietor of the premises. Hello, Sweetheart. The cat winds around her legs, flops on its back and writhes. You are a sweetie, yes you are. Stella has attention to give.

What's your name, Honey? Would Silas name you? She picks the cat up and pets it to purring. Puts it down when it starts to squirm. It twines itself around her legs a bit more, stretches, digging its nails into the floorboards. Scratch marks there: the cat has been resident for quite some time. Silas too, apparently. Not very permanently, it seems, because the place is bare but for a bed made of boughs covered with a single thin grey blanket, a kerosene lamp, a bamboo fishing rod, some dishes and pots, a gunny sack. The cat finishes scratching and curls up on the sack.

Cats always like to curl up on something, if they can. Stella's mother would never have a cat in the house. Because they shed. She must have had a cat at one time to know that. What if they do shed? Their fur is soft and they purr when they're contented and they keep you company. They are more continuous as company than a tree boy, though they have just about as much to say for themselves. A cat in the house would have been nice.

Her mother has a past. Well, everybody does. You start to have a past the moment you're born. She imagines babies reminiscing about their pasts. You know I liked it better where I was than where I am now. It was warmer there and, I don't know, more, how can I put this, fluid. I know just what you mean. It was rocking, rocking, rocking all day long where I was. And I don't know about you, but I never got hungry once. Not once. I'd go back there in a jiff, I would. Well, dearie, I'm afraid that's all gone. It won't come back again.

Stella's babies talk like little old ladies. Well, why not? If they're going to talk at all.

Lying on her back on the rough floor of Silas's intriguing hut, Stella looks up through the overarching trees to the sky. She has to shade her eyes against the sun, which is well up now. Silas is the last person she'd be with, if she were choosing to run away. Not that this is running off, running away. This hut will never hold her illicit marriage bed. A four-poster would fill it right up. On this raft floor it would be like a boat. Whatever Silas wants, whatever his reason for bringing her out here, he isn't going to go for her. Silas is safe.

She would not choose the swamp to run to, either. But here she is, no longer angry, but curious. Silas is gone again. He glided away in that remarkable canoe as soon as he delivered her here. Deposited her. Not so much as a gesture, not even some Silas sign meaning Stay. Well, he knows she can't walk away from here, not even if she wanted to.

Does she want to?

This is as good a place as any, now that her life is over. And even if her life were not over, she has at any rate been abducted. Having been abducted, Stella was obliged to miss school today. It's out of her hands.

She stands up and tests her blouse, hanging on a twig off one of the branches composing Silas's hut. Dry. And her skirt too. She looks hard at the entrance to the pool, listens hard. Silas won't be back soon, she's pretty sure, but who could tell? And who else might happen on this place? Hearing nothing, she peels off her union suit, hangs it up, dons the skirt and blouse.

Her entry into the river was unplanned, pretty much like her whole day so far. She stepped into the bow of the canoe, apparently off-centre, because it rocked to the left. She threw herself right. Instinct. But one needs instruction in these matters. Don't overcompensate. Lower your centre of gravity, quick! Down on the seat. That's what the seat is for, to sit on. So get down!

Lucky there was no gramophone in the gramophone place.

Silas might have tried to communicate all that. Signs and gestures can do a lot. But Silas is not used to conversing, not by any means whatever. So when Stella overbalanced, making one desperate, indecorous effort, rump in the air, to grab the gunwales, Silas, just stepping into the stern, was pitched into the river as well. They were both immersed, but the water just by the bridge is shallow. Nobody will be drowning there. Silas wasn't fazed. He picked himself up, still holding that paddle with the garish picture painted on it. He tossed the paddle to shore, picked up the canoe by the side, rolled it over, drained it. He set it down, urged it gently to the bank. Stella was headed toward the bank as well when he caught her from behind, grabbed her by the waist—not again!—and held her out of the water until *she* drained. My god, but this is humiliating, she thought. I might as well be his doll.

It would have been simpler to let her wade back to the bridge and drain on the bank, if she had to be drained. Maybe he didn't trust her to step into the canoe again, though, because he rotated her until one of his arms was around her back, the other beneath her knees. Pietà, she thought, but I should be carrying him. Then he placed her in the canoe, bottom first on the seat. The canoe wobbled when he got in, straddling the stern, placing his own rear end on the seat, bringing his legs in from either side, but it didn't tip. She had another tense moment when he leaned over to pick up a strange piece of driftwood, and yet another after they got going when it seemed they were about to crash into the bank, but instead burst right through the bushes at the edge. After that, the going was good, best when she sat and Silas walked, pulling or pushing the canoe along.

Her front must have been very obvious, with her clothes all pasted against her body. Silas didn't even glance there. Just grabbed and lifted. When they reached the hut, she saw that he had removed his shirt and spread it on the thwart to dry. Before he put it on again, she saw his muscled chest and torso, the powerful shoulders and back. He has a beautiful body, she thought. Smooth and hairless, almost olive. His natural shade, or augmented by sun? Easy to imagine living the life primitive out here. She has never in her life been anywhere but in her bedroom wearing so little.

She had the tiniest bit of disappointment. I looked at you. You didn't look at me. Well, she thought, that changes nothing, Tree Boy. You are Tree Boy still, Silas, and I'm what? Swamp Girl, River Lady? Hardly. Miss Foul Mouth. Miss Gone and Forgotten.

Miss Abducted. She won't be missed, not for hours. And then? Well, which of them will know to seek the abode of the Erl King? The sleek and muscled Erl King, demon abductor. She dangles her legs over the edge of Silas's floor, swishes her feet in the water. It's very quiet here, and pleasant in the sun. And if they do find us, the Erl King, the chaste Erl King and his Abducted, his Equally Chaste Companion? If they do find us? Let them all discover how anxious the Erl King is to entertain suitors, after all these bitter years of, of searching. For what? Never mind what. We don't know what. Not yet. I don't know what. Ah, but she has riches untold, the Erl King's – the word should be – *bride*. Bride of the beast. The story is mixed up. It's hard to keep straight. There ought to be riches untold. Vaults filled with gold in sacks marked with dollar signs. Sea chests bulging with jewels so bright they dazzle the eyes.

Well. No gold and jewels so far. No animal servants. That's something else she should be able to count on. She would be good to the animals. Well, there is a cat, oddly enough. Where did that cat get to? You always take good care of the animals, you listen closely to what they have to say, though not to gain anything, certainly not, and then you can count on the animals to come to your assistance in time of need.

No Erl King. No Demon Lover, Mother. Just this hut in the swamp, and Stella alone in it because Silas has some kind of bee in his bonnet.

Bonnet!

There's something in that sack. You'd think the cat could find somewhere more comfortable to curl up, paws over its nose, but the sack is in the sun, where it's pouring in the open side of the hut facing the pool. The angle of the shadow on the wall is climbing toward the vertical, though. It's moving toward noon. Noon and the bell. The bell and classes out. Lunchtime. On a day like today, everybody will be outside for their lunches, those who don't go home for it. Stella every bit as much on her own there as she is here. It's just as well her school days are over, just as –

Regret pours into her. Oh, what a terrible, terrible loss. There are, there have been, days when she exults in her aloneness. She always reads through lunch, or else pretends to read. Sometimes she just wants to think, when the morning has been interesting. Either way, reading or thinking, very often thinking *about* the reading, the closed world seems to open and open. Right now she sees herself standing with arms open. Open and raised, those arms are a sign of sending her mind and her heart out and out, far out into the infinite field, the fields, of knowledge, and welcoming all that back, all she can reach and absorb.

Tears are coursing down her cheeks. What she has lost!

She doesn't realize how much of her reaching depends, in her lively but pinched mind, on her and on nobody else except teachers, whether people or books. Others have closed her out; she has closed them out. She is friends with nobody. She is superior and unworthy. In her solitary meditation, no picture forms of Stella with arms reaching out to another person. Wrestling with Silas, that's not it.

Speak of the devil, conjure the sleek devil, here is Silas back. Stella blots her eyes with the sleeve of her blouse. Silas paddles up to the hut, steadies the canoe, then lifts out a whole wheel of cheese. Stella involuntarily snorts. You didn't get that cheese at home, Silas. Old cheddar, she hopes. She has not brought a lunch to Silas's summer home. No lunch and no book, and the chances are very slight that Silas has returned to her house, marched up the stairs to her room, and retrieved *Great Expectations* from her dresser. If she had her Dickens here, she and her 'bad side of human nature'—it's a lovely fat book, days and days of delicious reading yet—she could stay out here for, well, for days, happily enough. Not starving. But Silas tosses up no novel, only a straw tick, and then another.

Two ticks! There was only that bough bed before. Why is

Silas bringing mattresses? She picks up one, folds it double, then the other. Places them at the wall. More comfortable to sit on than nothing. Silas flicks a huge butcher knife, point first, into the floor of the hut, where it shudders briefly. Stella meets his eye. He tilts his head, one side, the other. What? Well, it means, it must mean, I am a boy, and no boy, not even one without hearing ears and speaking tongue, no real boy ever just tosses a knife out flat when he can stick it into something. It also means the knife is for the cheese and *not* to cut anybody's throat. Thank you, that's a relief.

That is the most Silas has ever said to me.

Stella is only half kidding. What a strange new thought: if you spend time with a person, say that person doesn't even speak your own language, and that is the case with Silas, after all, Silas is a foreigner, if you had to spend time with them, with him or her, you would have to figure out what that person was saying. Maybe you would never learn each others' language and yet still come to discern the other's meaning. That big knife, best to be careful with it, yes, but I believe Silas has just said don't worry beyond that. So I won't.

Silas — there he goes again. Has he got other things to pick up? Silas is the only foreigner she knows. She doesn't *know* the gypsies. She has merely encountered them. Can she learn Silas's language, as she learns Latin and French? Not out of a book. Silas and books are at opposite ends of the spectrum. What colour would books be, then? The bright end, surely. And Silas? Indigo. Yes, that fits.

Maybe *Great Expectations* won't be necessary. There's lots to think about here. She piles one folded tick on the other and sits down.

What are these ticks for?

He's not going to keep me here, is he? Overnight? Night is what a lantern is for. But he didn't bring the lantern. That was here already. If I do stay out overnight, if I don't go home at all, will mother be upset? Not likely.

Stella has been on her own at home for so long, she has difficulty imagining her mother even noticing her absence. There are fewer humans odder than Stella's mother, with her towering laugh, her strange getups, her mysterious independence and complete lack of predictability. Never any knowing whatever will she say next. At home, Stella's mother is no problem. The two of them have settled into their own lanes. What mostly passes between them now is silence. Out in the world, Katherine Bush is a caution. Stella has learned to abjure her mother's company anywhere outside the house, or else experience extreme mortifying embarrassment. An original in a small community, some caricature person out of Dickens, is a freak, a joke. Stella lives with a freak, has done so, just the two of them, for so many years that she is inured. As long as her mother is contained in the house.

Speaking of foreigners—her mother! An English-speaking foreigner not much given to speech, not at home. Will she miss me at all?

What is in that sack? The sun has left it, and so has the cat. What should that cat's name be? It's too soon to tell. If it comes back, she will think about that too.

The sack doesn't belong to her. It's not her property. Well, Stella does not belong to Silas. Silas has stolen her. Silas is a thief. Does a thief deserve respect for his own private property? Still puzzling that one through, Stella leans forward and grabs a corner of the sack between thumb and forefinger. Drags it over.

A gunny sack belonging to a thief. She draws it into her lap and the strong smell of jute rises to her nose. She reaches inside. Getting to know you, Silas. If I'm to learn your language, don't I have to find out more about you? What does the Tree Boy have and hold? Let us inventory the goods and chattels appertaining to said Tree Boy. What are chattels, Miss. A? O, Miss A. All gone. Won't come back again. The mind is treacherous. The mind has a mind of its own.

The inventory is disappointing. Some bones and a stick, a few other items that might interest a boy but excite Stella not a whit. Not a whit, she thinks. Whit is quick. It whistles to a stop. There are some yellowed clippings that spill out of an envelope, and what would Silas be doing with these? Newspaper clippings about sports from, it looks like, American newspapers. Sports! If they were about anything else, she might read them. Stella will read almost anything, but there is, and of course there ought to be, a limit. After a cursory glance, she slides the clippings back in their envelope.

That is a mystery, though. Silas with all those words. Surely he can't read. She spreads out the ticks, one on top of another, and lies down. Maybe she'll read those papers later. Maybe there's a clue in them somewhere. A clue about what? About Silas. Right now –

This is almost luxury, she thinks, as she stretches out. Stretches like a cat, but she won't dig her nails into the floorboards. It wasn't so very long ago she was doing her level best to dig them into Silas. He'd have been a mess. He'd have lost his eyes, for certain, she was that far gone. She can feel her body tense, imprisonment returning. I'll get out, I'll get out, I'll get away, you will not, you will never, never, never. Prick!

Ah. What a strange day. Cursing Stella, anti-Bella. Will not be facing Miss A.

They'll travel, she and Silas. Yes, this is the beginning. This is just a beginning. It must be. The two of them. They will something. What? Something they can do together. Silas and Stella. Stella and Silas. It sounds well either way.

They are back in the canoe. Where did all the miles go, miles and miles of river? They left the hut. She stepped into the canoe. The canoe did not so much as wobble, thank you very much. There was another paddle. Stroke and stroke and stroke. That was her. But where did the miles go? Because what is this ahead? A metropolis! The river would take them to Kingston. No! To Napanee. It's the Napanee River. But can that be Napanee, that towered, golden city into whose fabulous outskirts they are gliding?

Michael

MICHAEL HAS CROSSED the creek and turned into the west meadow. He has never been out here this early, the dew not even burnt off the grass, but it's not every morning he all but kills his father. He is fired pure, refined. There is a space surrounding his head, and in it a different sort of air than the air he breathes. How can that be? It isn't logical. And all his limbs hair-trigger, pert. There is a clarity in the new space that holds despair at bay. Some other part of himself wants to curl up, find a bed of moss and just lie down on it. Curl up small. But no. The energy of the argument still has him supercharged.

Coming at me that way.

His father, bearing down on him, lips compressed to thin white lines and eyes bright with rage, standing with his body arched forward, as though about to spring. Michael flinched. He couldn't help lifting an arm against the blow that didn't come. He took a step back. Humiliating. Just one step, though. Otherwise, he stood his ground.

Not so long ago, he might have turned and run off, crying, out through the sugar bush, over the stepping stones across the creek, to here, sanctuary. Something said stay. Stay, take the blow, if it's coming. Then what? Strike back? He was not himself. His face was burning.

The moment fires up in him. His blow, his father on the ground, stunned. Standing over him, fists clenched. Don't you ever do that again. Do you hear me?

Ah, to do such a thing. Even to think it. The thought shames him. Out here in the meadow, his parched heart rising to the white and orange and yellow flowers, the moss so soft, even the reindeer moss this morning, plumped by the dew. Now the tears do come. He leans on a tree in his weakness, the sobs heaving

144

out of him, unmanning him.

Behind him, Silas, just emerging from the spruce grove, stops and watches. He climbs one of the spruces to wait this out.

Michael cries himself empty. Where's the sense of it, he wonders. Took his hands off the teats to shift his stool and Aggie shied and kicked over the bucket. The wave of milk was pure white for just a moment, then browned in the shit and the straw. It was the startled barn cat leaping away that made him laugh, for Jesus sake! Laughing over spilled milk.

His father was standing over him in an instant.

Think it's funny? Eh? Think it's goddamn funny?

Sullen, he didn't answer. His father grabbed him by the arm, stood him violently up, flung the arm down. They stared at each other. And all Michael could find to say was Fine! I'm going west. Find somebody else to milk your stupid – That was when he was sure he was going to take a blow.

He straightens up, drops his hand from the tree. Deep breath. Now what? He's not going back there. How is he going to get to school? He will not sneak into the house for his lunch and creep out again. He doesn't want to see his mother, not in this state. His eyes are red, he knows it. He won't risk running into his father. Lost his hired man. *Hired*, ha. Lost his servant. Milk them all himself. But he'll be finished now, and Michael fears what might happen if they come face to face again. Hands in his pockets, he starts across the meadow towards the river. Peering between the branches, Silas watches him come.

The grass is thick out here, with the cows in the other field for now. Even so, it seems almost trimmed. He likes it best here when the grass is close-cropped around the boulders and the trees. The shapes show so much more clearly. It's a natural clearing, an opening in the wood midway between the curtilage and the river. There is something deeply satisfying about entering it, every time. It has everything he wants when nobody loves him.

Not fair to his mother, but he is not feeling especially fair today.

What about his father? A boy of his years, all but a man now, fair to his father? When pigs fly. When Tom Ritchie's boar gets airborne.

Look what sad silence and violence passes in this vale of tears between the fathers and the sons. What is the source of it all? Why does harmony not prevail when clearly it should? The Lord, once so lively and vengeful, having visited the iniquity of the fathers upon the children, must now be snoozing in his Heaven. That must be why all supplication falls on deaf ears. Harmony does *not* prevail here. Better accept the fact and deal with it, here, and not fob off the responsibility.

The guitar flashes into Michael's mind, that precious guitar. It's ancient, the top all scarred below the sound hole by millions of strokes of his father's pick. I'll smash it, he thinks, in another white-hot access of vengeance, I'll beat the goddamn box to smithereens on that rock right there.

Honour thy Father and Mother. Ha. Don't punch your father in the head. Don't knock him down and bestride the bastard like a colossus, Miss A. No, seek a polite way, gentle but firm, to make him understand that the wheel of power has lurched into motion. Now the ascendant is he who was under, down below and put upon.

That rock he is looking at is one of a grouping of rocks that he has walked past along the cow path for years. How has he never seen that it's one large rock, split? By some power of the earth, maybe frost? Whatever it is that forces stones up out of the earth in every tilled field, every single year, so you *never* find the field as clear in the spring as you left it last fall. The drudgery, every year of picking that rock.

There's something agreeable about that arrangement of stones—split and the fragments rounded by wind and rain, encrusted with lichen, grass and moss grown up between them like borders. It's one thing and it's many. He sidles around the complex. The look of it shifts with his changing angle of vision. What if he were huge? What if he had two hands huge enough to dig into the earth right there and pick up all those rocks at once, hold them together? What if he could press and press those fragments into one huge boulder. A big egg, it might be, standing by the path for anyone to see. No, he thinks, continuing his circuit, that's not right. Forcing together things that fell apart. You can't. A smooth boulder would look funny here.

Strange affection for the rock is whirled together with the giant his father, his father the guitar, as he moves toward the clump of spruce edging the meadow.

What can be said for insensate, insentient stone? Stone has its moods, extremes of ice and fire, iron cold in the depths of winter, summer heat. First came the rock. Then from the rock came everything else—everything but water and air—formed to the temper of the rock and subject to its moods. There are no extremes in any holy book not found in nature. Rock won't return Michael's affection. Neither will it attack or threaten to attack. But loving one's origin is proper.

Michael is under the spruces now, where Molly and Jerry often seek shade in the high summer. No Percherons here today, not physically, though Michael always remembers them here, swishing their tails at flies and shuddering them off, stamping their huge hooves under the branches, making a drum of the very earth. It doesn't occur to him to glance up into those branches he himself loved climbing, before school and chores took up so much more of his time. He doesn't see Silas sitting on an upper limb, watching him pass beneath.

Sunlight pours through the trees behind Michael where he lies on the bank with the rapids rushing past. He should never have raised that old argument. That was stupid. That argument is over. He was not and is not going out west. Where he is going is home, not this morning, maybe, and not to school, but eventually that's where he's going. There is nowhere else.

The sun rises a degree in its angle and lights up the spider web he has been looking at without seeing it, the intricate pattern still jewelled with dew. Beautiful.

Home, yes, but not to his comfort. Nothing will be said. They'll just tiptoe around each other in silence, allowing plenty of space. Finally there'll be some neutral subject, the cows or the fencing, whatever requires only a yes or a no, and Michael will grunt an answer and that will be that. They'll get on with their lives. That's how it goes. That's how it has been lately. Nothing changes.

A fly has blundered into that web.

Silas leaves the grove, heading in Michael's direction.

Nothing changes? Not true. Things are getting worse. Michael was so black-hearted this morning he almost lost himself. He might have done something terrible. Before going back, he wants to conquer every vestige of the black one that all but took him over. How to do that? What if it's not grim silence at home? What if his father comes down on him again? Finished the milking on his own, that won't improve his mood.

That fly is stuck. The more it struggles and buzzes, the more stuck it's going to get. He's seen this before. Now he's engaged in the fly's struggle. What about the spider? Spider bides her time.

'Biding her time' is his grandmother's phrase, though his mother sometimes uses it as well, that and some of Grandma's other expressions. When she does, something in the set of her mouth, a little humorous, a little ironic, tells him she knows she's borrowing. Imitating, really, the one she loves and suffers. More haste, less speed. It never rains but it pours. A stitch in time saves nine. There's one for every occasion. Proverbs spring to Grandma's lips. She seldom has to think anything up. One time she outdid herself.

The click, click of her knitting as she gossiped on, that time, his mother shucking peas and Michael doodling on the back of his exercise book, not paying much attention. Finding his ease in the company of women at their domestic tasks, present without being present. Attendance way up at church, his grandma was saying, young girls mostly, drawn like flies to that *Reverend* Smart. The emphasis shed doubt on the compatibility of godliness and manly magnetism. Married, mind you, she ran on, married with an infant, and they make those cow eyes at him. He was the wrong man to call, I said so at the time. A whippersnapper like that, I said. Hardly dry behind the ears, I said. But who listens to me?

Now, Mother.

Well, who? In my day there was such a thing as respect for your elders. What happened to respect, I'd like to know. Michael and his mother not daring to look at each other, the theme so tediously familiar. Then she passed on to the river. Why don't the men just go on down to Newburgh, she said, Newburgh or wherever it is, march right down there en masse and confront these mill persons? Douglas Stegner will listen to reason, I know he will. He's a lovely man, Douglas Stegner. Then to Lachlan. Why do the women always pick on poor old Lachlan? That layabout, she said. If you ask me, he's going to have to pull up his socks. He's going to have to gird up his loins and set his nose to the grindstone.

Too much. Lachlan sent too quickly through too many contortions. Michael snorted. The needles paused and his grandmother's gaze swung to him. What are you grinning about, you scamp? That was it. He rushed from the room, choking back laughter. Handsome is as handsome does, she called after him. He collapsed on the stairs, holding his sides.

In his room he laughed as quietly as he could until his midsection hurt. Handsome is as handsome does: one, what does it mean, and, two, what has it got to do with anything?

He had not fully recovered by supper time, but descended to his mother's second call. That call had the sharp edge in it. He found the women maintaining a dignified silence, and his father looking quizzically from one to the other. What's the matter, Mother, he said, cat got your tongue? Which is one of his grandmother's gems and could have started Michael off again. Better take the bull by the horns, so to speak.

Cat got mine, he said, and his grandmother glanced at him with just a hint of a smile. All right. Now please, Michael prayed, *please* let her say something original after grace. Otherwise, there goes supper. But the talk turned to immediate things. Pass the spuds, please. Certainly. Thank you. You're welcome. Thank the good Lord, there were no more strings of worn-out sayings.

Biding her time. The spider doesn't think, but it's hard not to imagine her waiting up there, wherever she is, out of sight anyway, thinking more haste, less speed, let Sir Fly tangle itself thoroughly, tire itself out. Come down when she's good and ready, not before.

Michael will have to stay now, stay and watch until she comes down and wraps the fly up and hauls it away. Then he'll go home.

The buzzing is weaker now, intermittent.

The west. Why on earth dredge that up again? They'd been over that. Like hell you are! I am too! Going west. To get the hell away from here! Meaning away from *you*! Ah, hell. He sits up. When is that spider coming down? A watched pot never boils. Thank you, Grandma. The fly can barely move. One of its wings tangled in the web stuff.

Silas, unseen, has crossed the creek on the same log bridge Michael used. The loud rush of water over jutting stones renders his already soft step inaudible. There has been no interruption of Michael's reverie. Silas has stopped and waited briefly, squatting behind Michael on the bank, arms folded. Now he rises, steps forward, lays a hand on Michael's shoulder.

Michael flinches and springs into the creek, landing on all fours, sliding and slipping on the submerged rocks, scraping his shin, struggling to brace himself in the current while he twists, twists back, trying to face whatever it is. Ahhh, he knows, he knows. His father. Followed me out here.

Floundering in the shallows, sliding here and there on the rocky bottom, arms up to ward off the blow. He finds a rock to brace his foot on, straightens, looks to the bank.

Silas!

For pity's sake! His grandmother's words again, even now.

Silas! Who is looking at him, tense and unsmiling. Anybody else who'd caused him to leap into the creek, one hell of a joke, would be hysterical right now. Bren would be rolling around on the ground. Not Silas. He's not joking.

Michael smiles, tight-lipped. Then he relaxes and laughs. He sits in the chilly water, back to the flow, both feet braced, water cutting around his back, letting the current float his arms.

Silas, you rotten turd! What in hell do you think you're –

Silas frowns slightly. He shrugs. One hand makes a slight gesture with his palm open.

What?

Talking to Silas. Where's the sense of that? Michael points to himself, raises his eyebrows. Meaning what? Meaning what the hell do you think you're doing. Silas nods.

Hell! Why not lift his feet, why not drop his hands, vault his backside over the rock into the current. His shin hurts. He's banged a knee as well. Stupid bloody Silas! Why not clear that rock and let go. Dead man's float. Just relax, let the cold current take him, slide him along, over and between the rocks. He knows the creek along here. There's nothing really in his way past this spot. Just slide with the current through the rapids into the swift deep part, down around the bend, and whoosh, into the pool beyond. Then climb out into the bush and over the fence and out to the road. Go on home. To hell with Silas.

But what does he want? Michael picks his way to the bank. Silas is already moving down the path. He stops, turns, gestures. Come with me.

Michael stands for a moment, hands on his hips. Then he follows, spider and fly forgotten, but of course he has watched that struggle before. He knows how that story ends.

WALKING THE CREEK, AUGUST 1911

(Bren Reynolds and Michael Deeks)

WHAT'S THAT?

What's what?

Way down there, under that stand of trees.

Which stand of trees? There's nothing *but* trees way down there.

Well, you see that really tall one, the elm, that's way up over all the others?

All right.

Well, bring your eye down to the bottom of it and then over to the left, say, well, hold up your hand and measure off the width of your hand to the left, and then tell me what that is I'm looking at.

I still don't – Oh. What *is* that?

That's what I'm asking.

It's moving around.

Yeah. It's in the water. It's *huge*.

What would be that big and be that colour?

We need a telescope. What colour would you call that? Lighter than brown.

Tan?

Maybe. It's in the shadows over there too. It might look different out in the sun. What in hell – Not a wolf. A wolf wouldn't be –

No, not that colour, and what would a wolf be doing in swimming, anyway?

Don't wolves swim?

I don't know, but it doesn't seem much like a wolf, to be in having a swim.

No, but what else would be that size?

A deer?

No, a deer would be taller.

Not if it was right down in the water.

A deer would come down to the water to drink. It wouldn't walk right in.

Bullshit. I saw a deer swim right across the creek once, right where it flows into First Lake, you know, where it widens out. A bear swam across there once too. And Mitch saw a deer swim right out to one of the islands on 13 Island Lake one time. He said it was raising two fawns over there.

Well. That still doesn't look like a deer. It's not the right shape somehow. Where's the neck? And a deer wouldn't just wade in the water like that. A deer would keep moving. What on earth –

Mike.

What?

We're stupid.

Why?

You know where we are?

Just about to Bellrock.

Close to Bellrock, yes. And who backs on to the water right at Bellrock?

What do you mean, who backs – Oh! Tom Ritchie.

And Tom Ritchie has?

Well, for – Tom Ritchie's big old boar.

Tom Ritchie's diving pig.

Ladies and Gents, I give you Thomas Ritchie's aquatic boar. World's biggest belly flop.

That damn pig.

Had us fooled, didn't he?

You know what I'm thinking now?

What?

Pig shit.

Pig shit. So?

Pig shit floating down river to the mill.

Ah. Where we swim. And what about the cow shit? Lewis's cows are always down at the back of their place. Remember the time one of them fell through the ice in the winter?

Yeah. That'd make you shit. You know those eels, the ones that Boumeesters catch?

Yeah.

Well, they eat shit.

Come on.

They do. And the Boumeesters eat the eels.

Where does your shit come from then, Bren? Because you're full of it.

And speaking of shit –

No, no. That's plenty of shit for one day. Let's get our shoes on and go home.

Bellrock, August 27, 1912

D.B. Stegner Esq

Napanee River Improvement Company

Newburgh, Ontario

Dear Sir

We had the fearfullest storm of wind and hail at Third Lake last Thursday afternoon about five o'clock that I ever witnessed. I was coming down Third Lake. Saw the storm coming and tryed to make the camp. Just got out of the lake and in the creek when the storm struck. If it had caught me on the lake the probibility is I never would have got ashore alive. I could not have been in a better place as in the creek as I dare not go ashore for the dry trees and limbs falling. It ondly lasted about five minutes and the ground was covered with ice in lumps as large as small hens eggs. After it passed over the watter in the lake and creek was covered with leaves whitch the hail cut off. The weather was warm and stayed warm and at sun down thair was plenty of ice on the ground whitch had not melted. It gave me a great pounding. Thair was none of it at Bellrock. I hear it was far worse in Bedford than at Third Lake. I suppose you have plenty of watter.

Yours Respectfully

Mitch Deeks

P.S. Some one is giving me a lot of trouble at Third Lake dam.

Think it is the Crowleys. I am good for them though

MD.

THE MOMENT OF THE HERONS LIFTING, as the canoe nosed among them, rising in such numbers, then scattering, will eventually form a nightmare. The awe Michael felt then will remain, but intensified and darkened by a sense of forbidden entrance. There, and not at the creek, he will think, *there* was where the journey began. He will be haunted until, years later, he finds a way to retrace it and open it into a clearing of words.

He is filled with wonder. That heronry. The Drowned Lands.

The Long Swamp, they call it, but he prefers the Drowned Lands. When he was a kid, just hearing the name gave him the good shivers. Drowned Lands. But the barren lake that used to form in his mind, with here and there the tip of a tall tree sticking out, the whole world drowned like after Noah's flood, this is nothing like that. The channel is narrow and winding, often no wider than the canoe is long. The edge of the bank is often impossible to fix, as they glide along. Sometimes it's bordered by the bushes they slipped right through, Michael grabbing the gunwales, bracing for the shock, but zipping through into the hidden channel—bushes that have those spiky white globes of flower in summer—but obviously that's not the real edge. Sometimes there are openings that might be spurs of the channel. The trees are mostly standing in water. Here and there an eminence pushes up, occasionally even bare rock, but generally the water creeps out over the edges of the creek—you'd hardly call them banks—and who knows how far out into the woods.

This is no place to be walking. He could more easily have imagined the swamp as a marsh, with reeds and cattails and red-winged blackbirds, than this forest drowned at the roots, the dense tangle of undergrowth and deadfall, and, above, the canopy of trees that sometimes filters the sunlight to dapple the water and sometimes all but shuts it out. Sometimes they are sliding through a forest cave, with branches darkly mirrored in the water. In such passages, the silence is pronounced. Birdsong seems suspended, and the mysterious noises that call his gaze to them, a rustle in the trees, a sudden splash, all seem eerier. The Drowned Lands are far more beautiful, much more various and far more sinister than he'd had the remotest idea of.

Silas drives the canoe unerringly on. Silas in a hat! Where'd he get the hat? Not to mention the canoe. That was a revelation, as he shoved it out from under the bridge. Wood strips over bevelled wooden ribs, a long beauty. Must be a sixteen footer. Unusual too, the first he's ever seen with the bow seat low and a back rest made by the curving covered deck. You're obviously supposed to sit facing the stern, but he isn't. He wants to look ahead.

Silas never had a pot, as Michael's grandmother is fond of saying of people who have a lot more than Silas. Silas has nothing. He is nothing. Michael's Grandmother is too re*feened* to say never had a pot to piss in, nor a window to throw it out. That is vulgar. She would never say, like Mitch does, He don't know shit from tar. That could also be said of Silas. More than once, this morning, Michael has asked himself what is the point of following an idiot. He's curious, though—where did the Silas who has and is nothing get this beautiful canoe?—and anyway it's too late for school.

But Silas knows what he's doing at the moment. Silas and the Drowned Lands—there's more to both than Michael knew.

For each stroke of the paddle there is a liquid whisper.

Occasionally the ghost of a wave slaps the bow as it cuts into the stream. It's a mesmerizing rhythm. Behind them, the wake ripples out to be absorbed by the receding banks. Soon only a line of bubbles marks their course, then the bubbles pop and disappear. What sign of their passing remains? A trace of foam, then nothing. In his mind's eye, Michael can see the herons circling above the trees, returning to their roosts. There were at least a dozen, maybe twenty, beating up into the air without so much as a squawk, long legs dangling. Great Blue Herons. And turtles. There were more turtles sliding off downed trees in that place than any other. The strangeness wasn't only the herons heading every which way. There was something stark and foreboding about the heronry. The trees were dead there. That must be it. They were sticks of trunk and sticks of branch cutting the sky. Handy places for herons to perch, a place of dead trees. But to see so many herons at once, and so close, because the canoe was right among them before they knew it, how amazing.

Here is another of these gigantic root walls, at least twenty feet high, a barrier of roots and soil and rock thrown up when that great tree overbalanced, tore up its roots and fell. He is grateful finally to be useful, guiding the canoe with his hands through gnarled, twining roots and branches.

They could be lost in the forest-swamp primeval. But for the familiar flora and fauna, they could be on another planet. That is how it feels out here, though they can't actually be very far from Bellrock. Which way are they headed? There have been too many twists to be sure. If this were the river – but how could it be? You'd never drive logs through here. But if it were, the Cameron Cut would be somewhere up ahead. Then the mouth of Hardwood Creek, which could take them to Verona. There is a rough map in his mind from the stories he'd heard, but it seems that he and Silas are off the map. He can't square what he knows, at least what he's heard, with the constantly changing strangeness of the constricted channel they are passing through.

When the canoe sailed out of the shadow of the bridge into the sunlight, Michael's face and shoulders were instantly wrapped in cobweb. He tore at the stuff, blowing and spitting. He grimaced and rotated to show his comical grimace to Silas. That was when he saw the hat. Also the paddle, which had something painted in bright colours on the blade. Just a glimpse of both, out of the corner of his eye. Silas in a hat. Why should that be strange? Why should a hat make a civilized man out of a savage? Somebody upstream going hatless now. No pot, Silas, but now you have a hat to piss in. There is no history to Silas, no way to pick him out of background. There wasn't, until today. He went in under that bridge and he came out somebody else.

Who?

Silas is so quiet that, even in the same canoe with him, Michael loses the sense of his presence. Of course, Silas is in the stern. He's the unseen motor, the propulsion. Thinking about Silas now, his invisibility—because he has been all but invisible until today—it occurs to Michael that he fits this place. Here it's right to be silent. Nobody would laugh at Silas here. Better not laugh. Better take heed, pay respect.

Respect!

Because otherwise, how are you going to get back?

Yes, how? Where are we? And why?

This is the moment when the sky alive with herons begins to turn, to change, as something dark and primeval seeps into that picture of huge sticks stark against blue sky, not a cloud anywhere to rescue the eye from the two-dimensionality, the sun above and behind the trees, so they're silhouetted. He had to shade his eyes. Until this moment he has been looking ahead, anticipating curiously. Now he is looking back, thinking back, to his home.

There, it's suddenly late afternoon, while here it's still well before noon. But the sun is slanting down the opposite way in his mind. His father is nowhere. His father need not appear in this moment, nor his mother. Anyway, he knows where she'll be: in the summer kitchen, scouring the churn. Here come the cows. They trudge out of the trees toward the barn. Now they have reached the yard. They are milling a little before the closed barn door. Why is that door closed? Why is it *closed*, he thinks briefly, impatiently, before it registers that no Michael Deeks is there to slide it open so the cows may amble in to their stalls. Now the cows pick up his impatience. He hears first one, then another, begin to bellow. He sees distended udders. He sees his mother pause at her scrubbing and look up. What under the canopy?

Silas!

Michael makes to turn around on his seat. Pauses. Draws a deep breath. He rotates, leaning on the gunwale with one hand while he points down the stream with the other, then shrugs his shoulders and holds his one palm up. He can't ask any more clearly than that. What are we doing? Where are we going?

Who are you?

That's an afterthought. No need to answer that. And how is Silas going to respond back there, anyway, impassively driving the canoe forward? Even if he stopped his paddling and laid the paddle across the gunwales in front of him, even if he were to answer in kind, with signs, what could he convey to his passenger? Up ahead there is a hut? There is a cat? Someone else is there? That is a lot to say, try to say, with hands. You'd take so long, trying to say that much, first in one way and then another, that the canoe would drift sideways and maybe lodge, broadside to the current in the channel, which is barely wider than the canoe at this point. It's the tight place, with the shallow bottom, just before the pool where Silas almost drowned, where the canoe drifted out ahead of him and he discovered his fins. So why bother with signs? Most of the answers are just around the bend.

Not all of them. Not the lights. Not what the lights mean, which Silas still can't tell. Not why he has drawn Stella and is drawing Michael to his hut, his sanctuary. To make them safe. Safe from what? He has a great fear. The unintelligible message of his lights has made him stony, even more impassive in expression than usual. He does not raise his hands, and Michael can read nothing but determination in his face.

So Michael is his prisoner? Prisoner of Silas. The silence has a chilly side, like a rock with a snake under it. You never get used to seeing that. No harm to a snake under a rock. Just leave it. Replace the rock carefully. Snake likes the cool. None of your business. But the cold thrill always clutches you, sets you back. How is it possible for one moment to feel so different from the previous one? What was fascinating is now frightening.

He doesn't know Silas. He never did. What Silas might think, what he might do. He has never made fun of Silas, not like most of the others. Once he helped Silas up when Bren pushed him down. They were all little then. Silas was a ragamuffin. So his mother said. She called him a ragamuffin and a street arab. Poor thing, she said. Maybe Michael caught her compassion. Maybe that's why he took Silas's part. But Michael is not remembering that in this moment of apprehension. He doesn't remember being the mouse who pulled the thorn from the lion's paw. Oh, but that thorn hurt. The lion couldn't get at it, nohow. No wonder he roared and roared. No wonder he befriended for life the small one with the strong teeth who eased that torment out.

Michael has heard that story, but it's far from his mind right now. Right now he is thinking opposites. Silas is opposite to me, he thinks. Where Silas belongs, I never could. Unanswerable questions are rising now, rising in useless words. What if he shouted? The swamp would swallow the sound.

But Silas isn't dangerous. This is only Silas. This is nobody.

Not convincing. Silas has been in charge ever since the touch on the shoulder, the leap into the creek. Michael was humouring him, so he thought, doing so when nobody else he knew would have played along for a second. That was his weakness. Easy to see that now. Play along and play along and where does that get you? Deep in the Drowned Lands with an –

That's not right. Silas *is* in charge. He knows what he's doing. He has the upper hand. He's no idiot at this moment.

They have run aground. The water is too shallow here even for the canoe. Michael twists around again, what now? Silas is stepping out of the canoe. He's wearing those moccasins, which Michael now sees as appropriate, handy. They feed his troubling sense that Silas belongs here and he does not. He will not step out of the canoe in his almost-dry boots. He removes boots and socks, rolls up his pant legs, steps over the side. Silas is walking past him. He'll take the bow. Strange to think how, in a canoe, you can lead from the stern, but that's what Silas has been doing. Michael catches hold of the stern now, as the canoe slides ahead.

That paddle has some trees and a wavy lake or stream painted on it in odd blues and greens. And there's a moose or a deer, or maybe a bear—something four-legged, at any rate. Michael is contemplating the scene on the paddle and wondering if Silas is the artist when the channel abruptly widens and the bottom drops away. Good thing he has a hand on the stern. He has missed seeing Silas slide into deeper water. His next step is deep, as he plunges in, up to his neck.

TWO

HALF A STORY

STELLA IS MOSTLY AWAKE, dozing. The first of the many times she awoke, she was cold and pulled the second tick up over her, went back to sleep. No pillow. Every time she rolled up the head end of the tick for a pillow, it unrolled. Silas on his boughs, with that thin blanket under him, not over, has no pillow. Maybe he doesn't know about pillows. And he was gone before dawn. His little cat moved to her then. She liked that.

Busy, busy, busy, Silas. Silas, what is your plan for today? What is your itinerary?

He didn't light the lantern last night, and she was eventually glad of it. Even a little light could have closed them in and shut out the night, made it menacing. Though the moon was almost full and the sky clear.

She was listening through the evening for two, so she felt. Sitting across from her, later reclining on his bough bed, Silas was immobile but not relaxed. He almost seemed himself to be listening hard, though she knew he couldn't. Using her ears for Silas, she was unusually alert. There was nothing very unusual to hear, nothing she hadn't heard at night along her own stretch of the creek—frog song, splashes, a pair of owls hooting to each other. There must be fish in the pool. After she accepted sleep, she did wake twice, terrified by familiar sounds magnified. But with her eyes open, the moon shadow was beautiful, and she sank back again into strangely peaceful, dreamless sleep.

Dozing now in the sunlight this morning, she could almost believe herself safe and warm in the make-believe four-poster, under the heavenly canopy, sunk deep into a comfortable mattress under a thick down coverlet.

Splashing now across the pool. A sound of the night translated into day. She opens her eyes. No canopy. A rough ceiling made of saplings covered by some sort of bark. She looks at it for a minute, a vision of log shanty forming. The splashing continues. Silas?

Silas doesn't splash.

She flings off the tick and springs to her feet. Presses herself against the wall and edges toward the opening.

The canoe. That's a relief. But Silas is swimming with it, why? and—no!—another boy is swimming at the stern. She rushes to the back of the hut in a flap, peers this way and that out the other open side. Where can she go? Nowhere. Cornered. With her back to the pool, she pats down her clothes and pats her hair down, anger rising. This is intolerable! She has resigned herself to Silas. She wants nobody else. Not even Patrick Lewis would be welcome in the flesh. Whenever he visits her imagination, that is *her* show. She turns as Silas reaches the hut and grabs the floor. The canoe swings around parallel, the stern propelled by Michael Deeks.

Michael Deeks!

Michael had caught movement inside the lean-to as he and Silas swam the canoe across the pool. Someone else out here? A dress. What is Silas doing out here with a woman? And then Stella Bush, looking down at him through that mop of yellow hair.

Stella Bush! Flea-bit Stella, the Brain. Shit.

She looks away, as she always does, but not before he sees the distaste. Silas scrambles up onto the floor of the hut, reaches down for Michael, hauls him up.

Here he is. Here she is. Something has to be said. She darts a glance at him. Hello, she says.

Hello.

169

She immediately bends to the bedding, picks up a tick, folds it, reaches for the other. He watches these domestic activities with wonder. Stella Bush sleeping in the swamp with Silas?

Well, he begins, not knowing what more to say.

Well? She echoes.

This is not promising. Of all people, Stella Bush. He is bad at talking to girls, and Stella never even talks to girls. That is not logical. If it were one of Miss A's syllogisms, the third term might even be: therefore, Stella Bush might condescend to speak to Michael Deeks. Or vice versa. The proposition is untested. Logic has never been Michael's strong suit, but he's too uncomfortable right now to think straight anyway. Bewildered, he's even more awkward than usual. And she has no more to say than he.

Finally, she breaks the silence.

Fancy meeting you here, she says. Her tone is scornful, as usual. She hardly ever speaks, in his hearing at least, but when she does there is almost always this acid. It gets your back up. Right now, she obviously means that nothing whatever is fancy, nothing is remotely pleasing about his turning up here—he looks around—in this swamp house. She watches him inspect the place.

Have you, she begins, I – have you ever been here before? She rushes on. Because I haven't.

But didn't you –

Sleep here last night. Yes I did. It wasn't my idea. It wasn't my idea to come out here at all.

Well, then, he thinks, what are you doing here. He asks, Was it Silas?

It was Silas.

They turn to look at Silas. He is busying himself with a gunny sack. He opens it, looks inside, closes and folds it carefully, puts it down. He steps off the edge of the hut onto the beaver dam, squats down to pet the little cat that has leapt from stick to stick towards him.

Silas brought me here too.

Why?

I don't know why. Do you?

She takes one tick off the other, folds it up small and sits down on it.

If I knew why, would I be asking you?

Oh. No, not at all promising. I just thought that you – He gestures at the tick she is now sitting on. Just like it's her house. Next she'll be saying, please take a seat. But he is not prepared for what she does say. Neither is she. He really should not let his own sentences trail off if he doesn't want them completed for him, in ways he neither anticipates nor enjoys.

O did you. Well, isn't that just like you.

That stops him cold. Just like me? What are you talking about. You don't know anything about me. You don't know what I'm like. But turn the other cheek, Jesus says. 'I say unto you.' That's how he begins. He seldom just speaks up. Well, I say unto you, Stella Bush, when thou answerest a question with another question, verily thou reameth my arse – But the words of Jesus are now saying unto him, 'resist not evil: but whosoever shall smite thee on thy right cheek, turn to him the other also.' Or her.

That verse was far from his mind this morning. Smite, smote, smitten. It would have been blow for blow if they'd gotten started, he and his father. Well, how can he fight with Stella? It's unthinkable. He will be tolerance itself.

There's no need, he begins, but she cuts him off.

You and your filthy mind!

Filthy mind! That's not fair. He is breathing fast now. It's hard to speak at all, let alone reasonably, especially after the morning he has already had. Listen, he hisses, but what is he going to tell her? Why should he explain anything to her?

Look, he continues, here you are, is all. I didn't expect that. I didn't expect to be coming here myself. Here I am, for god sakes. What do you think of that? What do I care what you and Silas are up to?

There you go.

What?

Silas and *I* are not up to anything.

Well, what if you were? What the hell is that to me?

We are *not!*

All right!

All right!

All right!

My god, he thinks, I knew she was touchy, but this beats all. Here we are, yes, and this is my second argument of the day. Offer the other cheek, see what it gets me. He turns, helplessly, toward Silas, who is disappearing off the far end of the beaver dam. That's right, he thinks, bring me out here and drop me and then bugger off. He lifts his hands, drops them to his sides. It's clammy in his wet clothes. He'd take them off if she weren't here. He sits down with his back to her.

What on earth is going on?

Silas — the inkling forms against great reluctance — you didn't bring me out here for her. Did you? If so – but that couldn't be. It makes no sense whatever. But if you did, Silas, you sure as hell should have let her know about it. Not to mention me.

Silas, Stella thinks, what have you done? What is this all about? If you brought him out here for me, and me for him – what kind of sense does that make? She envisions Silas with a silly grin on his face. Now that's unlikely in itself, Silas grinning, even smiling. She wipes the smile off his face. She sees him solemn, serious, ceremonial, grasping her hand and Michael's hand and joining them. Maybe Silas should have a circlet of leaves on his head, or a crown of some goddamn weeds, to perform this ritual of joining. She pulls her hand away, and not just in imagination. Michael doesn't see that, not with his back turned, radiating hatred. He hates her. She knows it. He would have no more truck with a joining ceremony than she would.

None of this makes sense, but she begins to have an inkling of the cause. It's her. She caused all this by falling away from herself. That must be it. What else? The right thing to do, always, the only thing ever, is keep yourself to yourself—your pain, always. Never, she tells herself, never let it out. Never loose it. What else would have permitted her to hand in that foolishness and filth to Miss A. Of all people in all the world! Who is calling Michael Deeks filthy? The pot, that's who, the pot addressing the kettle. They all are, though, all those boys. Filthy. Minds in the gutter.

Which takes some doing in Bellrock, where there are no gutters, nor ever will be. Next year, the Verona and Bellrock rural Independent Telephone Company, but gutters? Never.

Silas doesn't have that low mind. Is something missing from him, or does he possess something the others don't? That is a strange way to think of Silas. As having. Not nobility. He is no Galahad. No, it's more like, whatever it is, he lacks it. Some kind of bluntness that will not sharpen and refine. Even Patrick Lewis has that, she has to admit. She has yearned for him anyway, vainly, knowing better, despising herself for it. How can you live—it comes to this, and something just loosened and slid when she felt it, and she altered that poem in a cold, despairing fury—how can she live in a world so divided? Male and female. Not people, not individuals, just – blunt blanks. The stones and the pebbles. O, Miss A, you are the only water creature I know.

No, Stella knows another but can't see her. Living with her mother, Stella is too close. Looking for it everywhere, says the Chinese proverb, carrying it on my back all the time. Who will introduce Stella to her mother? Time does that, when there is time. And luck. The meeting of mother and daughter necessarily takes time when the mother is a cipher, a riddle, an outsider, when she is one more affliction in the life of a young woman already marked and needing no further sources of mortification.

Meeting. Relaxing into an understanding. Never to replace the absent warmth of heart-holding, a gap that can never be filled. But if the moment of understanding were to remain open, the daughter might truly become the mother. She might mother herself.

Katherine Bush is water if Miss A is water, if water is rushing and sparkling, if water is mystery and mystery is at the core of all. Stella cannot shake things out so that her mother and Miss A, for all their differences, fall into the same category. Who can blame her in this difficult moment in the swamp, with a darkness opening up in her? This is the worst moment yet in a life in which something is about to come to a head, fabric to rend, the centre to release its grasp, the worst possible moment to be stranded in the swamp with some complete stranger she happens to have known all her life. Known? They started school in the same year, that is all.

She has gone limp. All the will has drained out of her. She topples sideways on the tick.

Why? Why is this new arrival the last straw?

The camel's back is breaking.

Why?

Dear Lord, she begins. Dear – If she could pray. Even if she could go back to yesterday. Yesterday she had her fantasies. The gentle beast, oh give her the beast any day before Michael Deeks. The beast has the strength of ten. He has limitless reserves of passion, a deep, deep well of passion, but she controls him. Beast would do anything for Stella Bush.

O, save me. There is no one to address. All of her own tenderness—yes, Michael Deeks, my tenderness. If I were to touch you, you would know. But I'm torn. What is tearing me? The metropolis, yesterday's towers, the circus at the edge of that jewelled town: that was, that would have been, a tent full of the most graceful acts imaginable on the face of the earth. Silas and Stella would have sat side by side on the bleachers within. Hand in hand, maybe. Yes, why not, chastely hand in hand, united in total wonder, the beautiful bareback rider, the extraordinary flights through the air. Such danger! Such precision!

Today? What was merely impossible, but shining and sustaining, is ridiculous. She is ridiculous. She is unfair. She has crushed the young lad opposite. He had it coming. Who says that?

Nothing she imagines is true. There is no beast but Stella. Uncaged, she goes with her nails for the eyes. She goes with sharp words for the heart. Stella is the beast. She doesn't deserve to live. She doesn't want to live in this world that has no natural place for her. Oh, please –

Why should he stay here, where he's not wanted? Where he doesn't want to be. She doesn't want him. He doesn't want her. He could pull that canoe out and get into it and go. He could find his way back.

Well, why not? He and Silas just arrived.

But this is not his territory, his ground. If there is any ground. He knows the creek well enough between Bellrock and First Lake, First Lake and Second. And he's been tenting at Second, and north of Second with Bren. The swamp is different. All those openings they passed on the way here, what if the wrong channel looks like the right one when you're travelling the opposite way? Sometimes the channel was wide enough—those herons—and sometimes there hardly seemed to be a channel. He gave no thought to a return journey. Can't drop bread crumbs into water. What if he got lost out there? God damn it.

He unbuttons his shirt. He would undo his belt as well, slide his pants off, if she weren't here. Out in the swamp with a girl, for the love of Pete! He can see Silas across the pool, where he has walked along the beaver dam. The dam almost encircles the pool. How old is the dam, he wonders. He knows that beavers were trapped out of this country ages ago. He doesn't know they'll be coming back, taking up residence again, repairing breaches in their dam, shoring it up. If it were the middle of winter here, he could walk out over the ice. Maybe. Even that would be chancy, if the ice weren't frozen solid. Art Bookman used to run a trapline in here. Michael has a dim memory of pelts hanging from a clothesline, or on a shed door. Or was that in a photograph? Anyway, one winter Art went in and didn't come out. They asked Joe Compton to go in after him and he refused. Too dangerous.

He is gripping Silas's floor, the poles of his floating floor, with both hands. Did Silas make this place? He looks up the wall to his left. Leans over and grips one of the uprights resting on the beaver dam. Solid. There aren't any nails that he can see. Instead, the wall is constructed of sapling uprights with branches woven between them. The place is a big basket. Michael stands up and grasps two of the saplings. He can't shake the wall, not even with both hands. He is not looking at Stella, he would rather not, but he sees in the corner of his eye that she is on her side, legs drawn up under her chin. She's a baby.

No she isn't. No baby has a tongue like that. She's her mother's daughter, though, something he could not have thought until today. Until today, Old Lady Bush was the loudest, most ill-tempered, least considerate person he has ever met, and Stella just the most withdrawn. Smart, everybody knows that, just uncommunicative. And now there she is, poisonous and clenched up, small as she can go.

As he looks around the hut, it eats at him, Stella curled up like that. As if he had attacked her and so she made herself small, and not the other way around.

Clever how the roof slants off to the other wall made by that upstanding root system. Here and there Silas, if Silas did build the place, and who else would have, Silas has scraped soil out of the root system to create niches, shelves. He has placed objects in them. One is a stone bigger than his hand, with a band gouged out around the middle. He has set shards of mirror here and there, bits of a broken blue plate, some clay pipes. The roof has slabs of elm bark lapped like shingles over sapling rafters. There is enough pitch so that rain would run right off it in a storm.

He looks at her. She won't see him, not with her whole face

hidden under that storm of hair, and covered with her hands. She is the spit of misery. What made her curl up like that?

He sits down across from her, softening. He is looking at her almost with compassion, he is almost ready to present another other cheek, when Silas steps into the hut. He pulls the lid off the cheese box to reveal – a cheese. Why should that be a surprise? He cuts off a slab and offers it to Michael, who takes it gratefully, then steps over and touches Stella on the arm. She jerks away. Silas steps back, looking down on her, glances at Michael, who shrugs. Silas cuts himself a chunk of cheese and sits down beside Michael. Both of them looking at Stella.

It's not right to stare, Michael thinks. He turns his back to Silas and stares out at the pool. He *would* like to talk to her. She is the only one he can talk to, after all. If they could talk, maybe they could figure out why they're here and what to do about it.

I'm sorry. He could say that.

But he's not. She should be sorry, not him. She did sleep out here with Silas. Not that the arrangement feels like that. It doesn't feel – dirty. He could tell her that. He could try. It was almost what he was saying before. But she wasn't listening. There's no talking to a girl who won't hear you right. Why doesn't he step over there and touch her on the arm and say Don't you think you ought to apologize? Don't you owe me an apology? Sure. She'll uncurl very sweetly and bounce to her feet and offer her hand like a posy of daisies and make everything right with softly spoken words of regret. Sure she will. Just like she did when Silas touched her.

Maybe nobody has to apologize. Maybe they could just –
He swings around to face her again. Clears his throat.
Wait a minute. He doesn't have to talk to her.

Silas, he says. He could touch Silas's arm and address him directly, but what's the point of that? He keeps on looking at Stella. Silas, he says again. She has to be listening. She must be interested. What could he possibly have to say to Silas?

Before, he goes on, Before – uh, just a while ago, she and I got off on the wrong foot. You were over there, over yonder doing something, doing whatever you were doing, and we – there was a misunderstanding.

He can tell she's listening. Has her body not relaxed just a little? What now? Well, there's what he wants to know. Maybe she knows it. Maybe she'll sit up and answer. Maybe she'll speak for Silas. Maybe she can. Enough about the misunderstanding. He can hold the apology in reserve. He just has to draw himself together, so as not to feel foolish, saying to Silas what he needs her to hear. Which *is* foolish. Here he is, just like Mrs. Bitzan, saying all kinds of things to her dog whenever there's anybody to overhear. Now Winston, she'll say, go no more a-roaming. Stay here, my darling, stay here by your hearth and home. The woman is ridiculous. Saying things like that to a dog. Winston is clearly unimpressed. Winston goeth where he listeth. Michael is more than unimpressed. But here – it's worth trying.

Well, he picks it up, You brought me here. You brought us both here. No other way a person – Ah, this is silly. He breaks off. But – Silas, what is this about? Damn, this is ridiculous. He glances at Silas, who is chewing placidly. When he looks back at Stella, he can see that she has unclenched a little. Encouraged, he starts again. Silas, he says, you've got two people here, three, including yourself, two plus one, you see I can add –

She stirs. Then she sits up, but her head is bowed and her hair spills down over her face. Haystack, he thinks, haystack, straw stack. There hasn't been a comb near that hair since when? Her hair must be hard to control at the best of times with all that curl.

Yes, he continues, and it seems important just to keep on talking, I am competent at addition, subtraction, multiplication and division. I have a way with fractions, to boot, and can calculate decimals, which, as you know – actually, I guess you don't know, not having had the benefit shared by my, ah, friend and I here, of years and years and years of –

All right, she says, glancing up. I surrender.

I was just –

Just getting started. That's what I'm afraid of.

Now, I hope you don't mind me saying this, but you shouldn't finish my sentences. I might –

You might have a different, I'm sorry, a different ending.

Am I too slow for you? Is that it? He's got her talking, and he doesn't want the conversation to go sour again, but conversation with her is not predictable.

I'm sorry. I am. You're right. We got off on the wrong foot. Can we start again?

He sighs, loudly. He doesn't care if she hears his relief. In fact he wants her to hear it. He sighs again. She is looking at him now, hand on her cheek, her eyebrows raised in a questioning. It's not a warm gaze, far from it. It's tentative, wary. But a vast improvement.

I was hoping you'd say that, he says. They gaze at each other briefly, then look away. Fine, she thinks, you start.

Well, he thinks, you were here first. You start.

Bellrock, September 1, 1912

D.B. Stegner, Esq

Napanee River Improvement Company

Newburgh, Ontario

Dear Sir

I am not a Christian nor never made a profession of religion
nor never belonged to a church in my life but I consider my self
too mutch of a man to stand up and lie to people and go back on
my employer and work a mean underhanded game to please Mr.
O'Donohue. Anyone who knows me knows that what I aim to do is
what is square. There is no use of Bob Henry denying what he done
at Burnt Mill dam last Thursday night. I can prove the whole thing
even to the colour of the horse him and Delaney drove and the very
spot they left their horse when near the dam and the very hour they
left Enterprise and the very hour they got back to Newburgh.

I know it was Bob let off the water, and now the company will
hear about it. Wheeler was at my place. He says his hay is flooded,
and he intends to procicute the Company immediately.

Now I could of been at Petworth when Bob come here. I had a
letter from Mr. O'Donohue telling me to go to Cameron Cut. There

was some obstruction there he said please remove it. But that letter never arrived until after Bob come up and removed those three stop logs, so it happens I caught him red-handed. Mr Stegner could you not tell other members of the Company not to send me instructions. I take my instructions from you and you alone or else it puts me at sixes and sevens.

There was a man at my camp yesterday from Colebrook. He says the stop logs are in at Petworth dam and says he put them in to hold up the water in order to repair the dam at Colebrook. It is a great waste of water to let off water from the lakes when the stops are in at Petworth, as the water will back up in the drownded lands and run in places where it will cover acres of land and never run out again. Mr O'Donohue would not understand that. From what I can learn those stop logs at Petworth have been put in frequently this summer. We may calculate that every day they are in the water now running from the lake is lost. Would it not be a good thing to get someone to keep an eye on that dam and have those stop logs taken out immediately. I cant get a boat of any kind at Bellrock to go down.

Yours respectfully,

Mitch Deeks

IT ISN'T EASY to start talking, of course not. There is much that neither wishes to divulge. Michael does not feel, as Stella obscurely but firmly does about herself, that he is the author of his fate, meaning this swamp destination. But he is ashamed of himself now. The strangeness of the swamp and the flare-up with Stella have put the argument with his father into perspective. So much unexpected emotion on a single day. Even his father, resentful and silent as the grave, is better company than this. He'd go back now, if he could. He might even apologize for what was not his fault. Maybe not. Maybe just go back. If he could. Maybe an apology would come his way.

What can she tell him? Silas came and got me.

Why did you go with him? That's what he'll ask.

Well, I tried not to. He's too strong.

But why did you go with him? He won't let that alone. And she will introduce the abduction factor.

You mean he –

He grabbed me and lifted me up and carried me off.

No! Silas?

I fought. See if he doesn't show his shin sometime. But I asked why did you – He didn't carry you off, did he?

No. I just came along. I – don't know why I came.

Then they'll sit for a while longer, each of them contemplating what the other has said.

She was stolen away. She was. She resisted as best she could. She couldn't have fought to the death, which is what Sport here seems to expect. Well, if Silas hadn't been so much stronger – But there's no fighting when you're immobilized. And to fight Silas to the death when she had no idea what he intended? No. Not when she's in her right mind.

He came of his own free will. Is he the greater fool? It didn't come to a fight. If he had fought, perhaps he could have won. Maybe he and Silas would have fought to a draw, and he'd have limped back to the farm, too late for school anyway. Yes, he would have been no pushover this morning, no matter how strong Silas is. Perhaps the way to deal with your father is scrap with someone else, drain it off, all that anger. It didn't happen.

There is all that to say to each other. There is the journey to share, the mystery of it. They both want to talk about the herons. The strangeness, the beauty, and, for him, if he could find a way to say it, the ominousness. For him, the scene of the herons has begun to darken. Not for her.

Don't you need to dry off, she'll ask. Aren't you cold?

I'll just stand up and wave my arms and legs about, he says, and he will. You got wet too?

Yes, I tipped the canoe.

With many stops and starts, each will bring the other up to the present moment, avoiding at first the difficult question: why? Each has already gathered that the other doesn't know what induced Silas to bring them here. It is not within the capacity of humans not to speculate, so they have that exploration ahead. That is why Michael opened his mouth in the first place, after all.

It's a remarkable thing, the two of them being here in this hut of whose existence they were unaware, with something even more remarkable opening between them: conversation. Nothing in their lives adjacent to each other has made that possible. In fact everything in their time and place has conspired against it. The conspiracy would be more than figurative if any one or any thing were responsible for creating such barriers. The most remarkable thing in the world is real communication. These two normally withdrawn, uncommunicative youngsters, living in a declining village that will continue to slip, as will the whole unproductive area, whose population had already reached its apex in 1851, until it becomes a sleepy dormitory town in cottage country—they were stuck in this village until today when they were released and thrown together aslant the set patterns of interaction.

They are who they are. Sailing will not be smooth.

And Silas? If Stella and Michael knew how little Silas knows of the why of their presence here, they would be more bewildered than they are now. If Silas understood the nature of the danger he feels, if he could tell them what that clear danger is, what form it will take, they would make preparations. They would make ready.

She begins before he is ready, his mind having detached, disengaged, floating in contemplation of the brilliance of Silas's raft floor.

Pardon?

What do you mean, 'Pardon.'

I'm afraid I was thinking.

Ah yes. 'Mister Drifter.'

No, he thinks, she is not going to quote Miss A at me. Just because he became distracted for a moment, looking at Silas's hut, admiring it. That floor is floating, but steady in its place. The hut started him thinking again about Silas, how different Silas has come to look in a few short hours. But these hours have felt long. Short hours pass without passing. Time flies when you're having fun, they say. One for his Grandma. Fun! But he has entered what seems like another time entirely.

Please, he says, not that. Not that Mister Drifter is wrong. He has just proven it again. Mister Drifter, said Miss A one day, you are afloat, a-floating, in inner space. Would you care to share your thoughts with us, Mister Drifter? Snickers running up and down the aisles. Mister Drifter, good one. Nobody ever wants to cross Miss A, and Michael had done it by doing too much nothing. He did not want to share his thoughts about Amanda Cross's auburn hair, newly curled, cascading down her back where she sat in the seat just ahead, and how would you tease those, what are they, ringlets? And then his eyes had dropped to the desk where Patrick Lewis's name used to be carved so deep that it couldn't be scraped off but had to be gouged out. Patrick Lewis! Patrick could get away with anything. And Ronnie pissed his pants in Grade One. Michael was sitting on the same bench that day and the piss had reached his seat by the time Ronnie started to bawl, ugh, but those ringlets –

He'd loved those ringlets then, Grade Eight, when he loved anything at all that was done to Amanda Cross's hair, or done *by* Amanda Cross, because –

He's doing it again. It's not that he isn't listening. He can hear her speaking while his thoughts follow their own path. But he isn't hearing, so how can he blame her for assuming the voice of Miss A?

Are you with us? she says. Mister.

There is something wrong with me, he thinks. Allows himself that one thought more before wrenching his attention back to her. After all, he wanted her attention, and got it, and then he started squandering it.

Silas has rolled up his pant leg and is rubbing his ankle. That's a terrible scrape he's got there. Michael touches his own sore shin.

I'm sorry, he says. But the curtain of silence has dropped between them again. Goddamn it.

He'll make me bite his head off. He'll make me. And then how will we talk? I thought he wanted to talk. We need to talk about being in this fix. It wasn't a fix before he got here. Was it? Silas and I were comfortable enough together. Once we got beyond our initial misunderstanding. Misunderstanding is a good word for a fight. Once we'd had our little tiff. Tiff is a good word for I'll tear your goddamn eyes out, you – Well, it's a fix now, no question about it. Now she seems to be expected to communicate with this one, who can't even pay attention. Oh, Miss A. The patience of Job. Where do you find such patience? Did you always have it? It cracks once in a while, though. Mister Drifter, Mister Dreamer, Mister Lost Boy. Miss A plays variations.

Mister Lost Boy is the best of these names. 'Mister' and 'Boy' don't belong together. That's why Stella likes it. Miss A likes Michael Deeks. She doesn't play favourites, no, but she has a degree more patience with the dreamer, a slightly lighter tone for him than for the troublemakers.

Stella is a dreamer. Why has she never been drawn to Mister Boy? She never has, that's all. These things are not logical. Suffer less disappointment, accepting that. No, it's Patrick Lewis for Stella, Patrick the unattainable, who has set his cap for the unattainable Miss A. Now that he's out of school, he seems to feel licensed to try for her. To moon after her. Breaking the hearts of all the girls his own age and many of those younger. Hearts that *would* break, at least, if there were any substance to them. If they weren't soft and flabby, flabby and repulsive, like purple pieces of raw liver!

There I go. There I go again.

Patrick Lewis, though. That thick head of wavy blond hair that always looks so lovely, no matter how long it gets. Running his hands through it, combing it without a comb. Oh, let me. Well, they all want that, all the girls. And nobody much wants Michael Deeks. Who would? There isn't much to him. Stella has never paid him much attention. One horrid box social together, in Grade Three. Not her idea. She has idly wondered, once in a while, after Miss A hauled him out of a reverie, Where have you been, Mister Boy? Where did you go? Into some kind of a blank, probably. Nowhere she would want to go. And she has felt contempt for him. Letting himself slide that way in school. There are no public lapses for Stella, none. She does not permit it.

At other times? Miss Drifter, Miss Dreamer. Miss Lost Girl?

I'm sorry, she says.

What?

I'm sorry.

Yes, I heard that. What for? Isn't it me who's sorry?

It's her turn to throw up her hands.

And why shouldn't she, he thinks. This is futile. Why even bother talking? Just sit here and see if I can't ignore her. Just goddamn well sit. Wait until the situation clarifies itself, because she is obviously going to be no help. No help whatever.

Why is she like this? Her mark? Hard to live with that, probably. Harder to live with her mother. Never see them together any more. Mrs. Loud. Mrs. Speak-your-mind-whatever-is-on-it. And no father.

Well, that could be an advantage. His own father bursts into his mind. Huge, overinflated.

She doesn't have a normal life.

A normal life.

Whose life is normal? Am I normal? I can't stay on the one track. Every thought opens into another thought and I follow that and get lost. I can't think straight. That I cannot.

But I don't deserve this. Deserve what? Her attitude, that's what. I don't deserve her speaking to me the way she does, and thinking about me the way she does. What's the point of trying to talk with her?

Silas rolls down his pant leg, rises to one knee, then to his feet. He steps into the canoe and pushes off.

Can't talk to him, can't talk to her. One and one is two, two out of two is one hundred percent. Yes, I'm good with percentages. Did I mention that? I didn't? Odd.

He's driving me to it. If I bite his head off, whose fault is it entirely? It's his fault. And why should I even be having to bandy words with some boy I never talk to, who never talks to me? He's tongue-tied most of the time. Cat absconded with his tongue.

Tongue-tied she would not have said before today. It's an impression. She is confident of it. He and his father, old Stone Face. Mister Stone Face, father of Mister Drifter. The one of them more abashed than the other. Well, abashed is a word for ladies, really, ladies betrayed into immodesty, into immodest speech, probably, and sorry about it. Abashed. Eyelids lowered demurely. Abashment: the state of being abashed. Something causes that. Somebody has to act toward you in a certain way, or has to say something to you that abashes you. Makes you regretful. The word and the thinking that courses out of it takes her back to yesterday morning, sitting on her mother's vanity chair with her back to the vanity mirror. She could imagine being abashed then, or causing it in another.

She has not been abashed this morning. Bite my tongue or else I'll bite off his head. This day might well have been an eternity without him here, if all there is to do is sit and wait. And what else is there?

She was preparing to think, but has forgotten that.

This is apparently no stop on the way to somewhere else. There is no circus in Napanee. Not in April. Not even an imaginary circus. No, this appears to be the destination, and nervous awkwardness is going to draw the day out, drag it out interminably.

WORMS ARE NOT SO EASY to come by in the swamp, but Silas knows a place. To reach it he has to rejoin the main channel and paddle east, past the Cameron Cut, almost to Hardwood Creek. Concession 9 on the Portland Map of 1878, it's a hogsback that dips south, the only piece of high ground in the Long Swamp. Digging for worms there, Silas found his stone hammer and arrowheads. On the 1878 map, strangely, no one is listed as owning the one hundred acres of Lot 14, the only farmable piece of the whole swamp area, while the rest of the swamp, surveyed on the standard grid, in lot sizes between fifty and two hundred acres, is all owned, some by the government, some by the Canada Company, most of it by individuals. For what purpose or reason? Did they come by their parcels sight unseen? If so, where are the Long Swamp jokes to match those about being fooled into purchasing drowned lands in Florida, or the Brooklyn Bridge? Apparently few consulted deputy surveyor Samuel Wilmot, who completed the geometrical survey in 1809, and wrote in his Field Notes, that 'all the Land Lying North of the 8th Concession is absolutely not worth Surveying, being a body of Hills, Rocks and Drowned Land....'

Silas is in a hurry today, or else he would stroll around here, as he usually does. It's the only spot he's found in the entire swamp with a climb to level ground. He seldom ventures from the bush near the creek into the cultivated field north of it, and then, as now, just to the edge, where worms are easy to find. He feels bolder when the corn is high. The place is ambiguous. The tongue of high land reaches into the swamp, but is not of it. It's the edge of civilization, owned now, and worked, and for Silas fraught with potential discovery. Of him and his canoe. But there are those arrowheads he has collected for his sack. He doesn't know the history of the arrowheads, but he understands their function.

The man who farms the land in the 1920s will turn up a host more artifacts. There are no government archaeologists yet in place to stay the farming on an Indian burial ground. There are few Indians to take notice, nary a militant. In 1851, the Portland census recorded twenty Indians, still or again resident in the area. In 1861, there were none. But what about Joe Compton, latter-day shaman, with his divinatory powers? What about Silas's grandfather and Silas himself? His parents gone. So the three families who had come from further east, from the St. Regis area of New York, and settled on the island in Petworth, where they were known for making baskets and eking a living by selling them—they were assimilated. Yes, no Indians left in Portland. When is an Indian, one you can clearly see is an Indian, not an Indian? When he's a gypsy?

Katherine Bush knows better. What is wrong with her?

That is another one for the ballads. Come all ye Portland farmers, and hearken to my tale while Silas makes his way back to the hut with a container of worms. What is time to Silas? What does time mean to Silas in the swamp? There is no time, only space. Isaac Newton ought to get a load of Silas. Einsten ought to study him. True, Silas is hurrying the canoe back to the hut. Time for him is something wrong. Here is what is wrong: time is teetering over his space, a wave about to come coursing through it. The gate to the garden is trembling. The detail of angels draws nigh –

While Silas makes his way back, then, hearken to the ballad of Katherine Bush, the ballad of Katherine and Frank, Katherine, Frank and Mitch.

BALLAD

(Katherine and Frank)

WHO CALLS THE BUSH woman Katherine? Only Mitch Deeks now. Then is Mitch Stella's father? There are rumours to that effect in Bellrock. He is not, though he acts as fatherly towards Stella as Katherine lets him, out of respect for his brother, who *is* her father and was lost to the river before Stella was born. Out of respect also for the bereft Katherine, who was and remains his difficult friend.

The three of them were second generation in this country. They grew up children of pioneers, which is very like growing up children of parents who suffered the Great Depression. Deprivation of any sort breeds repression. It marks you for life. It marks relationships with offspring, with the future. Their present is your future come to be. All they have ever known is what you built, and continue to build—for yourself, yes, but also for them. You knew another way and left it, by choice or compulsion, and spent the rest of your life divided between there and here, the past and the now. Des Deeks, the eldest and heir to his father's farm, perpetuates the split and the anxiety. Drank it with mother's milk. Leo, the second son, hasn't a brain in his head. He will never be anxious about anything. And the younger ones, Mitch and Frank Deeks: like Katherine Bush they were not so divided, not having had to earn their place and their present. They were impatient with their parents and their parents with them.

Katherine's parents were latecomers and they didn't last in the country. She sprang from different roots than the others, but even her parents wondered about her. How, if she were no changeling, could such a wild sprite issue from such moderate but superior British stock?

The three were inseparable, Katherine, Mitch and Frank. The two brothers squired the lady almost as one, but it was Frank she finally cleaved to. Mitch understood that, for the most part, and accepted it. He was then what he is now, a mild man shaded by his volatile brother. He accepted Katherine's love for Frank as he accepted everything else life offered, with a dull sense that if he rose up and demanded more, if he were not complaisant but demanding, like Frank, he would be shot down.

Whenever Mitch and Frank went anywhere together, Mitch saw that all eyes were drawn to Frank, and that Frank was oblivious to the attention.

Were Katherine's eyes going to be any different? Of course not. The woman you love loves your brother; no need to hate him. Frank was twenty-one and Mitch nineteen the day Katherine showed up. All those years of their closeness, no, she was not going to split them.

Frank was throwing to Mitch when she happened by, the new girl with the strange, fetching accent. She was arrested by the smack of the ball against the drive shed. Wham! The idea was not to hit the drive shed, but to hit Mitch's glove. But Frank was wild. The ball would get away from him unpredictably. Fast and wild, that was Frank's pitching, and other things as well.

She was slender then. She had her hair cut strangely short. It framed her round face. Round and pert, it was, her hair dark and her eyebrows dark and her lips red and full. She didn't speak, that first time, just watched the taller one hurling at the shorter one. When Frank became aware of her, his control disappeared completely.

Jeez, Frank, Mitch protested, ease up, will you, or else hit the damn glove. You're going to take my head off. Or worse. If she hadn't been within earshot, he'd have mentioned his marbles. Better lose his head than his manhood.

It was a bad afternoon for both boys, Mitch stretching and leaping and blocking. And when he couldn't get his glove on the ball: Wham! Wham! Frank feeling his focus drawn to the road, where he was sure the new girl was laughing at him.

She wasn't. She had no idea what they were doing, or why. But she was drawn to the athleticism. She responded strongly to the physical intensity of these good-looking boys. She made enquiries, showed up at the next game, became a regular. Eventually, she became vocal. She made more noise from the edge of the field than any of the players on it. She hollered encouragement to Frank on the mound; she denounced in detail members of the other team. Her remarks were not always sensible. Her foghorn voice and uninhibited tongue became part of the entertainment, though other spectators gave her a wide berth. Frank was peacock enough to like her bizarre behaviour.

They were seeing each other. A skating party that first winter clinched it. She arrived at the pond with borrowed skates and a determined attitude, but her legs flew out from under the moment she stepped on the ice. Luckily, the snowbank at the edge broke her fall. Frank raced up and slid to a stop on one blade. You'll kill yourself, he said, lifting her up with both hands. He grabbed her every time she lost her balance for the rest of the afternoon, which was agreeably often. For touching, it was even better than dancing. They were pledged to each other from that day on, without a word of it having been spoken.

She was as odd as she was beautiful. She took the lead in things. She was not reticent. She was a freethinker, brazen. Without the loyalty of Frank and Mitch, she would have languished in the community. She would have stayed an outsider. With their support, she flourished, and did so on her own terms, abetted by her parents, who were rather too good for farming. They had plummy accents and superior attitudes and commenced to running a decent spread into the ground. When the place failed, they moved back to England. Katherine refused to leave. Her accommodating parents rented the pasture to Bill Cobb, rent to be paid to Katherine, and she stayed on in the house.

Not long after, Frank was lost. Some said it was on a dare, and it certainly came out of a boast. Frank claimed he could ride a log the length of the river, the slides of every dam included, with only a peavey for aid. This was in the high water season. He was working at the logging, as most farmers and their sons did, cutting during the winter and driving in the spring. He almost made good on his boast, too. He made it almost the whole way, passing each of the witnesses he had stationed at the dams, waving his hat in salute, his teeth flashing. He was uncharacteristically wearing a sash, and that may have been a clue to his bravado. Nobody, not even the Finns, could ride a log like the French. Frank was French for a day. And the last witness, as he hurtled down the slide at Burnt Mill, was Katherine. He wanted her stationed there to witness his triumph. So she was the one to see him finally lose his gamble, all the money he had bet against his skill and his life. He wasn't Frank when they fished him out of the millpond at Bellrock. His soul had flown.

Katherine had been freethinking enough to entertain his advances out of wedlock before he was killed, but she managed to hide the pregnancy and even the birth so well and so long, that nobody could surely connect the child with Frank. Mitch offered again and again to pose as the father, marry her in fact, but she would have none of it. He persisted for years, and his loyalty earned him the name of father in much of Portland Township, though the more thoughtful among the rumour-mongers felt that something did not fit. If nothing else, Mitch lacked the character of a man who would ruin a woman.

The baby was marked, a pretty little thing but for that. The mark may have confirmed Katherine in her strangeness. It was certainly what caused her to begin fending off her daughter, who was irrationally but firmly linked in her mind with Frank's death. But Katherine had always been unusually self-contained, even in her public displays. She and Frank were two blasts of strong ego drawn to each other. Neither was much interested in family or community. Their future should have been in some Bohemia far from here. Frank broke the seal to her containment by brute force of personality. When he was gone, she began to spiral in on herself, at least at home, her loud public appearances all but confined to baseball games and hockey games, where she became notorious as The Mouth. Listening to her, who would ever divine that she was, and will always be, lorn? That she has passed the loss on to her daughter like a package, like the unwelcome baptismal gift from a relative uninvited and vindictive.

THE SOUND HAS ESTABLISHED itself gradually. With a start, Michael realizes that he has for some time been hearing something not of the swamp. Something regular, repeated, sustained. Nothing he hears in the swamp is like that. Nothing is scheduled. Not even her breathing, opposite him. She is there, she's alive, she breathes, just as he does. He was very aware of that breathing for a while, the more aware because he has not been looking at her. Has been avoiding that. So then her breathing, like his own, neither of them especially noisy at it, became part of the scene. He can't make her fade into the background, now that she has emerged from it, though he'd like to. Of course this is no more her background than it's his.

Having been alternately resentful and forgetful, he is suddenly alert, tense, straining to hear.

What is that?

He glances at her. Her head is still sunk on her chest. She doesn't hear it. He stands, grasps one of the uprights of the hut, tries to pinpoint the sound. It could be coming from anywhere. Something scraping. Squeaking and scraping. He can't identify the sound, but he knows that it's human. No noise of nature is that regular.

Now he hears the whisper of cloth as she rises. He can feel her right behind him. He half turns, finger to his lips. He doesn't want to lose contact with that sound. What is it?

And what is it that is growing in the pit of his stomach. Fear would be too strong a word. Apprehension? More like it. Has he gotten so used to this new environment as to be worried that it might be invaded? Despite his discomfort, is there something very agreeable about the quiet here, in the sun, raised just off the water but so close to it, surrounded by trees? Has something of what Silas feels for this place been borne in on Michael?

ANYONE WHO HAPPENED on that hut in the swamp would have marvelled. Almost anyone. Stella has accepted it without much thought. Michael marvels. That it is here. That it is so cunningly constructed of materials to hand, and that it is so much, so very much at one with its immediate surroundings. Anyone would have admired, deeply admired, its maker. No question.

No one would have questioned the wisdom of a free-floating floor. Ingenious would have been the judgment. No more than the admirable builder would anyone foresee a swell of the pond beneath the floor, a surge of the creek into the pond, a surge and swell strong enough to set that raft of a floor to rocking.

That marvellous hut, little more than an elaborate lean-to, really—it takes one back and back and back to some place improvised into being and deliciously safe, you could live there forever, as in a book, and the beavers, had they not all been trapped out, but they'll be back, the beavers would be your friends, and sex, the light and dark of it, the sun and moon of it, would never rear its fascinating head like a Massasauga Rattler, and you would never wish to hit anybody or even dislike them.

This is not the first choice of habitation for your regained innocence, is it? That would be a tree house, wouldn't it? Or a nice dry cave. Or a big raft with a tent on it. Nevertheless, this hut in a swamp, so cleverly taking advantage of the root system of a fallen tree, this simple basket is the life original.

NOW SHE WHISPERS, What's that?

He raises a hand again, not to his lips. Shh, it says, I don't know. I'm trying to figure it –

Oars. Yes, clink and then creak. The rhythm regular, uninter-rupted. He listens some more, looking down at the floor as if to focus his hearing by scanting his vision.

Oars, he whispers. Oars! Somebody coming in a boat.

If it's a boat, she whispers – Neither of them thinks it odd that they're whispering, and it isn't, though neither knows why.

It is a boat. It has to be.

Well, then. We could get away. Couldn't we?

He doesn't answer. He is listening hard. The sound, the clink and creak, is coming closer. How close will it come? There must be a wider channel out there if there's room for a sweep of oars.

Something wrong. What? A boat out in the swamp, today. So? But today is not yesterday, when there was nothing new, nothing strange in the offing. Yesterday, there was no need to wonder about such things. No need whatever to sharpen one sense at the expense of another, no need to focus so intently. What is this, need? Someone is rowing in the swamp, that's all. Nothing sinister about that. Is there?

The sound is growing louder, coming closer. Michael turns, looks hard at the screen of bushes behind the hut. If he looks hard now, but he won't plug his ears to augment his eyes, will he detect water through there?

Who could it be out there? Travelling which way? The sound is hard to place and hard to follow. Somebody out in the creek in a rowboat, just rowing along.

A touch on his wrist. He shakes it off without thinking. Thinks better of it. She wants to know what he wants to know.

I don't – he begins, but the growing sound of the oars distracts him again. He can envision the scene plainly now, not the boat, nor the one at the oars, but the rowing action. Clink, as the oars scoop the water, scrape, as they slide along the gunwales, then again. As he concentrates, now, he can hear that the sound is not so regular as it seemed. There is a hitch in it sometimes.

It can't be – he begins again, meaning a search party. There is no talking. Searchers would be talking amongst themselves. You would hear them.

It's not a search, he finishes. His voice is sharp, but tiny, unimaginably soft. The rower is a blank in his mind. It's a man, that goes without saying. But this is eerie. And now the sound stops. Clunk, the oars are shipped. Michael's heart leaps into his throat. Involuntarily, he reaches behind him, brushes her skirt, her hand. She takes his. He squeezes it without knowing what he's doing, holding his breath, as though the rhythm of his breathing had become the rhythm of those oars, just slightly irregular, arrhythmic.

It's hide and seek. It's hiding in a good spot, such a perfect spot that whoever is It could tiptoe right up beside you, so close you'd have to hold your breath, because just breathing would give you away, and hope and hope that It would move on, move away. Choking the shout of laughter back down your throat. Pent energy. Any second it could burst out. Boo! Then running and running. Home free!

There'll be no running from here. Release of breath, long open-mouthed rush of exhalation as the oars start up again.

Who? It can't be a search. Somebody is just rowing from one place to another.

Mitch? she whispers. He considers that, eyes narrowed and lips pursed. She has his hand. The fact now registers dimly. He shakes his head. Who else it could be he has no idea, but he doesn't think Mitch. He doesn't know that Stella saw Mitch heading north only yesterday, or he might wonder at her asking.

Now the boat is very close. The main channel must be just through there, the sound is so near. Is that movement he sees? It is, but only the bushes shifting ever so slightly in the breeze. A hitch in his breast, as a red-winged blackbird alights. He concentrates with all his being on the spot where that boat should appear, if it's going to.

She lifts his hand and shakes it. Damn it, he thinks, leave me. He looks around sharply, then back. Her eyebrows raised. What are you going to do? Aren't you going to speak, to yell? Aren't you going to stop that boat?

He makes no decision. He doesn't speak. The boat moves past. Maybe there was a flicker of colour through the bushes. Black, blue? Nothing decisive. And the sound begins to diminish and fade. Moving toward Petworth, Bellrock? So many meanders out here, you could never tell from sound alone.

And now, her hand! He looks at their two hands together, drops hers as if it were scalding. He can feel his face go hot. To have been holding that hand at all and then to have dropped it unceremoniously! She tucks both hands into her armpits, as if to hide them, Don't try that again, Mister. But she was the one to take his hand, and she wasn't thinking either. Holding herself tightly, she twists away and then, as if spring-wound, twists back.

You didn't call! Her whisper is a hiss.

No more did you! he spits. He is opening and closing his hand. Don't do that, he admonishes himself. But the feel of her hand is still imprinted like foreign matter in his.

Call out yourself, he thinks, if you want to. If you want it so bad.

She has stiffened and turned away. She has retreated to the

folded tick and sat down again. He can hear that without turning. He feels the tension drain out of him. The sound of rowing is fading, but still audible in the distance. He dismisses it, but reluctantly, almost in panic. It was a chance for rescue and it's gone. He could still holler! He won't. Why didn't she! Stupid! No, not stupid. You can't say stupid about her. That's what his father calls him when he's angry, and that's wrong too. It's wrong! He is angry himself, gripping the upright of the hut now until the knuckles on his left hand, the hand innocent of hers, whiten. The tension of suspense is gone. The tension of anger is back.

Where is Silas now, he wonders. He has trouble thinking of Stella, the hand-holder, as being in this with him, in this predicament.

How very strange. A door has opened into some other world and they've stepped though it and all the rules are changed. How could that be, when they're just a few miles from home as the crow flies?

As the crow flies over swamp so thick and treacherous it swallows you down if once you set foot in it. That's what they say. The death of Art Bookman is only the most verifiable tale. It's historical. The hero of that story has a name. He has relations still living in Bellrock. He is the verification of all the other swamp lore Michael has from his grandmother, supported by his mother, who listens to the stories with him, knitting away, contradicting nothing, neither by word nor gesture. So they must be true, the stories of fools or children or drunks or fugitives who wandered into the drowned lands and never came out.

His grandmother could bring the swamp to life, dark and dank, with many treacherous ways of grasping your limbs to suck you down, down, down, a quagmire full of dreadful life.

Corpses. Quicksand!

This is not that nightmare swamp. Of course he was guided in, so he hasn't had to cross any of those stretches of deceptive ground that give way under you, and hold your feet in a dreadful suck and inexorably pull you down. But there it is again: a story for a winter's evening, sitting in the kitchen with the big stove blasting, listening to stories about somebody else, not Michael Deeks, not Silas, not Stella Bush, no, stories of others lost and frightened to death in the Long Swamp.

There's creatures in there.

What kind of creatures?

Never you mind. What kind of creatures is no concern of yours, long as you stay clear of that swamp.

I bet you don't know what kind of creatures, Grandma.

A word to the wise, young man. Listen to your elders and learn. And stay away from that swamp.

He had. During the day. The night was something else. At night, he imagined the swamp pulsing with lights, moving, shifting like fireflies, lights sliding from place to place, blotches of eerie light on the move. You couldn't trust anything that was host to that kind of shift. At night it was not so much what he'd been told that fed his imagination. Most of it came out of some book with a setting remote from here. After all, there are no books about where he lives.

She spent last night here. If he is here tonight, maybe it won't turn out to be so comfortable to be thinking about the drowned lands of his imagination.

One or two men might have tried to get through here on foot, at night—it would always be at night, in the dark and against their will. Yes, they might have been driven in here. Dogs could never track them in here, but they would want to. Their yelping would sharpen as their masters restrained them. He can hear it where he sits, perfectly safe in Silas's hut in the company of – not a maiden. The maiden in the stories he knows is always beautiful, golden-haired as a rule, and ready to love. He can hear that yelping raised to a frenzied pitch and he can almost hear shouted the very names of those dogs, bloodhounds, as their handlers call them off.

Let 'em go. Once in there? Goners.

Carrying a chest full of treasure? They wouldn't even get *to* the swamp.

The picture is silly, but it persists.

A maiden might be just the thing for tonight. One thing about holding on to a maiden, hugging her close to keep her from being so frightened, is that she doesn't have to know how scared you are. Does she? The hero in those stories is never scared and the maiden is. You'd think the feelings could be a little more evenly shared.

Stella Bush is no maiden, except in the technical sense. If he sees her coming tonight with her hand out to hold, he'll shove his own hands into his armpits.

He is exhausted, as if he'd been walking all day, or picking rock behind the stoneboat. The sounds of the swamp have returned to normal, the raspy *konkeree* of the red-winged blackbirds, the sigh of wind through the trees overhead, the odd splash of a surfacing fish. He sags, letting the tension drain from neck and arms. His chin sinks onto his breast. He lapses into a puzzlement both familiar and strange. He might as well be stopped at a crossroads with no sense of which way in the world to go on.

When Silas returns, his captives, if that's what they are, are sitting like skeletons in some fantasy, with legs straight out in front. There is meat on their bones and resignation, defeat, in their postures.

Sit up straight, Stella! Her mother's voice? Her own voice. Down here, she thinks. I am down so low. The day is not touching her, not now. The wheel has turned and she's at the bottom. It's flat there. Yes, there is a bottom landscape, flat and grey. That is her scape now. What has green to do with her? Or blue? Ripples on the water. Bright red over there, cardinal flower. The water is restless. The birds are busy, especially that diving, chattering kingfisher. She is stalled. School? Corridors of an ant heap far, far above. She contemplates it without emotion.

Low. Flat. Grey. She cannot go lower.

What is that she glimpses in the distance? Who cares? Stella Bush doesn't care. She does not care about anything that might form in the grey distance of this grey place. She *is* care. She is careworn. Even so, what is it she sees? Against her sullen will, despite the sodden heaviness of her body, she lifts her head. She is looking in the direction of the boy across from her. If he were to meet her gaze, now, but he won't, it's the last thing he wants, to be looking at the harridan who so recently appropriated his hand, but if he did meet her gaze he would have to turn away again. Because she is staring as if blind. The eyes of a blind person meet your eyes unwaveringly. You know they don't see, but as they never need to move their gaze from your face, it's unsettling. Stella Bush, looking hard at Michael Deeks, is seeing only her own private, solitary landscape. Something indistinct in it has broken from the background, crumbled out of it like ash, and is moving. Coming closer.

She is sitting up straight.

Closer and closer. It's no boat. There is no sound, not of oars nor anything else. Ears don't work down here.

Closer it comes, begins to take on shape.

Not it. Her. Shape of a dress. A slow stride, the head down. This person trudging. Her legs must be heavy, heavy, heavy. A grey girl in a grey landscape.

Who approaches and stops. She looks up. She is here, looking up, meeting Stella's gaze.

She *is* Stella!

This all happens. It does. But it takes place at the edge of consciousness. When it's over, Stella will not remember. She is dreaming awake. She has gone down, down, down. She will never be so low again. Who turns the wheel?

Stop.

That's the wrong question.

In the waking dream, Stella confronts Stella. The one who is sitting in Silas's hut, across from brooding Michael Deeks, scarcely notices that Silas has fixed a worm to a hook dangling from a homemade bobber and has flung out his line on the end of his bamboo pole. There in the pool the bobber twitches, a carved wooden ball with a blue feather sticking up out of it, donation of a blue jay, waving in the fresh mild breeze across the pool. Stella is sitting up very straight now, concentrating, looking hard at the other Stella.

She is so much like background. Her complexion is grey. Her hair, her clothes—grey. Her eyes dull. She is standing with difficulty. She wants to collapse. What is keeping her upright at all?

I hate you!

Stella hates that one. She doesn't move, that sullen grey one, and yet she seems to reach out. She would lift her arms if they were not so terribly heavy. She wants an embrace.

She wants to close with me, the straight-backed Stella thinks. She wants to close me.

Abandon hope all ye.

No!

With a moan, Stella scrambles to her feet. Michael looks up at her and tenses. Back in the world, she sees him tense. The other one is gone. You know who she was, and is. She is the victim, the prisoner. Her sky is always grey. If there were stars in it, how would you know? Grey stars against a grey sky.

Thank God the other one has vanished. Thank the good Lord this one remains to be thankful. Stella. Where has she been? She doesn't know. She does know she is on her feet and feeling a vast relief. Something has turned within her. Something closed and something else opened.

And now she is looking frankly down at this boy, looking at him with curiosity. He is looking at her. His upper lip has slid over his lower and it punctuates the wary expectancy in his expression.

Plain as day.

Yes, she is back inside the day. It's a beautiful day. You can get any kind of day in April in eastern Ontario. This one—what is that scent? It's sweet. Lilac? Unlikely. Borne on the breeze, whatever it is. This day dismisses grey care.

She has banished the grey one and come back to herself and the intensity of her gaze is frightening Michael Deeks while Silas fishes on. She relaxes slightly, the intensity diminishes. She smiles. Brilliant teeth between full lips, an infectious smile. It begs to be returned, but Michael is in no mood for that. His eyebrows lift in astonishment. His own lips open slightly as if he is about to speak. He doesn't have to speak. She can tell what he is thinking. He is thinking, What the hell! A smile from this one, so recently at loggerheads with him, what in Hades can that portend?

It's funny, his bewilderment. Her smile widens. A smidgen wider and it would be a laugh. She has banished the grey one and come back to herself, but which self? This is not the one she has carried since she was very young. That one stopped looking at people so as not to be scrutinized in return. This one, smiling, is not self-conscious, not just yet. She is on the verge of chuckling when he decides she *is* laughing at him, she thinks he's funny. She sees him beginning to take offence.

There is this acuity. She is filled with energy. She could look and keep on looking. She can read this boy now. Name him. She can read Michael Deeks. She knows what he is thinking because she can look at him. She is amazed. But he turns away from her. She will have to speak.

What will she say? Nothing about this change. Which is unfathomable. How can, how could anyone change so rapidly? On top of the world. How very, very strange. No, she has to speak, but not about that. He is frightened and huffy now. He will have to be talked out of it.

But first. She puts her hands on her hips. It's a posture for looking. Looking around her: the pool, the bushes edging it, the parting in the bushes where the canoe comes in and goes out —she turns, slowly—the root wall of Silas's hut with all the little mirrors and things; the open back of the hut where not so long ago they were straining to see the boat that passed just a few feet from them; the built wall of the other side of the hut, upright saplings with willows woven between them, a vertical basket very sweet to the eye; below it the brooding boy, still avoiding her eyes; Silas, fishing.

Fishing. Something deep and warm spills open within her. She steps to Silas and places her hand on his shoulder. He turns his head, can't see her for the hat, takes one hand off the pole and removes the hat. She steps around so he can see her without twisting his neck. She looks into his eyes, as she looked into Michael's. Silas is not so easy to read. He never was. But maybe he can read her. She gathers into her expression all that she has just felt, which must be – forgiveness. She is saying to him, I am with you now. I'm here, I'm fully here. Forgiveness, certainly. Maybe even love.

Does he read her? Impossible to say. His line jerks. His bobber is going crazy. He stands up to work the rod properly. Michael stands up as well. Must be a big one.

Michael and Stella watching Silas play the fish.

She is going to have to speak, and now, before shyness returns. She will have to speak. The impossible silence must not be allowed to continue.

It's my turn, she thinks. My turn.

Hello.

Hello? He looks at her sidelong, frowning, keeping one eye on the struggle between Silas and the fish.

Yes, hello. I thought we should speak. It's high time, I thought. For us to speak.

Pardon? What –

We are starting now. Until now we have been silent. Do you see?

He rubs his chin between the thumb and forefinger of his left hand. That, she realizes, is his most characteristic gesture. I could identify you, Mister, she thinks, from a long way off. All you have to do is squeeze your chin that way. Thinking, are you?

He is thinking. Hello. Strange way to put it, he thinks. More interesting than his own 'got off to a bad start.' Never *got* started, rather. The belt kept slipping. More tension needed on the flywheel.

Hello. He is testing the word.

That's right, she encourages. A very good day to you. A pause. Actually – no, let's leave it. I was going to say 'sorry,' and I meant to mean it, but I think plain 'hello' is better. Hello, hello, hello. Will you join me?

What? Hello, hello, hello?

There. We're off on the right foot now. Don't you think?

Not so much as a word –

A discouraging word –

He looks up. A few wisps of cloud up there, but not what you'd call cloudy. The weather is right. His spirits are lifting.

Silas has been letting the fish run, back and forth, tiring it. Now he sets down his rod and, hand over hand, pulls in the line. Stella and Michael peer over the edge as the fish comes into view.

That's a good size, says Michael. Pike. He kneels down to help land it, but Silas waves him off. He reaches for a stick with a branch off it cut short and sharpened. Holding the line with one hand, the pike flopping weakly, he gaffs it under the gills and hauls it up.

Could be six or seven pounds, says Michael. Nice fish.

Yes, Stella says. Nice fish, she says to Silas, patting him on the back. He nods once, as if he has heard, then threads a stringer though the gills, tosses the fish back in the water, loops the stringer over a post. He picks up the pole and twirls the line around it, stands it up where it was.

One is enough, I suppose, Stella says.

One that size is plenty, Michael says. Feed a whole family.

What came over her? He knows that something did. Jumping to her feet, looking so hard at him. That was startling. She could change back. He'll have to watch her. He'll have to keep an eye skinned, but yes. He'll give her a yes.

So, he says. That's not a word to stand on its own. Something always comes after 'so.' But the something could come from her as well as him.

So, he says again.

Silas fillets the fish, with the others watching. Guests for dinner, Stella thinks, cheese and now fish, a varied diet. A bull snake glides off the beaver dam and on to the platform. It pauses beside Silas, who does not start, as his guests do. The bull is a water snake, harmless to humans. It hunts fish and frogs.

This snake opens its mouth wide. Big flat mouth, top and bottom rimmed with sharp teeth. Silas tosses a bit of fish into the maw. The snake closes its mouth briefly, then opens it again. They can see down its throat. The bit of fish is going, gone. Silas tosses in another piece. Lots of fish for everyone.

Isn't that something, Michael says. The cat surprised me a little, but – in fact where is the cat? Cats like fish. They both look around. No sign of the cat.

Maybe the cat and the snake don't get along, Stella says.

I'll bet that's it. Well, Silas can save her some.

Is it a she?

Good question. I just assumed. She's—it's—quite small. You're probably right.

Silas tosses the skin and backbone into the pool. There's a sudden splash.

Holy cow, Michael exclaims. That must be a mistake. Whatever it was, I hope it didn't swallow.

Ugh. Stella is thinking of a fish swallowing the backbone of a fish. A two-backboned beast.

Silas puts half the white fillets into a Mason jar and lowers the jar into the water on a string. The rest he puts into his frying pan and covers it. The snake still has its mouth open wide. Silas tosses in one more scrap, then taps the snout lightly with the pan. It coils suddenly and slithers into the water.

That is amazing, Stella says. Have you ever seen that before?

A snake being fed? Never. I wouldn't have believed that if I hadn't seen it with my own eyes. I did see a snake catch a big fish, though. Well, I didn't actually see it happen. I didn't see it strike. It was just above the swimming hole. There was a lot of splashing near the bank. I thought it might be snapping turtles. I saw two snapping turtles rolling over and over one another once. Great big turtles. Huge. I don't know if they were playing, or what. Anyway, this great big snake had caught this fish. It was a pike, the fish, not so big as this one here. Couple of pounds, maybe, but far too big to make a meal for a snake. Its head was just stuffed into this snake's mouth. Too big. Way too big to swallow. But that snake wasn't letting go. Helluva struggle. I don't suppose either of them survived. My grandma would know what to say about that. Maybe you've heard this: 'your eyes are bigger than your stomach.'

Oh yes, I've heard that. Fits the snake, doesn't it?

Yes. But, you know, I wonder if that snake *could* have let go. I don't think its mouth could open any wider, so those teeth would just be clamped on that fish's head.

Bad decision.

Very bad.

You'd be much better off taking your fish from Silas.

You would. Though I don't think a snake needs its fish cut up into dainty little bits. I think they expect to haul a big lump of something in there and kind of digest it whole. Did you ever hear a bullfrog scream?

Yes. Ronnie caught one once. He was holding it upright, with the legs dangling down, and instead of a croak it let out this sad, wild scream. It sounded almost human. Ronnie was so startled that he dropped the thing and it got away.

Hmm. I heard one scream when a snake got it. Snake got it down, though. No screaming from inside.

The belly of the beast.

The what?

I'm trying to remember where that's from. The story of Jonah. Jonah gets out, though.

Out of the whale's stomach.

Yes.

Well, that fish, the one I saw, couldn't get in, couldn't get out.

Impasse.

Impasse.

Silas is away again, leaving Stella and Michael as suddenly as before. Busy, busy, thinks Michael. Never an idle moment. Where's he off to now?

Stella is thinking about that snake-fish encounter. She can

see it clearly. Two different tails thrashing, one head lost inside the other head. A savage picture. Bite off your head, she was thinking not so long ago. He wouldn't have been thinking of her, speaking of that snake, would he? Could he be as 'subtil' as the original snake? If the serpent actually was a snake, the serpent in the Garden. The serpent lost its legs, apparently, for being the tempter. Down on his belly, to eat dust all the days of its life. And all the days of its descendants. Not that the Bible says anything about legs. The Bible is a thick book, but it could be a lot thicker if it went into detail. Try to imagine a beast called a serpent that doesn't look like a snake. Impossible. And it's very unlikely Michael Deeks is so 'subtil.' She is. She proves that by thinking it at all. Stella is the snake here, if snake there is.

But there isn't.

Still, that fish stuck in the snake that could not disengage from the fish—a very good emblem for two people with no sense. Bite your head off, indeed. I won't. Not now. If I can help it.

The cat is back and has gone for the sack again. No more than Stella is Michael going to be able to resist looking into that sack. There is something in it, what? The real incentive to look inside things—boxes or rooms or chests—is somebody telling you not to. 'Under no circumstances must you ever—*ever*, do you hear me—open that door, lift that lid, enter that dark forest.' Nobody with any spunk ever passes that test. And oh, the trouble that ensues. Interesting trouble. Is curiosity healthy? That depends. How does it all turn out?

Nobody is saying don't open that sack right now, and Michael doesn't have Stella's scruples about it. He has more truck with sacks than she does, and no reason to associate such a receptacle with personal belongings. He picks the cat up, chucks it under the chin until it purrs, sits it down and grabs the sack rather roughly before the cat can reinstall itself.

Stella looks quickly at him. Is he going to look in there? He has no conscience, then. But she's curious too. What will he make of it? She'd like to say, Be careful, there's delicate things in there, but then he'd know she's been in it herself. She doesn't know that he wouldn't care, so she stays quiet, watching. He upends the sack, dumps everything out. She winces, and he sucks in his breath as the bones hit the floor along with everything else.

Careful. She can't help saying that much.

What's all this? He stands looking at the lot for a moment, then bends to one knee and picks up an item Stella missed in her own inspection. It was stuck in a fold in the sack. It's a flat, circular piece of metal with a ring at what must be the top. It has four sections cut out of it, in a shape something like a four leaf clover. A movable arm is anchored at the centre. Michael moves the arm one way, then the other. Stella approaches for a better look.

What is this, do you think? He hands it to her. Some kind of a compass? She examines it. The circumference is marked off in degrees, twelve degrees in each quadrant. The movable arm is sharpened as a pointer. If it's a compass, where is north? She turns it over.

One six naught four, she reads. Sixteen-oh-four.

What is that?

A date?

The year 1604? How could that be? It's probably a serial number. Something made in the foundry at Newburgh.

But what for? And what is Silas doing with it?

Silas doesn't do anything with it. He doesn't know what it's for either. He dug it up on one of his worm junkets and added it to his collection. What it is, is an astrolabe, a little larger but otherwise similar to the one Samuel de Champlain lost on a portage at Green Lake on the Ottawa river system. It was a boy, Edward Lee, who found that astrolabe too. He sold it for ten dollars. That was the deal, at least, but Edward never got the money. This was in 1867. Champlain's astrolabe passed from hand to hand until, in 1989, the Canadian government acquired it for the Canadian Museum of Civilization.

Who first owned Silas's astrolabe? In 1673, Fort Frontenac was completed on the site of present-day Kingston, under the supervision of René Robert Cavalier Sieur de la Salle. Maybe the astrolabe was la Salle's. Nobody is going to find out, because Silas won't be making Edward Lee's mistake.

Stella sets the trinket down gently. You'd better put these things back, she says. Here, I'll help. She begins with the bones, gently picking up each skull first. None of them seems to have been damaged. The bones, the stick, the snakeskin. The arrowheads. She and Michael examine each item before it goes into the bag.

Where would he get these things?

Don't know, she says. She hands him the envelope.

Now what's in here, he asks. It's not a real question, he's just talking aloud to himself. She doesn't have to answer. He puts down the sack to open the envelope and draws out the clippings. He flips through them, then sits down and begins to read. Halfway through the lot, he looks up at her. Gabriel Monture, he says.

Who?

These are about a Gabriel Monture. What is Silas doing with them? His name is Williams.

Not a relative, you mean.

Well. Maybe an uncle or something, with a different name. But listen to this. This man was really something. 'Seventeen to nothing' is the title of this one: 'Monture pitched a splendid game,' it says. He is pitching for a team called Boston and Montana. This is, in, let's see, Great Falls. Where is that?

Great Falls, Montana, she says immediately, and he looks at her in irony and admiration. What doesn't she know? She doesn't know what that compass thing is. She doesn't know things that Silas knows, presumably. Silas knows how to do things and make things, and Stella knows? Everything else. Either of them could make you feel ignorant. Or lucky. You could learn things from them both. If you didn't mind always being the one who didn't know.

Well, he knows baseball. And he does know that Montana is a western state, northwestern.

Hmm, he says, I wonder what Boston has to do with Montana. Well, he goes on, 'Monture pitched a splendid game, and was almost perfectly supported. He did not give a base on balls, did not strike a batsman and fanned eighteen. Only four hits were made off him. He had superb control, only once apparently getting himself in a hole, and then he steadied down and did the business.' Helena, that's the name of the other team. That's an even stranger name than Boston and Montana.

Helena, I think – well, never mind. No need, she thinks, to be pedantic.

No, what?

I think that's another place in Montana. Helena, Montana.

Oh, that's a relief. I can't imagine playing for a team called the Helenas.

Why not?

Well, it doesn't seem very –

Masculine? I didn't know that baseball – this is baseball we're talking about, isn't it?

It is.

Well, I didn't know baseball was a display of masculinity.

It's not, he retorts. Have you ever seen a game? His voice is rising in grievance. Does she think we strut around like peacocks? What about the beauty of the game, the teamwork, the discipline? But he thinks suddenly of Uncle Leo, incensed at being called out at home plate and screaming at the umpire, "I'll tear your fucking heart out and stuff it up your arse!" What's that a display of? Good thing Leo immediately started laughing. The situation could have deteriorated. He's foolish, Leo is, and he has a really bad mind, terrible, but even he saw the humour in that particular situation. The umpire threw him out of the game, which was *really* funny. Old Lady Bush giving them both a ripe piece of her mind.

My mother goes, she says mildly. I don't. I went once. That was enough.

Oh.

No need to say more. Weird Mrs. Bush. You can hear her all across town, calling down the opposing team players, and once in a while her own. She has this voice that cuts the air like a wind-axe. She's a joke, no two ways about that, though she's also part of home field advantage. Not everyone is self-possessed enough to play his best with burning ears.

Stella knows she needs to redeem herself. She felt his back

go up. Their truce is not so very old. She'll pretend to be interested.

Does it say there whether the Helena team has a name? The Helena Something. Somethings?

He scans the page. "Flood, the much touted twirler for the visitors … a disappointment.' Seventeen to nothing, I guess so. No, nothing about the team name.

Well, never mind, it's not important.

No. You're right. Anyway, this goes on. The Chief – He's called the Chief.

Indian, I suppose.

I suppose. 'The Chief was particularly impressive facing Helena's cleanup batter, Bowering. Aside from one towering foul in the eighth, Bowering was no challenge to the B & M twirler. He swings for the fences, the Chief averred' – Averred. That's a new one on me. The Chief – said, I guess.

Averred, opined. Said. That's right.

Opined!

Opinion, you know. Expressed an opinion. Opined.

Sheesh. Well, the Chief averred. What's that from?

Averred. Averred. I'm not sure.

Well, what he averred was, he averred that the big stick man for Helena was not so hard to out-think. 'It does not hurt to possess your speed, either, this reporter hazarded, and the Chief smiled his agreement.'

Michael reads on silently. 'Monture is a pitcher far above average and during his residence here has earned a gilt edge reputation on the diamond.' Michael picks up another clipping and another, reading intently until he has absorbed the whole collection.

Stella looks at his hands holding the papers, at his arms. Golden hairs on them. She is not interested in sports. Much of what Michael has just read or said is unintelligible. Twirler. Cleanup. Fanning and supporting. Big stick man. A base on balls. Swing for the fences. That reporter is addressing the cognoscenti. That is a word, she thinks, I will not try on Michael Deeks, even though he is obviously knowledgeable. Michael Deeks is in the know. He is actually concentrating. Fine golden hairs on his arms. She didn't last a whole game with her mother. The others were laughing at her.

Huh, Michael exclaims. This fellow was really something. I said that. But look here, here's his picture. She looks, to oblige him. There is no resemblance to Silas, but then the photograph is taken from the side. The man has one bent leg in the air and there is a triangular something on the toe and heel of the uplifted shoe. He is wearing quilted pants that come down just below the knee, and long stockings. A short-sleeved shirt with a long-sleeved shirt beneath it. She can just make out a large M on the front of his shirt. The M of B & M, no doubt. And then there's a funny little cap with a short peak and stripes around the crown. An altogether ridiculous outfit. And there he teeters on one leg like a stork. No, a heron. What a silly business. Michael clearly doesn't think so. Well, he plays the game. She knows that much, but has never seen him at it.

This man, the Chief, Michael says. He must have been really hard to hit.

Pardon?

I said hard to hit.

I know you did. Who wanted to hit him?

The batters! Whatsis name, Bowering here, and – oh, I see

what you mean. You don't know baseball, do you. Well, this Chief, he's a pitcher. He's the one, the pitcher is, who throws the ball.

Pitches it.

Exactly. Pitches the ball. He stands up on the mound in the middle of the diamond—that's what they call the field, the infield anyway. There's also an outfield. Well he, the pitcher, is right in the middle of the playing field and he throws the ball to the catcher, who's also on his team. But he has to try to throw it past the batter for the other team, who tries to hit—there you go—*hit* the ball, you see, as it comes by. Comes, phhht, comes in at a great speed, with a fast pitcher like Chief Monture. The batter only gets three tries at hitting the ball, not the pitcher. Well, I mean he has three strikes. Phew. There's a lot more to explaining it than I would have thought. I could tell you more if you like.

I'll think about that.

What she is already thinking is something she knows better than to say, now, because he is obviously enamoured of this silly pastime. What she is thinking is, wouldn't that be just wonderful. Wouldn't it be really fine to spend a good part of the day discussing the asinine game of baseball. She doesn't know what her peers among the girls have learned without ever studying the subject, the importance of pretending to be interested in what boys like. Let them talk and talk. No need to show much interest in the subject, just as long as you make manifest the depth of your interest in them.

Well anyway, Michael continues, and she rolls her eyes, the batter tries to hit the ball. The pitcher doesn't want him to, you see, so he tries to throw hard, so the batter will swing at it and miss. Or else he makes the ball curve or drop or jump. Good pitchers are tricky. The batter never knows what's coming. I heard once, let's see – Oh, yes, the pitcher wants to make the batter *understand*, too late.

Now that was unexpected. And interesting. There is a mind at work there. The pitcher must have a mind. He has strategy. It must be more than physical, this game. That's an interesting thing to say and an interesting thing to know, Michael Deeks. But not quite interesting enough.

Hence, she says, in a clipped tone she hopes will suggest finality, hard. to. hit. There. We've come full circle.

Fast.

Hmm?

He could throw heat, as they say. He could make his fastball jump.

And that's good? She should shut up. There must be a way into some other subject.

It's very good. And it says somewhere here – He flips though the clippings. Yes, it says his out didn't just curve. It snapped.

His out. Is there no end to the jargon?

An 'out' curves this way, at least if you're a righty. Sorry. If you're right-handed. An 'in' curves the other way. If you can make the ball move this way and that way, you can really keep a batter guessing. And then there's the change-up, the knuckler, the spit-ball, the drop.

I think I'm getting the picture.

You're getting the pitcher.

She groans. Please, she says, what I mean is, why don't I just treasure up the valuable information you have already vouchsafed me, and when I've completely absorbed it all, then I'll be in a position to ask for more.

Vouchsafed! The sarcasm, yes, that edge in her tone, but right now it doesn't cut. He has already said more to her than he has ever spoken to any girl. Filling her in. Instructing the smarty-pants. No wonder he has said too much. She isn't interested. She doesn't want to listen to him talk baseball. Why should she? So he is free to chuckle at 'vouchsafed.'

Yes, vouchsafed, she says. Many thanks. Vouchsafe me no more, is what I'm getting at.

He chuckles again. That's the first time I've vouchsafed. That I know of.

Quite a Voyage of Discovery, isn't it?

He gives his head the diagonal nod and wink that can mean any number of things. It can mean, I see you, Ould Sod, and I greet you. It can mean, Isn't that a caution? It can mean, Yep. Right now, supplemented by his smile, it means, Voyage of Discovery, eh! You said a mouthful.

He stuffs the clippings back in the envelope and replaces them in the bag. Replaces the bag where it was and calls, Kitty, Kitty, Kitty. The cat is curled up with its back to him and ignores him. Have it your way, then.

Voyage of Discovery. Sharp, yes she is, but she can be funny too.

And discovery is right. Silas with all this stuff, but no way of finding out, not from Silas, how he came by it. What is Gabriel Monture, the twirler, to Silas Williams, the –

Bellrock, October 13, 1912

D.B. Stegner Esq

Napanee River Improvement Company

Newburgh, Ontario

Dear Sir

There is a family row in progress at our post office and all things are going wrong as a result. As soon as I can I will send you Mr. O'Donohues letter that you asked for. Surely Mr. O'Donohue would not act so low as to send Bob Henry to do his dirty work and he secretary treasurer. I can't believe it. But I will send the letter and you may judge.

Burnt Mill dam wants cleaning out and facing up with lumber. It wants an oak jamb put on the bulk head each side. We need 700 foot of lumber for Burnt Mill and 400 foot for Third Lake. I estimate 427.00 in all including transport and my son Harry to work at half price. Please advise.

Yours respectfully,

Mitch Deeks

NEITHER OF THEM HAD ROOM for pie after Silas's fish dinner, but they had pie anyway. They are finishing it off, eating with their fingers as they ate the fish. Silas has tin plates but no cutlery. He is already washing the plates. He collected them as soon as his guests had their wedges of pie picked up. They have agreed that tonight's fish, with bread and cheese, was the best meal they ever had. Out here! With Silas their cook! Silas threw a bit of fat into the pan over the fire he built on the dam. His fireplace is made of flat rocks, limestone, a bottom and sides, blackened from previous fires. The fat sizzled and spat in the pan.

They had to be careful with the bones. Pike is a very bony fish. Had Silas brought the pie out to display before they'd had their fill of fish, they might have saved more room. He pulled it out of another sack.

Where is he getting all this stuff? From his home?

Not the pie, they're pretty sure, though neither of them has ever been in Silas's shanty. Their eyes widened when they saw the pie, and they looked at each other in astonishment.

You don't suppose – Michael began.

He's been baking? Before today, I would have said no, automatically. Now –

He nods. Me too, he thinks. Still, he says, something tells me that pie is –

Pilfered?

Pilfered! Where do you find these –

A pilfered pie. It just means stolen.

I know what it means. I'm not completely ignorant, you know.

I don't think you're ignorant.

Well, thank you. And I wasn't bothered by 'pilfered.' I just wasn't expecting it.

Don't you think we might suspend our expectations? For now? Out here? I mean, I didn't expect to be coming here yesterday. Today I didn't expect you to be joining me. I didn't expect to be talking to anybody. And, speaking of that, I didn't expect to hear from you—don't take this wrong, now, and also please don't think I'm asking for any more palaver about baseball—I didn't expect you to say anything so interesting as, what was it? about how the pitcher fools the batter?

Wants to make him *understand*, too late. Yes. I like that. Old Mr. Williams told me that. Why do you like that, when you don't like baseball?

Why do I like it? Yes, why? I need to think about that.

It doesn't matter. I just wondered.

It is interesting, though. I mean what makes it interesting? We both like it. Why?

I never thought about it. The why.

We could both think about it.

We could. But right now I want to eat. Just smell that fish.

I love raspberry pie, she says.

That wasn't raspberry.

It was too. Raspberry. Certainly.

No it wasn't. It was rhubarb. Rhubarb and something else. I don't know what.

Rhubarb! She laughs. A surprising deep rumble of a laugh that catches him off guard and makes him smile. Apparently they can disagree about pie without turning into a pair of cats. Silas's cat had a good feed too. That cat must be every bit as contented as the humans in this hut. Curled up with its paws over its head, it certainly looks like it. Who wants to fight with a full stomach?

But where does she get raspberry from? Maybe that's the other taste, the one he can't identify.

He has never heard her laugh. Is that possible? She must have laughed in his presence at some point, but he can't remember when. Who records when a person laughs? Until the subject comes up and you wonder. And then you lack information.

Stella always went her own way. I won't look at you, you don't look at me. The birthmark is bad, but you get used to it. It's not the only thing she was teased about. 'Stella Bush has flea-eas.' That used to be the chant, because she never had pretty clothes or even clothes that fit very well and she lives with a crazy mother and no father. Somehow all that meant fleas.

He was a companion of sorts once, and once only. Neither his idea nor hers. The box social in Grade Three. Just like the grown-ups. The money went to buy socks for the soldiers. Or tin? For the war in South Africa? Maybe it was for tin. All the girls brought a lunch wrapped up in plain paper, and all the boys who could afford it brought a nickel. No bidding, just names drawn out of a hat, and he got hers and had to sit with her and share her lunch. His heart sank when her name was read out, then his, and she stood up to a chorus of whistles and catcalls.

They sat on a log outside in the sun. He could see the smirks and hear the snickers and he knew she could too. What could they do but try to ignore them? But there was something about being there on that log beside her that he almost liked, despite the awkwardness. It wasn't her he liked. It certainly wasn't conversation, because there wasn't any. Here, she said, and handed him a sandwich, and Thanks, he said, accepting it. That was it. Still, there was this sense of virtue. Wasn't he good to sit right beside Stella Bush like that without any fuss, just as if she were beautiful and well-dressed like Amanda Cross and had no fleas. He was almost holy to sit with her and eat those awful baloney and mustard sandwiches without gagging.

No butter with their bread tonight. Silas might have brought some butter. And milk to drink instead of creek water.

Spilled milk. The cows!

Well, it's not his job tonight. It can't be.

Mustard and baloney is a terrible waste of good bread. He'd forgotten about that box social. Plenty of teasing after it, but a lot less than there would have been if he hadn't been so serene, meek and mild. Blessed are the Deeks. He has put that particular beatitude behind him, but the experience showed how to be patient when teased. Don't even show that it's getting your goat. It's no fun for others then. Teasing is a poor sort of fun anyway, that kind of teasing. Michael's got a girlfriend, nya nya, nya nya, nya. He has seen Bren's little brother drive him wild just by wiggling fingers at him and sing-songing, Doodie, doodie, doodie, doodie. Which of the two is dumber, the one who doodies or the one driven crazy?

Amanda Cross. He hadn't thought much about her in years either. What happened to stop him daydreaming about Amanda Cross?

It has to be rhubarb.

But rhubarb is sour.

Well, you put sugar with it. Doesn't your –

We never eat rhubarb.

Ah. Maybe I would be the better judge. We have lots of rhubarb. Four or five different patches. Did you know that whenever you move your shithouse to a new spot because the hole is filled up, right there, in the old spot, right out of all that shit, the rhubarb shoots up even though nobody planted rhubarb?

Oh! Are you trying to make me throw up? Now I know it was raspberry.

Rhubarb.

Raspberry.

Rhubarb.

Has –

He puts up a hand, palm out. Stop. Tell you what.

What? She giggles. It's possible to giggle over a dispute involving pie. I'm not sure I want to listen.

Sure you do. What do you say to rhubarb-raspberry?

Um. Say raspberry-rhubarb and I will accept.

Fine, deal. Shake.

They do. Her small hand is soft, but her grip is good. He pumps the hand once and lets go.

That's that, he thinks. Dinner over, dessert over. It must be gone six. The sun is low, just dropping behind the trees, casting long shadows across the pond. Silas has washed up and laid down on his bed of boughs. Michael and Stella sit down, each on a folded tick. Now what? That's that, what now?

He has never taken a girl's hand in a handshake. In a square dance, yes. You hold on to your partner or your corner, one hand in hers, one hand on her waist when you swing. You grasp the hands of all the women when you circle or allemande left.

He was walking past the Murphy house last fall. He glanced over and saw Lizzie Murphy framed in a window, turned side-on. He saw her big round belly, her head bent down to it. She was bending with some sort of attention or care towards her belly.

Some kind of sadness too, maybe. Mother and child, he thought, though the child was still inside the mother. Still in her womb. A sickle moon cradling a baby in its arms out of some old picture or song. The trace of a memory he didn't know he possessed. He stood on the road, observing Lizzie, seeing her for the first time as more than herself. Not thinking much about it, just looking. He wasn't prepared for her to glance up and see him. The last thing he expected, as he blushed and made to move on, was her sultry smile. And she beckoned.

He pointed to himself, Me? She nodded.

At the window she looked at him for a moment where he stood with eyebrows raised, wondering what he was doing there, not wanting to be seen having anything to do with Lizzie Murphy.

She pointed at his hand, his right. He looked at it, looked back at her, shrugged. What? She pointed again, then raised her arm and placed her own hand on the pane. He looked at it. There was her whole life, laid right out before him. Not that he could read it. Try the gypsies for your fortune. But the intimacy! How could she show the heart line and the life line and all that to a stranger?

She looked into his eyes, pointed again to his hand and nodded to her own. Why not talk? He could have heard her through that glass. Her mother must have been home.

He caught on. He placed his palm on the glass, fingers spread to match hers. Hers were shorter. She dropped her hand then and, before he thought to drop his, pressed herself to the window where her hand had been. Both of them looking down at her full breast flattened slightly against his palm. For a long, long moment. When he looked up, he saw that her eyes were on his now, and dark. They were smouldering. His hand suddenly felt scalded. He jerked it away. As at a signal, she turned and left the room. He hurried away from there, his face red and his cock hard. Carrying the baby around the village now, she never catches his eye. He avoided her for a while, but eventually realized he didn't have to. She is not trying to avoid him. He's invisible, just as he was before. He looks at her, though. Who would not? Just as well she doesn't see him. One of these days her fancy man will be back. So they say.

Fancy man. A strange way to describe Bob Henry. Every time Michael hears that name he sees a figure in the dark, the flare of a match, prominent cheekbones in sharp shadow, slit eyes, furtive drawing on a cigarette.

Anyway, they say he'll be back, tail between his legs. To face the music. The tune of Lizzie. Michael has his doubts. Bob Henry doesn't look to him like the facing kind. Nobody else he knows looks so much like pure danger. Just as well Lizzie has forgotten about Michael. He wants no part of Bob Henry, if he does show his face again. Bob is no fancy man to other men, whatever he is to Lizzie.

Michael keeps seeing Lizzie, though. He revisits that moment by the window again and again. It's like standing at the edge of the cliff over the old 'spar quarry, with the pink and white rock walls circling out and away.

Jump. Jump!

Something wants that, something within urges him to step back and gather himself and then leap! and his heart races and races as though he will, as though he's going to, he's really going to rear back and fling himself out over the edge and down and down and down, his arms windmilling until, just before he strikes water, pull them in to his sides and stretch the toes of his feet downwards, and –

No. It's too far down. You'd break your legs. You'd pitch forward on your face and knock yourself out and drown.

Yes, it's falling and falling. Sometimes he imagines a different ending to the episode at the window. She motions him around to the door. She is alone inside. He enters the house with his heart pounding.

To get his skin. If he could find out how. It's what the fellows talk about. Elmer Slade especially. He got plenty of skin off the prairie farm girls when he went west. If you can believe him. What is it, this skin? The one he knows about that is not to ask.

And he knows not to stand up until his item subsides. Good thing he doesn't have to.

SILAS HAS HIS SACK. Things in his sack. Sitting on the floor of his hut, he thinks about them. Bones, machine, stick, skin, papers. The man with the ball. In his mind, Silas does the pose. He does it with longing. His grandfather makes corn soup. Once in a while, when Silas sleeps at the shack, there'll be a pot of it simmering on the stove. The old man sleeping in the corner. He sleeps most of his days with his face to the wall now. Once his eyes opened. And closed again, quick. Don't want to see me. No soup anyway. Silas turned and left.

The things in his sack. He likes to think about them, even when he isn't setting them out on his floor. Floor of his hut. The two of them here.

She let him watch her. He could walk up the creek from his grandfather's shack and step out of the river at the back of her place.

He stays apart from the others. He looks at me.

They are here. Cat gone again. To ramble. Won't need a mouse tonight. Cat don't like cheese.

Here.

He doesn't feel good.

He lies back on his spruce branch bed. Tremors in his body, this time, rippling through his body, sparking from one end of him to the other. His arms leaping. It's happening. Why? He groans. He is pinned to the boughs as the first lights pour into the air. Sun still overhead. He can see the sun beyond the lights, worst thing ever. Sun up in the sky. Light around the edges of the belt of pulsing lights. Worst. Each light is a sound. Lights in a kind of speech. He groans and thrashes side to side. His head thrown back. Tendons rope out in his neck. A speaking of many sounds. A telling. His body ripples to it. The sounds playing him. His body lost to the mayhem sounded by the lights, deeper and deeper, passing and pulsing overhead. He is stretched, taut. He has no choice. His whole body in spasm, eyes bulging.

He brought them. He knew that. They came.

And still the lights, still the lights, still.

THEY GLANCED at Silas when he first laid down on his boughs, but otherwise took little notice. After dinner nap. Though that's what old people do. Silas is young. But there is no recognizable pattern for him. He fiddled with his sack and then stretched out.

234

At the first groan, their eyes are snatched to him, startled and amused. As he begins to thrash they rise quickly. Stella grabs his arm. Silas! She shakes it. He doesn't respond. She grabs his other arm, shakes both. Michael slaps him lightly on the cheek, then harder.

Look, his eyes are wide open. Can he be asleep that way? What's going on?

I think he's having a fit. Silas! Silas!

What can we do?

I don't know. Throw some water on him? Michael reaches for the frying pan, changes his mind, snatches up Silas's hat, steps to the edge of the hut, scoops up a hatful of water, dashes it on Silas's face. No effect. Silas is still convulsing, head now stretched all the way back, lips drawn back over his teeth. The teeth are grinding.

That's no good. What now? Michael looks around and around the hut, as though the answer is there somewhere, if only his eyes would happen to light on it.

I don't know, I don't know. Here, hold on. Hold on to his legs. Maybe we can stop him shaking.

Holding him down, they can both feel the hardness of his body, every muscle tense. And leaping. There is no control. They can't prevent his head from whipping back and forth, spit flying. Spasm after spasm racks him, but he utters no sound. Stella does, moaning a little with each of his shudders. Neither she nor Michael notices.

Gradually, the thrashing does begin to abate. Little by little Silas's neck relaxes, his teeth release their grip. He has yellow teeth, yellow and crooked. It's wrong to look in someone's mouth like that. He must never use tooth powder. His eyes close. Shaking becomes twitching. There are bubbles of froth on his lips. Stella wipes his lips with her thumb, wipes the thumb on her skirt. He sighs deeply, raggedly. His arms and legs are abruptly limp, as though he has given up. Or succeeded? Whatever his whole body was struggling with or trying for, the struggle is over. Stella and Michael release him. They remain on their knees, watching, until his breathing steadies and deepens, his eyes close.

Silas, Stella says quietly, her hand on his forehead. I think he's asleep now.

Michael straightens, draws a deep breath. Have you ever seen him do that before?

No.

How did you know it was a fit?

I didn't, but what else could it be? She looks up at him. I think he's all right now.

He moves back against the wall and she follows. They are both unsteady in their relief, shaky. That was scary, Michael says. You know, a lot of people call Silas an idiot.

Yes.

But I've been thinking. That canoe, which he can really paddle. This place. It's really well built. It's smart, intelligent. You have to be really smart, and you have to know things, to figure out how to do some of the things he's done here. Weaving with those willows? Silas is no idiot.

No, he – Michael raises a finger to stop her. There is a thought he doesn't want to lose.

What was it you said? 'Voyage of Discovery'?

I was joking, but yes.

Don't you wish we'd known this long ago?

About Silas?

236

Yes. I mean –

What does he mean? Where is he going to take that thought?

A thought to hold close and pull out from time to time, to look at. There is knowledge in it. Knowledge doesn't always come flashing in, fully formed. Sometimes you experience it, you don't think it. These two young people sit together in thought, regarding Silas with a compassion that, if he only knew, would confirm the unfortunate rightness of bringing them here. They have been bounced out of the standard course of life. To bounce out or step out, so compelling and insistent is the standard, the normal, to slow the moment and *look*, to see it new—that is a gift, even when not to your liking.

I'm sorry, he says. I lost the – Um.

Track, she thinks. Anyway, she says, you're right about Silas.

This new Silas is a marvel. He lies there, beyond them, though he has also come into their ken, having acted on them, whatever his intention. Which remains obscure, and will until, years later, Michael finds the inner resources to imagine it.

There is Silas on his bed of boughs, in the aftermath of his fit, Stella having spoken of a forerunner, the epileptic visionary Prince Myshkin. Silas is no prince. Visionary? Shaman manqué? A reasonable branch of thought away from this moment. Of course, some of these potential thought-paths never do open. What is opening for Michael now is a conception of life as more complex than ever he had thought. Far more complex than meets the eye. When the time comes for *him* to open the eye of vision, he will see far beyond far.

A LANDSCAPE NEW *to him. The great river hurrying him along
with his canoe. The great, dark, rushing river. No need to paddle.
The paddle is a rudder. Never before this great speed. Too fast. Rapids
now. He has to look alive. He knows still water best. Back there in the
swamp, miles and miles away behind him — behind? he hasn't paddled
his way here — the channels and eddies and meanders of his beloved
swamp. Gone for this north, this north broad rapid river propelling
him. Where?*

*The falls. He is mid-river, too near the centre of the current to
manoeuvre out. He could not have anticipated this. Now he is on the
brink and everything slows. The canoe noses over. He looks not down
but out, out and away into the beautiful gorge, trees on both sides, and,
far out ahead and far below, white water stretching into the distance
between banks of solid green. And the falling is*

floating, down, down and down.

*Ashore, he is on solid rock, a rounded hump of granite. There is
a river behind him. The same river? Ahead is a small clearing, and
in the clearing a cylindrical structure made of thick saplings with
smaller branches woven between them. The low opening in it faces the
semicircle of spectators. He steps off the rock on to grass, sits cross-legged
behind the others. The basket-thing is seized by a strong wind, whipped
violently this way and that. It strains and creaks in the wild thrash of
its possession. Outside, it's quiet, calm and warm in the sun. But the
basket is tormented. A crackle of noise bursts from it. Voices. Different
voices in a language he doesn't understand. He hears it. He doesn't
comprehend. Sometimes the people laugh uproariously. Something
funny spoken there, but not always. Some great power drawn to that
enclosure.*

*He is inside it, within a halo of intense light, his arms extending,
reaching long, palms up, sparks shooting off the ends of his fingers. He*

238

is that storm. The storm rolls out of him and streams back in. His mouth opens and he speaks. He is aware of speaking, not of what he says. Responding to questions and remarks from the seated people, delivering messages that he receives without understanding.

Far away now, in another tent, this one canvas, curled warm in a cocoon of living flesh, he is a worm, a caterpillar. He stirs, flexes. He is inside, feeding. It's not time. When the flesh is consumed, when it thins to a membrane, then it will be time. Then he will break out. But pressure is already building, the walls of his enclosure breathing, expanding. He is afloat between the walls. The pressure growing, pressing. The walls burst and he is expelled, flung forth, ah, into a blackness. Then he is floating down, down, down in a new air. Not falling but sinking. It's water. He settles on the bottom. Golden sand. A slight current rocks him, fœtal. By littles, the darkness lifts. A brightness above. He rocks. The shadow of a huge statue falls over the creek. From that other basket-tent. Towering over him now where he curls and rocks. Watching over him, rigid and monumental, arms folded, peering grimly into the distance.

We are here, we are here. We are.

TWILIGHT DESCENDING. Not a ripple across the pool, just water skippers streaking here and there. The trees are hushed. Silas's cat is stalking something halfway down the beaver dam. Michael and Stella are watching Silas as he sleeps. His breathing is regular. There is no sign that he is in danger now, but they can't tear their eyes away, not after the shock of his seizure. It's time for the foreordained conversation

Silas is your friend, Michael says, isn't he?

239

She hesitates. Of course she was close to Silas. Once was. Told him everything she ever thought and felt. Why not? He never heard.

I suppose so, she says finally. He was company for me sometimes, when we were small. Are you wondering why I'm here? Is that it? Because I wonder why you are.

Well, yes. I'm curious.

I don't know why. I didn't just come. Silas sort of captured me.

What, carried you off?

Literally. Look. She shows him the scratches on the backs of her hands. I was pounding him, she says. He had me over his shoulder and he backed up to a tree.

Over his shoulder!

Well, I told you. I wasn't about to go quietly. I had to stop pounding when he got my fists pinned to the tree. I did get him to set me down, finally, and then I gave him a swift kick.

Ankle? He is enjoying this story. He'll show her his own scraped ankle when his turn comes.

Yes, ankle. Not a good clean kick or he wouldn't be able to walk. Oh, I was furious.

You couldn't get away?

Could she have got away? She considers. Just up and run? Nobody outruns Silas, but she didn't even think of trying. Run? No, I – I guess I got used to the idea of going with him. I was thinking I, uh, wouldn't go to school today anyway.

School. That quiets them both, considering the difference of this day, with school and their own homes so distant. Captives of a sort, the two of them. Captives of a sort of friend who has transported them into his own world and given them a feed of fresh-caught fish. If you read about this in a book, you wouldn't believe it. Michael is on the verge of saying so, but she speaks first.

Isn't Silas yours?

My –

Friend.

Well.

It's not a word Michael has ever used for Silas. Bren is his friend, he supposes. They spend a lot of time together, despite their differences. Michael is friendly enough with the other fellows, gets on with the men on the ball team. More people might call him a friend, come to think of it, than he would call them, if he were being strict about it. When it comes right down to it, he's not that close even to Bren. He keeps a lot to himself. A friend is someone you can talk to. Can't talk to Silas, how could Silas be a friend? But maybe Silas thinks otherwise. Michael doesn't pick on him like most of the others, that's about it.

But it wouldn't be friendly to say Silas is not his friend. He doesn't want to say that to Stella. I haven't thought much about it, he says finally. That much is true.

But I came along with him. He just signalled me to come, and I did. I didn't fight. Not with him.

With someone else?

He shouldn't have added that. She's too quick. Too late now. Well, my Dad, he says. Let's just say it wasn't the best kind of morning.

His countenance darkens. She sees trouble there. It makes her curious, and surprised to be so. Other people's lives. You live your own life beside them for years and years, and what do you know of them, really? Desmond and Emma Deeks and son Michael. Respectable farming family. The son never says boo. The father never smiles. The mother is pleasant enough.

Nothing more to be said. Apparently there was, there is. But she lets it go.

So you have no more idea of what Silas is thinking than I do?

Do you have any idea?

No.

Well, neither do I.

They have broken bread together. Breaking bread is a sacrament. It reaches back—is this right, she wonders?—to the Last Supper. Nobody said grace this night. For what we are about to receive. For tasty food to fill up an empty stomach you surely have to be thankful. Just to sit down and eat with someone else is a holy thing. There is courtesy and hospitality in it. Generosity on the part of the host.

Silas as a host with guests.

Every time she turns this situation around, looks at it from another angle, and finds words for that particular angle, it thickens up. This day is nothing like most days. Normal days have their differences too, but most of the changes are so small that one day looks and feels very much like another. You have to stand back and rise above the days and look at, say, the changing of seasons. Then you understand how much change is happening around you, outside you. But even the seasons go round in much the same way every year. It's a round, a circle, a cycle. So you have to dive back in again. Have to? Why have to? Want to is more like it. Have to want to. Standing back, rising above, where you can see very clearly the changes –

She is trying to apply this sacrament of the meal shared with – strangers. That is not exact.

But she has been moved by this evening's meal. She is moved.

Her heart is strangely open. Her heart leads to her brain. Her brain is working in the accelerated way she loves. She is glad of silence at this moment. That too is novel, this much comfort with others, so that she can be with them and still think.

It won't last. She shouldn't have thought about others, about strangers. The world is full of strangers. The world is not friendly. She has estranged Miss A. She is a thwart disordered torment to Miss A. She is in exile.

Meanwhile, though. Meanwhile.

It's very easy to get lodged in a paralyzing thought, but there's too much energy in today's difference. The wheel of her thinking lurches back into motion. Back down, up close, she comes.

Is today so very different? Yes. But what if you looked and looked at any one day, one day as demarcated from the previous and the next. Might the differences not stand out as much as the samenesses? If they did, could you possibly formulate a theory about that? Would you need a theory? You would want some watchword or motto or epitaph—no, epithet. Those two words are easy to mix up, and the drag of epitaph on epithet makes her aware that epithet is not quite right either. Paradigm? Better. There is another ep-word that will not quite come.

What if Stella thinks of this day not as strange, but as typical? That's the ticket. Hold on to that idea, now, test it in and against the future. But hold it like something golden in your guts. Warm and glowing golden, replete with potential. My God, she thinks, the possibility! Today is a typical day!

It stills her. She will not move for the next few minutes, so as not to dislodge her new golden thought.

A moment of silence, such as is declared *in memoriam*, is never empty. A moment of worshipful awe is in no way empty.

Thought might be stilled, stalled or paused for the sake of pure intellectual sensation. The story not unfolding but spreading, allowed to seek its own level.

We don't stay. The moment snaps. On we go.

Stella is days, she is weeks beyond the dream of escaping down-river with Silas. He is her friend, her stranger friend. He is safe, yes, but he may be a danger to himself. There is something wrong with him.

In that dream, Silas would have delivered her somewhere like a package and then left.

How does she know that?

She doesn't see Silas in her future. I'm no seer, she thinks. The very idea amuses. But I look for Silas up ahead and I don't see him. Not with me. Where is he, then?

Right now he is lying there on the bough bed. Is he going to sleep through the night? What if he has another fit? He needs care. He needs to be taken care of. Who is going to take care of Silas? Doctor Morse must be told. She will tell him. He will give advice.

But he's strong, Silas. He could be a worker, with a body like that.

Say he delivered her to Napanee. The metropolis of Napanee. Or Deseronto, nearer the big river. Might a boy who can't hear and can't talk find work in a shipyard? Or on a ship? Going to England, say? One of those ships carrying on its deck, because the hold is too small, that tall pine that Mitch's father was always talking about, the white pine that he cut and trimmed for a mast, and if only that tree had got on board that ship, but it never did, the profit would have set him right up. Mitch shaking his head, telling about that. His father's pipe dreams. Mitch as solid as the

Shield. How does a father like that get a son like Mitch? Mitch's mother was his anchor.

A ship. One of His Majesty's ships. His Royal Majesty's Navy. Some of Those Majesties are in Canada right now. Union Jacks all over the country. The King and all his relatives are above all the English people, so they must be far above the people of the pink Commonwealth. We look up to them from way down here. We look up to Mother England. Somebody's mother can be very tiresome about that.

She is humming 'Hearts of Oak,' one of her mother's favourite patriotic songs.

> Hearts of oak are our men
> Hearts of oak are our ships
> We always are ready
> Steady, boys, steady
> We'll fight and we'll conquer
> Again and again

Michael's head swivels to her. What's that?

Hmm?

That you're humming.

Oh. 'Hearts of Oak.'

I thought so. Why 'Hearts of Oak'?

Well, I was having a thought that I suppose is foolish.

About trees? About fighting?

About Silas. What if he were on a ship? What if – I wasn't thinking this, but what if he joined the British Navy. 'Hearts of Oak,' you know. He's got a body of oak. Or ash. He is hardwood.

Don't be stupid is what he thinks, but keeps to himself. Silas a British sailor? I have a fairly strong feeling, he says, that that won't work.

Oh, I know. It's a fantasy. But I was thinking, I got to thinking, what *is* he going to do? He isn't fit, I mean he isn't fitted for anything.

Fit. They both catch the other meaning. She is embarrassed. He chuckles, but says nothing.

Silas sits up quickly. He unlaces his moccasins and rises in one easy motion. He steps to the edge of the hut and sits, bare feet in the water. Bends and scoops a handful of water, rinses his mouth, spits off toward the dam, scoops another handful and swallows.

He was asleep, Stella says. Does he know we're talking about him?

How could he?

I know. He couldn't. Still –

She stands and moves to him. She touches the shirt that covers his admirable upper body. He turns to her.

It's nothing mean, Silas, she says to his face. It's just talk. She holds his gaze for a moment. His brows knit a little. Otherwise, his expression doesn't change. She bursts into tears. She kneels beside him and clutches his arm.

Oh, Silas. She presses her forehead to his shoulder. His free arm lifts and he holds his hand in the air, as if to emphasize some retort, but the gesture is unfinished. His speech is all in that movement. It cannot be completed except in touch as he reaches across his body and cradles the back of her head with his hand.

At that, tears spring into Michael's eyes, a lump into his throat. He should not be seeing this private moment. It's embarrassing. And there is something else. Silas's gesture is so mature. An instinct Michael knows is true has shown Silas how to give comfort. Michael is jealous.

Beyond Silas and Stella, the last of the light is stark above the trees across the pond. 'Like three warriors reaving home / The plunder of a burning town.' The line comes to him out of some book. Something from school he is surprised to remember. He understands it now, seeing what it shows, and there is a pang of surprising pleasure in the match between words and scene. A streak of sun lights Stella's hair where it cascades over Silas's shoulders. Her sandy hair is abruptly golden. If Michael were Silas, he would run his fingers through it. Silas does not. His cradling hand doesn't move.

Missing out, Michael thinks, not seizing the day. And then, yes, what will Silas do? What will become of him?

Does Silas have to do something? Does he have to find a job? Will he need money to live here in the swamp, if that's where he will live? He has no oven here. He can't bake his own pies. He can't make his own cheese. Could he live on fish? He could trap in the winter. No. Too dangerous. And you can't live through the winter in a basket.

Yes, what will Silas do?

What will Michael do? Follow Patrick Lewis to Toronto? Michael can hear and he can talk. He goes to school. There is always some kind of a future for the likes of him. Farming? No.

He will not stay home and work the same old round, year after year, with no wages, just his board. There's nothing weak about his father. His father will be The Farmer for the whole foreseeable future. He is a bear with his paw over the sun of his son. The paw of the Pa.

Always booming the life of a farmer. Best life there is. Your own boss. Nobody to answer to. Make your own schedule.

Yes, your own schedule, but what's in it besides work and more work? Once in a while a dance that leaves you exhausted and grumpy all the next day. And no leaving early when you and Jim Shibley are the orchestra. Michael himself on bones. Not much talk in this great schedule, either. Mostly silence. And the weather: too dry, too wet. Warm weather too early for syrup, too late for planting. There are still branches to clear up in the sugar bush from the ice storm.

Michael doesn't know how to put the weather into perspective. He doesn't know how much his father likes calculating his chances, working those things he can control, trying to anticipate those he can't. He is always trying to prepare a cushion of some sort, to stay a little ahead. He is moving, consolidating, settling. It's a complicated game. It requires those interminable discussions that Michael finds so boring. They are information sessions. What kind of seed for the land and the conditions. Whose bull to improve the stock. The latest in machinery and how, with few resources, to get access to it. Hear about that New York Land Exposition? First, second and third prizes for Canadian wheat, and the whole of both Americas in the competition? Of course that's western wheat out of prairie soil. Yes, but still – On and on and on, gathering information and applying it to the circumstances, adjusting, adjusting, adapting. An art form that melds the farmer and his land.

The real farmer, Des Deeks might say, if he knew how to put such matters to himself, let alone to Michael, has a mind for soil, for livestock, for corn, a mind like a maple tree, like the sun and the moon. The real farmer's head is packed with formulae and facts. His hands—look at his hands. They are landscapes in themselves, worn knotted as his face is worn, weathered, leathered, by shaping the land in his own image.

Even Bob Henry understands this, some of it—Bob, who

everybody knows as some kind of a villain, who will never have a chance at farming, but who loves horseflesh and understands horses by an instinct he doesn't understand. It was Bob saved Belle's foal the year before he up and ran away. Belle was too skittish and the foal too weak. It stood, but she wouldn't let it suck and soon it fell and couldn't rise. It was Bob went for the bottle and the nipple and got himself stepped on getting some milk. It was Bob who urged the foal to its feet and herded mother and foal into the chute where Belle couldn't shy away. Cut her own baby on the legs, even so, stamping about. Pine ointment on the cut. Bob done all that, Bob, the British husbandman from the London slums. There is more to Bob than anyone in Bellrock knows. There is always more, to everybody.

Shaping the land, Des Deeks, shaping yourself to the land. For your son to repudiate.

And no talk possible between them on these matters. No theory of farming to share.

And this territory so hard to work. Not like the fertile west that Michael wants so badly to see. Three days on the train an adventure in itself, then the Rockies! The mountains look so good in the posters, and they are so identified with the west, that many a worker who makes it no further than Saskatchewan wonders where they got to.

No, you never know enough about the factors involved in farming, so the challenge is constant. It's a fair challenge, a worthy struggle. You could wake up in the morning charged to meet it, body and mind. Des Deeks used to. He still accepts his marginal land, with all its limitations, but it has become clearer with each passing year that the river company stacks the scales against him.

These goddamn sharks down the river, he raves. And Mitch. Even Mitch. See if he don't build himself one of those fancy stone houses in Bellrock!

Now, Des. Emma Deeks can only stand for so much of that kind of talk. Family is family. It's a job for Mitch, she says, you know perfectly well it don't make him rich. You weren't down on Mitch when you were helping him burn that bar of slash up to Second Lake.

Yes, well.

Yes, well I know things have changed.

They *haven't* changed, woman. They haven't changed enough. It's been the same thing for too damn many years. Just wait and see how much good these petitions do.

It's not *things* that have changed, no. She stopped herself, but Michael could see the signs. He sees them frequently these days. Her own temper fraying. Pinched about the mouth, she was, as though actually clamping her teeth on a retort. *You're* the different one. That's what she thinks. *You're* what has changed. I know why, yes. Not your fault, but try living with yourself. Spend more time with that fool guitar than with us. Cows and the guitar, guitar and cows. Come up out of those minor chords. Come out of there and talk to me about the future. The future used to be your favourite subject. Slack those keys off, Des, and come over here. Let me make you a nice cup of tea and let's talk.

His Dad's petition was a threat. He tossed it on the table before breakfast one morning. It was addressed to the despised BS: 'Dear Sir,' it ran, 'Take notice that I calculate to come on the Napanee River Improvment company for damage done me by the Third Lake Dam going out so you had better come or send some one out to apprise the damage.' Embarrassing. But Michael could only nod and say, Fine, it's fine.

His Dad stomps off to the barn and mutters at the cows.

When his mother boils over it's Michael who gets the brunt, but at least she always apologizes, and makes excuses. Times are hard, he feels a lot of pressure. We both do. Don't be so hard on him. Which hardens Michael more. Sends him out into the meadow, this morning's meadow, with the broken rock and the spider and Silas's summons, and all that led to Silas and Stella not exactly embracing here, but almost. Michael has less and less time for his beloved meadow, his place of reverie, because there is always some urgent, unnecessary job to do. Let Al Reimer fix that fence. If our cows get into his field, let them eat hearty. A good feed is just what the doctor ordered. Not what his father wanted to hear. Barking at him again.

Michael is working himself up, building up steam. His lips are pursed, very like his mother's, his hand unconsciously working his chin. Under his breath, he hears himself say, This'll show them. They'll be sorry they –

They what? Drove him away? They didn't. His father won't care anyway, no, but his mother will be frantic by now. By now, everyone in town will know that he didn't go to school, missed his chores. Everyone in town will know that Stella is gone too, and how is that going to look? Stella and Michael, with no history between them. There'll be stories.

Nobody needs fact for that. Everybody loves a mystery. Enlivens a dull existence. Michael Deeks disappeared, Stella Bush disappeared—it don't make sense. Murder! Somebody off his nut, some drifter, he killed them both, killed the both of them and carved up the bodies and hid them. Poor Emma Deeks. Just sitting at the kitchen table with her back to the door and the dishtowel over her eyes. And Des? Out looking. Of course. With the others? On his own. Couldn't bear to be with the others. Joe Compton notified? Yes. And Old Lady Bush?

That one!

No one would be searching for Silas, of course. He comes and goes at will. He's like the wind or the rain. He's like weather. Comes and goes as he pleases, his grandfather having given up on life. Silas never enters his dreams. His life is nothing much else now but dreams. They flail him something fierce, the good dreams of youth and flying, the gumbo dreams, the quicksand-and-fog dreams. He can't see and he can't move, and none of this has anything to do with Silas. Silas is beyond his range, beyond anybody's range. Nobody worries about Silas.

Somebody should. He has just had a seizure. He has no friends, only this pair. What about her, weeping on his shoulder? But she's the one needing comfort, and he offers what he can. The other? He looks on at the tableau, boy and girl in awkward embrace, almost silhouetted now in the falling light. He watches silently, no part of that intimacy and wondering, almost scornfully, that he should feel so left out.

He wants to go home.

But nobody is going anywhere, not tonight. Foolish to consider at night a course he decided against by day. That's a full moon rising behind him, a huge moon hulking just above the bushes back there. The light will be very different soon, and there will be lots of it.

Ah, but the swamp in the night. Shadows everywhere. Moon and sun shed such different light. The shadows are so different. No. Tomorrow. Tomorrow he'll have to snatch that canoe when Silas goes to spring a leak.

But Silas just had a fit. Leave him in the swamp without his canoe? Taking Stella? Would she come? Looking at her now, he has his doubts. If she did come, would that be a rescue?

IN HER AGITATED STATE, Dorothea miscalculates the height of the low porch back of the Bush house and lurches off it. Arms flailing, she hops a couple of steps to regain her balance. A near pratfall with no one to witness. Katherine Bush is not seeing her out. Dorothea strides away. She marches up the road to her own house.

Still trembling after the interview—confrontation—with Katherine Bush, she flings herself onto the settee. She wraps her arms around herself in a fury. To be told she is 'after' Stella! Has the woman no proper maternal feelings? Her daughter missing, no constable notified, then to attack one who is apparently more concerned than she is! Completely, utterly, wrong.

And yet. It floored her. She had to stare. Her mouth must have dropped open and stayed that way. Of all things under the canopy—a predator. Dorothea Asselstine? And yet.

Drawn to Stella, yes. For many reasons. But no, not that way, never. Teacher and pupil, no, no. Unthinkable.

Dorothea is trying mightily to bare herself to herself. Has she ever—ever!—behaved improperly? That woman!

Never. The relationship blossomed outside of class, yes. Otherwise, how could Stella possibly be fed to anything like her capacity? Within the constraints of the classroom, impossible. Stella hides.

Oh, God, she is hiding now.

Yesterday was different. Yesterday, unable to maintain her conviction that Stella was crying out in that ridiculous poem, yesterday it was, You will come to me. Yes, I see there is a problem, but you come to me. You come. After tendering the apology you owe me – Oh, Heavenly Father, a soul in distress, Dorothea, and all you can think of is debt. Decorum and debt.

And Michael Deeks gone now too. Something in the township is opening its maw and swallowing our children.

She unwraps her arms, stands up, paces.

Stay away from my daughter. Oh, it hurts. To have been so discreet, to have suppressed so much of herself. With complete success, so she had thought. Found out by such a woman.

Maybe she doesn't – She's jealous. Maybe she's just jealous. Abdicating the role of mother, another woman picks it up, puts it on. She resents it. Dog in the manger. Another woman, more mother than –

Than? More than what? No, no, no.

Dorothea paces and paces. She pauses in her restlessness only to twitch the curtain aside and look out. What does she expect to see out there? All she does see is the empty school, late afternoon sun transfiguring the front, the side in shadow. Light and dark. A painting by – she can't think who, not tonight.

Transparent! To a woman as indiscreet as Mrs. Bush. If. If she wasn't just lashing out.

All this heat for the wrong reason. Where is Stella? Where is Michael Deeks? Two children missing and no explanation. That's what we should be discussing, she and I, that and nothing else. 'After' Stella, indeed. Dorothea would go after Stella right now, if she knew where she was. Bring her back to that harridan, her 'mother.' Then what? You stay away from my daughter.

You hear me?

She stops between kitchen and parlour. She will join the search.

She should. Everyone should be searching.

If she does, though, what about her lessons? What about her other students, her other responsibilities? Somebody has to represent solidity and continuity in these desperate times. Somebody has to embody it. The school out there. That meeting, the plot – none of it could possibly have anything to do with this. Still. The trouble has gone medley. She has a terrible presentiment. She wants to drop down, right where she is, just let go and fall and curl up on the floor. If she can't stand up, she can't go out.

Because she is afraid. Face it, she says to herself. You cannot bear to go out there. Because they will all look at you. They will look right through you.

But her classes. Even the Brens and the Ronnies. They will be in class tomorrow, and so must she. And, oh, Michael and Stella might be there as well, and the relief! This night revealed as nothing but a bad dream –

She hauls her small self up off the floor of her mind, stands it up straight. She lights the lamp on the kitchen table, sits down, opens her textbook. Elbows on the table, she stares at the page with head in hands. Not a posture for preparation. She straightens her back, chooses a pencil from the cup on the table, concentrates.

It's a grim-faced Miss Asselstine tonight, but anyone passing her house will see the light on, just as usual. Burning the midnight oil, Tom Ritchie always says. You work too hard, Dorothea, he says. Too hard, she volleyed just the other day, smiling back, what is too hard? What you do, he replied. Take some time for yourself.

For herself. What self? She is her vocation. That is all she is. Even so, she can never do enough. Never. She cuts her losses, every single day. It is never humanly possible to do all she needs to do on any given day. Large or small, there is always a residue, nothing to do but absorb it. Nights at her kitchen table, she draws heavily on her foundation of word, of number, of thought. So solid it has seemed, blocking up, strong to build on. Tonight it seems insubstantial, fluid, more water than stone. Water slips, it slops. It flows away.

Something is cracking. A very delicate balance has been lost.

Except with her beautiful mind, Stella never moved toward Dorothea. Stella shies.

What if she hadn't?

I HAVE A TWIN, you know.

No, I don't know. How could I know?

Well, that's just a way of putting it. 'You know,' I mean.

Well, why haven't I heard about her?

Oh, it's a him. Nobody wants two of me.

He leaves that. There's a danger glow around it. But he has to say something. Not saying it, right now, is agreeing. What has wanting to do with what you get, though, especially when it comes to babies? He could say that.

Has this got something to do with Silas? Silas sitting on, with his legs in the water of the darkening pond. She wiped both eyes on the shoulder of his shirt before disengaging and returning to her seat beside Michael. Drooping, like a fatigue had entered her bones.

Ah, he begins, what happened, what –

Happened to him?

Yes.

Lost.

Lost? Who loses a child? A baby, was he?

He was two years old.

When he got lost?

Yes. I can see him. I see him with his arms lifted straight up. He wants up. There are tears on his cheeks. Rolling down his cheeks. That's what they say, 'rolling down.' It's more of a slide, isn't it? Tears don't roll.

Michael nods.

If I were asking somebody for a hug, reaching out my arms – She stops, and Michael fidgets in discomfort. She isn't asking, is she? Surely he isn't supposed to volunteer. Nobody hugs in his family. His mother and father never touch, not that he's seen. They must at night, the same bed. He doesn't care to dwell on that. He doesn't want to ask himself what it might say about their intimacy that he is their only child.

Sorry, she says, I'm not asking.

How does she know what he's thinking? The idea of her divining *that* thought confuses him.

Well, he says.

Oh you would, would you? She has cocked her head at him. There is a small ironic smile on her lips and the one eye he can see looking out through the screen of her hair has a twinkle in it. He shifts, grabs his chin.

I'm teasing, she says. And don't worry, I'm really not. Asking.

I'm remembering, that's all, remembering my little brother. Well, he's always little. He will always be a little boy, raising his arms. Pick me up, he says. Pick me up and wrap your arms around me. He wants to be held. He's stuck that way, always with his arms raised. Why doesn't anyone pick him up? I'd pick him up. I'd hold him tight –

To his great surprise, Michael feels the lump in his throat again. Such longing in her voice. He swallows. This is delicate ground. He has never had to deal with such a delicate matter. All the fellows, every one of them, they never depart from the usual. There are never any surprises.

Well, there was the one evening Bren climbed up on the roof of his shithouse, wouldn't come down. What got into him? Surely not having to wear the truss. Who cares about that? One time and one time only, crying and carrying on, insisting in this strange gravelly voice, no one likes me, everybody insisting no, not true, you're a fine fellow, don't be silly. Come down. Come down and we'll play something. What would you like to play. You can choose. What?

The girls were better at this than the boys, but the silence of the boys was part of the persuasion. When Bren finally relented, it was Kick the Can, perfect for the twilight, and he got to be It.

Easy-going Bren, of all people. That kind of surprise you can do without. But never having to think what to say? Ever? The patterns for conversation are all laid out for every single day. You pick up the script as soon as you leave the house. The weather—well, that's more the grown-ups. He has that delight to look forward to, endless talk about weather and crops and the government and religion. Now it's girls and baseball or hockey and so on and on. And nothing more interesting from the girls: boys and clothes and boys.

But this one, now that she is talking, is all surprise. It's not comfortable. He has to be on his toes. He doesn't like the conventional talk, but there is something to be said for it. You know what to expect. You don't get yelled at.

Does she really have a twin? Did she? How could they live all their lives so close and he never heard anyone breathe a word about that. What if she's making it up? But the sadness is real.

How—I hope you don't mind me asking this—how was he lost? I mean, I don't like to call it careless, but.

I know. 'Lost' is the word I like. It's my word. I can always hear it calling to another word. I always hear 'found.' 'Lost' is only half a story.

Yes, but –

But what are the facts? That's what you want to know.

Yes, and if you might, by any chance, be –

Making it up? Making it all up?

I might just as well sit here and think at you. You know what I'm thinking.

No. I have no idea. Nobody knows the mind of a gull, as they say, and, no, you're not a gull. That just came into my mind. I shouldn't just let things come, but I do. I mean nobody knows what's in somebody else's mind, and a good thing too. It's odd, but I seem to have had this conversation before. Probably with myself.

She has been talking to him, but looking ahead, down. Her voice, thank goodness, has lost that grating edge. He has been watching her talk. Looking as well as listening might help him gauge her veracity.

In the pause, Silas rises, goes to where his kerosene lamp has been sitting. It really does seem as though he's listening, his activity somehow timed to the rhythms of their conversation. He swirls the glass container to test the level of fuel, lifts off the chimney, screws off the wick holder and adds some fuel from a jar. He picks up a box of matches, Michael and Stella following his every action. They scrutinize everything he does for clues about his well-being and his intentions. What are they going to learn from his lighting of a lamp?

He slides back the cover of the matchbox, chooses a match.

Every stick a match, says Michael.

Every match a light, responds Stella, and together they intone:

Eddy's Silent Parlour Matches.

Come into my parlour, says Stella.

Said the spider to the fly. Michael looks around. Not what comes to mind, thinking parlour. We do have light, though. At least Silas has a light.

Now that the lamp is lit and the wick turned up, the night is excluded, made larger, darker. Three young people in a halo of light. Stella's face, what Michael can see of it, glows reddish now in the light of the lamp.

There's so much I don't know, she says, but I couldn't be making it up. How could I, when I see him so clearly? I see the little blanket he used to drag around everywhere. My mother mooned over that blanket, afterwards. She used to put it to her cheek and the tears would fill her eyes. Did we talk about him? That's your next question.

Is it? You're actually getting ahead of me. That's a good one, though. Did –

I think so. I do. Not exactly talk, maybe. I know I used to ask, and she – He's been, he is, a lump of something sore I carry with me all the time. He's so much part of me, always with me, that I'm used to it, so used to that little lump, or maybe it's a hole, a piece of me – She pauses. Her hands are in her hair, raking through it, as though she might tear some out.

Tearing their hair, he thinks, without knowing why or where it comes from. Sackcloth and ashes. The language and the actions of lament.

A piece of me, myself – gone. I've accepted that. That's the way it is. I had accepted it, and here I am thinking about him again. It's easier – her voice cracks – not to.

The tears are streaming down her face now. They are not rolling. She lets them fall.

I remember asking and her not saying. Never. Never saying. Like with your father. So you don't know? What happened. What happened. No.

The lump is in his throat again. He would reach out to her if that were thinkable. He hasn't the courage. He could wipe away her tears. He could offer her a hankie, if he carried one. He never does, except a bandana for his neck during haying. Never one of those monogrammed handkerchiefs like Eric Friesen has, the pig, to mop his sweaty, piggy brow. Blows his nose into it too. How could you blow snot into a square of fine linen? He could use a hankie like that right now.

I'm sorry, he says.

She looks at him with gratitude, keeps on looking. When has that ever happened before? Her eyes are shining, tears in them catching the glow of the lantern. He has to look away, his heart pounding.

261

Sorry, he thinks. Such a simple thing to be, such a simple thing to say. The right thing. Lucky.

THE TEACHER CAME. Mitch came. Where is Stella?

The teacher stared at her. Why? Something spoken when she wasn't herself. When she was beside herself. But she spoke quite reasonably to both. They came and they went. They came about Stella.

They think she doesn't care. They think she has no heart.

She has no heart.

Let them take care of their own daughters, that's all. Let them attend to their own affairs, tidy their own houses and lives, those that have houses and lives and daughters. Her – she hardly ever uses the word, hardly ever thinks it. Daughter. To think daughter is to think mother. That is not – What is wrong with you, she thinks. Katherine Bush, what is wrong with you?

What?

If she were her daughter's mother in every respect, she might well now be thinking how sharper than a serpent's tooth it is to rear an ungrateful child. But that was a thought for yesterday. Yesterday was for thinking ingrate, because – why? Where was the disagreement, the argument? There was none. There is no –

Nothing. She has no heart. The serpent in this story is – no, she is not – But she is gnawing herself.

Where has Stella got to? Where would she go? Not to the teacher, no. The teacher was here. She stared and left. Her mouth was open and her lower lip trembled. Why? Katherine spoke very reasonably. She always does. Mitch came. They both came about

262

Stella. Let them mind their own –

Nothing, no one, no Stella at Stella's rock. Stella's novel upstairs on the bedside table. Wherever would she skip to without her novel? Nowhere Katherine knows to look. What does she know?

She knows nothing.

Stella should be upstairs right now, reading that book. Burning the midnight oil.

What is wrong with me?

It has been years since Katherine Bush thought of herself as daughter. She is reaching back and back, imagining herself as the daughter now. Where would she go, fleeing, if she were Stella?

Or is that wrong? The wrong question. If she were – if she'd been stolen – there would be no choice. The likes of filthy Bob Henry. Bob Henry and the Murphy girl. It wouldn't be a failure. No one could blame –

Her thoughts a-tumble. To come out into the world – flesh of her flesh lost in it. Please God, only lost. Lost might be found. Please, please.

What is wrong with me?

IF I WERE INTERSTELLAR, Stella says, I'd be Venus. I'd go to Venus. You can see Venus right now. That bright star there. Planet, actually.

He looks where she is pointing, shading the side of his face from the lantern glow. Which makes him think to ask Silas to turn it off. Nothing to see by lantern light now, anyway. He waves a hand at Silas to attract his attention, points at the lantern, turns his thumb and forefinger counter-clockwise. Silas obliges. If he can see you, you can communicate with him.

They have been talking about the heavens since Michael cleared his throat just to clear it and startled her. Oh, she said, I was on Mars. Mars? That is where her mother places her when she daydreams.

Daydreams! He is supposed to be the dreamer.

Well, she never permits herself to dream in school, not unless at recess or noon hour, when she might as well. Nothing else to do then. Eat lunch and read. Or dream.

He raises his eyes in the renewed darkness. She dreams, he thinks. Another dreamer. They study the sky in silence, the quadrant they can see out of the hut. There is the good old dipper, the only constellation he is sure of when Orion has slid out of view. It's a beautiful night for stars. When the lantern was lit, it was hard not to look at that, eyes naturally drawn to the brightest, nearest light. The stars are better to look at, you have bigger thoughts looking out than looking in, and it's not something he does often. He and Stella have never been stargazing with each other. She has the big word, interstellar. He repeats it. There's her name in it. She must know that. He asks her.

Maybe, she says. But I don't think my mother had stars in mind. Stella was my grandmother's name. My mother's mother, in England. It's possible that she, my grandmother, was named for Mary, the mother of Jesus. Mary is sometimes called Stella Maris, Star of the Sea, which is very beautiful. It would mean that my grandmother was Catholic, I think, because Mary is much more important to Catholics than she is to Protestants. My mother and I are nothing.

No religion?

That's right.

We're Methodist, I guess. At least that's the church we'd go to if we went. Well, my mother still does. She used to make me go, but I gave it up after my father did. I feel like I'm nothing too. Also.

'Nothing will come of nothing. Speak again.'

What?

It's from *King Lear*, and I hope you don't mind me mentioning Shakespeare, because I know most people hate Shakespeare.

Not me. Well, I find it hard to read sometimes. But listen: 'Why, man, he doth bestride the narrow world like a colossus.' Remember that? 'The fault, dear Brutus, is not in our stars,' he waves his hand dramatically at the heavens, 'not in our stars but in ourselves that we are underlings.'

I do remember that.

I remember entertaining my parents with it. Prancing around the kitchen. They thought it was funny, though it's not supposed to be. Well, they thought *I* was funny.

Michael Deeks, a thespian!

They both laugh.

King Lear is my favourite play. Do you know it?

No.

Though I love *The Tempest* too. 'Yarely, yarely, men! We split!'

Yarely?

I have no idea. But the ship is being wrecked in the storm, the tempest. It's coming apart, splitting.

Yarely. He chuckles.

Anyway, she continues, 'nothing will come of nothing' is where Cordelia is having trouble telling her father how much she loves him, because her sisters, who don't love him at all, are lying about that. They speak first, and since they not only don't love him but actually hate him, because Cordelia has always been his pet—she's the youngest, you see, and they're jealous—so they use the floweriest language imaginable and flatter him shamelessly. He loves to be flattered. And if Cordelia does that, the same as her sisters, it'll be like she's just as false as they are. So when he turns to her and asks what she has to say to earn a bigger share than her sisters – I should have said that he's planning to divide his kingdom between his daughters and kind of withdraw. Retire. He doesn't want to be king anymore. So he has already decided to give Cordelia a bigger third.

A bigger third. He never took Maths from Miss A.

Over eighty years old and never took Mathematics. Hasn't got much common sense, either. Anyway, Cordelia can't stand to sound like her nasty sisters, so when he asks what she has to say, she says 'Nothing,' which really takes him aback. His favourite daughter, you know. So he says 'Nothing will come of nothing. Speak again!'

Give me a better answer.

A better answer for a bigger third. And she won't do it. And he flies off the handle and banishes her and divides the whole works between the false sisters and everything starts to go wrong for him.

Sounds like he has it coming.

Well, he does and he doesn't. It's complicated. He's too foolish and they're too awful. It's a tragedy.

He has the flaw.

The tragic flaw.

They are both back in school. She is still with *King Lear*. Most people in it are flawed. Well, some of them are almost all flaw.

For some of those creatures, flaw is hardly the word. When you put out somebody else's eyes pretty much for fun, that's not just flawed. That's evil.

Michael is thinking of Oedipus. Is it chance that gives him another blinded man to contemplate just now? One story draws another, that's all.

Tragic flaw, he thinks. It doesn't fit Oedipus so very well. Everything is against Oedipus. That's all very complicated too, but he isn't. He didn't have it coming. Not being blinded.

Anyway, he says, returning to the conversation, I don't suppose you really wanted me to speak again.

Well, no. Your 'nothing' reminded me, that's all. I've got us sidetracked. What was it I was – Oh yes, my grandmother. She lived in England, in a county called Suffolk. The village of Sudbury. That's in East Anglia. You know, where England bulges around into the North Sea, the east coast? No?

'Fraid not.

Well I know it because I used to look at the map of England and dream.

Dream! For the second time tonight! I don't suppose you'd call that, oh, say, *drifting*, this dreaming that you do. No, I don't suppose you would.

All right. I apologize. Go ahead, call me Miss Dreamer if you like. Go ahead.

No, no. I wouldn't think of it. Really, I couldn't. I could not bring myself to be so cruel.

Fine, then. That is your tit for my tat. Do you mind if I continue?

Tit is teat, he thinks, the tit should be hers. But he won't risk saying that. He is amazed to be talking this way. She says something, and he says something. Dialogue. You see it in books, but you don't do it. He never has. Not this back and forth. It keeps you on your toes. It calls something out of you.

It wasn't dialogue at first. It was sticking the knife in and then wiggling it. That's what she was doing. It drove him back into himself. His standard place. He's glad he found his optimism in there. That's what sprung him out. Now they are conversing. Actually engaging in conversation.

Please, he says, be my guest.

Yes, *they* are the guests. Silas's guests. To explore the moment further, though such exploration is as yet more Stella's purview, he might observe that words are stepping stones. They invite you on. Sideways is Michael's particular step along the unmarked path. Which could be traced after the fact, by another if not by him. Or—why not?— by him, years hence, his apprenticeship to language having been served. Given the enabling words:

> Who curseth Sorrow knows not her at all.
> Dark matrix she, from which the human soul
> Has its last birth.

…Then drawing his nightmare word by word through the needle's eye. Remembering especially from this evening what he has yet to feel in it: Everything, coursing through him. Achieving, finally, a measure of rest.

Guests. Not captives.

But she has begun again.

I was at the map. The map of England. I'd like to go there, England. I'd like to go to Sudbury. Mother said once that there's a church in Sudbury called St. Peter's, just a little church, she said, and if you go up behind the altar you find a tiny door at eye level on the stone wall and if you open that door, and apparently just anybody can, there inside is a little niche in the stone, and in the niche is the skull of Simon of Sudbury. He was a priest who was beheaded for his beliefs. And his head, what's left of it, the skull, is right there. Isn't that fascinating?

You've been dreaming, right?

We could just drop that, I think. There is warning in her tone.

Yes. Or – What am I trying to say? Or we could – Well, there's no need to make fun, but – I don't know. I've never talked to a dreamer before. That I know of. Drifter and Dreamer. You know?

It's her turn to ponder their conversation. He is talking to her, actually thinking and talking. Can it be that most people use only a fraction of their mental capacity in conversation? Is everybody capable of much, much more? Does she have to look at everybody, now, with that in mind? She is now equipped with a view – Equipped? It bears more thinking on, but if it holds up, this view of everyone as more than they show – Well, Ronnie might actually be less. Already there are holes in the view from the swamp. She will call it a work-in-progress.

We have agreed, she says, on raspberry-rhubarb. I have suppressed my hesitations on that score. I believe I can meet Mister Drifter halfway.

She stands. Mister Drifter, she says formally, may I present Miss Dreamer?

She offers her hand, dropping a courtesy, which she holds until he scrambles to his feet, inclining his head in a slight bow as he takes her fingers, just her fingers in his own, in what he imagines is the courtly way, his other hand raised in a foppish wave.

Where do Canadian village boys and girls learn to pose thus, like familiars of the courts of Europe? They do not. Curtsey and bow, yes, even in rural Ontario. Curtsey or bow when accepting applause for any performance. Girls, you spread your skirt or your dress with each hand, place one foot behind the other, toe to the floor, and bob once. Looking always ahead, never down. Now boys, with the left arm, hand open, across the waist, the front of the waist, and the other arm behind the back. Now bend smartly from the waist, down and up.

But anyone looking on at Stella and Michael, posed in the light of the full moon now risen among the stars, surprised by themselves, anyone might well imagine them otherwise, her in a full-length spreading gown of silk jacquard with square neckline and gathered bodice, a tiara sparkling on her coiffure, he in richly embroidered tailcoat and waistcoat, with velvet breeches and long white stockings. The beauty spot affixed to her cheek possibly a mole in the low light.

The only onlooker is Silas, who lacks all knowledge of the courts of Europe. But he has some small experience of posing. Seeing his friends, his guests or captives, rise and stand, he rises also. He sets himself, then rears back, lifting a leg and an arm, the other arm behind his back, and freezes. Now they are a threesome, a tableau of moonlit statuary, a riddle in the round. Stella and Michael, fingers still linked, turn to Silas, astonished. Then they look wide-eyed at each other, drop their hands, and dissolve into laughter. Silas holds for a moment more, then relaxes and sits down again.

Does Silas understand hilarity? Of course he does. Neither of the others see his face clearly in the dark, but he has a smile on it for the first time in what seems to him, now that he feels his face relax, days.

They are here. They had each other by the hand. They were laughing. Good. The tension he has not been able to lose lets up a little.

What was that, they have asked each other, seated again, and again watching the impassive but unpredictable Silas. What else has he got in his repertoire? They watch him with smiles on their faces.

Waves are slapping lightly beneath them. The bullfrogs are starting up. Simon of Sudbury in his niche is forgotten.

Did I mention *The Swiss Family Robinson* before?

I don't think so. You mean the book?

Yes. Did you ever read it?

No.

Coral Island?

No.

What about –

We're not in school, you know.

We certainly are not, and we were not in school today. We were truants. And we may be truant again tomorrow, unless – But books aren't school. Books are salvation. She giggles. Now you'll say 'we're not in church.' I love stories, that's all. Nothing I've ever read is like my life. My own life – She trails off.

He is not the reader she is, but he likes stories too. Who doesn't like stories? Life stories or legends, woven together, braided, the way we still live out the myths. He knows some words about stories, words like 'tragic flaw.' If he put his mind to it, he might even be able to recall the Greek for that. It's hard enough having to remember the English without having to remember Greek words as well. It doesn't help when Miss A writes the words in Greek letters on the chalkboard. She knows languages, Miss A. She likes to write them out. Verboten. That's a German word that Ronnie knows pretty well now. So do they all. Verboten. Forbidden. Don't do it. Do it and you'll have to write it out hundreds of times. Hamartia. What is that? Is that the tragic flaw? If so, his father has it. His goddamn temper. Well, it's a flaw. Maybe not tragic.

But no, his life is nothing like a story either.

Robinson Crusoe, she says abruptly.

Now I know that one, he says, relieved. He was closing up before, with her naming books he hasn't read. Here's a space he can open into. Stuck on an island, he says. Footprint in the sand. Friday.

Yes. He's marooned, Crusoe. He is really glad to find that he's not alone. Marooooned. She draws the word out, relishing the sound. The point is, don't you feel a little like that? This could almost be an island.

Who's Friday, then? You weren't so happy to see me. Maybe if I'd shown up first as a footprint.

And if I'd been alone for, what was it, years? But you didn't want to see me, either. Did you?

Didn't want to see you. And now – Miss Dreamer, may I present Mister Drifter. Do you catch my drift?

I do.

Dreaming, daydreaming of bones. Bones and Mrs. Bush. He'll tell Stella about that. It will explain a few things. There are fuller versions of their adjacent lives—separate in any way that counts—and he sees that he might fill her in. He could give her something of himself. It would not only be talking, then. It would be more.

He might give her something important, talking, trusting that she would keep it. A keepsake. Can he trust her? They have known each other for years, for hours. Minutes, maybe, the first hours here having had little to do with getting acquainted. Can he trust her?

He was ten when his father washed off a couple of spareribs after supper and carried them out to the drive shed, telling Michael to come along. He didn't say what he was up to there, scraping off all the gristle, trimming the bones same length, humming the while, but Michael knew that he was somehow included. Something soft in the lines of his father's face, something relaxed and gentle about his working with the hack saw. There is a warm kind of silence that includes. Michael will gravitate to it all his life. His third lover will be the first with self-confidence enough to coast with it, their relationship the first to survive it.

Michael forgot about those bones, but not the moment in the drive shed. It can flash out its warmth at unexpected moments, as right now. He hates his father? Sometimes. He can almost but not quite use that word. He approaches much nearer that word than he does love, which, once in a long while, he feels emanating from his father, being returned. Michael will be quite good at forbearance when he is less churned up about life.

He found the bones set one on either side of his plate at supper a couple of weeks later, like auxiliary cutlery. They were dried out, shined up and polished. He looked up at his mother, who was smiling, but it was his father who spoke. There you are, he said, nodding at the bones. Once upon a time, he said, those bones helped hold up Bossy's guts, but most of Bossy is spareribs and steaks and roasts, all nicely stored in the ice house now. She won't be needing these. King wanted them, but I said no.

273

In a small reverence, every slaughtered cow becomes Bossy in the Deeks household, serving beyond life under a generic name. An earlier Bossy greets Michael's feet every morning in the form of a rug. King has no cause for complaint. He does very well by Bossy, with a steady supply of bones to gnaw, to bury, drag around and snarl over.

A familiar ache, thinking of that time, that father, the one with the sense of humour. Guitar player, square dance caller, step dancer. The one he wants to stay proud of. He would never smash that guitar. It *is* precious.

After supper, his father showed Michael how to hold the bones curved away from each other, one each side of his middle finger, how to snap his wrist to clack the bones in reel-time or jig-time. They kept slipping out, at first, but soon Michael took to it. You've got rhythm in your bones, his father said. You're a chip off the old block. Chip would be a good nickname, Michael thought. But he didn't mind 'Bones.' He carried those bones wherever he went that whole summer. He could always fish them out of his pocket on the way somewhere and snap out a beat to go with some mouth music. Bones, they called him, or Bonesy, or Mister Bones, until Mister Drifter took over. Mister D sometimes. He was both Mister B and Mister D the time he ran into Katherine Bush on First Lake Road and frightened the hell out of her.

He got smart enough with the bones to accompany Jim Shibley and his father at the dances. He liked it when his father was the centre of attention, dancing, while Jim fiddled and Michael clacked. Your Dad, Jim used to say, he can leap over a divan and never lose the beat. Your Dad is a light tower.

Michael was a tot of five the night he woke up in the school where he'd fallen asleep on the coats, astonished to see his father in the middle of the floor, nimbly footing it to one of Jim's jigs, with everyone clapping him on. He never cracked a smile, not that night nor any other. His dancing is serious. He might dance fancy, but he's no showman, not like Jim. He's a man doing the best job he can, that's all, offering the people what he has. He dances like he plays guitar at the dances, to accompany the fiddle. When Michael got old enough to clap along with the others to his father's rhythms, he always got a wink. He liked the acknowledgement. And then came a time to be part of that. You can catch more beats with bones than feet. Grace notes, descant beats, for his father. On some nights, they'd be talking back and forth, feet calling, bones in reply. Or bones stitching a counterbeat all around the foot work. When they were both inside the rhythm.

The proper place to be inside the rhythm—inside and fully awake and free of yourself, like his father at times with the guitar—is at home. They agree about that without ever discussing it. At the dance, they do enjoy themselves. Playing is a pleasure any time. But the dance exposes them too much. First Lake Road, he found out, is even worse for such exposure. There ought to be a prohibition: Forebear To Dance Down First Lake Road.

I don't suppose your mother cares much for me, he says, chuckling.

A pause before she answers. Where is that coming from? I don't know, she says finally. Why not?

She never complained about me? She never said how I cost her a jar of pickles one time?

Pickles?

Pickles. Listen, you remember the time I burst out laughing

in school and had to be put out?

I certainly do.

Well, it started with your mother.

You were laughing at my mother?

He hurries to correct that impression.

No, no. Listen. I'll tell you about it.

He was all by himself, deedle-de-deedling along the road to school, clacking the bones, his feet jumping out every which way. Prancing and kicking up dust like a fool. He was thinking of his father, the time he made them all late for church because he'd cranked up the gramophone and put on a catchy fiddle tune and just had to dance it. Michael and his mother at the door, in their Sunday best, watching him with smiles on their faces. Where was all the impatience then? Of course he was hot and sweating from dancing and then hurrying along the road to the church, but he couldn't help himself. Music in his bones. Got to rattle them.

Well, there was Michael on the road, snapping his bones, jigging and leaping around the curve by Hooper's Mill, and here was Mrs. Bush suddenly right in front of him, confronted by this mad young dervish. Her eyes bugged out and her big face stretched out lengthwise. Her mouth was a huge O as she shrieked. Up went her arms—Michael demonstrates to Stella—up over her head, and up, way up, went a jar out of her hands. Up went his eyes, following the arc of its flight, fascinated, up and then down and smash on the road.

Sweet pickle, it, ha, it looked like, he says. Peals of laughter from the two of them. They laugh themselves sore.

Mrs. Bush had lost all her breath out of that enormous hole in her face, and she was panting. Her hands were flapping wildly at her chest when Michael tore off past the mill. He didn't even say sorry. He had to run before the laughter overflowed. Behind him, Mrs. Bush caught her breath. He could hear her hoarse hollering. Then he fell into the ditch, helpless, laughing until his sides hurt.

Oh, she'd have been furious.

She was.

And that's why you –

That's why, yes.

My lord, she says. It gave us all hysterics.

Yes, and gave Miss A the fits. Sorry, Silas.

Old Lady Bush's face and those airborne pickles had popped into his mind without warning at school, made him grin. Stop that. He couldn't. Without warning, the grin widened. Clamping his teeth on the volcano within, he released a groaning sob. All eyes swept to him. He was grinning so hard his eyes must have been slits, his mouth closed tight on the welling laughter. No! he was admonishing himself. Not now! He was shaking and huffing, eyes brimming.

It was seeing himself as the others must see him—alarm in some eyes—that made him lose all control. The high, giggling trill that escaped him shocked everyone else into shouts of laughter, all but Miss A. Even she couldn't hold back a smile. She recovered herself quickly, but the class was already lost to an orgy of laughter. She was shouting, then, but no one was hearing. Her face passed through red into purple. Finally, she hauled out the strap and slammed it, wham! wham! on the desk. She was throwing her whole body into it. The sight of that, even more than the noise, got everyone's attention. She stood, rigid, waiting out the residual titters, then addressed Michael.

You. Pick your face up off your desk, she said, and get out.

And stay out, she said, until you can control yourself. His face was flaming as he made his way down the aisle and out the door. She might as well have said, Go home, nitwit, laugh yourself empty, sleep on it, whatever it is, and come back here tomorrow prepared to listen and learn something. He tried to gather himself outside, sitting on the school steps. Unfortunately, Reverend Smart happened to pass just then, and shot him a reproving glance. Only reprobates are exiled from class. Michael dropped his gaze, embarrassed. When he looked up again, the pastor was mincing down the road and Michael found himself thinking pickle again. Not sweet pickle. Big fat cuke. Right up his arse.

Which set him off again, the answering chorus of howls from inside the school cut off by Miss A's yell of rage.

Later, late for chores, the cows bellowing and his father angry, his sides were aching from laughter and suppressed laughter and hard concentration on neutral subjects during detention.

Worst day of my life, he says ruefully.

Yes, I can see how it would have been. And there we were, the rest of us, enjoying it. I never thought to mention you to my mother, or else I might have got her side of the story. She never spoke about it. She never expects better from any of you boys. Well, not from anyone. She complains. She complains about her indigestion, about her aching bones, about Mitch Deeks, if you can imagine that. Her only friend, and she dresses him down, in person or otherwise. Where's the gratitude? Poor Mitch. Of course she complains about me pretty much all the time. 'Ungrateful whelp.'

Whelp!

All right. Bitch. I'm a goddamn bitch.

It's like a slap. How can she say that? That kind of language from a girl, it puts his guard up. And tattling on her mother. Reticence is so ingrained in his own family that tact or taste in such matters need never be mentioned. He is offended. In return for his story of frightening her mother, she gives him profanity and disloyalty. Elsewhere, in other times and places, and also here, when he's older, he will take cursing in stride, whoever does it. He already expects it from the fellows. He knows filthy jokes about Old Lady Bush he would never in a million years divulge to Stella. He never repeats them, just as he never passes on any brutality to Silas. Brutality is somehow in the air again.

She knows he has gone silent. She doesn't like it. The word hypocrite flitting through her mind. Chances are very good that she will let it light on him. Very good chances. Michael Deeks, with his own family troubles. We aren't getting along, he says of his father, and then to sit in judgment on her. A storm gathering. She can feel it. She can feel the bright day of their concord whitening, thinning, going milky, all the good blue, the blue and green, sucked out of it and a front gathering. It isn't jolly Boreas presiding over such tempests. No. How could she think the poor king on the heath would be subject to the breath of a round-lipped, slightly comic wind-spirit. A windbag. The suave, level world has buckled.

Hell is a blackness. It's a night season storm. You see it coming, you know the angry blue-black skies are going to overwhelm you. She will not call to it. She will not, not, not encourage it. There could be entrails. Entrails. This young hypocrite, Mister Whatever, this silly little beast of a boy, tiny in the shadow of her towering.

Don't say intellect. Do not. Please, my pride, go down.

279

I don't want ripping. I don't want him decimated. For what? To what end? In whose interest? Oh, God. Hold me. I've given too much. I have exposed myself, Miss A, and now –

It's a long and a long way off, the voice. A tunnel and that voice so small, almost inaudible. Her name. It comes to her that it is her own name. Now rushing at her. A word she can see, rushing at her, spiralling down the tunnel, speeding toward her down this contracting tunnel, a barrel, and it hits her, penetrates her like a shriek, and she shrieks back, WHAT?

Jeez, he says, starting. There's no need to shout.

Who's shouting? She says it more quietly, but sharply.

You, he says. You! he repeats, as if suddenly occupying the word, his tone accusing.

Don't you judge me, she spits.

Judge? But he knows what she means. It takes the wind out of his sails. But he doesn't want to admit judging, either. He is removed from the mode of giving. He has retreated, withholding. What was he going to say to her, anyway? He was going to ask her something.

But saying her name. And her shouting at him. He said her name. He has never said her name to her face, not until now. Never once in seventeen years, until now. And she shouts. He can feel that name on his tongue like a betrayal. How could he have named her? To her very face.

She is shaking. What is it, fury? Silas, what do you want with this fury? This goddamn fury, this bitch. There it is. Goddamn. Bitch. Never until now has he had a single positive thought about Old Lady Bush, the pickle-tosser, the cut-knife voice, the crazy, and now his mind has an insect boring into it the thought that Stella has it coming. He is standing with her mother, denouncing the bitch, her daughter. This is where he is to say nothing. He knows it with a rapidly shrinking part of himself, the part bearing his sense. Going, going, gone. Bang of a gavel.

What?

Your mother gets down on Mitch Deeks?

So what?

Mitch Deeks. You know what they say, don't you, about Mitch?

About Mitch they say many things.

Well, but do you hear them? He won't say bitch. He'll think it, but he won't say it. Do you hear them say Mitch is your father?

She goes for him. Good thing he is tense, hair-trigger in his tension. He rolls away from her nails, and up onto his feet. She ends up in an ungainly sprawl on his tick, then recoils. She had one strike in her. Silas has risen quickly to one knee, astonished.

There they are again, the three, posed in another triangle, this one rigid, tensile, as if suspense were cast in bronze. It lasts and lasts.

Bellrock, October 31, 1912

D.B. Stegner Esq

Napanee River Improvement Company

Newburgh, Ontario

Dear Sir

I am so up side down this morning and you wont wonder at it when I tell you that my house and about everything I had in the world except my family was burnt up yesterday noon.

I had just got home from Burnt Mill. I had dinner about one o'clock. I had just finished eating when my wife noticed smoke but not in the house just outside of the door. She drew my attention to it. I went out side and looked at the chimneys. Every thing looked all right but I could not tell where the smoke came from. I then came in and went up stairs. In one of the chamber rooms it was like a furnace. Every thing on fire. I run down stairs and got the children out of the house and got my desk and papers but I couldnt carry that and two guns worth $55 so I had to leave them. Some of the children then got excited and began to scream and ran a round the house. The smoke was very thick by that time and my wife thought they ran in the house by a side door. She then got perfectly wild and ran in the house and up stairs. By the time I got her out a person could not get near the house. The neighbours had arrived by that time. It was blowing a gale and every thing went.

Mr. Stegner I never thought I had one half so many friends before. Many has come forward with clothes and other help that has not been giving me the time of day. For shure a time of trouble can heal some wounds. An ill wind does blow some good. Everybody seems so kind and good to me and my family. The greatest of all blessings is friends. I know that for shure. Friends and relations. My brother didnt come but his wife did with blankets and some of his sons clothes for Harry.

Please drop me a card next week and say how the water is.

Yours respectfully

Mitch Deeks

EVENING IS A GENTLE WORD, a lovely, gentle word. Like slumber. The evening is deep now, sunk beneath flotsam, a wreck. It looked so promising. Stella and Michael have retreated into themselves. Where is the difference now between the two who can hear and speak, and won't, and the one who can't. Now he is watching them.

Nothing can be predicted, not with certainty. Silas has inklings. They were so strong. They could not be disobeyed. Now he has these guests. One minute they are posing. He liked that. He likes it. He offered them his own pose. The three of them, posing.

They are all waiting. He doesn't know what for. He wants them waiting with him. Something of him will be lost if the danger takes them.

If he could say that, even to himself. If only he didn't need to have that said for him. It makes one lonely, having to say that about him, to say it for him. Silas, you are beyond your maker. He is searching for you. He loves you. He loves them. They do what they must. He has set them free. They go for each other, then, when he wants them to – to what? Is it his business to create harmony? He wants them loving. Is that ridiculous? Yes and no.

It's a bad evening now. It would be quiet but for the night sounds of the swamp. The two of them with functioning ears greet each sound with contempt. They will take no interest in those noises. The noises push them back, away and aloft. They are black-hearted, both of them. Silence bulges from them. Their angry auras are touching. They are ready to flinch away.

What a long way they have to go.

The burping frog isn't comic to them; it's stupid. Stupid goddamn frog.

Say that to him.

Say it to her.

Who can help hoping? O belovèd, hoping can't be helped. Within is where hope goes when assaulted, hounded, outraged. Hope is inviolable still, but deeply distant and thoroughly obscured. Dark and heavy curtains. But they shift about so. They are purple. Deeply, darkly purple, a bruise. Highlights of scarlet. Deeper, deeper, deeper. Deeper, if red at all. Hope so gone within.

But bright. Always day there. Always full sun. Inviolable and lost.

Silas watches them. Relight the lamp? Not while the two of them share that shaft of moonlight. He can see them. He needs to do something now. He reaches for his sack, pulls it toward him. He can see them both perk up. Watching him. He pulls the sack into his lap, looking first at the one, then at the other. They meet his gaze, expectant. What's he doing with the sack? He fiddles with the lip of it. They know what's inside. He doesn't know they know. He might take things out. He might spread his things out and look at them. They could look. He knows they need something else. They hate. It's not what he wanted.

Not the sack. He folds it in two and places it gently beside him. He looks from one to the other. He opens his hands on his knees, resting on his crossed legs. The open hands attract their attention. What is this, a show? He is in shadow, but they can see his movements. What is he doing, what is he going to do?

He stands, facing them. Thinks better of that, bends to one knee, then to both, and walks on his knees across to them. He picks up Stella's right hand in his left, Michael's left in his right. He holds their hands for a moment, then nods at the space between them. If they would join their own hands, there would be a circle. He feels both grips tighten, no. They know, but they won't.

Silas, she says. It's her warning tone, but Michael can't believe how glad he is to hear her voice. There was going to be no speech between them, ever again. This is not between them. It's for Silas. But Silas can't hear. There is a precedent for speaking through Silas. His joy surprises him, because silence beats hell out of savagery. She can't be predicted, she can't be trusted. He wants to talk to her. He must be crazy.

Silas sees her mouth move. That is something. He drops their opposite hands, grasps the two they refused to join, raises them high in the air. If it were a boxing match, and it nearly was a fight, does this mean they both win? He drops their hands, which touch briefly and jerk away, as if scalded. But they are relenting. They are convalescent. One of them will speak now.

Silas stands before them. He raises his left knee high. His leg then glides into the long step, his right arm windmilling around and down, and he follows through, his right leg lifting, having delivered nothing into the dark. He straightens, stands looking for a moment in the direction of his non-throw, then sits down again, cross-legged, looking at them.

Oh, says Michael.

He was throwing, she says.

A baseball. Like the man in the picture.

Ah.

Mitch comes over, she says. He visits. Never for long. I wonder if his own family likes it, his wife especially. He just drops in. He might bring something, a pint of maple syrup, maybe, a jar of jam. Once he brought a piece of bark he found in the creek. Just as an excuse. It was smoothed by the water and there was a sort of pattern on it. 'Reminds me of something,' he said, 'I'm not sure what.' I thought it looked like waves. Waves of wood. Well, bark. I guess bark is wood. It was pretty. She threw it in the stove right after he left.

Mitch might be our only company for a month. It's so quiet. You forget how to talk. I love Mitch. He's a gentle soul. I do love him dearly. He's the man in my life, the only one. My mother grumbles at him, sometimes shouts. There is something between them. But my father? No. All the father I have, but no.

I don't know why I said that. I'm sorry.

Why you said it is that other people say it.

Yes, but –

It wasn't nice, no. And then I wasn't. Look at us. Babies, or worse.

Worse, I guess. You're the first baby that scared me to death.

We're both sorry. And I'm scared too. I frighten myself. To jump that way.

I was mean. I had it coming.

No. People are mean all the time and you can't – I can't be trying to scratch their eyes out. Why you, anyway? I mean, I heard what you said when I was tiny. I heard it first from Ronnie. Ronnie, as you know, has always been the soul of tact.

Michael emits an appreciative snort.

It wasn't about Mitch. It was just 'you got no Da.' That was at Sheila Clarke's birthday party. I remember she had a light green dress on with some kind of netting over the skirt and some spangles in the netting. I thought that dress was just magnificent and I coveted it. Instead, I had Ronnie Pilk saying, 'you got no Da,' and, while he was at it, as though the two things were connected, something about my –

A gust of wind rushes through the trees above and he cocks an ear to it. Is she listening too? Is that why she stopped? But the subject is delicate. He will help. He takes a deep breath.

Your face.

He takes another deep breath, and holds it, but she says, Thank you. My birthmark. I don't think Ronnie was even being mean. I don't really think he is ever mean, intentionally, but he has no brains, and he says what he 'thinks,' and he thinks only what he's been told. So I knew, I knew it immediately without anybody having to spell it out, that people were talking. I gathered that at a very early age. It made me shy. It's bad enough to be a certain way without everybody gossiping about you.

Stella has fleas. Don't touch Stella. Poopy-face Stella. Stella is a bastard: that never seemed right to him. You call a man a bastard, a woman a bitch. But the words don't match. If you're calling somebody those things it usually means you don't like them. She called herself a bitch. Her mother did. Bastard: got out of wedlock. Wedlock sounds like prison.

So it wasn't Mitch.

I think I'd know. I can't tell you how.

I wonder how that story got started, then.

Well, the visits. But something tells me he knew my father. Maybe he'll tell me some day. She keeps him quiet. There are certain subjects she prohibits.

Verboten.

Verboten, our one German word, except for Tannenbaum, and how useful it is.

Actually, Michael has learned another German word from Bren. 'Donkey, donkey,' says Bren the linguist. Thank you, thank you. But 'donkey' doesn't belong in this exchange. Michael is puzzling over what she has said. No father. An absent father she knows nothing about. Nothing?

Nothing at all?

I have thoughts, she says. Are they memories? I can't tell. I think about him. I don't think he died. Surely she would talk about that. If she talked at all. I think he must have left, and I can't blame him. I'd leave too, if I could. I'm always thinking about leaving. I think about starting over.

With a skull?

She purses her lips, contemplating that. No, not the skull. But it is perceptive of him to bring that severed head into this. That head in that niche in the church in the village she often imagines is her true home, where she would be welcome and, of course, unmarked. A princess of East Anglia. The East Anglian Maiden.

He shouldn't have said 'skull.' It could be dangerous to say what just comes into his mind. Or maybe not. She is only thinking. That's all right. Why should he not make her think, whenever he can. She with her big brain.

Not with a skull, she says. But that particular skull, when I think of it, does not represent death. That's interesting. I don't follow a father to Sudbury, though. In my mind. That is my mother's family. I don't know where I'd go to trace his side. I have so little of him. I might be making it up.

Not your brother, though.

No, not him. Never.

No?

No. I know what you're saying. Lost brother, lost father, what's next? But I have more of my brother. I can *see* him.

Not your father? I can see my father. Right now he looks mad as hell. He had to do the cows. He'll be beating on his guitar now, I suppose.

That's his refuge?

Refuge. I suppose it is. Escape. Refuge.

I don't see my father. Sometimes I think I hear him. Or feel. It's hard to put into words what he is, if I'm not making it up. It's warm. And safe. Like something all around you. Around me. And humming, a sound of humming.

A tune?

I don't think so. Just what you might, I don't know, what you might kind of mutter under your breath, you know, when you're concentrating on something else.

A lullaby?

Half a day he has known her. Years and years, and half a day. Strangely, he now knows her better than he knows anybody. With his mind, that is, with his heart-instructed intelligence. He knows his parents with his body, his instincts. They *are* him in ways that no one else is now nor ever will be. But he could not *say* them. Even his mother never speaks her deepest thoughts to him. He is secure in her love. He knows that, but he doesn't know her. He knows Stella better. In half a day, he does. He knows things about her he would rather not know, things he would rather not have heard and seen. He doesn't understand all that he has learned. She tantalizes and frightens him. She has almost made him forget the bizarre circumstances linking them on this day.

But he doesn't know enough to be prepared for her sharp intake of breath. He is completely taken aback by her collapse into tears. Her rending sobs, her wailing. She has lost her body, lost her bones. They won't keep her upright. She falls with her head on his knee. She could have fallen anywhere. Her wailing would wake the dead. It rings out across the swamp. There is no other sound in the swamp from one end to the other. Of course the swamp has no clear end. It merges so gradually with solid ground that the edges of swamp and rock, soil gaining purchase on the rock, could never be fixed. There is no sound but wailing in the vicinity of Silas's hut. Everything nearby is stilled, listening. The floor listens, the fallen tree roots listen, the beaver dam listens, the pool is perfectly still with the moon path stretched across it, listening. All creation is listening to this primitive wail of grief. It must be. She is gone to it, emptying, years and years and years of it, emptying, spilling out of the deeps of her.

His heart is in his throat. Her head on his knee, convulsing.

This is harder by far than Silas's fit. He is crying himself now. He can't help it. The tears are flowing and he is gulping, shaking. He is ashamed. Blubbering like a baby, second time today.

A baby could tear you, this kind of baby.

She has her knees up to her chest again. He places his hand on her hair. He begins to stroke her hair, her head, absently, as though she were King, who lays his head on Michael's lap in much this way. Love flows between them so, dog and boy. King's brown eyes look up, as only a dog's eyes can, eyebrows twitching with extreme sensitivity, acute interrogative alertness.

Her face is hidden. The wailing is less strident now, but her body is still racked with convulsions. It's a kind of a fit, it must be, a primal grief possessing her and shaking every bit of her body.

He recovers first. He strokes her still. After a long spell, with her breathing heavy but more regular, she brings up a hand and rests it on his knee.

Silas, he thinks, there you sit. Watching the two of us, thinking what? Is there some part of you that picks up sounds as sharp as those she was making. Have you been hearing her? Do you cry, Silas? There must be a grief that you feel. Can you let it out? There is so much hurt that people have to carry. Michael isn't carrying much, not really. He has *no* problems. He should be able to drop his difficulties. Why can't he? He can speak and hear. He'd often rather not, but he can. He is not marked. His parents are ordinary.

Once Miss A was reading to them in French. Don't open your books, she said, just sit still and listen. These are words you can understand, she said, without understanding. He remembers the thrill of apprehension he felt, hearing that. How can anybody understand without understanding? It made him tense, alert. Was that the idea? Scare them into listening? And he didn't understand, neither what the words were saying nor who they were being said to, but his guts contracted when the voice, Miss A's voice inside somebody else's words, began to rise. Somebody in the story was shouting, shouts packed tight with tears. Somebody was angry, angry and sad. Miss A was really putting it on. She was living that story, right up to where the shouting almost turned into sobbing just before it stopped. It echoed, pulsing in the pause that followed. Nobody moved. Every single student in that classroom scarcely breathing.

And then came quiet, tender, soothing words. What *those* words were saying he still couldn't tell, but what a change. What a relief. Was it an answer? It must have been. There must have been a new speaker, an older one, calm and wise. Gentle words, comforting. Hearing them, you could easily imagine that one holding the other.

He would speak like that now if he could.

Now he is thinking about his hand stroking her hair. He is willing tenderness into it. He is highly conscious of her hand on his knee.

Silas, Silas. Why, Silas?

By his alert stillness, Michael can tell that Silas is attending to them. His friends. Why yes, they are friends, friends all three. Silas's friends all but embracing now. They are taking care. Michael's eyes well up with tears again.

Thank you, he breathes. Whatever Silas has in mind, now there is this. She is shivering against him.

Are you cold?

She shakes her head against his knee, a gesture so intimate that his heart swells. Thank you. But now he's afraid. Silas, whatever you're thinking, you are not afraid. Not like this. This can't go back to town. Cannot. He knows a word. Michael knows a word. The word will not go back to town, where everything is now exactly as it always was. Except two people are missing. Three, but one will not be counted.

When they return, the ruffled surface of life will calm. Soon it will be unpuckered. He can see all the fellows right now, lounging under the pole light at the store. He can hear the talk. Stella Bush? Bullshit. You're joking. What is he, out of his mind? The proper line, then, the way back in, is just to haw haw with the rest of them. Yes, it was a laugh, haw. No, no, it was nothing. Change the subject.

Betraying her.

Oh, Silas. I never thought I'd wish I were you, sitting there with nothing on your mind, nothing like this, not torn up, not so full of different feelings you're like to burst.

The moon on its own course has left them, but moonlight still silvers the trees, shadows everything. The middle part of Silas's body is latticed with light and shade where he lies on his bough bed, having decided that his friends, his guests and captives, are calm enough now. His head and feet in darkness. Sandwich, Michael thinks. It is ages since he and Stella were holding Silas in his convulsions on that same bed.

Venus still where she was? Stella would know. The whole night sky will be worth watching now. Might there be shooting stars? Not in April, probably not. He doesn't want to change position, not with her head still resting on his leg, though the leg is going numb. His hand still playing lazily in her hair, her breathing regular now.

The bullfrogs are in full cry. Earlier, there was the occasional blup of a frog and how different the sound was back then. Shut your trap. Leave me alone. Now the comedy is palpable. Chains of deep-threated rob-oo, rob-a-boo across the pool and out the other way behind them, out into the other pool or channel where the oarsman passed by, so near they might have reached out, parted the bushes, and looked into a startled face.

Whose face? Why, Bob Henry's. And then? Pleasant or otherwise to conjure the upshot of that coincidence?

Frogs chugging and booming up and down the creek. There is one basso right beside them. Whenever it lets go, Michael can't help chuckling softly. Guiltily. He should not be laughing. He and Stella haven't moved, haven't spoken, which is why that bass voice joins the ambient chorus. They have been silent and still now for what seems like hours.

There is no breeze. The night air is warm and damp. There'll be chill later, not yet. Once in a while a heron releases its jagged squawk, as if suddenly choked. A saw-whet owl is velvetly hoo-hooing on and off not far away, and once they were startled by raccoon shrieks. Their silence goes on. He won't speak until she does. What if he has to sleep like this, sitting up?

Three years ago, almost to the day, he and Bren were tenting at Second Depot. Michael had trouble dropping off to sleep on the hard ground in Bren's tiny pup tent. Scanlon's men had finally doused their light. The arguing and joking had died out and the night noises swelled up to replace them. Sudden splashes that might have been frogs leaping from the bank, or small fry breaking surface in the shallows. Sounds inaudible by day magnified in the night. Though a mouse scampering through dry leaves can be surprisingly loud during the day when you're still and quiet.

Before he dropped off to sleep and added his annoying snores to the nocturnal medley, Bren said that the whistling rush passing just overhead at intervals was ducks. Teal, he said, and Michael could see them, necks stretched out like arrows and wings a-blur, the very image of speed in flight. Blam, said Bren softly. The duck in Michael's mind folded its wings and dropped out of the sky. Over and over again, until he was finally asleep.

Up to his neck in water and kicking for all he was worth just to keep his head up. He had no arms. Where his arms should be were stubs, stumps, bumps. He was somehow reaching with them anyway, and at the same time hovering over himself, looking in wonder at his armless shoulders. His legs were exhausted from the effort, heavy, heavy, heavy.

How long could they keep up this pumping? His chin kept slipping under, his neck arching back to lift his head, hold his mouth in air. Clouds up there. Wispy clouds in the deep placid blue of the sky.

Then there was a tattooed man in only a loincloth, also with no arms. He was at the market in Kingston, drawing on the macadam with a chalk held between his toes. Michael still kicking, thrashing for all he was worth. He noted the long arcs of the armless man's muscular calves, his muscled thighs, drawing with one foot in front of the big tent, outlining a ballerina in graceful lines. She was a wonder as he shaded her in, one leg gracefully drawn up so the foot rested on the other leg just below the knee, head also demurely inclined down and to one side. Tutu pink and slippers pink, stockings white, hair yellow. Yellow hair pinned up in a bun. Michael's whole body undulating now, the body of a pike! He will fling himself to the bank! He cannot. But one above, on the bank, reaches down. His head is grotesque, reptilian, eyes bulging out on either side. How can he see ahead? That one must pull him out, because he is dead tired now, thrashing and tired in the bone, but help from a monster? No!

The air cracked open.

He came to, jackknifed straight up, drenched in the morning heat, heart drumming in his chest, and what, and what?

Again. The shrill whoop of a whip-poor-will perched on the apex of the tent just a foot from his face. Its shadow on the canvas.

Relieved, exhausted, he laid back down, to watch the shadow and catch his breath. Wisps of dream evaporating, burning off like fog above the creek where you'd be looking into the mist and the heron would materialize on the rock out there like a photograph forming out of the chemicals, and if you moved, say lifted a hand to scratch your ear, the grey-blue body on those long, long legs would deliberately dip, the wings unfold and beat into air, neck drawn into that crazy Z. Like those dozens of herons up the creek on the way here. Too many herons. How could you attend to them all? Far too many.

The ballerina faded last. She never moved. Of course not, a chalk figure? Her arms arced over her head in very poise and grace. She faded and faded. He almost cried out. Such piercing beauty gone for good. Why would anyone say 'for good' of such a grievous loss?

Bren slept on. The sleep of the dead in the canvas heat-trap.

He'll have a cramp if he doesn't shift his leg. He slides his left hand beneath Stella's cheek and lifts her head. He needs a change of position, just bend his leg a little. He doesn't want to disturb her, but she sits up, hugs her knees up to her chest, rests her head on her knees.

He stands up stiffly, squats several times, shakes out the leg, stretches as high as he can reach. He could warn her about the whip-poor-will. This place is too open to trap heat, though. Plenty of ventilation, and the sun won't be in their eyes, either. The hut is at right angles to the travel of the sun. They were not squinting into it during supper, and it won't be in their eyes come morning. Because they are going to be sleeping here. That is clear now.

What time of day is it? He is bone-tired, wrung out, but it must be fairly early yet.

She has sat up, stretched once, hugged her knees. She has moved. That is as good as a word, every bit as good as a sentence. He can speak.

Why don't I lay these out, he says, indicating the ticks they have been sitting on. Looks like Silas has his bed, he goes on. A bit lumpy, but there it is. His question hangs in the warm air. Fine. He can wait. He has never felt more patient. He kneels at the edge of the hut, scoops up a handful of water to dash on his face. Another scoop for his mouth, rinse and, about to spit, thinks better of it, swallows.

Want some?

Her head is still on her knees, but facing him when he looks at her.

Michael, she says.

Yes. He answers as if that were nothing, her saying his name, but it's much. His name on her lips, and that throb in her voice. He can feel the answering pulse in his forearms.

I'm so sorry.

For –

You must think I'm crazy.

No.

Well, why not? I bite your head off, try to scratch your eyes out and then bawl my own head off.

You really –

I really did.

But it's okay. Really. What if I roll these out? Hard on the back, I expect. Maybe better than what Silas has. Okay?

She nods, and rises. He spreads the ticks out side by side.

Would you like to lie down? I think I will. Try these out?

ONE SIDE OF THE SCHOOL on the hill above Petworth is starkly bright in the light of the full moon, the other is shaded. Two horsemen rein in on the shadow side. One is tall and thin, the other tall and huge, a bulky man whose horse stands seventeen hands high. He swings out of the saddle with ease and watches with amusement as the other disentangles his feet from the stirrups, lifts his leg high over the horse's neck, rather than the haunch, and slides heavily to the ground.

Okay, Doc? Walter is bending backwards, hands on his hips, stretching.

Fine. I'm fine.

Not too –

I'm fine, Lachlan. Let's get to it.

No.

What do you mean, No?

Lachlan takes his pipe out of the breast pocket of his overalls, digs in another pocket for his pouch.

One, he says, that moon, and two, no wind. We'll set down here in the shadows by the mill and wait a spell until the wind comes up. The wind'll bring us cloud and the cloud'll give us cover. Right? Three, we still got lots of time before she goes up at Fifth.

Methodical Lachlan. He'll do it his way and he'll do it right. How can a man so methodical live so like a pig? His place needs the touch of a woman in the very worst way, a substantial woman with a cast iron stomach and a tree-sized broom. Couldn't keep the wife, no wonder. Lachlan's woman, the men call her. Walter once overheard Tom Ritchie's wife call her Beulah. If she wasn't referring to the cow. If Lachlan hadn't named the cow after his lost wife. If they were even married.

Lachlan is always on the mind of every woman in the township. So it seems to Walter. Lachlan is a project. Has any woman

299

actually visited Lachlan's place in recent years? Let him once greet a respectable farm wife in combinations with his posterior hanging out the flap and see how long the encounter lasts.

Walter sees Lachlan's ex-wife—Beulah—sees her as petite, a tiny creature Lachlan could pick up like a doll, far too small to keep abreast of his messes. He sees her overwhelmed by a mountain of trash, one forearm raised in a vain attempt to ward off the toppling tip. Walter himself is neat by nature. He is methodical too, as befits a man of science, but he picks up after himself. No woman need object to him on that score. But he is no woman's project. He is womanless. Rebuffed, rejected, shut out, stalemated. Balked and baffled.

Lachlan is homespun, Dorothea said once, he never ruffles. She was all in white that day. Slender and graceful, as always, dressed all in white. Even her hat was white, though with some delicate pale pink artificial flowers on it. Serving lemon squash at the Women's Institute picnic, and there was Lachlan in his overalls, talking to her as easily as to a horse or a cow. It made Walter shiver to imagine Lachlan stroking her gently, combing her hair through his fingers like the mane of his big horse. It almost made him sick to think that, sick of himself as well, at the utter unlikelihood, the uselessness of such imaginings. She was only conversing with Lachlan, talking pleasantly, that was it. There was obviously no attraction, not on her part. Lumbering Lachlan was going to be no rival. Not for her affections.

But why, why, why does she turn sardonic when it's his turn to converse? Well, they got started off on the wrong foot. He was stiff with her when they were introduced. He can make himself sweat, remembering that. He was in love instantly and what did that make him? A pompous ass. And now, all she expects from him, at best, is the exercise of wit. In which she herself is adept. And so he can never say anything to her that matters. Which matters not a straw to her. And of late, she has been impatient, even angry. And on Monday –

Lachlan leads the horses to a patch of grass behind the mill and hobbles them both. He sits on a stump and Walter does likewise. Lachlan covers his stump completely. Best go round by Hartington, he said of the evening's route. It's longer, but safer. It was too long for the comfort of Walter's backside. His skeletal frame is no kind of a fit for a saddle and he is no rider at the best of times. He knew what to expect of the roads, though. He has seen the township map of 1808-9, with all the road allowances laid out on the standard grid. A perfectly geometrical exercise in surveying that ignored the terrain, whether rock, lake, river, or swamp. Lay the actual terrain over the survey and everything starts to twist and bunch. To make a short story long, the round-about way from Verona to Petworth is a good eight miles. You wouldn't dare take a boat through that swamp at night. Maybe Mitch Deeks would, or could, but Walter doubts it.

If the roads in this township are ever to be straightened, there will have to be a hell of a lot of blasting. The pathmaster will be making good use of the likes of Lachlan.

Lachlan might be growing out of that stump. In the light of the full moon he might be a tree. Or a troll. A huge troll, pipe aglow in the dark, placidly puffing, patient as the hills, content to wait for his moment. While his companion fusses and fiddles. Gets up and paces nervously, back and forth.

What about tomorrow? Lachlan is not thinking about the aftermath. He can't be. He blows the dam, fine, and maybe the two of them escape without being observed. But Lachlan's blasting is known in all quarters of the township. Mighty Lachlan. He can blast a face of 'spar neat into the box of your wagon, so they say. He can blow the wallet out of your back pocket and never singe a hair of your arse. The job at Fifth Lake is different. Amateurs can manage that. Just break into the powder house at the mine, help yourself to the dynamite. Or lift it from the railway crews blasting up near Parham. But a solid concrete affair like this one—you need a man who knows explosives.

He settles his sore rump on the stump again. It'll be sorer yet before he's home. What if he had meat on his bones? Would that give him, have given him, a better chance with Dorothea? Who likes a skeleton? Skeleton with formal manner.

It took over two years to win the people of Portland Township, insofar as he has, and it would have taken longer but for the rescue of Brendan Reynolds. Not even that, but the manner of it. And he doesn't know what called him to it. It bewilders him. He has never admitted that to a soul. He has imagined himself explaining it to Dorothea. That is what he wants, after all, wants it overwhelmingly. Release from his isolation. He wants to share his deepest thoughts and concerns with her. He imagines that he would be able to. All that's needed is wedlock. One flesh and one mind; for better or worse; for richer, for poorer; in sickness and in health, 'til death do us part. Under the canopy of those sacramental words, his soul to be unlocked to her, and hers to him.

A skeleton with an angel! Still, he wants to tell her. He wants her to know how he woke that time in the middle of the night, his second winter in Verona, a fierce blizzard howling outside. He remembers every detail of that night. Often, ancient mariner with one imaginary listener, he does tell her. That sort of telling is no release.

He was warm enough under the heap of blankets, maybe too warm. Whatever the reason, he woke in sweat and fear. Fear of a giant walrus, for goodness sake! In the middle of the continent! An immense walrus that stood upright and menacing on its tail flipper. Wrapping himself in a blanket, he got up from the daybed near the stove, which was cold by then, not even ticking, and tried to see out the window. It was frosted thick, top to bottom. He could hear the wind shrieking out there, feel the house shudder, ice pellets flung in waves against the pane. And for some reason he had the feeling he was elsewhere. Something—what?—shifted and he was in a different house.

Behind him in that other house, as he stood with thumb pressed on the frost to open a peephole in his own window, was a source of heat that was not a fire. Not even heat; it was sound: moaning, then screams, then moaning again. Rapid breathing. He must still be dreaming. He placed both palms on the window. No dream is ever that cold. Palm prints in the fronds of frost. Nothing to be seen out in the street, not even the buildings across the way. Lost in the whiteout. And then the other house was gone. One is one and all alone and ever more shall be so. Ever more?

Bed, he thought, shivering.

He was sitting on the edge of the bed. He had the covers drawn back, prepared to swing his legs in, when he locked up. He wanted back in that bed, badly. Something wouldn't let him. Then Mrs. Reynolds entered his mind. It was just about her time. But they would not send for him. No, they would not. Not him. Not for that.

Bed.

He couldn't.

If they had sent for him, at least there would have been a horse and cutter, a robe over his knees.

He lectured them sternly next day, gave them his doctor's lecture: any time of day or night, do you hear, any kind of weather. He didn't have to preach. Appearing when he did, half-frozen, having struggled all the way to the Snider Road on his new snowshoes—that won them, that and the life saved. Goes to show you, said Tom Ritchie, shaking his hand vigorously a few days later, a man looks like the Grim Reaper might just be, he just might be on the Good Lord's side after all.

Grim Reaper? An atheist on God's side? There was nothing whatever to embrace in what Tom said, not with the mind. But the good intentions and the warmth, the endorsement, were most welcome. He felt gathered in at that moment, accepted. He could begin to serve. That should have been it. The news spread like a grass fire in a dry summer, but it didn't take every-where. Mrs. Gagnon still crosses the road rather than pass him close by, upright Mrs. Gagnon whom he once saw in transport. Glanced into a travelling revival tent from which gutteral sounds were emanating, and there she was, rolling on the grass. She's a religion-heated fool, but his nemesis nonetheless. He is ashamed of the non-medical use of strychnine that invades his thoughts about her. Hippocrates would not approve.

Baby Bren would not have survived with the cord around his neck. Now he's a hellion like the others his age, too old to be called Little Walrus. Walter has stopped that. Nobody ever asked him why only Bren, of all his babies, was a walrus. Walrus is apparently as likely an endearment as any.

What he wants Dorothea to hear, and then consider and

perhaps explain to him, and with no reference whatever to God and His mysterious ways, is what it was that put him in that other house, in the room of labour. A dream inside a dream, well that's not so uncommon. But he *was* awake. And a house inside another house, the outer house that of a rationalist—well, it troubles him. Nothing in the medical literature touches it, nothing he has found.

That delivery did change his life, he has to admit. The sweet taste of belonging was briefly his. It made him ravenous for more. But nobody fraternizes much. He has their respect, even their trust, but he lacks the common touch. Nobody seeks him out. With Dorothea, everything would be different. His life needs – Well, he thinks bitterly, why dwell on that? Why indulge in self-torture?

If he ends up in the hoosegow, who would care? Really? Nobody important to him. He tries to imagine her visiting him there. All the way to Kingston on the K & P just to see me? More haggard even than usual, he looks up at her from his seat, the thread-bare blanket on the hard edge of the bunk. The pathetic political prisoner, his conscience clear, sequestered in his dank cell.

Pathetic is right.

Moping is pathetic. He wouldn't mope. He'd read. Never be caught without a book, says Emma Goldman. Time spent in a cell may thus be useful. Walter knows the very book for perusal in his cell, dank or not—*Prison Memoirs of an Anarchist*—though he can't get it. Mother Earth books are stopped at the border.

He slides off the stump. It's no good as a seat. Maybe it'll support his back. Lachlan smokes placidly on. The breeze is picking up, as he predicted. Walter looks into the sky. No sign yet of the promised cloud. With the whole beautiful romantic canopy of the heavens above, here sits Doctor Morse in the shadow of Petworth School with his companion of the night, not Alexander Berkman of the memoirs, but a placid, pipe-smoking galoot in overalls.

IT WASN'T IN YOUR TIME, Stella begins, and it wasn't in my time –

Those times would be about the same.

Be quiet, Mister. Mister Pook. I christen you Mister Pook. Shut your mouth and listen.

This wasn't in our time but it was long ago. There was this man, a traveller, and he was walking up the First Lake Road. He had passed the place we will call Pickle Point. He had passed the mill and crossed the bridge over the creek. He was trudging wearily down the road, late in the evening, and he was wondering wherever was he going to find a place to stay that night. So finally he came to where he could see a track running off the road to his left, just two ruts, really, with grass between them, heading off towards the creek. And he stopped and wondered about that track. He looked up ahead, debating whether to keep on, but something said to him, turn and follow that track. So he did. And a goodish way into the trees, well away from the road, he found a little cabin with an old man sitting on the stoop.

'Good evening, father,' said the traveller. 'I've been walking and walking. I walked all the way from Peters' Mills today. Did you know that Peters' Mills was the old name for Colebrook?

Now who's interrupting?

Well, whose story is it, Pook? 'All the way from Peters' Mills,' he said. 'I'm very tired,' he said, 'and I wonder would you have room for a tired traveller in your good house tonight?'

'I'm not the father of the house,' said the old man. 'You'll have to step inside and ask my father. Go right in. You'll find him sitting by the fire.'

So the traveller opened the door and stepped in and, sure enough, there was a very old man in a rocking chair, warming himself by the fire. 'Good evening, father,' said the traveller, 'I wonder could you put me up for the night?' The very old man looked up from the fire and said, 'I'm not the father of the house. You'll have to ask my father. That is he over there, lying on the daybed.' He gestured toward a corner of the cabin. The traveller moved over to the daybed where a very, very old man was lying. He was reading a heavy old book and he could hardly gather the strength to turn the pages. 'Good evening, father,' said the traveller, 'would you be so good as to provide me with a bed for tonight?' The very, very old man raised his eyes from his book and in a quavering voice said, 'I'm not the father of the house. You'll have to ask my father. Go through that door into the other room. You'll find him in there, smoking his pipe.'

The light was very dim in the next room, but the traveller finally picked out a tiny, wizened figure in a large chair. Wreathes of smoke were rising above him. 'Good evening, father,' he said. 'I'm weary with walking all day long, and I would be most grateful if you could offer me a bed for the night.' The ancient man removed the pipe from his mouth and spoke, so softly that the traveller had to lean close. 'I'm not the father of the house,' was what he heard. 'You'll have to ask my father. He is lying right there in his cradle.' He pointed with the stem of his pipe. The traveller stepped over to the cradle. Inside was a tiny figure with a beard curled all around and over him like a blanket. So still he was, and so silent, that the traveller wondered if there was any life in him at all. But 'Good evening, father,' he said, 'I badly need a bed for the night and would be much obliged if you could spare me one.' He stood over the cradle for a long time. Finally, he heard a breath exhaled and in it he could just make out: 'I'm not the father –' Another breath: 'Ask my father –' A third: 'Hanging in the horn on the –' The voice faded out to nothing.

Looking about him, the traveller spied a hunting horn hanging on the wall. He approached it and peered in. Something white as ash and tiny as could be was in the horn. A human face, wrinkled beyond belief. Astonished, the traveller turned to regard the bundle in the cradle, then the ancient man, still smoking, in the chair. Through the door he could see the very old man turn a page of his dusty book. Outside, the sound of chopping. The first old man cutting wood to warm his father at the fire. He turned back to the horn and cried out: 'GOOD EVENING, FATHER. COULD YOU BY ANY CHANCE PUT ME UP FOR THE NIGHT?'

The voice that answered was sharp as a cricket's. 'Yes, my child,' it said.

At that, a table appeared, laden with delicacies and fine wines. The traveller sat down and tucked in. When he was satisfied, in came a bed all covered with furs. He laid himself down and sank deeply into it. As he curled up to sleep, he thought to himself: it certainly is a wonderful thing to find the true father of the house.

It takes a few beats before Michael realizes she is done. The swamp sounds have taken over from her voice. Talking of half a story –

Hmm, he says. Hmm. That's, that's – different. Where did you learn that?

It was in a book Miss A lent me.

Does she often lend you books with strange stories in them?

All kinds of books. I have to give *King Lear* back soon, but I don't want to. It was a prize book. On the fly-leaf it says Dorothea Asselstine, First Class Honours in English Language and Literature, 1895. She'd lend you books too, if you asked her.

Coral Island and those? I doubt it. She doesn't like me.

Now, that's wrong. She does like you.

Phooey.

She does. And even if she didn't, she approves of reading. You know that.

Anyway, that's a very strange story.

Isn't it? That's why I remember it, I think. All those old men, older and older.

The very oldest one shrivelled up like a prune.

A transparent prune.

But he's the one.

Yes.

Father of the house. Thought he wasn't going to show up. Some kind of a trick being played, I thought. Very strange.

Did you like it?

I don't know. I was expecting something more to happen. How many generations of old men in that house?

She counts on her fingers. One, two – six.

Six generations of men, and nary a woman.

The story comes from Norway, if I remember right.

Not from here?

No. I just put in First Lake Road.

And Peters' Mills and Pickle Point. Thanks for that.

Sweet Pickle Point.

They have women in Norway, right?

I believe they have women everywhere.

Not in that story.

No.

And you like it.

Yes. I do. I've been thinking: so many fathers – That's not why I like the story. I like it because it's unusual. It doesn't have a moral and it doesn't end with 'happily ever after.' But so many fathers, and me without – I wonder. Well, it's kind of nice to be left hanging for a change. Don't you think?

Take some getting used to, that sort of story. But thanks for telling it. You did a very good job.

Thank you.

You're welcome.

You'd need patience, he thinks, to keep asking old man after old man. Most people would be on the road again after just a couple of them. He certainly would. Getting darker out and these old codgers playing some kind of a joke. Whereas the traveller— you don't learn much about him. He's a tired traveller, that's all. Needs a bed. Coming from Colebrook, Peters' Mills, but he probably doesn't live there. No. What makes him so persistent? He keeps asking long after any normal fellow would have given it up. And then! Not only the bed, but a feast. Good thing he kept on. Strange, strange story.

That table, she thinks, that table with all those foodstuffs, suddenly just there. And wines. How much wine would a man need? Out here it would be milk. She should have said milk. She should have put bread and cheese on that table. For the Pook. Strange to have thought of calling him that. And, drat! There should have been pie for dessert. She knows exactly what kind.

Now you.

Me!

Don't act surprised, Mister. I told you a story. My very first. Now it's your turn. Doesn't have to be a story. A recitation, a song. You don't happen to have your bones? No, I didn't think so. Fared forth into the world without his bones.

It must be close to bedtime. The one thing she will not be asking for just now is a lullaby, so, perversely, he is thinking lullaby. Not that he can bring anything back, not enough to sing. He racks his brain. 'Incy wincy spider.' His mother always tickled up his leg with that one. Up Stella's leg? Just to illustrate the rhyme? Probably not.

How about 'Taffy was a Welshman, Taffy was a thief. Taffy came to my house and stole a piece of –

Beef?

I'm no good at this.

It doesn't matter. I just thought.

I need practice. I haven't been told stories for years. My mother used to. There's one about a hen – Wait. I know. There is something I know quite a lot about, and the subject is close to your own heart. It's not a story and it's not a song, but it's –

It's baseball. Isn't it?

God damn it!

A peal of laughter from her. Sorry, she says. I should have let that come from you. Not that I want to. Hear about baseball. But perhaps you were thinking how to put me to sleep?

But how did you know what was coming? Did I let you know somehow, did I tip my hand? You know what you're like? You're like one of those dogs – now hang on. I know what you're thinking, but I'm thinking about Max, Bren's little dog Max.

Have you ever seen Max dive?

Dive? Swan dive? Jackknife?

Tom Ritchie's diving boar.

Excuse me?

Something I was reminded of. But it's not a story.

Sounds like it should be.

If the pig really did dive. But it doesn't even swim. It wades.

He pauses. How do you make a story, anyway? *Is* that pig a story? What if he didn't throw it away, as he did just now? What if he built it up. A thousand pounds springing gaily into the air over the creek, front trotters clasped together in the ever-so-graceful Hog Dive. Hmm.

Anyway, he continues, whenever Bren dives off the dam, Max dives. At exactly the same second. Exactly. You can't fool Max. Bren might pretend to be just dawdling, you know, dum de dum de dum, not an idea in his head –

Not difficult for Bren.

Ha. But there must be something in there, and Max must know it, because Bren dives and, boom, Max dives with him, *right* with him. Every single time.

So I'm like Max.

Max is like you. He reads Bren's mind. You read mine.

No I don't. Don't be silly.

Well, how do you know what's coming, what I'm going to say. It's –

Uncanny.

God damn it!

Sorry.

No. I was joking. That time.

See.

See what?

I think you're taking evasive action. Because you trapped me.

I trapped *you*?

You gave me that word, 'uncanny.' It was lying there on the tip of your tongue and I scooped it up and you pounced on me.

That's good.

Good, eh? He's not sure he's following. Well, he doesn't know any stories.

I don't want to be –

You're not.

Boring.

He lets that sink in, down and in. It's warming. He has never heard that, never expected to hear it, certainly not from her. Not boring. Is that as good as being interesting? To ask would be fishing for a compliment. But no need to ask. She's in his head, she'll answer.

She's quick. Lightning quick, they say. 'They' apply that one fact about lightning to other things. Lightning *is* quick. It comes and goes in the sky piled high with those angry dark blue clouds. Cumulonimbus. Today was cirrus. No lightning in cirrus. Stella is like both kinds of cloud. The big blue ones can be terrifying. She can be terrifying. And she can be placid. Yes, she's quick. Not a mind reader, but fast. Strikes quick, like a snake.

If she really were in his head, she would now see a poem appearing there. She would see lines beginning to form. 'The outlook wasn't brilliant for the Mudville nine that day.' He does know one poem from beginning to end. The wrong kind.

There was ease in Casey's manner
                         as he stepped into his place;
There was pride in Casey's bearing

and a smile lit Casey's face.
And when, responding to the cheers,
he lightly doffed his hat,
No stranger in the crowd could doubt
'twas Casey at the bat.
Oh yes, the whole thing, the whole last inning of an inglorious day at the plate. But baseball *is* boring. To her. In deference to her, he will not recite 'Casey at the Bat' this evening. If he knew her better, he'd know that he could. Normally, she would rejoice to hear anything stanzaic and rhyming. But if he knew her even better yet, and she had confided how she flouted Miss A's assignment, he might not risk any echo of her own recent poetic effusion, expulsion from school, the grievous loss of Miss A. The balances rise and fall, rise and fall, in a mind so capacious and volatile. Mostly there is rising at this moment of this night in this strangest of all places to be sojourning.

Will she confess about the poem? Sharing such a diminishing, shameful thing? Time will tell.

No 'Casey at the Bat,' and therefore no annotation such as only an aficionado of Frontenac County baseball could supply, the story that the inspiration for Casey was a Casey, nicknamed Jumbo, who played third base for the Syracuse Stars and summered in Newburgh. Michael could hardly recite the poem without mentioning that. Boring. Best avoid the whole works.

And there is another delicate point. He first heard the poem when he was in Grade Two, at a concert at the school. Bill Madden recited it, that and 'The Shooting of Dan McGrew,' to the usual thunderous applause. Applause can also be like a storm. The recitations came before the scheduled performance of 'O Tannenbaum' in German and English, by Grade Twos cleverly

314

arranged on stage behind a green paper Christmas tree, three kneeling, two standing, and one, Stella, standing on a chair. They were looking out at the audience through round ornament holes cut in the tree. Stella was to have a solo. Was it nerves about that, butterflies churning up her stomach, or was it the larger shyness? Whatever the cause, before the performance even began, she puked on the ornament directly below her and the whole tree dismantled itself with cries of disgust. He hasn't heard her sing since then. Nice voice, as far as he can remember.

Bellrock, November 3, 1912

D.B. Stegner Esq

Napanee River Improvement Company

Newburgh, Ontario

Dear Sir,

I can never forget your kindness about my house. And family and friends here has all pitched in as well and lumber from Scanlon. My wife and children are staying with my sister at Parham, we had a bee to clear off the mess a sad business I asshure you and then the new house went up in a couple days, the frame of it. We will not be out in the cold this winter Mr. Stegner as I thought we might if we didnt pull up stakes and head south.

We just about lost Donald Fleming building the house. He should of left the roof to them with better balance and there is plenty in this territory experienced barn raisers but there he was on the peak of the house before the rafters was covered and he lost his footing and would have been head first on a rock but My brother Des took a dive for him and sent him off into the grass. Just winded the both of them but Donald would have had his head broke and his brains out but for my brother. Mr. Stegner it made me proud to see my brother do that.

You know we have not been speaking this summer. I didn't expect
him at the bee, him and his son but they both come and it choked me
up I don't care if I say it. And Des made Donald climb back up to the
peak of that house right away and Donald says how grateful he did or
else he would never have climbed so mutch as a ladder ever again.

Found the Third Lake dam totally burnt up. Some person set the
dam on fire Sunday as Nick Boyd saw the fire from his place. I think
Joe Crowley is the man that burnt the dam as he has made threats
repeatedly. It is really too bad. The dam was in splendid shape.

I hear that some person has burnt Rathbun's camp at Davey's hole
it is an epademic.

Please let Crowley go to thunder or to the law whitchever he likes.
There is six inches of water all over the land Crowley claims damages
for and the bed of the river perfectly dry at Crowley's bridge what do
you think of that. I took three men and showed them Crowley's land
with the water still on it. We found that wonderful well frozen over
and the ice had not been broken for three days so you see they don't
use the water out of it. We traced a gully from Crowley's field to the
lake. Found a natural dam halfway from field to lake and a big fall all
the way from there. The three men will make oath that to the best of
their belief Third Lake does not damage Crowley one cents worth.
But now it seems he has taken matters into his own hands ondly we

don't have the proof and there is plenty of men around those lakes who would think nothing of burning a dam or a man rather if they thought they would not get catched at it.

Yours respectfully

Mitch Deeks

NOT BORING IS GOOD. But he is not performing, either, not helping to pass the time. There'll be no joy in Bellrock, if Michael Deeks strikes out.

Something is coming to him, though. From his father. From the lullaby so painful to contemplate. From the circle of the sun and arms around. From the word 'love' that cannot, repeat, *cannot*, be carried back to Bellrock. From the negro his father heard singing with his guitar on the platform at Verona when the K & P got stopped there, held up until the track ahead could be cleared. The chance encounter between his guitar-playing father and this guitar-playing negro, the song that his father brought home.

I could sing you something, he says.

Good. I'm sure there are no songs about baseball.

Oh you are, are you? How about this: 'Take me out to the ball game.' I'm not fool enough to sing any more than that, but I'm afraid there is a whole song about really loving the whole idea of going to a game of baseball. It's a waltz.

A baseball waltz, now. Will wonders never cease!

A waltz of baseball. You're tempted? No? Well, it's not what I had in mind. What I had in mind was, are you ready?

Ready.

Put your arms around me like a circle round the sun
I want to love you, baby, like my easy rider done
You don't believe I love you, look at the fool I've been
Believe I'm sinkin, look at the hole I'm in.
Stealin, stealin, pretty mama don't you tell on me
I'm stealin back to my same old used-to-be.

There you are.

Is that all?

No, there's another verse.

Well?

Oh, that's enough.

Thirty seconds worth, and the night yawning before us. Sing some more. I like it.

Well –

> That woman I love, she's bout my height, bout my size
> My special rider comes to see me sometimes
> You don't believe I love you –

And so on. It goes on like that, back to what you've already heard.

So you're telling me I've now heard all the words.

Uh huh.

Is that the point of a song, do you think, just to communicate all the words? But you're embarrassed. You have no stories to tell—though I'm still curious about Tom Ritchie's boar—and you are too seldom asked to serenade members of the so-called fair sex. There are so few troubadours hereabouts, so little serenading along Depot Creek.

What about Malcolm's tom?

Thank you. Romance is not dead along these vernal banks. It persists in feline form. Where has Silas's cat got to, by the way?

Swamp romance?

Swamp mouse? I think we've heard the sounds of slaughter already this evening.

Listen to her talk! That's what he'd rather do than sing, but he's easy enough now to sing the song through, both verses and the chorus.

It's not the same without the guitar, his father's guitar, that is. His father has been working out the guitar part, a new style. He was not picking it up overnight, having heard Delta blues for the first time in exotic circumstances. The Delta via Chicago now returning from Ottawa via Pembroke.

'Blues my life,' the negro said to Des Deeks, the only listener who stood rooted on the platform the whole time he was there. 'Your life too?' Des didn't connect the colour with the music. Kinds of blue, he thought, shades of it. A blue life? He nodded, at a venture, and the negro nodded back. He could play and talk at the same time. He was caressing the strings. 'Blues my life.' Drop the verb, make it hard for a Canadian farmer to pick up your sense. But Des was getting the music, taking it in. He would need it and use it all his life, use it and change it.

The music mutates like language. Take a language from there to here, give it time, pretty soon you need a dictionary to fix that language moment, spread it out for inspection. As if it could ever be kept from growing.

So tonight Michael Deeks offers Stella Bush a rumour of blues, blues at third hand, blues with growing pains that, in this case, transforms a jug band tune. He knows the song from his father's playing, over and over, with and without the words. Working out with his thumb and fingers, rather than the flat pick, the syncopation between low and high notes.

'Never heard that before,' he said at the dinner table, unusually animated. This negro had got down off the train with his guitar. He was a passenger. He had a ticket. That was already strange. There are negroes in Harrowsmith. They work for the Gordons and live above their big carriage house. Michael has heard about them, never seen them. If he had gone west, he'd have seen negroes on the train. They work on the train, according to Elmer Slade, who did go out, but he called them niggers. Michael knows it's negroes. Maybe you could say nigger respectfully if you didn't spit the word like Elmer does.

Well, that negro got off the train, his Dad said, got off and sat down on the bench in front of the station and just started in. What was it like, hearing that kind of music? Michael would have liked to be there, just to hear what it was that enthralled his father. Though it was annoying too, his going on and on about it. Boring. Is a certain amount of any subject, no matter how interesting in itself, quite sufficient? Probably. Depends how much of a welcome the listener extends. Michael is ready now to listen to almost anything Stella might say. And he has a perverse itch to try making baseball interesting to her. He'd like to find a way. Just to leave blank such a huge interest in his life, that can't be right. Could Silas play? He can run. Runs like the wind. He wants to pitch, it looks like.

What about the two of them, Silas and Michael, in a game of catch? Leave Stella alone, maybe, when it comes to baseball. Teach Silas the game. Or Silas could be Exhibit A. This man redeemed. Lost in darkness, teetering on the verge of the bottomless pit, friends and neighbours, then found, r*edeemed*, and by who-um? Not by *who-um*, ladies and gents. Ask not by *who-um*. Ask by *what*. By *what*, you ask? Why, what else but the bestest game what am, my Honey Lamb. Now you know what I am about to name, good Christians. Let us all together name it.

MICHAEL IS IN REAL DANGER of drifting right now, baseball being many things for him, including a physical mystery that he often mulls over. When the time comes to speak sensibly, meditatively, of some of his physical feats, speed and timing will be two essential words. Speed, because who officially won the race that Silas disrupted? That's right, Michael Deeks was Runner A. What if Michael and Silas were to race head-to-head? Silas would win, but Michael would be in it.

Timing? What about that day in centre field, one of the few times he played there, shifted there from left, just for the day. Coach waved him in to shallow centre for a supposedly weak batter who then, unexpectedly, caught every bit of a fast ball. Out it flew towards Michael, high and long. Had there been an outfield fence, it would have been pointless to go after a ball that deep. Just ruefully watch it go, nothing to be done. But Michael was not thinking fences. He wasn't thinking at all. At the crack of the bat, he turned and ran for all he was worth. He ran and ran, like a demon. When he turned, still running, and looked over his shoulder, there was the ball, descending, still well above him. He was not going to make it. He leapt. He soared, good god, what a sensation, his arm fully extended, the ball dropping neat into his glove. Robbing a so-called light hitter of a certain homer.

Speed, timing, and some kind of instant, instinctual, positional calculation. Ball and glove meet at precisely the same point at exactly the same moment. No margin for error. There is no error. The impossible catch is made. What was the mind doing all this while? Switched off. The body taking over.

He won't be telling that now. The best he could do now, even to a listener knowledgeable and interested, would be recount the event. Even a listener more engaged than Stella might think he was merely boasting. Stella would be rolling her eyes. Merciful heavens, can't you spare me? No, first learn how to step outside the act and ponder the mystery of it. Then, thinking slant, find the words.

It's not just his own performance Michael would be brooding on if he allowed himself this drift. The game is in his blood. Even his dad played, not as much or as long as his uncles, but Michael remembers him efficiently covering shortstop before the dairy wore him down. The Verona team was almost two-thirds Deeks at one time, if you count the brothers-in-law. Michael comes by his talent honestly. Know me, he might say to Stella, know my forebears, baseball players all.

His dad was waiting for him after the game of his highway robbery in centre field, fell in beside him on the long walk home. Eventually he cleared his throat and said, 'Good catch.' Two words from his father worth volumes from anybody else.

HIS DAD SAID THERE WAS a poet got off that train too. Who discovers such things? A negro and a poet on the same train! In Verona! The poet was a curiosity, easy to dismiss. Supposed to be a *Canadian* poet. Unlikely. Maybe he was English. Or American. An American poet on a tour. A tourist poet. Ugly enough to be a poet, his Dad said. Now why say a thing like that? Michael didn't like it.

His father didn't like the smartly-dressed young man wearing spats and impatiently consulting a watch on a chain hauled out of his vest. He didn't like the fellow dropping a remark about coons before re-boarding the train. Michael could see his father standing rapt in front of this negro, listening for all he was worth, full of admiration, and smiling with the others when the negro answered the young man smartly with the guitar. Never missed a beat, his father said, but made a kind of nyah, nyah by bending the strings way up the neck. Called that young whippersnapper an ass, and never spoke a word. The negro was better dressed too.

There was his father in the living room, struggling with that song, a far cry from 'Strawberry Roan,' Michael's favourite, and all the other western songs his father knows. Or the jigs and reels he can pick out. 'Smash the Windows,' 'Mussels in the Corner.' In this new music there is wanting, both in the words and the tone of the guitar and the voice, judging by what his father was starting to get, with the lower strings talking to the higher ones.

There he was, Mister Early-to-bed-and-early-to-rise, a dairy farmer no less, bending over the guitar long past bedtime. Something very annoying and slightly embarrassing in that solitary concentration, his father with red-burnt neck and gnarled brown hands poking out of his work shirt, hunched late over the strings for the third night in a row. His mother tried to jolly him away from the guitar at first. Des, she ventured from the bedroom, it's ten of the clock. Time all decent folks was abed, and rogues a-joggin. Finally, she lost her patience. Des, for goodness sake, she shrilled, put that thing down and come to bed! Nobody else can sleep!

Circle round the sun, Stella says. I like that. Circle round the sun. What's an easy rider?

He turns to face her. She is on her side, facing him.

Easy rider, special rider. I've been wondering that myself. He wants to love this one woman, the one he's talking to, like he loved another one. 'I want to love you, baby' –

I don't suppose the baby is an infant.

Doesn't sound like it, no.

Baby, he calls her. But she's a woman.

That's right. I'd say.

Not a baby.

No. And the man is having trouble. She won't believe he loves her. He's digging himself into a hole.

And stealing. What's he stealing?

He's stealing back –

Oh, yes. Of course. Stealing back—that's nice, stealing for sneaking—back to his same old used-to-be. His old sweetheart?

Used-to-be. I guess so.

So she's the one he wants to love? Or does he want to love the new one like he loved her? And what way is that?

Or love the new one like the old one loved him.

They give the question some thought.

It's confusing, she says finally.

Yes. I like it, though.

Oh yes, I'm not saying that. Circle round the sun. I like it very much. It was a real serenade. I am very much in your debt, sir. She pats his hand, hers lingering, and eases on to her back.

He stays on his side. He keeps on looking at her because she seems content to lie looking up, and with her mark-side towards him. He was first to lie down, so maybe there was no choice, and it's dark as well. He can't actually see the mark with her face in shadow. But he can see her profile clearly enough, how lovely her features are.

He grasps her hand, shifts to his back. He will not make her uncomfortable with looking. He has been vouchsafed his vision.

He can hold it as he holds her hand, the look of her shapely nose and full lips.

Lizzie Murphy has full lips like that. Pouty lips. Those lips and eyes. Her lips were apart that time she was looking down at his hand on her breast. Through the glass.

There it is, for god sakes, the familiar awakening. Not now. Stella Bush is not that kind. She is not any kind that he knows, but not like that. Surely not. What kind is Lizzie, for that matter? A mink, according to the fellows. Goes like a mink. No, not Stella.

There are other things he wants right now. Right now it's not his body that wants. Or it wants Lizzie Murphy. Mind of its own, Bren likes to say. Never mind all that. There is thinking to do that Stella's hand in his will allow.

It is astonishing.

Lying here, side by side with a former stranger, and Silas – a chaperone? Holding hands with this – She is a stranger still, but he has been intimate with her. Astonishing. This feeling he has is excitement. He feels himself expanding. Not his cock, but his, what, his heart? his soul? This enlargement, this engorgement of heart or soul—it has to do with laughter. Not the thing itself. He is not going to open his mouth and guffaw. Not like that other time, pickle time, when he'd have given anything to hold it in. Even thinking of it now makes his face flush, though he's glad at least that one other person now knows what the fuss was all about, the pickles at Pickle Point. He is not going to fling across the pool any shout of exultation like Silas expelled the first time he swam. No, and nothing to match Stella's wailing earlier. Not laughter itself, but the potential of it. Pent laughter, the sign and signal of joy.

He knows, lying as he is inside this huge contentment, unalloyed for the delicate, threatened, inviolable moment, that he can do – anything. He knows or will know all the forces and impulses in the world, all the elements, the people and places and the animals and rocks and trees, the very spiders and snakes and chickadees and especially the rose-breasted grosbeak, all the music and stories and dancing, and the liquid diamond water of the creek—everything attached to him by invisible lines of force. He could reel it all in. He won't, but he could. If he did, he would *be* Everything. Every single thing. At once. He could do anything and be anything.

Bellrock November 30, 1912

D.B. Stegner Esq
Napanee River Improvement Company
Newburgh, Ontario

Dear Sir

I let off more water as directed but the shanty men arrived in
Bellrock last night. They are going to blast out a lot of rock where
the old saw mill stood above the village whitch will interfear with
my work as we will have to shut off most of the water at Burnt Mill
for a week. Rooke will not let them build a dam hence the blasting.
Yes Mr Stegner I am going west with my family to Oregon on the
picific coste. I have thought the mater over carefuly and have made up
my mind to go. What is the use of me staying here. This part of the
country is played out. If a person buys a piece of land and puts five
years hard work on it and good Buildings they cant sell it for what
the buildings cost. I can give the names of twenty two young men of
this neighborhood most of them good hard working boys. Why did
they leave there native land Parents and friends? For pleashure? 'No.'
Because they could not make a living here and lay up a little for a time
of trouble and old age. This is not a good farming country. It is not
a mining country. The timber will soon be gone forever. The ondly

regret I have in going is in leaving my old parents and my good kind friends. But I have come to the conclusion that in duty to my self and family I should go. I have got a good friend and a man I can depend on who is a guide in the timber country of Oregon and I can depend on what he says and he advises me by all means to come. He owns a lot of timber land and will give me a job with him as a guide to private locaters and prospectors and I can buy or locate some land of my own and have all the pine timber on it as the country is not cursed by a timber limit-law whitch gives all the timbers to land sharks and the rocks to the poor man.

Of course I would not think of going without seeing you and will come and see you some time next month. I don't think my brother would suit the company to look after there work.

Plese have Mr. O'Donohue send up the balance of my wages for the season.

Respectfully

Mitch Deeks

P.S. Did you get the letter I sent re Mr. O'Donohue?

MD

I am not turned reformer. I am a good Tory yet and when war comes I can attack the yankeys in the rear if I go to the coste.

THREE

DARK MATRIX

BALLAD

(Bad Bob)

BOB PLOUGHED INTO THE BANK twice today, rowing his zigzag course, better than that first time, first and last time in a boat until today. No horse and no train neither, O'Donohue said. False whiskers won't fool nobody during the day, he said. Never know who you'll run into, can't be too careful. No, it's boat or nothing, he said. Deeks will be at Burnt Mill today. I seen to that. Keep an eye skinned for Scanlon's bunch. Not likely to be that far down with most of the drive still in the upper lakes. But watch out. Watch out how? Headed backwards all day. Looking back the way you come, making all that racket.

Nobody in that fucking swamp anyway.

First boat he was on was a ship. He was hanging over the rail and puking. Then he let go and tried to straighten up but the ship lurched and he hit a wet patch on the deck and went down hard. He cracked his head. There he lay, rolling with the ship. The bleeding sailors were still laughing when he came to. He could have rolled right into the fucking ocean, for all they cared.

Off of that ship and onto that train and right into hell. Cobourg. Somebody going to pay for Bob Henry having to walk from Colebrook to Petworth and row all the way from Petworth to Bellrock.

Mitchy.

Bob has got dreams mixed in with the facts. He could not be

convinced of that, and anyway who's going to tell him? Who is going to say, Now Bob, that crossing was perfectly safe and you know it. That crossing on that ship was heavily supervised. You didn't like it, Bob. You especially didn't like sleeping down below. It stunk down there. There was always the smell of vomit, some of it yours, Bob, but you never vomited over the rail. You were never allowed near the rail in heavy seas. You dreamed it, Bob. You must have. You're a weasel, Bob. Look me in the eye, now, and tell the truth. That crossing was safe! Dr. Barnardo wouldn't have it any other way. You know that. And as for Cobourg, why didn't you tell the inspector, Bob? How could we change your placement, how could we have saved you? Because we would have saved you, Bob, we would so. We would have come and saved you, but we didn't know. And why didn't we know, Bob? Because you didn't tell us, that's why. You little weasel, Bob. You've got nothing on us. Admit it.

Who's going to say all that to Bob now? And what good would it do anyway? One thing for sure, nobody's going to say I'm sorry. Wouldn't that be a thing worth saying? Bob, look at me now. Just stop that and look here a moment. Bob, I'm sorry. We're sorry. It *would* be worth saying. Bob is a father. He doesn't know. Would it even be sensible to let him find out?

You never know. What's best? You just never know.

Bad Bob under a big tree, his back to the trunk, hidden by a bend in the creek from the first houses of Bellrock. He knows the kind of tree, not the name of it, not for sure. A maple or a beech. Not a birch. Birch has the white bark. There's a bunch of them over there, across the river in that field. Hogan's field. He can see some of their sheep from here. One of those birches is bending from the top. How long before it snaps? Sapsuckers love those birch trees. If he crossed the river and went up close, Bob would see pecker holes evenly spaced up and down and around the bark.

His back to a maple or a beech just off the river, the boat pulled up. Goddamn boat. He should of brought gloves. BS should of give him gloves along with the whiskers. And the gasoline. Scared the hell out of BS last night, where he was sitting under the single bulb with that green eye-shade over his eyes. Little round glasses on his nose. Pipsqueak. Never know how much trouble he was. Never expect an accountant to be so much trouble. Time to visit Mitch, he said. Time Mitch don't have any place to live. Again.

Listen, he said. Things are getting worse. You know Stegner listens to Deeks. Fool enough to pass those letters on to me. Those are Company letters, Company letters come this-a-way. With excuses, of course. Deeks is a good man, he says, Deeks is doing the best he can. Deeks can't be right all the time. Well, no, he can't, and no, he isn't. Most of the time he's wrong. *Respectfully* Mitch. But Stegner doesn't hear. Bernard, Bernard, he says, it's not just us. It's not just you and I and the others down here. I'd like more water too. The foundry is down twenty per cent this year, and last year fifteen. I know what you mean, he says, I do. Knows what I mean! My orders backed up and not enough water to turn my wheels because Deeks is holding her back upcountry!

A silence. Bob was not going to speak. Not going to prompt. He had the upper hand. He doesn't often have the upper, Bob doesn't. No, Bob is a lower hand man. He was lower hand as infant, child and youth. Selling matches on the streets of London and sleeping nights in an alley when Dr. Bernardo's man

334

stumbled on him. Bob never wanted to leave Stepney Causeway. He liked it there in the dormitory with the other boys. He didn't have to work for his meals. They could play games there. Over a year at Stepney Causeway, and then on to the goddamn train to that goddamn ship.

Lizzie Murphy's knee rising out of the tall grass in the meadow between Ball's and Goodine's. A naked knee. His pecker stirs, remembering. If he had any control over his thoughts, any control whatever, he would shut Raymond Bowe right out. The last thing he ever wants to think about when he has the upper hand is sick Raymond Bowe. And why is fucking Raymond so often right there, distracting, eating at Bob's brain, just when he's least wanted. Talking to BS last night, there he was.

We've got to do something about Mitch.

What?

Mitch Deeks

Oh. Yeah?

Mitch is bad for us. We've got to do something.

Go on.

Bob is taking his rest, rubbing up his palms. Missus BS packed a lunch, for god sakes! Bad Bob and a packed lunch, that don't fit. What's her name? Ethel? Myrtle? She brought the lunch to him this morning as he was brushing the straw off his clothes and fixing to look in on BS's team. He could smell them all night. All night long the good strong smell of horse flesh, and the memory of beautiful Belle, so why on earth dream of big fishes? Myrtle or Ethel, or whatever her name is, she must know something. BS himself never showed. Take the boat above Petworth, he said last night, said where to find it, where to leave it. So she must know something. She looked him over pretty good this morning, but that's not it. He'll remember. The Missus knows something. Might come in handy to know that some day. Surprises him about BS, that's all. Not very close to the chest, bringing the Missus into it.

But a lunch, wrapped up neat in the newspaper. Bad Bob is not touching that lunch. What he wanted was not lunch but a pair of good gloves. Palms and fingers blistered raw before he even got through the swamp.

Might as well throw that lunch away right now.

Bob rises, steps into the boat, picks up the lunch by the string wrapped around it. Wrapped in the newspaper, neatly tied with string and a neat bow, for god sakes. Fire the damn thing into the river. Bob's left arm reaches back across his body. Sail that lunch away. He pauses with the package held close. Could you skip a lunch? Could you hook a big fish with a lunch for bait?

There wouldn't be any fishes here like the fishes in his dream. They were so big, and there were so many that you heard them coming before you saw them. The whole creek was stirred up with them. They were headed upstream where First Depot runs into the creek, where it narrows. Those fishes made so much noise because they were swimming half out of the water. No fishes swim out of the water, so what the hell?

Bob lowers the lunch package to his side.

They all rushed to that place where the creek starts, but they didn't exactly go into it. They just disappeared. All that noisy rush to get across the lake, and there must have been hundreds of big fishes, because the lake was packed with them. You'd think they'd get in one another's way, but no.

What about tossing bits of lunch into the creek? Bob is thinking fishes. There'll be some fishes in the creek. Pike this time of year, for sure. He amused himself most of an afternoon one day, watching until Spotton left his house by McCumber's Bridge, catching frogs, tossing them into the pool where a big bass would rise up, whoosh, gobble them down. You could feed up a bass to be huge that way. Would a bass jump for a bit of lunch? Depends. Let's see.

Bob sits down against the tree, pulls the string off the package, unfolds the wrapping. Puts the newspaper aside. Mutt and Jeff. Maybe look at that later. Damn, he thinks, it's beef. Fish don't like beef. Not with horse radish. Not on pieces of bread so thick. He should fire bits of that lunch into the water anyway, just to see. Or the whole thing. To hell with it. But Bob, being no fish, not even a Pisces, Bob likes a bit of roast beef, with horse radish or without. He shouldn't have opened the damn thing. Now his mouth is watering. His mouth is letting him down.

Well.

Where else is he going to get a bite to eat without stealing it? Bob is changing now. He *is* Bad Bob. He has to be. Bob is Mister Night, even in the broad daylight. And what makes daylight broad? Some days it seems like you can't understand anything.

Bob knows Hunger. He met it first sleeping in the alley in Cheapside. It came up to him. It slid up to him in the middle of the night and stood there. You could see right through it. There was nothing to Hunger, nothing at all. And yet oh, how heavy Hunger was when it came aboard him, so he couldn't and couldn't and couldn't get up. And then he did get up. He woke himself up and then he could rise and shake himself like a dog, and lie down again. And either he never had woken up in the first place or the Hunger was waiting just out of sight, because there it came again and pinned him. The Hunger used to come in the night at Stepney, too, even though he was fed there. It never showed at Cobourg and he barely ever had enough to eat at the Bowe place. What kind of sense does that make? Raymond must have kept it off. Between the Hunger and Raymond, give Bob the Hunger every time.

Things he doesn't want to do he sometimes has to do. Lizzie's naked knee rising up out of the grass and then falling towards him. Opening her legs. Bob starts in on the sandwich. He is weak. He can't help it. There's cut carrots in there too, wrapped in waxed paper, and what else? Some kind of a tart. What does she think I am, anyways? Who?

But his heart. Chewing that good roast beef, he can't help but let it change. With BS, it's all business. Pipsqueak. But you have to be business *with* him. Otherwise stay away. Bob hates that he needs BS. He has forty dollars in his pocket right now. He'll pick up the rest after. Clear out. Is it just business with Missus BS? Myrtle, or – give it up. Maybe she don't want anything from him. Maybe she just wanted to help. Dr. Barnardo did. Why couldn't he stay with Dr. Barnardo? Why does he have to be a Canadian? He never will be a Canadian. A Canadian is nothing. Travel anywhere, call yourself a Canadian, see what it gets you. Laughed at, that's what.

Missus Bowe didn't want anything from him. She had those soft eyes. She had mother eyes. But never a peep out of her. And he stopped seeing her. She used to feed the chickens, she used to cook, then stopped. She was always upstairs then. He knew that. He could sense her up there, though nobody said boo about her. Then the girl came. She was from England too. She was the cook and Bob took care of the chickens and Belle and just about everything else outside. And when she came, Bob had to move

338

out into the summer kitchen. He had to sleep out there even in the winter, goodbye to the stove. You couldn't say any good of Raymond but that he was warm.

Why didn't the girl ever want to talk to him? They came from the same country. Mrs. Bowe hardly opening her mouth, first to last. She had soft eyes but beaten. She was the wife, what did that matter? She wasn't boughten, but she was another slave. Married to Satan, simple as that. Old man Bowe. Marry a slave or buy one. Or get them to give you one for free. Never thought he'd meet Satan. Where is the girl now, Bob wonders. Would Raymond go after her once Bob made off with himself? Probably.

No grub for fishes today, little fishes like that lucky bass, or big fishes out of a stupid dream. Bob is starting to feel like Bad Bob again.

He remembers that smell of bread baking at the Bowe's. The bread never for him. He never had a taste of it unless somebody in the house might leave a crust. He lifts what's left of the sandwich to his nose. Yes. That rich smell. If he'd been able to eat some of that bread hot. He has never had hot bread in his mouth. Fucking Raymond. Raymond had lots of that bread. His stomach hung over his belt. Raymond was a fat pig already. Bob will never be fat. There will never be an extra ounce of fat on the body of Bad Bob.

Bad Bob. He likes it. O'Donohue got one thing right. Bad Bob, he said. Thought he was making a joke. Raymond, you fat pig, you fat sow.

Mitch is a pig too. No he isn't. Mitch is a lovely man. Lovely! Who said that? Mitch don't know that BS reads those letters. Mitch may know that BS has different ideas, but he don't know the half of it. He don't know that Bob Henry is Bad Bob. You're a woman, Mitch. Sit down to piss. Scorch your ass, Mitch.

Why is a word Bob doesn't use much, not very much, but it's a word he owns. Why, why, why. If you ask, and no answer comes, or an answer comes that you cannot abide—why, it tears you up. So that's where Bob's Why stays: inside him.

What's the point of asking, anyway, when you just have to swallow the answer, or the lack of answer? Bob doesn't know what Dorothea knows and Walter is pretty sure of; he doesn't know what Stella and Michael are just discovering, that answers are not even what matters. Answers! Who has answers, really? To the big questions. Dorothea has her faith, Walter his skepticism. Neither has answers; neither has certainty. No, answers are not it.

What is? Why, directing your question to some other human being who listens. Have that person take it in, take it seriously, take it on. What a sense of loosening then. It starts within and ebbs without. Even your limbs begin to relax.

Bob? Never. Why ask? The consumption took his parents, so he was told. Dr. Barnardo made enquiries. So there's Bob, at the age of five with nobody. Why? Why Bob? Why couldn't Bob stay with Dr. Barnardo? He would have done anything to keep his name off the Canada list. Then why the Bowes? He never once sat with them at their own table, not even once. Why the pig, crawling in with him at night? Yes, Bob is entitled to ask. Perhaps he deserves answers. Perhaps everyone does. First, know your question; second, find someone to ask. Your own listener. Bob has none. Lizzie a listener? No.

Something else. Why is Bob out here now, waiting for night? Why, on this day, when so much is going forward that neither he nor BS has any inkling of? If there were any choice in the matter, wouldn't it make sense not to place him here, within easy walking distance of Bellrock, when the 'gunpowder plot' is about to blow up? If it blows up in Bob's face, that will be another big Why in his ledger, will it not? That would be a terribly unfortunate coincidence. It's coincidental anyway that Bob is here, just across the road from Bellrock, gathering himself to cross it and enter the village. He has the false whiskers on, he's wearing an ugly hat.

Bob is on his own time. Any time tonight will do. He might try to see Lizzie. Back of the house is where she sleeps. Knock on the window. O Bob, you scared me silly. Ha ha. How was I supposed to know it was you? Fooled you, didn't I? Maybe she could come out. Why doesn't he do that? Why not do that first? Does he want to? If he could just think of Lizzie without fucking Raymond sliding in, shoving it up his ass.

If he did visit Lizzie, then he would find out about the baby. Bad Bob a father? That's got to knock him back. That baby could be an answer. You never know.

He couldn't take his trunk when he ran from the Bowe's. He misses that trunk. Trunk and nothing else. Not that you want to be hauling a heavy trunk around when you're racing all over the country. But to have a trunk to carry your things in, put things in and keep them. Keep them safe. Nice things. That trunk was made of alligator. It was strong. It was a beautiful trunk. Raymond and them can have the books, the Bible and the hymn book and *Pilgrim's Progress* and all that. The stupid traveller's guide. The same man must have made that up as gave the magic lantern show at Stepney Causeway. They were all supposed to like what they saw, all that about nature and farms, but he didn't. The Why in his stomach. They were all supposed to be going on an adventure, all those well-dressed youngsters trooping onto the train to Liverpool. Work hard in Canada, make us proud.

341

They had to undress first. Stark naked, they were, and the doctor called the nurse in to see them all skinny, so they could both have a good laugh.

That stupid dream of fishes. Bob Henry is a horse man. He's—what is it?—a questreen. That's Bob's big palomino waiting back at Petworth. That horse is full of ginger, and yet that horse will wait all night for Bob. BS said no horses. No horse today. Fucking rowboat. But that is Bob's big horse with the saddle, sterling silver pommel and silver all over the harness. Keep that harness in the trunk. Bob Henry's big, strong, spirited palomino. Or Black! All that silver against the black, think of that. Waiting for him back at Petworth. Beach this goddamn boat, one foot in the stirrup, and then! Let her see him then!

Why was that goddamn lake in the dream with the beautiful big fishes right next to the farm out of Cobourg? That he ran from. That he'll never go back to unless to burn them out. Whole goddamn family of goddamn Bowes. Ride his big black stallion over there some dark night. And then.

He should be dreaming of big black horses swimming across Depot Lake. Make some sense. He could be on that horse. No more goddamn rowing, ever. A horse is made for a man, and Bob Henry has the best big black horse, the best and the biggest and the fastest horse north of Kingston and Napanee and fucking Cobourg, Raymond!

Bob stands and viciously kicks a rock. Too big a rock. Jesus! He grabs his foot and dances a few steps on the other leg. Sets down the foot with the screaming toes, limps a few steps, sits down hard on the road, jerks off the boot and holds on to his toes with both hands, rocking.

Before the encounter with the rock, Bob's mood was sombre.

Crushing a footful of toes never lightens a man's mood. Bob is very bad at the moment. Who will benefit first from his present state of mind, Mitch Deeks or Lizzie Murphy?

Bob still doesn't know. Let nobody meet him now, is all.

MICHAEL WITH SILAS in the canoe along the creek. Sky thick with herons. So many herons. Not blue herons. Skin not feathers, flying lizards. They are zooming near. Silas is bolt upright, paddling placidly. At the bow, though he is steering. Michael sees his peculiar stroke, upper wrist twisting over. The creatures don't perturb him. A manic gleam in each savage eye. The air fills with raucous cries. Something else, a long-drawn-out moan that swells and swells and fills his ears, his head. It's the train, not distant, not way over to Verona, but just beyond those bushes, car after car, rattling west without him. Just beyond the bushes underneath the tall trees whose branches canopy the air, sealing these lizard-herons below. Broad daylight yet a crimson glow around each trunk. And a huge thump breaks into his ears. Not ears. His body.

Stella is holding on to Silas, one of his legs between her legs, and pushing her crotch at him, running her fingers over his abdomen, over and over. His stomach muscles. Then he is on his stomach above her, moving on her, and she is sliding her fingers down his backbone, slowly, vertebra, vertebra, vertebra. Muscle and bone. Not Silas. Patrick Lewis, and a sound rising from him. Laughter, growling. He has been asleep, and now he is waking, angry, savage. He rolls off her. His eyes widen in recognition, then narrow. She recoils at the hatred in his eyes. One more second and he will – what? His mouth is ugly. He raises a fist. His lips open. 'Tramp!' he snarls, in her mother's voice. 'TRAMP!' It's a scream.

She wakes in a panic sweat, suffused with shame. Her skirt is right up her legs. Was she rubbing? She quickly turns her head in Michael's direction.

Can't make him out. It's pitch dark now. She stares while her breathing settles. Wriggles her skirt down over her legs. Cold. She turns on her side, towards him, reaches out. Where are you?

He flinches, grunts, grabs her hand.

Sorry, she says.

I was awake, he says, thickly. I'm awake. He thinks he is. He has snatched her hand from his privates, still or again erect. He keeps the hand, gripping it hard.

I had a dream, she says. I didn't like it.

Mmm. His own dream is still fading. He will open his eyes. That glow will fade. It will fade and his eyes will open. He is running the fingers of his free hand over the back of hers. His fingers are tracing their way up her arm. He pulls her arm toward him. Come here.

Why is he pulling at me? Don't.

Don't do that, she says sharply. Pulls her hand out of his.

What? Now he is awake. What? What's happening? Why is his hand in the air?

You were talking to me. Weren't you awake?

What did I say?

I'm awake, you said.

Oh. He lets that sink in. Is that all?

That's all.

Let it go. He was asleep. Who was he pulling at? Pulling at a dream. A girl in a dream? She is wet. Oh, if he weren't awake.

344

But don't pull me so hard. Leave me be. Myself.

Pinch me, he says.

No.

Don't you want to find out whether I know I'm talking to you?

No. Go back to sleep. She is shivering.

You *were* sleeping.

Yes. I told you. I was dreaming. I didn't like the dream so I woke up.

Oh. I didn't catch that. Did you say what the dream was about?

No.

What was it about?

I forget.

Oh.

They might never have gotten back to sleep in the cool of the night, cold now, without his sliding on to her tick and pulling his over them. They lay awake shivering for so long. Finally, she said it. You'll have to come here, she said, and he did. At first they laid on their backs, trying to keep their bodies apart. Hands is one thing. Holding hands was nice. It was a lot. He laid there under the tick, beside her, hands over his crotch. How was he ever going to get to sleep on his back with his item sticking up? But on your back, stretched out straight, you take up less space. They don't have much space. Room for one, now serving two.

She lies rigid. Warm, thank the good Lord, but tense. Sleeping with a boy. How does Silas manage without blankets? If he did not, he might have thought of covers for his guests. But at least

they're warm now. Warm and tired, and, despite the awkwardness, their limbs begin to relax. Their breathing deepens. He
is gone first. There is a tiny regular click on his in-breath that
she listens to, annoyed. How is she going to fall sleep herself,
listening to that? And he suddenly turns on his side, dragging the
tick with him. She jerks it back. He mumbles at that, but stays
on his side, knees bent up. He wants the whole bed! All right,
she thinks. If that's how it's going to be. She turns away, holding
tight to her side of the tick.

That is no good, not without putting her feet over or
under his.

She is half asleep when her body tells her, fit yourself to him.
More than half asleep and past caring about such a little matter
as touching. She is drifting off against him, a pair of spoons,
her arm around him, hand resting open on his chest. Her cheek
against his hair. Her middle pressed to his bum, and no wonder
she drifts back into the dream that woke her. If it is a dream. But
it must be. But there is no mother, no Patrick, no Silas. It's waves,
rocking and rocking. If you were to lie down in the bottom of the
canoe in the middle of Second Lake, say, and let the waves rock
you and rock and rock you. If you let everything go, and relaxed,
it would be light blue, robin's egg blue, and Oh, and Oh, all your
limbs come unpinned, especially your legs, clamped together
yet spread wide. The creek flowing through you, through her,
Stella, and out over a falls. Oh. And so tiny she is now, is then,
the membrane of her shell infinitely soft. Curled up in it. Ever.
Ever. Ever. Ever.

NIGHT

4:30 AM. All the dogs in the township awake, yipping, howling or baying.

KATHERINE BUSH STARTS AWAKE from the rocker where she has passed the night so far, waiting up. She rises heavily, shuffles to the table, turns the wick of the kerosene lamp up high, lifts and aims it here and there about the house. She opens the front door, lamp raised high, looks out. The night is dark. Where'd that moon get to? Full moon. Overcast, must be. What's that racket? Something happening, but she can't see what. Stella? No answer. Stella! Her harsh voice is breaking. *Stella!* Nothing. Her back is hunched as she stands holding the lamp aloft, her whole body tense. Finally, she sniffs, turns around. Back inside, she trims the wick, replaces the lamp on the table and lowers herself heavily into the chair. Her cheeks are ravaged with tears. For two days, now, she has been all mother, levered by loss into the role she had abjured. *For granted, for granted*, is the refrain of lament coursing through her.

JIM SHIBLEY IS REASSURING the missus and the kids. It's nothing, it's nothing. Go back to sleep. It wasn't nothing. It was loud. Well, I'll go out and look. You stay here. He feels his way out into the lobby and lights the lamp. Leaves the door open so they'll see the light. He looks out the front door. There is light moving in front of Mitch's house. Mrs. Bush's voice cuts through the night. Her daughter run away. Her daughter and young Mike Deeks. Craning his neck, he can see past the school to the Ritchie's. Light in there too. They're gone to Kingston. Teacher must be up. He douses his lamp and tiptoes back to the bedroom. Nothing doing, he says, nothing to see. Go back to sleep. The darkness hides his frown. Where, oh where, are those kids?

MITCH IS STALKING AROUND his house with a shotgun. The gun is new, bought after he lost the other two in the fire. He hasn't used it yet. The shells in both barrels are loaded with salt. He knows a prank when he sees one. Hears one. Egg all over his windows last week, every damned one, and Martha begging him, quit that fool job now. Enough shilly-shallying. Quit and let's go. You won't have any friends left if this keeps on. Mitch? Mitch? And him reassuring her, it's just kids. I know it's kids. They're running wild. Have you talked to Miss Asselstine lately? If she can't control them – Now, now, things will get better. And anyways move where? I said Oregon to Mr. Stegner. Not there. Well, then. But the day after the egg attack, and those eggs stole right out from under Ritchie's hens, he emptied the shot from a couple of shells and filled them back up with salt. He was half awake, sleeping like a cat, with his pants on, when the thump hit.

What the hell? Suspenders up, he was outside in a snap. Lights began coming on in most of the houses. He could see shadows passing and passing the windows. Miss Asselstine's head poked out the Ritchie's door. You heard it too, she said. What was it? Dunno, said Mitch. Helluva noise, though. Certainly was. What are you doing with the gun? O, those young whippersnappers, you know, put the fear of God into them. If it was them. No sign of those kids? No. What do you suppose? I don't know, but I'm terribly worried. Oh yes, I know. Well, nothing doing that I can see. Goodnight. Night. Mitch goes back in and turns down the lamp, but he's not for bed. Too keyed up. He sits by the window with the gun across his knees.

BOB HENRY IS OUT of sight behind the school, breathing hard. He was sneaking up to Mitch Deeks's house in his slouch hat and false beard when it happened. Jesus Christ! He dropped the can and ran. Now he watches the illuminated upper body of Mitch Deeks circumnavigating his house, new house. Holds his breath as Mitch passes the can. What's wrong with the man that he don't see that can? Almost tripped over it. A man that stupid? Deserves what he gets. What he's going to get. He deserves it. So does she. What does she deserve? She let him love her. How could a woman be so bad and be so young? Into her drawers. You have a bad opinion of yourself. I do. I'm a very bad opinion. She deserves it. Deserves what? His mind racing.

LIZZIE SITS BOLT UPRIGHT. Bob? You back? You here? She gets up and pads to the crib, where Anthea is sleeping like a, like a baby. Your daughter, Bob. Where you been? Where did you go? And never said a word. And left me in this fix. No, no. Don't bother asking. It's too late. Far too late for that. She's yours, yes, but I'll bring her up myself. All I wanted was a word. Take advantage of me and then—gone. Too late, Bob. You hear me? Back in bed, her limbs straight out stiff, her arms across her chest. Tears running down past her ears, soaking the pillow. With a bang. I know that's how you'll come back. Bang, bang. Bob.

IN HER WRAP, Dorothea stands on the stoop, looking first at the school, the side not concealing Bob Henry. That is Morse, she thinks. That was Doctor Morse's dynamite. That was certainly his blast. They've got Lachlan in their pockets, the big galoot. Morse's revolution, Lachlan's work, I'll bet any money. Why did I think, right away, the school? They met there. They were plotting this. I didn't want particulars. I trusted him. That's his blast and by now everything that was meant to happen has happened. The revolution. Awake! We did. We're up. Where is Stella? Stella and Michael, what has happened to them? All those lights out here. It's like morning mid-winter, everybody rising in the dark for work or school. Stoking their stoves, dressing quickly in the cold. Sleepwalking to breakfast. But this is April, an April night more like high summer. Tomorrow will be scorching again, over eighty. Unseasonable. But this—she sits down on the step—one of the the loveliest things about this territory—no real demarcation between day and night in summer, except of light. If you could stay up all night, talking with the one you loved, supposing you had found her – But you couldn't. You absolutely could not. What a blessing to be awakened into this caress of cool air, if she weren't so deeply unsettled. She leans back against the door, her mind drifting over the last two days. What is she going to do with this guilt?

Oh, Stella.

DES HAD BEEN WAITING for it, but he didn't need to wait this way, fully dressed, lying in bed on his back with his hands joined behind his head. Emma finally asleep. Exhausted with the waiting and the worry, she didn't hear anything. Not even King's howling into the dark could rouse her from fretful sleep. Why pick tonight, tonight of all nights, to go missing? Well, the argument. And, long before that, drifting and drifting apart. My son. Lately, he'd been catching sight of Michael, and suddenly thinking, my son. Pride flushing through him, surprising him. Though he was more often impatient and heartsore. No talking to the lad. But had he ever? About anything he thought or felt? Not really. But they could be close without speaking. They could at one time. When had that come to an end, that comfort? You get into the habit of silence. Heart silence. But don't run away. Things get tough, don't run. Walk away angry sometimes, maybe, yes, burn it off. Whenever the old man stuck in his craw he'd haul the box back to the river and play until his fingers could take no more. Lost in the box. Like the man off the train. Blues his life. Yes. The old man made him a better player, give him that. But what happened to the promise he made himself? No son of mine.

Never angry like that. Michael. Des swings his legs heavily out over the edge of the bed and sits up. The cows are raising a hell of a racket. And! The loft! Warm night like this. Why hadn't he thought of that? He tiptoes out and down the stairs.

TOM RITCHIE'S OLD BOAR feels the jolt through the ground of his pen. His little front legs shoot out straight. Mmph? He scrambles onto his back legs. Front legs bent now, kneeling. His head swings from side to side for a few moments. Then he topples back onto his side. One big snort from his great round hairy snout scatters dust and straw and he is asleep. No more than the mind of a gull does you or I or anyone know the mind of a pig.

FOR SILAS THE CREEK is animal, alive, a character living and acting in his world, responsive to the heat and light of the sun, constantly moving, always travelling, even in the freeze of winter when it takes on temporary shape. Even then, water is always bright and active beneath the ice, and the rapids freeze solid only in the coldest winters.

There is no volition to water. Water has no mind. Water is an instrument of the planet. Leave it be, it does what it does. But impede its wonted flow, it will gather weight and pressure until, released, the walls of its vessel breached, it lunges free with incredible force.

Water is animal tonight, ponderous, gigantic, unconscious, behind the Depot dams. Water shouldering the dam tonight at

Fifth Depot Lake, and at Lott's dam miles south in Petworth.

For half a century Depot Creek, the Napanee River, has been a resource and a torment. Pent and released in controlled bursts, that water created the mills that spawned the settlements that grew into villages and towns. Those go-ahead places drew the settlers for whom custodianship of the water became an issue so contentious as to recall old stories in which one party's greed and indifference causes the death of another. Cain rose up against Abel, and slew him and the Lord said to Cain, Where is Abel your brother? And oh, the reply was chilling: I do not know, he said. Am I my brother's keeper? The Lord had only one culprit to confront in the first days.

Precious life, the flesh so frail! Who is the culprit on this now-dark night in 1913? The ancient story gone labyrinthine. Whom do we lesser beings accuse?

Pulverized by dynamite, the upper dam releases a glee of galloping wave. The crest, charging downriver, tears out weakened dams at Fourth and Second as it surges, tearing off bridge railings and fences and, above Bellrock, sweeping away an unmatched pair of unpenned cows. It pounds with such force into the Bellrock Mill that it smashes the waterwheel to smithereens, then leaps the low dam where Silas first glimpsed his canoe and surges on into the Long Swamp.

HAS LACHLAN FALLEN ASLEEP at the Lott dam? Isn't it time to blow up that goddamned nuisance once and for all? Perhaps it is time, but what does timing matter tonight? Take your time, Lachlan. Fifth Lake is far upstream. Perhaps it makes no difference at all. Perhaps the die were already cast. Perhaps they would have come up snake eyes, however the waters conjoined. But surely it would be better for the sleepers at Silas's hut to be merely swept off the floor as that up-river wave punched across it.

But the raft floor of Silas's hut is rocking now, the water beneath it having just been suddenly lowered.

Lachlan having risen and ponderously walked to his plunger and deliberately depressed it, and what a beautiful job of work! Rubble from that huge blast might have dropped on houses in Petworth, but no, Lachlan has flung it all downstream where it will safely lie submerged, contributing to no attempted reconstruction.

Water streaming out of the swamp has the raft floor rocking, gradually enough, not so much as to agitate the sleepers on it. The floor is merely set to rocking. In time, if time enough there were, that rocking motion, that lazy side to side, to side, would surely have entered their dreams. Sleepers in the staterooms of the Titanic triumphantly riding the gentle North Atlantic swells. Stella's unhoused babies, home again and rocking safe. Well might young dreamers, rolling this way, that way, gently in their sleep, have dreamt Mother Ocean. But the downstream crest, to be sure much diminished by its long night's travel and already searching out into the Drowned Lands, carries force enough, as it reaches the hut, to catch the floor on the rocking upswing

Three young sleepers. Two now as one, Stella pressed as close to Michael's back as clothed flesh will permit, and Silas, third man, chaperone, lying apart on his back with mouth open wide.

The wave lifts and hurls the floor in a somersault into the channel. Dumped into the creek, all three are pinned beneath it, so lately their bedstead. What a tangle underwater, what a thrashing panic as Michael and Stella tear at the water-heavy ticks that wrap them. Silas, less cumbered, quickly claws his way out. He surfaces, takes a deep breath. Drags himself back under. He grabs with one hand the side of the floor, seizes a tick with the other, pulls at it, what is it, snagged, he jerks and jerks, finally it releases. One-handed, he hauls and hauls and hauls it past him, unwrapping Stella. He doesn't know. She tumbles fast downstream. He reaches again, grazes a wrist, grasps it, pulls another mighty pull. Holds on for dear life now, clawing his way out and up again, dragging Michael behind him.

Now they are all free.

The floor is all raft now, carrying Silas and Michael downstream in the darkness, hanging on, exhausted, breathing hard. But for the drag of the canoe, still tethered to the floor, ribs stove in, sunk, the raft might almost move with the speed of Stella, now submerged in the dark beyond them. Michael and Silas, clutching the raft, clutching each other. An eon passes before Michael knows who he is embracing.

He thrusts Silas off. Where is she, where where *where*. It rises in his throat to a scream. Stella! he shouts at the height of it. Stella!

HEART IN HER MOUTH. *No. Her stomach. Up. A rising. The last, the ghost of a dream of a drifting, a wave, the crest of a wave that rises, rises, Oh! the foam, the sparkle, hesitation, sparkle, high and sliding, sliding, oh. Agh. The water. She thrashes in the water, it closes over her head and she swallows a mouthful, oh, and then out again, her head out again in the cool night air, air! but the night—there are no, how can she tell, no stars, no moon, how can she see—the clouds—and under she goes grasping and grasping again. The floor, it rose up and tumbled her over and clawing and reaching—Michael! Is it he she swept her hand across in the dark? Michael! or some—no, unthinkable, no. Or Silas? Where, oh, where is Silas, went to Bellrock for the cheese, for the bread, for the pie, it was Silas in her house, her mother's house, the doily, doily, antimacassar holler at the ball game, Chief who wanted to hit, no, no, not Michael—his quiet eyes, his hands, his arms with golden hair, and Silas's hands that stole her, stole her away, Demon lover, not Silas, oh! Something slippery, muddy, oh, and down she goes again, and the water, the creek, entering her mouth her lungs, her hair spread out, a tendril of root grasps her foot and holds, the floor of the hut is where the others are, behind her, beyond her, hair trailing out in the flow of the current, dark of the water, running, water running, then it gives, the tendril gives and Stella drifts, she drifts— free now, free of all resistance, slides with the current now into a pool beyond the pool. She is free and warm in the kitchen. There is a fire bright in the stove. The kettle is jiggling on the stovetop. She opens the firebox, tosses in two more sticks of wood, whoo!—hot. Soon the kettle will boil. She has the tea all ready in the cup. And turns away, untying the apron from around her waist. He is in his high chair, Mister two-years-old exactly, exactly the age he was the day he was lost and, O Salvation, now is found. In his high chair and pretty soon too big for that. You'll be too big for that, won't you, my Pook, my pookie Pook. Her pointer finger stubbing his button nose, he giggles. Who's my darling boy? Michael is my darling, my darling, my darling. Michael is my darling, the bold grenadier. Yes, my leafy Pook, Stella is with you. Stella will take care of you. She will never leave. We'll always be on the rise. Walking up the twisty trail—so many switchbacks. Just after the next rise, surely this time there'll be something to see, not one more switchback on the rising path up the side of this mountain, isn't it just about time we reached the top, my darling? It is. Hold on, hang on, Stella isn't too tired. Hold on, my Pookie. One more rise, a turn and oh! Look! There is the valley. Down down down below, the blue river meandering through the green of grass and tree. Just as if someone drew it, drew it all so green and beautiful and where—where over this last rise and the trail, down down down, more switchbacks, yes, my Pook, hang on, honey, more of these switchbacks but now it's downhill, down down down to where we'll see, we'll finally see, there in a meadow, a glade, a clearing—don't ask how I know, Mister Pook, don't ask. There is a house, a hut, a cottage in a clearing, waiting, prepared, dressed precisely for us. And on the stoop, an old man waiting, growing older and older and older, waiting, yes, for who to walk up? To trudge up and say, Hello my good man. Why, you, little tree-boy, you and I! To say, For my brother and I, dear sir, have you a room for the night? Ah, the magic words, the magic words. The old man replies, Pook, I know, don't ask me how. We're tired, Pook. Aren't we a little tired now? How many old men have we patience for, little Pook, my love, before we sink down, me to my knees, you on my back, until we sink and the dark wave rises, rises, knees to waist to chest to neck to head, before any haven of a leaf or a love, before any lovely fastness under a birch for leaf or love, dear Michael, Mister Pook, before it opens up, the lovely broad bedroom, wide wide room in the tiny cottage, opening, opening, spreading like a rug just now rolled out and the four-poster bed. Ah. Here we are. Thank you, sir. You are most, most, most. My brother and I, yes, this is my little brother in whom I am well pleased, yes, we are weary down down down to the bone and the time is upon us. I'll just remove these mocassins—bright and new they are, do you see, and I love, just love, the pattern of beads on the tops—the lovely curlicues of white—off with them, off, and see how deep you sink, deep*

*and deep, deep into the sheets, and the cover a quilt, log cabin, look!
and see, here you are and here I am, little piggy, my Pook. These are
your sleeping drawers, the very same you were wearing the day you
were lost and this is my garb the day that I drowned, a little bit faded,
just a little bit the worse for the wear. I was under for days, I was under
for weeks. No little men came. I thought they would, where I slept and
slept with my eyes open wide. No little men. But a rainbow above, and
fish above, and the sun by day and the moon and stars by night up
over top, and look, dear Pooksie, look up there! The whole night sky in
the canopy over your head. I'll slip out of this. The door clicks shut. I've
stepped out of this and, there, I've folded it over the chair, over the chair
by the bed, the beautiful chair with the caned back and seat. Folded
over, to dry. Tomorrow I'll shake the silt out of my skirt, my blouse.
Shake it out when it dries and don't you just love the maples? Overhead,
the leaves of the maples, beautiful, beautiful sugar bush. It must be
beautiful October again. Yes, give me your hand, I'll never let go. Oh
well, if you wish, if you'd like me to. But I'll hold your hand and I'll
lift you up and whoo!—fling you high in the air, the crisp air under
these maples, leaves of red and orange and rust, the whole and the
variegated, down the path to the creek, up you go, up, and down you
come. I'm catching you neat. We'll walk, we'll stroll the path to the
bottom of the farm, and there's the creek, our friend the creek, and
that tall cow lifts her head, mmm? Lifts her head to look us over and
we smile back. Back? That cow never smiles. No cow can ever smile.
And the fat little cow never never looks up, why should she bother? She
is fine, dear. Down at the edge of the creek there is a fish, a pike, and
a snake, a water snake swallowed the head of the fish and neither the
fish nor the snake, neither the snake nor the fish will survive. Isn't that
sad? It isn't sad when the snake has only swallowed its own head. That's
right, and now you could roll it like a hoop while the man rows by. The*

man rows past. He keeps and he keeps and he keeps on rowing past. Taking care. He is constantly, constantly taking care. And who is my father? He is my father, humming and humming and—no, Michael, no. A lullaby, no. My love, my father, rowing into the narrows where the creek swallows the lake—those logs, those fish, those loggers, that boat—swallowed into the creek, the Napanee River down to the down to the down to the sea, and there comes a time for rest. The time comes, my lovely Pook, dear brother mine, when we can rest. We can lie out flat. We can stretch out our limbs. Long, long limbs a-stretch. We can rest. Place your head on my shoulder, love. I'll rock you. We'll rock ourselves to sleep under this lovely canopy. Moon and the stars up there in the blue. And dreams, oh, the lovely dreams. Sheep for you and waves for me. The soft and white, the soft and blue. And the bright, brightest morning we are walking, quietly, walking to. The light that shines for us then, dear brother Pook, oh! And I'll never leave you in the navy. I would a maid-man go for you, disguised for your sake. A maid in disguise, your elder brother I would be. But no, my dear, my dearly belovèd, we will rise and dress in our clothes, now dry and clean. And hand in hand, when the click comes, door wide, light streams in, then hand in hand we go, my love, out we go, right out delighted into the day.

WALKING THE CREEK, APRIL 1913

(Michael and Silas)

YOU HAD ME.

I had you.

You had my hand.

I had.

My hand.

Yours.

But I can swim, Silas, why not hers?

Yes.

Yes, what?

Why not.

Women and children first, Silas. You never heard that.

No.

You wouldn't need to hear that. Would you? She's your friend. Yes, I know she is. You must have loved her.

Love.

Your first time for that.

That.

That word.

That word.

It means, Silas, I have to sit down, Silas, I'm scared to death, I've got to sit down here, look, this grassy place, I don't feel good.

Sit down.

No, no, I'm – agh! O God, there's pie in that, raspberry-rhubarb, raspberry loves the rhubarb, that word, it means, it means.

Pie. Cheese. Bread.

That you brought us, and the fish, and you brought us both out there, you, goddamn it, Silas, why? Why, you asshole, let me go, let go of me. I'm sorry.

Sorry.

I'm sorry, I can't say love, I can't say love, she was your friend, not was, she is she is.

Friend, she was blue. Blue. You were green, I was blue and green. I knew. They said.

What are you, Silas? I have no idea what you're saying, look in there, look. No, not. Silas, my skin is shrinking, my skin is tight all over, if it shrinks any more I won't be – I have to sit down again. You have to go yourself.

Alone.

Yes, alone. On your own, by yourself, *toute seul*, Miss A, solitary, all alone, all, all alone, where is she, Silas, why why why?

Why alone.

Don't ask me, Silas, tell. Tell me what you know, you knew. Did you see this coming? I don't believe you did. But say. Tell me. I can't stand this.

Mean, no. Blue and green. But all the others. A belt. Across the sky.

Silas, that's no good. I have no idea.

Across the sky, no. Just above, the air. It would come. I knew, yes *my* skin tight, my muscles, I knew. I didn't know.

You didn't.

Stop. It was hurting. They were all together, the big one and the thin one, red red red in the village, trouble, I could tell.

She was in trouble?

I could tell. You came here, you.

Yes, me. Why?

You.

You said that.

She was alone.

Did she. Want me?

Want.

Did she ask for me?

No, you were green, she was blue.

Did she want me, Silas, you bastard? What did she want?

You, two.

But I didn't want her, Silas, I didn't think about her. She wasn't. Not for me, not until. Silas, where is she? Why?

Where.

And colours.

All.

Your colours are saying? You can speak. I knew it. I didn't. What are you saying now? We'll play catch. I'll show you. But tell me.

The man.

In the paper? The pitcher? Does he have a – what colour? Oh, Silas, you're driving me crazy. *I'm* blue. Can't you come further?

Green. She was blue.

Was was was. What do you *know*, Silas. You know. I see you know. Silas, you have to say better.

Divers.

What?

Divers, their teeth, the trees, water, the pool.

What?

My.

Your what?

Tongue.

Yes, it could loosen. Yes, try. That's right, let me see. It looks, that little thing hanging down, it looks all right. I have one too. I don't like to see your tongue, all cracked in the middle, Silas, it's an ugly tongue, and your teeth. No wonder. But a tongue, it should speak. I can't say, try.

It's first, it's new, it's coming out, there is an egg. She's in the egg, curled up in the egg, you know an egg.

Yes.

Curled up tight in there. The little bones. That was bad.

Bones.

My sack.

Bones in your sack. Silas, fine, but, Silas, what about her? Where is she? You know things. Where? The love. I'm sorry, we'll keep on. The bones were squirrels?

Beast, my little. The other one killed them. I can think. I didn't think.

Not straight? Think crooked, Silas, think sideways, meander. You're a creek, Silas, find your level. Where is she?

I'm sorry. She's curled up tight in the egg. She's happy happy happy. Then no, she's not. She wants, she wants. She wants, she wants.

Out.

The shell.

Good, shell. Another word. I know. I don't know blue, or, yes, I'm green, and blue is her, but why? Why?

Wait. She's not out. She's coming. Coming out, ah! That is her, she's wet, she has her legs. She'll take a step.

She'll dry.

Yes.

She's out now?

Out.

Stella.

She. Loves, loves, loves, loves.

Stella?

You.

Me. Say Mmm. Say Michael. Say Silas?

No.

You don't see yourself?

No.

She worried about you. Silas, you didn't hear. She said last night, oh. She said, your friend last night said, What's going to happen to Silas? Blue, your friend. Love. Mine. Oh, I'm care, I'm ravelled, oh torn, Silas. Stella, a mother, blue and blue and blue, I know I know, look in here and here, you'll find her. Then, what's for the best, you didn't think, oh, hold me, hold my hand. Oh dear God, Silas, now I'm coming home.

THURSDAY, APRIL 17. 8:30 AM. Where did all these elm logs come from? Strays, they must be, lost from various drives, freed by the flood, now jammed together at this tight spot in Cameron's Cut, just before the channel opens out again. Michael and Silas, wet and shivering, are peering at that jam, forlorn hope.

A quart of that water, Michael is thinking, waiting with Silas, filling his mind with thoughts he can bear to think, right there in that curl of a ripple around the last log in the jam—if you could isolate a quart of water, or even just a drop of that water, but of course you never could, but anyway, *say* you could—a pickle jar full of that very water, or a drop out of that very jar, it might be pouring down the river to the St. Lawrence and then on down the St. Lawrence into the Atlantic, let's see, one, two, hmm, three – Oh, it's hard. *It can't, she just cannot be* – Maybe if you floated something down—a little square piece of wood with a ring of paint around it might be the ticket, or maybe a round piece wouldn't get stuck so easy, oh, a little round end of a pole you could pick up at the mill and mark with a bit of paint, what would be best to show against that green: red, maybe, or white?

Where is she?

A hard problem any day for the likes of Michael, his thoughts characteristically branching, branching, just like the river itself, usually trickling out into some cul de sac of an inconclusive tributary. Miss A would know how to work the problem out without getting sidetracked.

Michael's eyebrows are joined by v-shaped tension lines. Silas's face bears little expression. Only one who knew him well, and very few can say that, only a very close acquaintance would detect the anxiety new to his body. The night river took the one who knew him best, if knowing is the right word.

Someone like Miss A. Michael needs someone. Miss A. For the problem so very important to solve this morning. Silas is no help with this, despite what has so newly passed between them.

Under that jam? Could she have floated under there?

Any other day Michael and Silas, but not together, never together, might be standing by the creek to watch Lachlan come and blow the jam. Lachlan can blast a load of 'spar right into the box of your wagon. Blow the wallet clean out of your back pocket. That's what they say. And where is he? Where is Lachlan? Lachlan is late.

She could be all right, Miss A. She's alive for sure if she knew to lie limp and go with the surge. She might have grabbed a big elm like the ones bunched up here, one that got through. What is to say she would have gone down, pulled under? Nothing. Absolutely –

What she probably did was—relief crashing through him—she probably caught hold of an elm that rushed on through. She probably hung on and hung on and hung on all the way down to Petworth. Anyone smart as her. Why not? She probably stood up when she could, when her feet hit bottom at Petworth, stood up and stepped right out on to the bank. It's a long walk home, certainly it is. She might have started, though. Or somebody in Petworth took her in. Took her right in, dried her off, got her into borrowed clothes, wrapped her in a blanket—oh, those goddamn, goddamn ticks—wrapped her up warm and carried her to a buggy. Bellrock! Probably that's where she is right now. Back there, or on the way there. Dried out, warmed up, a passenger in some kind person's buggy.

But Michael and Silas won't leave the river they have been combing since first light. Probably there is no need for this search.

No. But just in case, they have been scouring the edges, wading in the creek when it shallows, wallowing or swimming, searching and searching for any sign.

Standing by the jam, they are not in the same world as Scanlon's men, come down from upriver, leaning on their useless cant hooks or lounging in the grass as they wait for Lachlan. Scanlon himself standing apart and cursing under his breath. The men don't care about the delay or what Mr. Rathbun thinks, but Scanlon has to.

How could those men be joking about George Hudson driving onto McCumber's Bridge, and the water swept him off it, him and his horse and buggy? Baby face, Michael hears, mama's boy. Georgie Porgie Hudson driving that fancy little trap that dragged his horse down. What is funny about that? The poor horse wouldn't have had a tinker's chance. Michael can see that, he has to see it, the horse still hitched in the traces with Hudson's trap pulled out behind her in the stream, one wide open eye staring up. He broke up sobbing when he heard about that horse. It was partly the horse and partly what it meant, that poor drowned innocent horse. Crying for the horse and not for Hudson! Well, the horse was helpless. The poor creature had no choice.

Yesterday he would never have let Silas take him by the hand away from the raft to flounder upstream towards the hut from the place where they fetched up in the dark, having abandoned the raft and the smashed canoe. It was together they hurtled down river last night, after Silas's strong arm saved his life. But her hand, *hers*, where was that? It was her hand he thought he caught. Everything happening so fast and pitch black without a moon—it was hold on, hold tight, and never mind how firmly

367

that other hand gripped, how it kept on kept on holding when he could feel his own hand numbing.

Some rogue part of him badly wants to break in and say, She's lost, oh, she's gone, and why? He couldn't want hard enough for it to be her hand gripping his. He hates himself for that. Sobs are jammed in his throat now. If Lachlan's dynamite looses sobbing along with the logs? He is free of himself for now. He wouldn't care.

Here is Lachlan now, pipe in his mouth. Here he comes, one foot, the other foot, slow and heavy. He moves like a Percheron. He wouldn't hurry if his house were burning up around him. He doesn't hurry anything, sleepy Lachlan. Yawning, shaking his head with it.

It's annoying to see Scanlon's men go silent, nudge each other and grin knowingly as Lachlan approaches. What is funny about Lachlan this morning? Nothing is funny about Lachlan. Michael loves Lachlan right now, because Lachlan will gentle the logs to move. There will not be any violence to those logs. Probably she was up out of the river this morning and off away home, one way or another, but say she floated in under that jam. Just say she did. She could be under there yet, unconscious maybe, but breathing at the cleft between two logs, two of those logs that are side by side. That is easy to picture. It could easily be so, and this man he loves like a father will be freeing her gently as a lover. Those two logs will slide downstream and then part and out she'll float, out from between them nice as you please.

Silas is plucking at Michael's shoulder, motioning with his head. When the jam lets go they don't want to be here. They want to be below, where the creek slows and turns. They slip up into the meadow to make their way down there.

Bellrock

April 23, 1913

D.B. Stegner Esq

Napanee River Improvement Company

Newburgh, Ontario

Dear Sir

What a sad bisness, Mr. Stegner. That little girl gone in the flood after they blew our dams it tears my heart up. I know what youll say its not my falt the missus says the same. Its not you, she says. You tried your best to keep those dams how many years. I had to think. About twenty five years Mr. Stegner isnt it? Nor you didnt burn your own house down neither did you. She never forgets that. Well I says we dont know who done that. We dont know who, you gomeril she says but we know why. Mr. Stegner, I never wanted to believe that but now I dont know. That little girl had nothing, nothing much, anyways. Her mother is poor and no father since she was a nipper. But she was smart. The teacher says she was the smartest ever. She come into this vale of tears with a mark on her face. If she hadnt of had that mark and different circomstancis but Mr. Stegner isnt that the way. A man has a hard job of it figuring why things is as they are what is fair. Mr. Stegner I no I count my blessings. Things has not been what they might for me and mine these past few years but we have each other and our health well, my rumatizm but that dont signify today.

Mr. Stegner I cant work the river, no more. Mr. Stegner this is my resignition. She's not the ondly one lost, you may be shure George Hudson's family will go to law. But I wont be able to do my work thinking on her, she was a friend. And this whole country we cant agree to share it. Mr. Stegner, it breaks my heart to leave that river I worked so long but I cant work her now.

By the by you know what I always said of Bob Henry? Well the teacher seen Bob outside the School with a can of gas. I was still awake after the bang woke me up. I heard the teacher yell and I hopped it outside. I had my new Shotgun filled with salt and this fellow running away, I had no idea who. My idea was it was some young scamp at his deviltry. Well I give him both berrels whitch was the second big noise. Next was Bob yelping. Hell be picking the salt out of his derier for some little time to come and picking it out in the jale down to Napanee. We got him dead to rights. The teacher was a witness but anyways the salt would have told.

But why last night? We cant figure it out. And burn the school? We know it has something to do with those dams blowen up, but what. Theres a lot of talk. Pete Swenson says nobody we know blew those dams, he wont say who. He ondly nods to himself and he smiles. But Pete Swenson has never in his life said one thing anybody paid any attention to. We think he just wants to make himself important.

It couldnt have been Doctor Morse, the Verona doctor. Somebody saw him near Petworth dam or that is the story. But what kind of sense is that? Hes too good of a man. People are quick to juge. I dont know if you ever seen Doctor Morse probly not, skin and bones and a long face never knowen to smile. But he served this community true, the township. But you know how nothing beats a jumping on a man if he would slip and falls and hobnail boots is best for that.

Well Mr. Stegner all things earthly has an end and our long corispondance in regard to the affairs of the company is about at an end I suppose forever and wherever I go one thing shure I will always remember the many favours and kind words I have received from you during the time I have been in your employ. Mr Stegner if everyone put their best foot forward like you the world would be a better place.

If you would ask Mr. O'Donohue to send up what is owing me I will call us square.

Yours Sincerely,
Mitch Deeks

P.S. There was two young boys with the girl. The one of them was deef and dumb, the other was my brothers son, Michael Deeks. They cant get much out of him what was they doing in the swamp when the dams bust. One thing shure, those boys had the living daylights scared out of them. Its a mystery, Mr. Stegner through a glass darkly so they say, then face to face. I wish I was face to face right now. They say He works in mysterious ways his wonders to perform but this aint a wonder like I think of a wonder it is something fine. No, I keep all my faith for me and my family just to keep going we don't know where right now.

And so Mr. Stegner, I remain

Your obdt. Servant

Mitch Deeks

THE MIND

TORONTO, JUNE, 1919. Dorothea and Elizabeth rise from their booth in the Angel. The restaurant is empty of patrons now, but for a man facing the back wall in the last booth. She and Elizabeth are out on the street before it strikes her that she knows the back of that man's head. She pauses. Wait a minute, Love, she says, and steps back in. The man behind the counter looks up, eyes her questioningly. Forget something? She shakes her head, walks past him for a good look at the solitaire.

Michael Deeks. All these years beyond the great divide in her life; his too, most likely.

She badly wanted to talk with him back then, but his tremendous silence rebuffed her. She never found the opportunity. There was no official inquiry, either. Only for that Mr. Hudson, and no good reason offered why not. How could the story ever come out? Michael was absent from the funeral. He dropped school and joined the Frontenac Regiment. Then she was gone. Others were leaving too. She hated taking cover from the exodus.

She whirls and rejoins Elizabeth on Queen Street, seizes her hands. Do you mind going home by yourself? There's somebody I –

Elizabeth looks in the window. That man? Why?

He's from home.

One of your suitors?

No, no. He was a pupil. I've told you about him.

Not –

Yes, he's the one.

374

And he shows up here? That's remarkable!

Elizabeth takes another look, a good long one. Oh dear, she says. She turns back, all tenderness. Yes, she says, you go back in.

I might be quite some time.

I shouldn't wait up?

Best not.

All right, Love.

Dear Elizabeth.

Dorothea lays a hand on his shoulder. He starts and looks up. His face is drawn, but he smiles. Your hair is short, he says. She smiles back. Do you mind, she says, indicating the booth. No, he says. He gestures to the seat opposite, but she shakes her head and makes a shooing motion. He shrugs and slides over.

She will not engage his eyes. For him or for herself? Both, she decides. And what to say? She can see that his life has been scourged. It might well have been the war. No doubt he has been through an ordeal. She aches to hear all about it, but will not approach all that tonight. She means to have just the necessary conversation, to have it side by side, as companionably as can be managed. She would love to speak as Dorothea. Call me Dorothea, she would say if she could, but she knows his shell. He won't be easily husked.

Stella, she offers at length, just the name. Name and subject, her only theme. He tenses, she feels it. Pardon me, Michael, she goes on, I've no small talk this evening.

Speak now, she thinks, or forever hold your peace. How readily that springs to mind, not so very appropriately just at this moment. Speak up, if you're going to, that's all. She is hesitant now. He may not want to hear. He says nothing.

The knuckles of his hands gripping the coffee mug are white, but curvature spreads the force. It will not break. She loves knowing the properties of things, their tolerances. To know the heart and soul of another with such certainty – To be certain how to proceed –

Go to the core.

I loved her mind, she says, and pauses. The pattern of the wood on the back of the banquette opposite is all diagonal. What kind of wood, and how was it cut? Why be asking now, of all times, for goodness sake? Is it veneer? She shakes her head to clear out the questions.

It was a remarkable mind, she goes on. It could have soared, if – Well.

She is arrested again. 'If only.' So much to sort though. He is tense and patient. There is no hurry. She can speak, revise if necessary, speak again. She sits for a few moments more, considering, then unexpectedly swerves.

So much mediocrity, she says. Bad people thriving. My faith collapsed. It went down. Oh Michael—her voice deepens, trembling—I loved teaching. I was called to it and to me no calling is higher. But without faith? A teacher needs a foundation for –

Drop that. Where's the good in such bleakness. Turn away from it. She has defeated the darkness. She has. And now she has probably confessed both too much and too little. But he shifts in his seat. He angles toward her. Has she touched a nerve? He has something to say. Silence while he scans her face and she lets him. She feels his gaze like heat.

So you – he begins. So you too –

There it is. She doesn't need it spelled out.

376

Yes, she says. I could hardly bear to live.

He lets that sink in. But I thought –

You thought I was Miss A, just the same as usual. It was my place to behave as if I was, so I felt. Apparently I was convincing. But no. Any one, *any* one of us, is vulnerable. Without something to stand on, without it – A clicking in her throat. You know?

I know. It's a sob. She has broken through. Oh, Michael, she thinks. Oh, Stella.

Her arm around his shoulder, she gathers him in. He clutches a deep breath, holds, releases in spasms. He is gulping, sobbing against her, back in Silas's hut, right back on the floating floor with Stella sobbing on his knee. Oh turn, he thinks, oh please turn.

Dorothea is not so often gnawed by guilt, not so very much now. No longer sunk in the futility. Why get up, she asked herself every morning then. Why even bother? For that matter, why bother going to bed? She had to drive herself through the simple daily actions. She has made a fragile peace, with herself if not with the world as it is, world without end, no end to the misery, the potential for it. Christ always on his cross now. Never gently lowered, never lovingly laid in that tomb. The stone never rolled away, the spirit-body not ever risen in glory. That story lodged in the agony, both Marys waiting, perpetually.

But, thanks be, she has Elizabeth. Elizabeth found her, helped her return to life. Now she is seamed with something mineral. Quartz? Obsidian. She has resources to share again. She lets him sob.

I – He tries to speak, but chokes on it. He tries and convulses again, but she has heard the trace of l-o-v. She leaps.

You loved her.

He nods against her shoulder. She inclines her head to his, touches his hair. There, there. She will never have a child, though she has had many, Stella preeminently.

No one should have to confess love like this, she thinks. Lost love to a third party? Never, not ever in the past tense.

Leave it. Elizabeth loves her. Together, with difficulty, and not so very high, they hold up the sky.

She raises her head. Listen, she says, we share this. We always will. You know what I mean. Who she was, her death. I share it with you. She will never, she'll never – It's Dorothea's turn for tears, his to reach out. He wraps his arms around her. Stella. They hold each other, weeping freely.

Footsteps approach, hesitate beside them, then retreat. If passersby on Queen could see them, but of course they can't, not this far back from the window, not this far from the street, but say they could. Misreading, they would smile. Lovers, they would think. There might be a double take or two. Two men? Then chuckles. No, but you can hardly tell the women from the men these days, can you? That's the war for you.

What is the hour? Late. The place will be closing. Dorothea sighs deeply. Sorrow, she thinks, dear Mother Sorrow, come to us now in the hour of our need. Sorrow stopped Dorothea in her tracks. It moved in, occupied her. Matured, Sorrow got her going, pushed her out into the world, away from home, her home so deeply loved but contracted, narrowed in a single night. Michael, she says softly, will you give me your address? I want to send you something.

He slowly unwraps his arms, wipes his eyes, pats a breast pocket. Finds a stub of pencil. No paper. She opens her bag, fishes out a receipt, gives it to him. On the back, he scribbles his particulars in the familiar hand.

That's where I am now, he says, his voice thick, but –

For how long?

I don't know.

She puts the bill back in her bag, snaps it shut. We were meant to meet, she says. I don't speak of Providence. I can't. But I do believe in design.

She should cross her fingers. She ought to make some sort of sign to rebuke 'malign,' the lurking rhyme. But this is not that. This moment has nothing to do with the hunch and tumble of truth, contorted, threatening to sweep her along and away.

Remember her, she tells him. We are all she is now.

No, she thinks in sudden wonder, *not* all. Where does that notion come from? What does it mean? All she knows in the moment is that there is more to this, more to Stella still, than she has words for. The crude version will have to do for now.

Are you with me, Michael?

Remember! he retorts. As if I could help remembering. But – But I think I know what you mean. We are to keep her.

Exactly. Keep her warm.

Side by side again, they sit in silence.

Michael, Dorothea says at length, I'm so glad we met. She opens her bag, picks out the receipt, writes her own address at the bottom, tears it off. Look, here's where I live. If you ever need –

Thank you. He puts the paper in his pocket.

A clatter of glassware goes on rather long. They gather themselves, rise. She waits while he pays his bill, then together they step out into the fresh Toronto night. On the street, she takes his hands in hers, looks into his eyes for a long moment. He returns her gaze. Finally, he speaks.

Are you walking?

Yes.

Then I'll walk you –

No, thanks, Michael. I'm just a couple of blocks away. I'll be fine. Will you be going home? To the farm?

I handed back all my kit. I've got my papers and my transportation chit. He pats his back pocket. But I'm still thinking. I haven't decided. In fact I can't decide.

Well, do you think we could meet some other time? We haven't exactly caught up.

We could.

Would you come by? Before you go home? If you do.

Yes. He thinks no.

Do, she says. I'd like that very much. *Very* much. Well, then – She smiles, drops his hands and turns. Hands in pockets, he watches her go north on Peter Street.

The lights of the Angel abruptly go out and he looks absently in. He realizes with a start that the man who served him and took his money—the owner? He's old enough—is at the dark window, staring out. Their eyes lock briefly. What is it Michael sees on that shadowed face? Longing? The question is lost as he turns back to Miss A, then crosses Peter and heads east on Queen. She finished my sentences, he thinks. I could have finished some of hers.

Half a block away, the thought strikes him.

Silas!

He pivots and strides back to Peter, but she has already turned off. He fishes out the address. He could find her. Or he could actually visit 'some other time.' Visit a teacher? But he's no longer

380

in school and she isn't teaching now, not by the sound of it. He is a man, supposed to be. Maybe he could. Maybe he will. Though she might not know. He stands, irresolute, his mind awash with recollection.

He began to doubt the impossible conversation the day after. He ground it over and over until he wore it down to some figment of his grief. But conversation or no, he and Silas were linked. The bond should have held. It should have been unbreakable. But he was numb for so long. He wanted to disappear and almost succeeded. He did succeed. He must have. No bullet finds a man who isn't there. He never went looking for Silas.

Silas, Silas. He should have.

Silas was always outside, the perfect outsider. But—an astonishing image darts in—*huge*. Monumental, capacious, obdurate. No statue, though he could pose like one. He could pose as a pitcher. Ah, Silas. Lost, and yet, like Stella, *there* all through the hell years, especially in dreams. But hadn't he always been lost, and wasn't he actually, in his own way, thriving? Here's to thriving, Michael thinks. At least he didn't have to win the stupid war. That detail was for the privileged, the lucky ones, those with all the advantages. Silas in the navy? No.

But having come so close, to let him go –

Michael will be awake all night, the evening slowly subsiding in him. He will crisscross Toronto between Queen Street and the harbour, walking and walking, his mind charged and whirling, returning again and again, bewildered, to the stones in the beloved meadow of his childhood. The large rock shattered into fragments, the pieces resting in permanent exploded relation. Those pieces, the whole: he will shuttle between them, agitated

and annoyed. So much is clamouring to be thought through—
Silas, Stella, the gift of Miss A—why be dwelling on a vestige of
the vast story of Earth in deep time, sorely scarred by latecomers
but millennial, impassive, enduring? He has yet to trust the gifts
of his mind.

He will sleepwalk through the next day, exhausted but also
alert on some level he has never experienced before. He will walk
and walk, and walk some more, then fall into bed at 8:00 PM.
Twelve hours later he will wake as if entering a clearing for the
first time.

GRATEFULLY ACKNOWLEDGED

TELLERS, LISTENERS, READERS
Anne Archer, Anita Best, Michael Crummey, Degan Davis, Kevin Davis, Kenneth de Kok, Beth Follett, Lois Grant, Holly Hogan, Helen Humphreys, Sean Kane, Don McKay, Earl Meeks, Dave Monture, Michael Ondaatje, Carolyn Smart

WRITING LOCATIONS AND SUPPORT
The Leighton Colony, The Banff Centre; Baptiste Lake, Ontario; Coffee and Company (St. John's); Dooney's (Toronto); Hava Java (St. John's); 191 Madison Ave., Toronto; The Toronto Archives; The Ontario Institute for the Study of Education; 13 Island Lake, Ontario; 113 Bond St., St. John's

The Canada Council for the Arts;
The Newfoundland and Labrador Arts Council

PUBLISHED SECTIONS
TickleAce 35 (Spring 1999); T. Anne Archer, Mary Cavanagh, Elizabeth Greene, Tara Kramer and Janice Kirk, eds, *On the Threshold: Writing Towards the Year 2000*. Vancouver: Beach Holme, 1999; *Talk That Mountain Down: Poetry from The Banff Studio 2005*. Orono, Ontario: Littlefishcartpress, 2005; *Open Letter*, Thirteenth Series, Number 1 (Fall-Winter 2006-7) (for Ray Ellenwood).

SOURCES
Kenneth Bagnell, *The Little Immigrants: The Orphans Who Came to Canada*. Toronto: Macmillan of Canada, 1981; Gus Cannon, "Stealin'"; E.R. Checkley, "Yarker and Vicinity." *Lennox and Addington Historical Papers*

and Records, I. Napanee: Lennox and Addington Historical Society, 1909; Mrs. C.E. Clancy, *My Early Recollections of Newburgh*. May 7, 1936; Gail Corbett, *Barnardo Children in Canada*. Peterborough, Ontario: Woodland Publishing, 1981; Isabella Valancy Crawford, "Malcolm's Katie"; Tom Cruikshank, *Rogues Hollow: The Story of Newburgh, Ontario Through its Buildings*. Editor and contributor, Peter John Stokes; writing, reseach and illustration, Tom Cruikshank, assisted by Robert Heaslip. Toronto: The Architectural Conservancy of Ontario, 1983; Bruce Dowbiggan, *The Stick: A history, a celebration, an elegy*. Toronto: McFarlane Walter & Ross, 2001; Frank B. Edwards, *The Smiling Wilderness: An Illustrated History of Lennox & Addington County*. Camden East: Camden House, 1984; Candace Falk, Stephen Cole, Sally Thomas, eds. *Emma Goldman: A Guide to Her Life and Documentary Sources*. Berkeley Digital Library SunSite; Emma Goldman, *Anarchism and Other Essays*. New York: Mother Earth, 1917; John Woodcock Graves, "D'ye Ken John Peel"; Helen Hutchison, *A Study of the Napanee River Improvement Company*. Toronto: University of Toronto Department of Museology, 1974; Ron Hynes, "Saviour" and "1962"; G.P. Maximoff, *The Political Philosophy of Bakunin*. New York: The Free Press, 1953; Nick and Helma Mika, eds. *Community Spotlight: Leeds, Frontenac, Lennox and Addington and Prince Edward Counties*. Belleville, Ont.: Mika Publishing, 1974; Napanee River Improvement Company Papers, Lennox and Addington Archives, Napanee, Ontario; Brian Osborne, "The Settlement of Kingston's Hinterland." Brian Rollason, ed. *County of a Thousand Lakes: The History of the County of Frontenac, 1673 to 1973*. Kingston: Frontenac County Council, 1982; William J. Patterson, *Portland, My Home: An Illustrated History of Portland Township*. The Township of Portland, 1994; *Portland Township Memoirs and Biography: Past and Present for the Future*. Young Canada Works Program, 1979 (Holly Emmons, Lisa Clow, Kim Grant, Mavis Flear, Heather Snider, Darlene Young); Dorothy Murray Sliter, *The Friendly Village*. Jackson Press, 1974; Jacob Spelt, *Urban Development in South-Central Ontario*. Ottawa: Carleton University Press, 1983; Ernest Lawrence Thayer, "Casey at the Bat"; Gerald Tulchinsky, ed. *To Preserve and Defend: Essays on Kingston in the Nineteenth Century*. Montreal and Kingston: McGill-Queen's University Press, 1976; Dan Yashinsky, ed. *The Storyteller at Fault*. Toronto: Ragweed, 1993; *The Kingston British Whig*.

In his letters to D.B. Stickney, of the Napanee River Improvement Company, now held in the Lennox and Addington Archives at Napanee, Mort Meeks's voice is so compelling that I was strongly moved to let him speak for himself. Fact within fiction, undissolved. An attractive idea still, but unworkable in this case. So I respectfully recruited Mort Meeks as collaborator, folding his words into my own. I have been at pains to be true to this decent and responsible individual and to the historical record in general, while telescoping dates, combining events and otherwise working my raw material in the service of story.

Now resident in St. John's, Newfoundland, Stan Dragland has published three books of fiction: *Peckertracks, a Chronicle* (shortlisted for the 1978 Books in Canada First Novel Prize), *Journeys Through Bookland and Other Passages*, and (for children) *Simon Jesse's Journey*. *Wilson MacDonald's Western Tour*, a "critical collage," has been followed by two other books of criticism, *The Bees of the Invisible: Essays in Contemporary English Canadian Writing* and *Floating Voice: Duncan Campbell Scott and the Literature of Treaty 9*, which won the 1995 Gabrielle Roy Prize for Canadian Literary Criticism. *12 Bars*, a prose blues, was co-winner of the bpNichol Chapbook Award in 2003, the same year *Apocrypha: Further Journeys* appeared in NeWest Press's Writer-as-Critic series. *Apocrypha* was winner of the Rogers Cable Non-Fiction Award in 2005. *Stormy Weather: Foursomes* (Pedlar Press, 2005), was shortlisted for the E.J. Pratt Poetry Award in 2007.

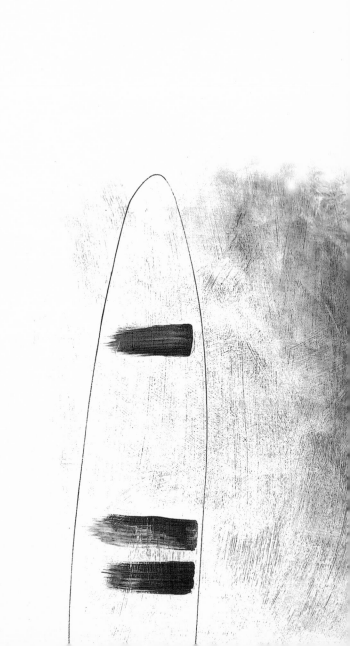